To Brenden
Kleiboeker

best wishes

FW Bane

July 2020

The Clubhouse

ALSO BY FREDERIC W. BAUE
order from pergolapress.com *or* amazon.com

BOOKS

The Spiritual Society: What Comes after Postmodernism

A Bibliographical Catalog and First-line Index
of English Poetry Anthologies to 1640

Creation: a Literary, Apologetic, and Doctrinal Approach

The Epistles of Herman Noodix

The Pilgrim: A Novel

Flight: A Novel

MUSIC

Too Deep for Words – Original Compositions for Guitar

The Great Dance – Church Music for Guitar

New Chestnuts – 19 Original Songs

The Bethany Hymns

The Clubhouse
a novel

Book III of The Diamond Quintet

F. W. Baue

Pergola Press
St. Louis

The Clubhouse
Copyright © 2019 by Frederic W. Baue. All rights reserved.

Published by Pergola Press
908 Brownell Avenue, St. Louis, Missouri 63122
www.pergolapress.com
fredbaue@gmail.com
(314) 307-6512

This is a work of fiction. Resemblance to any person, living or dead, is coincidental.

The name of Satchel Paige is used in a fictional sense, by permission of the Luminary Group LLC.

No part of this publication may be reproduced or transmitted in any form or by any means, without permission from the publisher, except by a reviewer, who may quote brief passages.

Book design by David Brinker
Jacket and author illustration by Abraham Mohler
Map by Aaron Shaefer

Publisher's Cataloging-In-Publication Data
(Prepared by The Donohue Group, Inc.)

Names: Baue, Frederic W., 1946- author.
Title: The clubhouse : a novel / F.W. Baue.
Description: [Second edition]. | St. Louis : Pergola Press, [2019] | Series: The diamond quintet ; book 3
Identifiers: ISBN 9780984807758
Subjects: LCSH: Theologians--Travel--Germany--Fiction. | Man-woman relationships--Fiction. | Hunting lodges--Missouri--Perry County--Fiction. | German Americans--Missouri--Perry County--Fiction. | Lutheran Church--Missouri--Perry County--Fiction. | United States--Social life and customs--1971---Fiction. | Perry County (Mo.)--Fiction.
Classification: LCC PS3602.A84 C58 2019 | DDC 813/.6--dc23

For Nigel Goodwin, who encouraged me

Erhalt uns, Herr, bei deinem Wort.
Lord, keep us steadfast in thy Word.

Martin Luther

Contents

Acknowledgments		xi
Preface		xiii
Principal Characters		xvii
Map		xix
Prologue	A Sense of Place	1
Chapter 1	An Injured Man	6
Chapter 2	John and Rachel, John and Rafael	29
Chapter 3	Another Injured Man	56
Chapter 4	Conflict on and off the Gridiron	86
Chapter 5	An Unexpected Guest	106
Chapter 6	The History of Mayangala	129
Chapter 7	Chortazo	152
Chapter 8	Old Methuselah	177
Chapter 9	O Tannenbaum	191
Chapter 10	Two Kinds of Confession	214
Chapter 11	The Argument	236
Chapter 12	The Fight	253
Chapter 13	An Easter Wedding	270
Chapter 14	A Sacred Meal	287
Epilogue	Healing	301
Clubhouse Recipes		305

Acknowledgments

A number of years ago we published the first edition of *The Clubhouse*—a small run, hastily put together, and full or errors. A beginner's effort, one might say. We were on a pretty steep learning curve. Since then, we have published two novels, a book of humor, and a collection of original hymns.

We are now proud to present our new, improved, second edition of *The Clubhouse*. I am struck by how often a reader will pick up one of our Pergola Press books and say "Wow!" before reading a line. Just the book *qua* book is in itself a work of art. The design of the dust jacket, the layout of the title, the cover illustration, the hard back, the cloth cover, the gold foil stamp on the spine, the binding, the font, the interior design, the 60-pound paper, the quality printing—all of these things go into making a book a thing of beauty. It is a tactile pleasure just to pick it up.

In this day of ephemeral electronic communication, where trivial words fly back and forth in cyberspace, I believe that the technology of the book has a great future. Think about it: the battery never goes dead, the software never crashes, you don't have to buy a new Kindle e-reader every few years because the old one is obsolete, and you can't take your laptop to the outhouse. If you keep a book dry, it will last for hundreds of years. As communication becomes faster and faster and cheaper and cheaper, a book of serious words rises to iconic status. That is why we chose to go for the highest production values in this series.

For all this attention to detail I thank my fellow Pergolites: chiefly our designer David Brinker, and illustrator Abraham Mohler, a successful sculptor working in marble, bronze, and other media, who drew the author portrait from life in one hour. Both Abe and David have contributed important editorial suggestions. Of course to my good wife Jean I give the highest praise for all the encouragement and support during years of struggle.

Thanks also to Jackie and Eddie and Debby and Chucky and Peggy and Randy and Janie and Kurt, the old Clubhouse Gang of long ago, who listened raptly as Uncle Rudy and Uncle Fritz told spooky stories before bedtime as we lay in a row on our army cots on the back porch of the Twin Springs Hunting and Fishing Club, established in 1911 by our grandfather, Emmanuel Hoffstetter. That blessed place is now torn down and lives on only in the memory of those of us who were children there. As it was the model for the Clubhouse of our present tale, I hope it will come back to life in the imagination of our readers.

Finally, we say with J.S. Bach, *Soli Deo Gloria*.

Preface

The Clubhouse, the novel you have before you, is Book III of *The Diamond Quintet*. "Quintet" because it consists of five interrelated novels: *The Pilgrim, Flight, The Clubhouse, The Last Game,* and *Ras Josiah*; "Diamond" because the theme of baseball is important to all the stories. The Preface to Book I, *The Pilgrim*, contains a fuller discussion of theological themes and literary devices in all five novels. Here and in subsequent volumes I will be more concise.

The Pilgrim traced the sojourns of Paul Gottlieb, a young pitcher and budding musician from the unique, German-heritage, Lutheran community of East Perry County, Missouri, homeland of the unique, German-heritage church body known as the Lutheran Church–Missouri Synod. It is 1966, and Paul is awakening intellectually to new influences in music and poetry and the culture at large. This leads to conflict within the family. Paul takes his guitar and hits the road. He lands in San Francisco, and starts a successful folk-rock band just as the Summer of Love is about to explode. But now conflict arises as a result of his own choices and actions. Paul finds that the path toward redemption is difficult to find.

Flight is the second novel in the series, but it is connected to all the rest. As such, it was necessary to add a section of correspondence, *The Epistles of Paul*, to bring the reader along in the twenty years that have elapsed between the two stories. *The Pilgrim* was set in 1966–1969; *Flight*, 1988–1989; and the *Epistles* begin in 1976.

As *Flight* opens, Reverend Mark Brandon (who is related to Paul Gottlieb), is in Tucson, Arizona, serving St. Mark's Lutheran Church.

It is his fortieth birthday. He records his thoughts in a journal, and keeps going for a whole year leading up to his forty-first. In that year he encounters his wife's mysterious illness, the trials and tribulations of a bad car, struggles with his pitching, his brother's homosexuality, and more. Then in the middle of all this muddle he wins a new Corvette in a convenience-store raffle...

Now we have *The Clubhouse*. We are back in East Perry County, Missouri, at the Friedensee Hunting and Fishing Lodge, known commonly as "The Clubhouse." Set in 2004, this is the story of John Mason, an LCMS pastor who has gone to Heidelberg, Germany, for doctoral study in theology. While there, he falls in love with the wrong woman—an African princess. In their passion they bring a love child into the world, a boy, and they name him Josiah. But she is living in exile from the country she was born to rule. Serious trouble develops, and John hurriedly finds his way home. He finds peace and quiet at the old Clubhouse, and time to write up his dissertation. But trouble is pursuing the child—and him.

To add verisimilitude, I have added a section of authentic Perry County recipes as an appendix.

Book IV is your basic Lutheran apocalyptic baseball novel, *The Last Game*. I am grateful to my wife, Jean, for suggesting the subtitle: *A Novel in Nine Innings*. That is, each chapter describes one inning of play, with the intrigue and the love story worked in between pitches, balks, and timeouts. Every year The Children of Abimelech semipro baseball team stomps the St. John's Lutheran Church Men's Club Nine. But this year, 2011, the team has a new coach: Reverend Carl Reinhardt. We saw little Carl as a child in *Flight*, where he asks his Uncle Mark Brandon to show him some trick pitches that have been passed down in the family. He does, and Carl becomes a standout pitcher in college and seminary. He is challenged by this Abimelech cult in theology, in baseball, in love, and in life.

The series concludes with *Ras Josiah*. You will remember him as the rambunctious little boy from Book III, *The Clubhouse*. He also showed up in *The Last Game* as a little dugout rat. Now it is 2025. Josiah has grown up. He is an amateur American baseball player.

He is a Cambridge scholar. He is an African king. And to prove his claim to the throne of Mayangala, he must kill a lion with an ancient spear, as have all his forefathers before him. Josiah is challenged by a man-eating lion, and also a monstrous villain, but is aided by not one but two ghosts, the love of a good woman, and the friendship of a legendary horse.

In all these works I endeavor to depict dramatically the fullness of reality in straightforward, American literary fiction. I aim for realism, both material and spiritual. God is unseen but active in these pages. A fellow pastor said, "These are not 'safe' books." Like the lion Aslan in Narnia, God is not tame, but He is good. Sin is depicted as it is. But so is grace. This, too, is part of reality. Let's call it theology in narrative form. May the reader be spiritually edified as well as entertained by reading these tales.

Septuagesima 2019

Principal Characters

Rev. John Reinhardt Mason, *Lutheran pastor*
✠ Elizabeth of Mayangala, *his lover*
Josiah Mason, *their son*
Rachel McFadden, *a neighbor, later his wife*
Ralph Mason, *mechanic, his father*
Betty Mason, *his mother*
Jasper Mason, *mechanic, his uncle*
Mildred Pope, *manager of The Clubhouse, his aunt*
✠ Herbert "Buddy" Pope, *her husband*
TD Pope, *their son and John's rival*
Rev. JJ Kolding, *Lutheran pastor and John's uncle*
Rev. Earl Gottlieb, *Lutheran pastor and John's mentor and uncle*
Paul Gottlieb, *musician, Earl's nephew*
Lori Gottlieb, *his wife*
Kurt Gottlieb, *their son*

Rafael von Päpinghausen, *John's enemy*
Sinan, *Rafael's friend*

Peter, Jacob, and Isaac, *princes of Mayangala, uncles to Josiah*
✠ Shadrach Teseney, *manservant to the king of Mayangala*
Miriam Seyoum, *his wife, maidservant to the queen*

Rev. David C. "Pastor Dave" Henderson, *Lutheran pastor*
Francis J. "Frank" Laclede, *businessman*
Benjamin Q. "Ben" Laclede, *businessman*

"Doxie," *a German Shepherd*
"Milton," *a Quarter Horse*
"Old Methuselah," *a catfish*

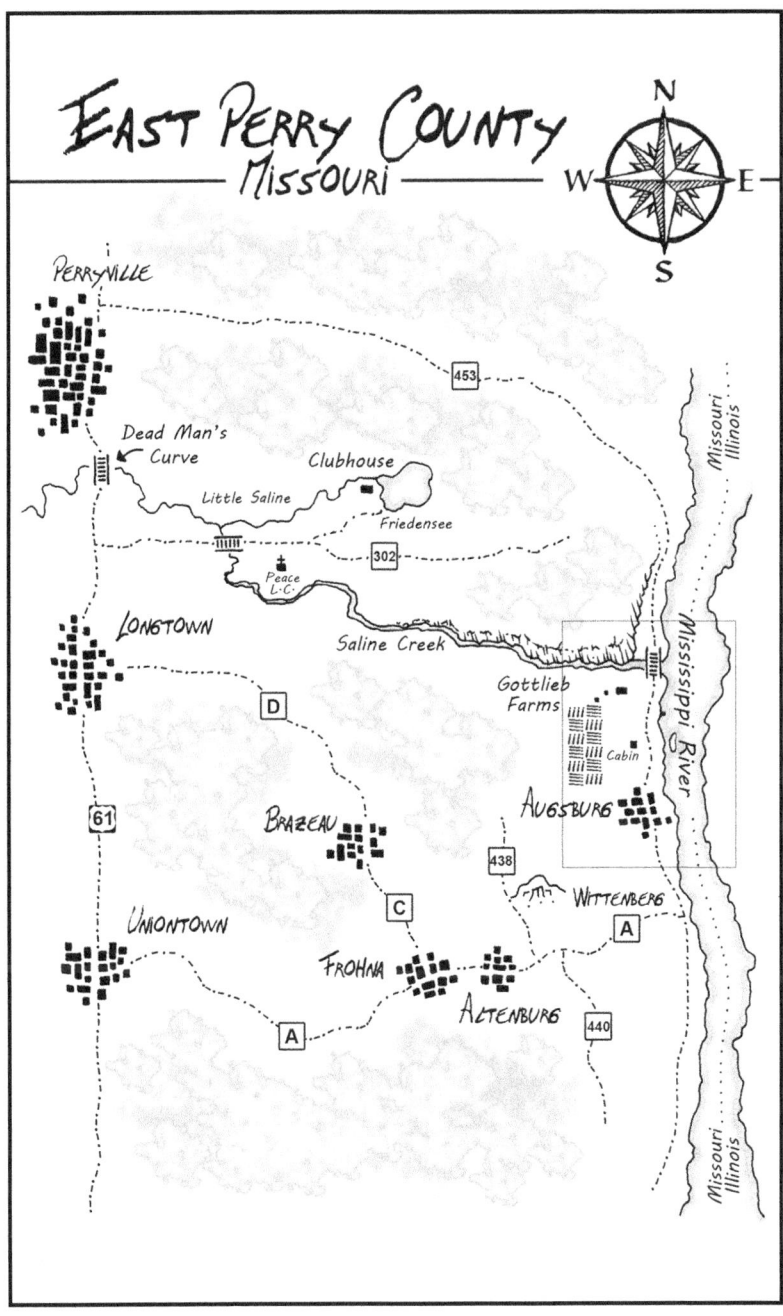

Prologue ◉ A Sense of Place

The lake is full—full of water, full of fish, full of stories. By it stands an old place called "The Clubhouse," and it, too, is full—full of memories and tradition. Its proper name is The Friedensee Hunting and Fishing Club, Perryville, Missouri, Friedensee being the name of the lake that empties out into the Saline Creek that in turn pours itself into the Mississippi River not many miles away. Hunting and fishing is the official activity there on its many acres. Everyone calls it the Clubhouse for short, and properly so, for the building is the heart and soul of the place. Nothing grand or pretentious, it is just sort of an overgrown lodge which several families of Perryville, Missouri (pop. 2,511), needing a place to get away from the stresses of life in the bustling county seat with its railroad and commerce and politics, had gone in on together back in 1911. In time it became a kind of refuge, a sanctuary for them. They kept the Clubhouse going through all the changes that were tearing apart the world outside—the Great War, the Great Depression, the forced change from German to English, World War Two, the upheavals in the Lutheran church. These came and went and affected everyone in profound ways, but the lake somehow retained its eternal calm, and the Clubhouse remained the same within its comforting walls. You visited the place and it grew on you and in you, and it stayed with you when you left.

When the children were growing up there, fishing along the lakeshore, tramping through the woods with their dogs and .22s, skinny-dipping in the creek when no one was looking, they were ignorant of the serious things that worried their parents. They were unhappy, as all children are, with the little miseries of their lives: the toy they wanted but didn't get, the boy they liked but were too shy to talk to, the playground bully that threatened everything. Great miseries and great mysteries would afflict them all as they grew up. But for a time they had a sanctuary, a place to be at peace and just be children. It was for them as it had been for their parents, for they, too, had been children there. They, too, had had a "Clubhouse Gang" of brothers and sisters and cousins and pals and dogs in their generation. And so they kept coming back, bringing the children and the children's children and grounding them in the traditions and stories and old ways they had learned from their parents and their parents' parents, paths of life and belief that though fragile somehow withstood the paroxysms of the modern world outside.

The Clubhouse is unpainted, its siding made of walnut planks rough-hewn almost a century ago from an onsite tree, and resistant to all weather, though now gray with age. About sixty feet long and forty feet wide, it has a peaked tin roof, rusty and patched here and there with tar and old license plates. When it rains, the raindrops on the roof make a sound like the voice of many waters, in harmony with the sussurance of the lake. There is a big woodpile, which Uncle Buddy always insisted be kept away from the house because it drew bugs. There are no utilities. Heat has to be made by hand in the fireplace and stoves. Light, such as there is, comes from coal-oil lamps that give a soft, golden glow to everything at night.

Inside the Clubhouse is a big central atrium with a high ceiling. The centerpiece of the hall is a great stone fireplace that old Godfrey Mason himself had built of the limestone that abounds in these parts. Above the hearth is a mantlepiece made from a single, hand-hewn plank of oak from an old barn. On it is a rack of pipes—each man knew his own and no one else ever touched it—and a tin of Carter Hall tobacco that everyone shared, a fragrant Burley and Virginia blend that wafted through the whole clubhouse, accompanied by the strong laughter of men telling stories after the hunt. Across the hall from the hearth is a beat-up old upright piano, and on it is a tattered Lutheran hymnal that Aunt Millie likes to play from, its weight doubled from the paper clips marking the dozens of her favorite hymns. The old folks still knew the German words, and when the mood struck them would sing *Erhalt uns, Herr, bei deinem Wort* and *Ein Feste Burg is Unser Gott** with strong voices in good harmony. On the wall by the piano is an old hand-cranked telephone that still works on a party line, the "number" at the Clubhouse being two shorts and a long. Whenever there was a call everybody else on the line listened in, so they knew to come over if there was trouble. That's how the community was alerted when there was that bad accident over at the McFadden place across the creek and Peter and his son Bobby were killed, leaving young Rachel and her mother to carry on alone.

The women regulated and ruled the Clubhouse as they do all places by controlling the kitchen. The men were free to have their adventures and range over field and forest in search of game. But if they wanted anything to eat they had to do obeisance and bring an offering—preferably field-dressed and ready to cook—to the door of the kitchen. In it was a big, black wood-burning Franklin stove, trimmed with ornate, nickel-plated frippery. Millie could tell when the temperature was right for baking by popping open the door and waving her hand inside. On the stove was the old blue tin coffee pot with its white-flecked porcelain finish, and from it came good black coffee to fill the heavy crockery mugs, the kind you used to get years ago in the country stores with a cake of shaving soap back when all men used straight razors, and when the soap was gone you had yourself a nice mug that kept the coffee hot for a long time. There were a lot of these old mugs at the Clubhouse, and they were always full of coffee and always in use.

On either side of the hall are small, rustic rooms. Each has a cast-iron frame bed that sags in the middle like an old horse, and complains with a groan when you lie down on it. On the washstand is a white porcelain pitcher and basin, the glaze crazed with age. By the window is a four-square wooden chair and a plain table with a coal-oil lamp. There is a peg on the wall to hang your clothes on, and a thunder

---

* "Lord, Keep Us Steadfast in Thy Word" and "A Mighty Fortress Is Our God"

mug under the bed. The little wood-burning stove has an isinglass window, endlessly fascinating to children when they look through and see the fire burning and making fantastic shapes of ghosts and goblins.

At the front end of the hall, just off the kitchen, is a large, screened-in porch, furnished with those old-fashioned bentwood chairs made from hickory branches with the bark still on. The walls are knotty pine, and inscribed with dates and trophies—a foot-long channel cat caught by Hilda Mason in 1938 while she was pregnant with Jasper, a ten-point buck taken by Ralph Mason in 1972 after he came back from Vietnam. This porch serves as the main entrance to the Clubhouse as well as the main sitting-and-visiting area, for it looks out over the lake.

The lake is not large, about nine or ten acres in area, and has limestone cliffs at the far end. It is surrounded by woods, mostly oak, typical of Missouri forests, but here and there stands a huge old sycamore, the white-barked "ghosts of the forest" as the old folks used to call them. In the highest of the trees by the lake are many heron nests, a rookery from which the great blue-gray birds would glide easily into the sky and depart in the fall and to which they would return in the spring to raise their young. In the morning when the water was as glass, a lone mourning dove nestling in the strong arm of a great tree would coo, and in a moment its mate would answer, and soon they would find each other and be at peace. And the lake as it lay sequestered between the motherly hills was often still and peaceful, though the fishermen sensed that large and mysterious things were moving down deep beneath the surface. The lake was deep, folks said, though how deep no one knew for certain, and supposedly connected at the bottom to a cave that trailed off into the hills and perhaps connected somehow to the Mississippi River. The story handed down in the family was that the old-timers like Godfrey had caught a glimpse of a catfish of immense size once years ago when the water was exceptionally clear and the sunlight was at just the right angle.

This is the end of the line. A narrow gravel lane leads away from the Clubhouse, squeezing between a mighty sycamore and the deep ravine near the stream that spills out of the lake, through a deep canopy of trees, then across a low-water bridge, connecting with this and that gravel road, then a county road so remote that it doesn't even rate a number, and somewhere beyond that a paved road that may or may not lead to a hamlet with a gas station/store/bait shop, depending on which way you turned, not that it made much difference either way, and beyond that Perryville and beyond that the great world. But people in these parts just didn't have much need to go anywhere, and didn't. They had about everything they needed; their wants were simple, their provisions right at hand. They could be described in the words of the old saw, *Wir bleiben beim Alten.*[*]

---

[*] We stick by the old ways.

Chapter 1 ◉ An Injured Man

It was September at the Clubhouse, late summer or early fall, depending on the mood of the weather. The days were placid and sunny, but at night there came a gathering chill that contained the tiny seed of winter to come. The herons had left for the south, though this year at Friedensee one lone old bachelor heron was wintering over, as sometimes happened with these birds along the Mississippi flyway. Always hungry, he plied his trade in the shallow water near the lakeshore, ever vigilant for a stray minnow or frog.

The tree frogs and cicadas became quiet for a moment and listened to the sound of gravel crunching under tires as a dusty, rusty red ragtop Jeep threaded its way carefully between the big sycamore and the ravine and pulled in to the Clubhouse yard. The engine coughed as it shut off. A lean man of about thirty unfolded his long limbs and maneuvered his way out of the car, hopping and balancing on his right leg as he reached behind the driver's seat for a wooden cane. He had to grope for the cane, which had slipped down between the boxes of books. His sunburned face tightened in a grimace of pain as he eased down on his left foot. He was wearing Levis and a red flannel shirt and floppy canvas tennis shoes, at least on his right foot, for his left foot was encased in an orthopedic boot. Above the square jaw was a long straight honest nose with a kind of notch where it joined the brow that gave him at times a fierce, tomahawk look, like an Indian on the hunt. His teeth were straight but a bit yellowed from too much coffee, his lips were medium-thin, and when he smiled, which lately had not been often, the grin tended to slide over to one side of his face. He had clear, penetrating, grey eyes etched with laugh crinkles but a brow creased from sorrow, a full head of brown hair that needed a serious trim, tousled from driving too fast with the top down, and a streak of early snow blazing up from his forehead.

His name was John Mason, and he had just driven in nonstop from New York, and before that had flown from Frankfurt, Germany, and before that had taken a train from Heidelberg, which he had left in a hurry. He had gone to Germany to study theology. Now he was back home, back at the Clubhouse.

Germany! John thought back to the first time he had seen Rafael. It was at the Westfalen Club. Dueling club, to be more precise. Dueling was forbidden but tacitly condoned. A vintage Mercedes 450 SL had driven up to the club's meeting-place, and out hopped this big strapping fellow with a live, squealing, suckling pig under his arm.

"A bribe!" he exclaimed. "A bribe to secure my membership application!"

The club meeting was still in session. Rafael set down the pig, which immediately began scurrying around the hall, with two men falling over themselves trying to catch it.

The president banged his gavel. "Order, order! All those in favor of admitting—um, what's your name?"

"Rafael von Päpinghausen."

"This fellow Rafael to club membership say 'Aye.'"

Unanimous, with two abstentions on part of the two men who had caught the pig and were going out to dig a fire pit. "And honorary membership for the pig!" said one as he went out the door.

As he settled in to club life, Rafael became notorious for his pranks. One morning John had tottered into the little ten-by-ten foot *Fernsehraum*[*] looking for a cup of coffee only to find all the furniture removed and the room completely filled with a VW. The TV was on top of the car. A VW is a small car, but in a room it is enormous by contrast. It must have taken Rafael and his band of merry pranksters all night. People were still laughing about it after a year.

---

[*] TV lounge

After the pig roast, John and Rafael drifted along the streets to a favorite tavern overlooking the river. They ordered Spätenbrau Optimator, a kind of dark, dark *Doppelbock* you almost had to drink with a spoon, like soup.

"So you are American," Rafael said.

"You could tell," John said wryly.

"Who else could speak such bad German?"

"I might be French."

"There you have me. And you are studying..."

"Theology. You?"

"Comparative religion."

"Interesting. Comparing what to what?"

"Islam and Christianity, particularly how the same hermeneutical problems appear in both systems of belief."

"Hm. And here I thought you were running for Class Clown."

Rafael nodded his head and raised his palms. "I humbly ask for your vote, and a small donation to the campaign war chest."

"Yeah, right," John said sarcastically. "When pigs can fly?"

Rafael was puzzled. "What is this expression?"

"American slang, meaning 'never.'"

"Hm. But seriously, Christians accuse Muslims of having an unreliable text since nobody was in the cave to verify what Muhammad claimed, namely, that Gabriel came and gave him the text of the Qur'an. Then again, Muslims accuse Christians of clinging to a New Testament text that has been corrupted by scribes and redactors down through the centuries."

"OK," said John. "So do you have a working hypothesis?"

"Yes. That Islam is the one true religion and everybody else is going to hell."

"No, Rafael. You are confusing Islam with the Lutheran Church–Missouri Synod."

They stared at each other. Then they chuffed. Then they cracked up laughing.

"Of course," said Rafael, "I am Muslim myself, so there can be no other conclusion."

"Of course," John replied. "And for me as a Missouri Synod Lutheran, it's the same. So. You're going to hell."

"And so are you." They lifted their glasses in salute, then drank. "But really, John. This is the essence of contemporary scholarship. Efficient and streamlined. You start with a foregone conclusion and accept whatever supports your thesis. Whatever does not, you reject."

"Brilliant!" exclaimed John a bit too loudly, as he was rather deep in his cups. "This cuts my research time down to practically nothing. Why, I can foresee finishing my whole dissertation by the middle of next week."

"Yes!" said Rafael, "and still have time left for dueling and wenching."

"I knew I was going to enjoy Heidelberg," John said, and the two men lurched out of the tavern and down the street arm in arm, singing drinking songs both foreign and domestic.

How did it happen? You think you know someone, then...

Gingerly he made his way to the front porch and put his hand on the old iron handle of the screen door, dark and smooth from long use. The spring creaked and twanged as he opened the door, and after he passed through pulled it shut again with a bang and three light afterbangs. John paused and looked around. Late afternoon sun angled in strong bars, with motes of dust floating quietly and lazily in random patterns. A late-season wasp, iridescent purple with its tender tiny legs trailing behind, flew sleepily toward the ceiling and its mud-daubed nest. On the shelf was the old clock in its ornately carved case, well-oiled and running smoothly, the pendulum moving regularly back and forth with a calm, slow and stately tic-toc behind the glass door. The hand pointed to III. *Kaffe stunde.*[*] On either side of the clock were two angels, carved of rich, brown Missouri walnut by Uncle Jasper, and the angels were kneeling in prayer and facing the clock, as if watching and waiting for the Last Hour to chime. On the wall next to the clock was the old picture of Custer's Last Fight. Anheuser-Busch used to give them away. Every tavern and clubhouse

---

[*] Coffee time

and cabin had one. Over the years people had put names on the characters. Custer was his grandfather, Irving Mason, who had started Mason's Garage in Perryville back in the Twenties, the shop where John's father Ralph and his uncle Jasper—both Indians in the picture, scalping a couple of regular customers—carried on the family business. For John today, however, the hand-to-hand fighting didn't seem very funny or quaint, for it represented serious men trying to kill each other.

Outside, the lake was glassy and calm except for some ripples down by the dock where the kids would swim on warm days. It was early autumn. Perhaps he would swim. It might help his foot to heal. Inside, everything was the same, just as it had always been, just as one hoped it always would be. He breathed deeply of home. Of tradition. Of safety. Of healing. The smell of coffee was in the air, strong and black in that ancient pot that had made coffee for generations here. As a wave of relief came over him, he almost, but not quite, began to weep.

At a battered rolltop desk in the kitchen sat an old lady. The top of the desk was littered with books of all kinds. She looked up when she heard the screen door bang. She was plump, with a soft round face and a snub nose, curly grey hair done up in a loose, careless bun with a pencil stuck in it, and wire frame half-glasses on a chain. She wore an old cotton house dress with a faded floral pattern, and over it an apron with big pockets, and the pockets full of useful things. Her name was Mildred, John's aunt by marriage. Her husband was, or had been, Herbert Pope, "Uncle Buddy." She got up as quickly as her arthritis would allow, yanked her neck to the left and right to get the crick out, then walked with a rolling gait to the porch, scratching her head absent-mindedly and still thinking about the grocery list she had been working on for the hunting party that was coming on the weekend.

"Hey, Millie," the man said with a ready smile and the hint of a Missouri twang, sanded down and polished over with years of education.

"Johnny!" she shrieked and threw open her arms as she rushed toward him and enfolded him in a deep, motherly hug. She smelled faintly of smoke from the wood stove. "My God! Johnny! Is it you? Good Lord." She stepped back and looked him over. "When did you get in? Why didn't you write? Have you seen your parents? Did you stop at the garage? Have you eaten? What happened to your foot?" She paused for a breath. "Here, sit down."

John eased down into a rocker and propped up his hurt foot on a coffee table. On it were old copies of *Field and Stream, Guns & Ammo,* and *Missouri Conservationist*. Millie licked her fingers and tried to smooth down a cowlick on John's forehead.

"My God, John, you look a fright. Comb your hair," she said as she plopped down into a chair beside him. He smiled again at her, and she at him. She shook her head in wonderment. It had been three years since he had left for Germany, and almost six months since anyone had heard anything from him other than a brief, occasional postcard. And here he was, presto, just like that, out of the blue, with no advance notice. John ran his fingers through his hair a couple of times and tried to pat the mop down and smooth it over.

"And here you are," Millie said, "just popped out of thin air, and nobody's heard from you in ages."

"Just a few months. I'm sorry. But I . . . "

"Well, that's too long," she scolded. "You're supposed to write every week. That's the rule in this family. Ages. What happened to your foot?"

He shrugged. "Oh, nothing."

She scowled and wagged her finger. "And you're too thin. When's the last time you ate? Haven't you ever heard of sunscreen? Your nose is peeling. Look at you. My God, what a mess. Just like when you were a kid. Here, let me get you some coffee."

He listened to the comfortable, decades-old sounds of Millie banging around in the kitchen, and as he leaned back exhausted in the rocker he began to drift off. Fresh thoughts of Germany floated incoherently and randomly in his mind, things he didn't like, a cursing man, a roaring dog, darkness and blood . . . then Millie was beside him shaking his shoulder as he came to with a start.

"John! John! For God's sake, wake up! What's the matter with you?"

"What, what?" John replied groggily.

"You were shouting in your sleep."

"I was?"

"Yes."

"What was I saying?" he asked, fearful that he might have revealed too much.

"A woman's name. It sounded like 'Elizabeth.' Who is she?"

"I don't know," he lied, "somebody I met in Germany."

"Then you were yelling, 'Get it off me. It hurts. It hurts.' What is this, John? What's happened to you?"

"It's nothing. I just had a bit of trouble, that's all."

She looked at him intently. Something was not right. She'd have to pry it out of him somehow.

"The apples began to come in heavy and early this year, so I've been making pies to make a little extra money on the side. Here, try this, John."

He rubbed his eyes and yawned. She set before him a large slab of apple pie, still warm from the oven, dusted over with cinnamon sugar on the top crust, with a thick chunk of sharp crumbly cheddar cheese on the side, and with it a steaming white mug of black coffee, made the right way, good and strong and clear from putting an eggshell in the pot. With alarm Millie watched her nephew eat: he ate like a wolf, noisily, with big slavering bites, chewing hardly at all. Where were his manners? Then he asked for more. He gobbled that down, then ate a third piece, slopping it all down with gulps and swallows of the coffee.

He looked up from his plate to see Millie staring at him. "Sorry," he said. "I just seem to be empty all the time. Can't get filled up." She shook her head. "Must have a tapeworm or something," he said with a shrug and a weak attempt at a joke.

"Guess you heard that Herbert passed away," Millie said.

"I'm sorry. I heard a long time after. I was preoccupied with a lot of things . . . I'm really sorry."

"Don't worry about it."

He smiled wryly and shook his head. "Uncle Buddy taught me to fish."

Millie's eyes filled with the memory. Old times of full weekends, the Clubhouse abuzz with activity, kids running around in wet swimming suits and soggy tennis shoes, banging in and out of the house between adventures to the swimming hole and the Old Burnt Mill, breathlessly bringing in newly captured frogs and turtles to the grownups, who populated the cool porches and shade trees, sipping Falstaff beer and playing pinochle, and talking, talking till all hours, until finally, like fireflies blinking wearily and settling back into the grass, one by one they found their way to bed. And John had been among them in those days, just one of the kids in the Clubhouse Gang, a chubby little boy, as silly as the rest, though given to reading and daydreaming, and one who somehow was a natural shepherd over the rest, so that the parents never worried if they all trooped off somewhere and he was along to watch over them. And because of his physical strength, unusual in one so young, he was given the honor of carrying the big watermelon down the long hill to cool in the spring for two days, then lug it back up the hill on Sunday afternoon—the great round cannonball watermelon, dark green on the outside and dark red on the inside, so cold and sweet, to be devoured with slurps and laughter and the shooting of watermelon seeds from between the thumb and forefinger in the sweltering afternoon...

Millie's eyebrows knit up in the middle with a look of sympathy. Time to give it another shot. "John, be straight with me. What happened to your foot?"

"A dog bit me," he replied guardedly. It was too painful to think about, much less talk about.

Millie looked at John with one eyebrow raised. "A dog."

John nodded. "A dog."

"Is that all?"

John shrugged evasively. Of course there was more to it. Much more. More than he could cope with, and certainly much more than he wanted to reveal to his relatives. Time to think fast.

"Well, let's see," he began, "I got into this sword fighting club in Heidelberg—dueling is very big there, you know—and we went out into the forest one day for a duel with this other club. And it was my turn to fight. So they gave me a sabre, and I squared off with my opponent, and we started hacking away at each other, and just when I almost had him, there was a shout from the men, and lo and behold this enormous gigantic wolf came bounding out of the forest, growling and howling and baring his fangs, and he bit me on the foot. I chopped his head off with my sword but he still held on. It took seven doctors three days to pry his jaws off me."

Millie clapped her hands and laughed. Here was John the storyteller, the one to whom the mantle had passed. "I knew there must be a reasonable explanation," she said.

"Listen, Millie, the doctor said I need to take it easy for a little while. Stay off it. Let it heal. You know. And I have some work to do on my dissertation. I did visit Mom and Pop when I drove in. I'd hoped I could stay with them, but they've got a full house. Mom's taking care of Billy now that Lou Ann has a full-time job, plus Katie's over there a lot. Besides, I like it here. It's quiet. I can think."

"That's fine, John. You know you don't have to ask. I need to run into Perryville tomorrow but Rachel will come over to look after things. She usually rides her horse."

"Rachel?"

"Rachel McFadden, you know, the neighbor girl who used to come over and join you kids. Part of the old Clubhouse Gang. You remember her."

He paused. Then it clicked. "You mean Little Beezer?"

Millie gave him a wry smile over her reading glasses. "Call her that now and you're liable to get your hair parted with a rolling pin."

John smiled and shook his head. "Little Beezer. With that funny little turned-up nose that wrinkled when she laughed. Which was all the time. And her two front teeth missing. And those freckles. I guess I was about ten or so when she started showing up. She would have been, what?"

"Five."

"Yes, five," John continued, looking out toward the dock. "And her dad had the farm across the creek and he grew melons. It would have taken a half hour to drive there but if you cut through the cornfield you could walk there in ten minutes. But, wow, that's still a long way with a big watermelon. Then she followed me back to the Clubhouse one day."

Mildred sipped her coffee. "Mm-hm." She took another sip. The dove, nestled in the arm of an oak, gave forth a soft cry. "Yes," Millie continued, "and there she was, like an extra bonus cousin, and then in the evening they'd all sit at your feet and you'd make up these wild stories."

"Right," John said. Only fragments were left in the bottom of the well of old memory. The bear that could talk, but only to children. The balloon that went to the moon. The giant catfish with magical powers. "Rachel McFadden." He chuckled. "Boy, oh boy. I think I saw her once or twice later on when I came down for weekends during high school. But not much. So she's still around."

"What?" Millie asked. "Your voice was trailing off."

John spoke up, louder this time. "I said, 'So Rachel is still around.' Do you still go skeet shooting without your earplugs in, Millie?"

Millie shrugged. "Yes, she is. She was working on her master's in English at Washington University but then there was that accident, you heard about it, when her father and brother were killed. And there was a rumor that she'd had some other kind of trouble, too, I'm not sure what. She never said. I never could pry it out of her. So Rachel came back to help out on the farm. And she started pitching in over here, too. That's the way she is. But now that we're past Labor Day I only need her one day a week. Except for deer season. She's taken up the guitar. You should hear her play. She's really quite good. It's just that she does wacky impulsive things, sometimes. Like going to Europe on a moment's notice."

"Guitar, eh? I'll be sure and ask her." He chortled. "Beezer!"

Millie raised a finger. "Give me your keys. I'll bring in your stuff," she said, glancing at his foot.

"Thanks."

He tossed them to her, she caught them left-handed with an effortless, natural motion, just as she had years ago when playing baseball with the boys, then walked to the screen door.

"A dog," she said, looking at him, and shaking her head went out.

◎ ◎ ◎

John awoke early in the morning as he always did, poured cold water into the wash basin, splashed his face, and dried off with a rough white towel that had been washed in rain water and put to dry on a line outside. It smelled of fresh air. It was cool in his room but not enough for a fire. He got back under the warm covers, took up his little pocket edition of the Bible—King James—and said his morning prayers, a simple devotion of a chapter, a Psalm, the Lord's Prayer, Luther's Morning Prayer, and the Sign of the Cross. Uncle Buddy had not only taught him to fish but also taught him to pray, showing him how to develop the habit, how to read the Bible, which passages to go to at which times—when things were good, and when things were bad—which was where he turned this morning. It was Uncle Buddy who was his mentor, much more than his actual namesake, Uncle John Kolding, even though Kolding was a minister. He turned to Psalm 103:

> Bless the Lord, O my soul: and all that is within me, bless his holy name. Bless the Lord, O my soul, and forget not all his benefits: Who forgiveth all thine iniquities; who healeth all thy diseases; Who redeemeth thy life from destruction; who crowneth thee with loving kindness and tender mercies.

It seemed to fit, after all he'd been through. Now to find peace and healing, both of body and soul. Millie was a caregiver, with her homey ways and kind spirit. She was a healer, in her own way. If only Uncle Buddy were here to sit with him by the lake and talk and wait for a bite.

"There's a big catfish down in this lake, Johnny," Uncle Buddy had said one sweltering day in August as he put a fresh worm on his hook. John had been about twelve at the time, and listened as he worked on a tangled reel. Uncle Buddy had been taking him fishing on the dock since he was a little little boy. "I never seen him myself, but I been told by reliable men. My Grampa—you know, old Godfrey Mason—come out here one time when they were building the Clubhouse, in 1911, this is back when everybody in these parts still spoke German, you know, and some guys hauled in a boat on a wagon and paddled all around the lake. Grampa said it was clear as glass that day, and they could see all the way down to the bottom. One of the guys was Gus Schmidtke, the banker, and he pulled a shiny new silver dollar out of his vest pocket and tossed it overboard. The men watched that coin all the way to the bottom, must have been thirty feet down. And way down there it looked like there was a log down on the bottom of the lake, just a big brown thing covered with mud. And wouldn't you know it, the coin landed on top of the log, and the log moved!

"It began to swim, great, lazy swishes of its enormous tail, slowly, slowly, in big circles, coming up toward the surface. It took the big fish a long time to come up to the top. The men were amazed. They had heard stories from the early settlers about huge catfish taken from the river—seven foot long and 300 pounds—but nobody had ever seen one for they were all inlanders, used to taking bluegill and crappie and panfish from the creek. Of course the men all acted like idiots, talking a mile a minute and trying to bait their hooks and get them in the water. But that fish just swam up to the surface and looked at them. It was a huge thing, they swore it was four foot long or more, with an enormous head and a huge mouth. And it floated there near the surface for a moment, just staring at them with big, dark, glassy eyes, gills wafting in and out, in and out. You better believe it. And the men all stared back like they was dumbfounded. Then the great fish sank down again into the depths, down back into the deep bottom of the lake, and went into a dark place, looked like a cave or ledge down there. By then the light was changing and a breeze had come up and rippled the surface of the lake and they couldn't see as well. So they went home and that's all they talked about for the next month was that enormous catfish. They called him Old Methuselah, and every time they came back to the Friedensee they hunted for that fish. They fished from the shore, they set out trot lines, they waved lanterns at night to draw it up from the deep. Chummed the water with turkey liver. Never did see it again, though several men got tremendous, line-snapping strikes from time to time that they just knew was Old Methuselah. So that's the tradition for the menfolk in our family, you know, Johnny, to fish for Old Methuselah, though God only knows what we'd do with him if we ever caught him. Nobody ever thought of that. We just have to try and catch him. He's in there, though, you better believe it. Them things live a hunnert years, them old catfish, a ranger told me one time. He's in there. My Grampa saw him. You better believe it."

As John got out of bed the springs squeaked and twanged. He thought he heard a horse whinny and a dog bark off in the distance. Probably came from the McFadden place across the creek. The foot was bad this morning, but all the same John hobbled on his cane into the kitchen and made some doughballs from flour and water and bacon grease. It was still early. Catfish had the habit of lying in the deep water during the day, then coming up to circle the shallows at night to feed. Maybe one hadn't found anything to suit him yet. He heard a splash in the lake. He felt the rising excitement that fishermen feel when they hear a splash. Could be a big one. Could be Old Methuselah, though John had reacted to Buddy's yarn with skepticism, like all older children who are wise to Santa Claus and the Easter Bunny. Maybe a doughball would be tasty to the fish. A nice cat for breakfast would sure be good. The sweet, white flesh of the catfish. Nothing tastier. Dip him in flour, then egg, then cornmeal, then fry him up in the big deep cast-iron skillet. Some fresh biscuits. A whole lot of coffee. For John was ravenously hungry again, and it seemed like the more he ate, the emptier he felt.

John selected a long cane pole and took the cork off so the bait would lie on the bottom where catfish like to find it. He took it slow, for the foot was hurting badly as he hobbled down to the shore. Leaving by the screen door on the porch, he looked at the big sycamore tree next to the ravine. The old tire swing was hanging still. John stooped to pick up a rock, then shied it at the tire swing but missed the hole. He tried another rock, and missed again. Forget it. Hearing another splash, he continued across the broad lawn and past the little copse of trees where a saddled horse—surely Rachel's—was grazing, and down the winding path to the sandy beach by the dock. It was a difficult walk, but it was worth it. There on the dock was a neat pile of clothes and a towel. And there was Rachel, swimming in the lake. John took it all in: the clear morning air, the wisps of mist on the water, the woods around the lake, the heron on the far shore, and the naked woman swimming. Not that he could see much. The water was dark green and there was a glare on the surface and she was low in the water, her body a pale blur, swimming outward with a lazy breast stroke just off the end of the dock. Then he was rewarded. As she executed a surface dive her round bottom came into view for an instant before she disappeared under water. In a moment she surfaced again and paused to tread water, turning slowly stroke by stroke toward the dock where John was standing.

Just before she spotted him he spoke. "Well, Beezer," he called out with a laugh, "you certainly have grown up!"

She shrieked, and the note echoed off the cliffs at the other end of the lake. The heron, startled, rose up on its great wings and sailed lazily up through the morning air to its nest.

"God! John, you bastard!" Rachel yelled as she found the shallow bottom with the sole of her foot and now was low and still in the water. "What the hell are you doing, spying on me? Get out of here! Millie said you'd sleep till noon." Her face was flushed and hot with embarrassment at seeing him. This was the same John who had teased her as a child, playing jokes on her and giving her nicknames. The John of her childhood, gone for so long, and now come back. She had so looked forward to seeing him. Sure, she'd had a little-girl crush on him, but that was long past. Just the same she wanted to see him on good terms and make a good impression. Why of all days did she have to pick this one to get the urge to go skinny dipping? Yet one more impulse that blew up in her face.

John raised a finger in mock admonition: "As the door turneth upon its hinges, so doth the slothful upon his bed. Proverbs 26:14."

Rachel came right back: "Oh, yeah? Well 'Whosoever looketh on a woman to lust after her hath committed adultery with her already in his heart.' Matthew 6:28. So beat it!"

John's laughter exploded from his mouth and echoed from the rocks. "Good, Rachel. You got me. You must have had Pastor Gottlieb for confirmation like I did. I apologize. Look," he said, lifting up his foot, "I'm a little stove up. I can't just run back to the Clubhouse. Come on up. I won't look." Then he swore by the ancient children's oath: "Cross my heart and hope to die, stick a needle in my eye."

As Rachel began to dog-paddle slowly toward the dock, keeping her body low in the green water, John turned his back from her and limped away, turning left at the end of the dock and walking past the sandy beach to the old fishing spot. He waited, facing into the woods while Rachel toweled off and dressed. There was the horse, still grazing. John heard another sound, perhaps a groundhog scratching around. When Rachel gave him the all-clear, John pressed a doughball onto the hook, cast the line out into the water, and stuck the cane pole into the mud, firmly and deeply. Just let it sit, was the old wisdom for catching catfish. Sooner or later a cruising fish would find it.

John turned and smiled at Rachel, who was still glaring at him. She was a grown woman now, shapely in the compact way women get from farm work and riding and swimming. A fly buzzed past. The air was warming up. The horse snorted and swished its tail. Then as he looked, distracted by the sight of the young woman, there came a sound behind him like the patter of small running feet, coming up very close to him before it registered in his mind that he was hearing something he should pay attention to. Like the explosion of a bomb it startled him—there behind him was a large black and brown dog, barking with a huge voice, the barks like thunderclaps echoing off the cliffs and filling everything everywhere with pain and fear and confusion. John reacted with a spasm that threw him backward as the maw of the dog with its ferocious teeth came closer and closer, barking and barking, louder and louder.

"Stop!" he pleaded, but his voice was faint with fear. "Stop. Go away. Go away!"

Then just as suddenly there was Rachel with a wet towel in her hand, swatting the big German shepherd. "Doxie! Doxie!" she shouted. "Down girl, down. Sit!" The dog hushed and sat. "There's a good girl, that's right, sit." The dog looked admiringly at Rachel, wagging its bushy tail as it panted with its tongue out, expecting a snack from its master like all dogs do all the time. Rachel reached into the pocket of her shorts and pulled out a dog biscuit and gave it to Doxie as she patted its head. "Don't bark at John, Doxie. Don't bark at John, you bad puppy. He's our friend. He's nice. He's good. He won't hurt us. No. No no no. John is good. John is good. John is good." She rubbed the dog all over as it lay on its back in submission, smiling with its whole body. "Sorry about that, John. Are you OK? God, you really reacted."

"Yeah, sure," John fibbed, still shaken. "I'm fine."

"I know what's the matter with her. She's about to drop a litter. Yesterday she took off after the mailman." Rachel stroked the dog's head and scratched behind its ears. "You're a naughty girl, sleeping around with those lowlife neighborhood mongrels. Naughty, naughty, naughty. Here, John, let me help you up." She extended a firm grip and he took it. She was strong and pulled him up easily.

"Thanks, Rachel," he said, and meant it. "I'm going in."

"OK," she replied. "I'll be along in a minute."

John made his slow way back to the Clubhouse. He looked again at the tire swing but decided not to throw a rock. Maybe there was a football around somewhere. Limping onto the porch, he sat down on the bench and looked out at the water in the early light. The heron in its high nest beat its great wings slowly and rose up in stately flight, then glided slowly and easily down over the surface of the lake and then away toward the creek. Some sparrows were squabbling and feeding at a pile of cracked corn Millie had set out for them next to the woodpile. Suddenly the birds scattered in a flurry as the pounding of hoofbeats came closer and closer, and Rachel on horseback leaped the woodpile in a graceful arc, trotted past, then turned and jumped it again, and again and again. She called the horse "Milton" and tied it to a porch rail, unsaddled it, gave it a quick brush down, and put on its nosebag. It was a lovely brown gelding, a quarter horse by the look of it, the kind most farmers rode in the county, buying them from Aintree Stables on County Road D.

Rachel came in and started banging around in the kitchen, something like Millie but with a different rhythm—energetic and brisk. And pretty soon the smell of fresh coffee wafted out onto the porch just like a hundred times before when John was a kid. With Rachel cooking, Millie was playing the old piano. As usual, she was playing a hymn and singing along. It was an old German one, *Schönster Herr Jesu.** Then, as he had the day before, John dozed off again, but only for a moment, not long enough to dream. He was determined not to make that mistake again. Even as he dozed he could hear Millie singing a verse from "Abide With Me," the hymn that was sung at all funerals, and no doubt had been sung over Uncle Buddy:

> Thou on my head in early youth didst smile,
> And though rebellious and perverse meanwhile,
> Thou hast not left me, oft as I left Thee.
> On to the close, O Lord, abide with me.

When he awoke, there was a cup of coffee before him and a plate of bacon and eggs, and Rachel sitting across from him with a book in her hand.

To John she was not what one would call a beautiful woman, though there was something attractive about her in a healthy, outdoorsy sort of way. An inner light seemed to come from somewhere under the surface of her skin, though perhaps it was just an illusion created by the tone of her skin. The freckles were gone, replaced by an even tan and a clear complexion. Her hair was light brown, tending to blonde from hours on the lifeguard stand, and cut short for easy care. Her eyes were a very deep brown, as brown as could be, the color of dark coffee and as warm and inviting. Though as she read her eyebrows knit up in the middle as if she were looking upon some scene of ineffable sadness. Her nose was small, turned up just a little, and when she talked or smiled there was a dimple in her cheek. Rachel

---

* "Fairest Lord Jesus," or, "Beautiful Savior"

was of average height and build, her breasts full and firm but not too large, her arms round from exercise and work, and her legs solid. She was wearing a folk festival T-shirt and khaki shorts, and hiking boots and thick socks. She was much more than just a farm girl.

John said a quick silent grace and took a couple of bites. The slab bacon was crisp, the henhouse eggs done over easy in bacon grease with a little salt and pepper. There was a slice of homemade bread with butter and homemade watermelon preserves, and a cup of black coffee.

"Mm. Man. Delicious," John said between big bites. "Thanks, Rachel. Mm. Wow. What are you reading?"

"Oh, nothing. Shakespeare's sonnets." Rachel looked at him with satisfaction. She liked to cook and she did it well, and she liked to see a man eat, though with a twinge of anguish she remembered for the hundredth time that day that she had no men to cook for any more. As she looked at John eat, it gave her pleasure to give him pleasure. But he seemed thin. He needed more good meals. And he was eating way too fast.

He put the plate down and slurped at the coffee. Three gulps, four, and it was gone. "Sonnets. Good. Read me one."

"No, you'll be bored."

"No, I won't, I swear."

"OK, here we go. 'When to the sessions of sweet silent thought/ I summon up remembrance of things past,/ I sigh the lack of many a thing I sought,/ And with old woes new wail my dear time's waste . . .' Hey!"

John had nodded his head and was pretending to snore. He came to when she yelled. "Huh? What . . . "

Rachel shook her head and chuckled. "See if you get any more culture from me."

Then they looked at each other. Where to begin? What to say? They were five years apart in age—insurmountable in childhood but now not so far apart. He was thirty, she twenty-five, both adults but not so far from adolescence and childhood before that. When they were kids he was a big boy and she was a little girl, and that was the limit of the relationship. At least for John. Then came high school for him and football and work during the summer and less time at the Clubhouse, then college and seminary and a hitch in the parish and then Germany. He really hadn't seen her for ages. They looked at each other, both at a loss for words, laughed nervously, then looked away.

"So how have you been?" they both said to each other at exactly the same moment, then laughed even louder with more jitters.

"OK," John said, "we'll draw straws."

"You go first."

"No, you."

"No, you."

"No, you. OK, I give. I'm terrible. I've been a pirate for years and years, killing and plundering up and down the Spanish Main, and I fell in love with a dusky black African princess and she broke my heart, and then I was mortally wounded by a sultan in a duel with scimitars and now I've come back here to die."

Rachel laughed heartily. Here was an echo of the John she knew, full of wild, impossible stories that kept the little ones hanging on every word for hours as they sat with him by the fire on chilly evenings. She had sat in his lap so many times. It was so nice, so secure to be in his arms. But that was ages and ages ago.

John knew that laugh at once. It was the same she'd had as a child, but now was deeper, yet with the same musical timbre of wind chimes in the breeze.

"Here," she said. "Let me get you some more coffee." She brought in the pot and filled his cup. Quiet surrounded them in the still morning with the ticking of the old clock. A slight breeze picked up, rustling the leaves in the nearby trees. The horse swished its tail. A duck flew in and landed with a splash, followed by her drake, then together they waddled up the shore toward the corn pile and fed together, casually conversing with low gabbling voices. Doxie came in from the kitchen and sat down beside Rachel. The dog looked at John and growled as its hackles rose. He tensed up.

"Doxie!" Rachel admonished. "Hush." She rolled her eyes. "Preggers. Though what I'll do with the puppies I haven't a clue. Just try to relax, John. Dogs sense when you're afraid of them. It puts them on guard."

"I know," he said. He'd always liked dogs, always got along well with them. Except once.

There was a pause. Again the slow ticking of the clock.

"So what happened to your foot?"

"Oh, nothing."

"Sorry," she said, "I don't mean to pry." This was odd, she thought. Normally people like to talk about their aches and pains.

"Oh, that's OK," he said reluctantly. "Well, a dog bit me. Sort of."

"Really! Must have been a heck of a big dog."

He nodded, looking for a way out of this corner. "So catch me up on yourself."

She took a deep breath. "Oh, boy. Let me see." She fiddled with a piece of paper she had absent-mindedly torn from a magazine, twisting it and untwisting it. So many things to say, so many things to conceal. "Nothing much, really. Farm work and all that. You know. Then in high school I was on the swim team and was a lifeguard in the summer, and then I got in at SEMO State and majored in English, and after that I got in at Wash U. and was working on a master's in English, even got as far as drafting a thesis. Then Dad and Bobby..." She drew a breath and stopped.

"Yes, I heard. I'm very sorry."

"Thanks, John. Then after that I pretty much had to come back here and help Mom."

They said nothing for a minute or so, but somehow neither one felt uncomfortable in the silence. Heavy deep dark water was flowing under the bridge.

"What were you going to do your thesis on?" asked John.

"You really want to know?"

"Sure. Fire away."

"No, you'll be bored."

"No, I won't. I swear. Look, I'm working on a dissertation myself."

She took a breath. By now she had wadded up the piece of paper into a little ball and was rolling it around with her fingers and looking at it. "You'll be sorry. 'Re-imag[in]ing the Silence of the Other in Shakespeare's *Measure for Measure.*'" She looked at him for a reaction. Once again John had dropped his head forward as if he were sleeping and as she finished began to fake-snore loudly. "Wake up, you!" she said with a laugh as she flicked the spitball at him, hitting him squarely on the forehead.

"Ow, good shot!" John said with his lopsided grin.

"That's twice," she said, wagging her finger at him in mock warning. She tore another piece of paper from the magazine and began to twizzle it. "All right, John," Rachel said, gesturing with her hand for him to begin. "Your life story."

He shrugged. What to say, what to hide? "Well," he began, "college in Milwaukee, then seminary in Ft. Wayne, then I got assigned to a little bitty congregation in Alaska. It's not as cold there as you'd think. And the fishing was unbelievable. Me on one side of the creek fishing, and a bear on the other. But I got a few articles published, and my old profs encouraged me to go on for graduate studies, and I got in at Heidelberg. And I went over there three years ago and finished the lectures and here I am to try and pull together a dissertation." It was the truth, as far as it went.

Rachel nodded. "On?"

"I don't want to say. You'll be bored."

"No I won't."

"You're sore at me. You'll sic Doxie on me again."

"No, I won't. Now go ahead."

"'The Third Use of the Law in the Systematic Theology of Phillip Melanchthon,'" he said, finishing the long title by speaking more and more slowly until again he was nodding and snoring.

Rachel laughed again, loudly and clearly as she jumped up. "You obviously need a nap," she said.

"Actually, a nap wouldn't do me any harm. I had a long drive yesterday."

"Where did you come in from?"

"New York."

She looked at him with her mouth open. He must have driven

twenty-four hours straight through. As she gathered the breakfast dishes she said to him with more tenderness than she meant to let out, "Well, you go tuck yourself in. I'm going back down to the lake for a bit, then I need to do these dishes."

"Any more skinny-dipping? I'll postpone my nap."

She clenched her fist and shook it at him in mock anger.

"OK, OK, I give. Check my line for me while you're down there, will you?"

"Sure. Can I help you up?"

"Thanks." And again she pulled him to his feet. He seemed so light. He needed to eat. She needed to feed him. John left the porch. She took the dishes to the kitchen, then left also, going out the porch door and pausing to stroke her horse's muzzle and whisper tender loving things into its soft ear while her thoughts tumbled around over that man inside. She looked at the old sycamore by the ravine. Here is the tire swing John put up when he began to get interested in football, so he could practice throwing the ball through a moving target, and he would push her for it seemed like hours at a time, talking about silly things and making her laugh. Then she walked toward the lake. Here is the woodpile where John hid the golden Easter egg that year she found it, and she felt so special, and he had made a big fuss over her in front of the other children and even though she was not a relative she was made to feel like one. Here is the little copse of woods where she and the other girls would have proper British tea parties with their doll house tea sets, and the little boys would make fun of them until John drove them away. She was five or six when her parents first started letting her come over to the Clubhouse, and John seemed like a god descended from some far Olympus, he was so big and confident and masculine, and she had worshipped and adored him. But that was a long time ago, and she had been just a little girl. So much had become of her in the intervening years. John it seemed had had some kind of trouble. But who was she to pry? She had had troubles of her own. Here was the dock where the kids used to sit in the evening and watch the sun go down over the lake. And here is the bank where John came down this morning with his fishing pole.

He had cast the line in the water and pushed the pole down into the mud bank just here. Or somewhere near here. She looked around as she snapped out of her memories and thoughts. There was a socket in the mudbank and there was the print of John's tennis shoe and pock marks from his cane. But the pole was gone.

Chapter 2 ⊚ John and Rachel, John and Rafael

Millie came back from Perryville about noon. The old Buick station wagon was loaded with groceries, and Rachel went out to help carry them in. There was a new broom and dustpan, some dishwashing detergent for the kitchen, Brillo pads, bars of Ivory soap for the rooms, toilet paper for the outhouse, Folgers coffee, stew beef, slab bacon and brown eggs from the country store, navy beans, flour, baking powder, plus things Millie had bought from farmers along the way: potatoes from Schultheiss, onions and bell peppers from Oswald, and tomatoes and carrots and two chickens from Ann Gottlieb, the pastor's wife who kept a large garden and henhouse.

The two women worked together like old teammates who knew the plays without thinking and could anticipate each others' moves. Rachel put the block of ice in the icebox and stored the meat while Millie threw back the red-and-white-checkered tablecloth on the long table to make space for food preparation. Rachel went out to the woodpile with the hatchet and chopped up a bundle of kindling, brought it in, and started a fire in the old stove while Millie cubed the beef. When the fire was going good Rachel put bacon grease into the large cast-iron skillet and browned the meat while Millie pumped water from the kitchen cistern into the big cook pot and set it on the back burner to heat up. That done, the two women sat down at the table to peel and chop vegetables—Millie the carrots, Rachel the onions.

"So did John ever haul himself out of bed this morning?" asked Millie.

Rachel nicked her finger with the paring knife. "Ow, dangit! Where are those Band-Aids?"

"In the cupboard next to the sink."

Rachel bandaged herself and sat down again. "Oh, yeah, he got up early. He came down to the lake while I was swimming."

"You weren't skinny-dipping again, I hope."

Rachel looked down intently at her onion and said nothing.

"Rachel!" Millie exclaimed. "How many times did I tell you you were asking for trouble, doing that?"

"Well," Rachel shot back, "you told me John was exhausted from his long drive and was probably going to sleep late. How was I supposed to know he was going to get up early and go fishing?"

"Young lady, you don't go running around naked when there's a man around. He probably sensed it in his sleep and that's what got him up." Millie shook her head in disgust. "Where is he now?"

"In his room, I guess," said Rachel.

"Probably napping," they both said simultaneously, and laughed.

Millie diced a carrot with expert fingers, scooped up the bright orange pieces, and tossed them into the big blue bowl. "Or daydreaming about naked women in the lake."

"Oh, come on, Millie, gimme a break. He didn't see anything. Besides, after I swore at him and yelled at him he was very gentlemanly and looked away while I got out and dried off and dressed. A funny thing happened, though. Doxie was off sniffing around in the woods when John came down, and we exchanged a few words, but then all of a sudden Doxie ran up and started barking at him. Nothing serious. You know the way she does when she's carrying a litter. John reacted like he was terrified." Rachel teared up. "Boy, these onions are strong," she said. "I couldn't understand him reacting like that to a little old dog."

"Really," Millie said. "Makes you wonder. He's been around dogs all his life. Strange that he'd react like that. You know, he's got his foot in that boot thing, and I'm darned if I could pry it out of him what happened. All he would say is that a dog bit him. What do you think, Rachel?"

"Well, what kind of dog could do that kind of damage to a man's foot? A bulldog has tremendously powerful jaws. They're bred for biting and holding prey. A bulldog could break bones if it got hold of you. My uncle Jerry told me about a friend of his, I guess this was back in the Fifties when they were kids, a bulldog got hold of his hand and wouldn't let go, broke several bones before they shot it, and even then they had a time of it prying its jaws loose even though the dog was dead."

"Sure," said Millie, "but a man would have shoes on. What kind of dog . . . you know, I should call Doc Kramer and set up an appointment for John, get that thing looked at. He must have had it treated in Germany before he left, and I'm sure their doctors are fine and everything, but he ought to see a local doctor. You don't need to dice those onions so small, dear. For stew you want them nice and chunky."

Rachel nodded and began whacking up the onions in big pieces. The two women worked in silence for a minute or so, both mulling over the problem of John. "This is going to be an awfully big pot of stew," Rachel said. "Isn't it just the three of us for dinner tonight?"

"Oh, I forgot to mention," Millie said, "John's parents are coming by later on. I popped in on them when I was in town. They have the grandkids with them. John had only stopped by at their house briefly before coming out here, so they wanted to come and visit and spend some time."

"And he's too thin," Rachel began. Though his tight black European jeans fit him well, she thought to herself. Very well, indeed.

"Yes," Millie replied. "He needs fattening up. Did he take some breakfast?"

"Lord, you should have seen him wolf it down." The memory of his ravenous eating was at the same time fascinating and terrifying, like being confronted unprotected with a ferocious animal.

"Well, that's a healthy sign. He has an appetite. He's not depressed or anything. That's bad for a man, to get all tangled up in his mind. A man needs to do, not think."

"What a brain, though. I told him the topic of my master's thesis, and then he told me the topic of his doctoral dissertation and blew me out of the water. It's just so puzzling, though, Millie. He seems guarded, somehow. He wasn't like that when we were kids. I mean, he made fun of me and called me Little Beezer and all that, but he was nice, you know. Now it's like he's, I don't know, what's the word ... wary. TD isn't like that at all." Rachel thought for a moment of the big man, Timothy David "TD" Pope, Millie's son. He had taken her out a few times recently, picked her up in his big Mercedes, wearing good clothes, smelling of nice cologne. They'd go to a fancy restaurant in St. Louis or drive through the hills in the wine country west of St. Charles. TD was unfailingly polite and wore his success lightly and easily, as if it came to him as a matter of right. And that car was really impressive.

"Well, I couldn't say exactly," Millie said guardedly. "Timmy's been around all these years and John's been gone."

"Yeah," Rachel went on, "I was so excited when you called yesterday and said he was here. I had hardly seen him in ... I don't know, what, fifteen years or so, since I was still a girl, about ten or eleven. And God, how I worshipped that guy, you know, little-girl crush and everything, and then he comes and he's all, he's just, well, ordinary. Except for all that intellect. And that Jeep of his is a hunk o' junk." Yes, she thought, who could be attracted to a man with a junk car?

"I don't know about ordinary," Millie replied, "Hand me some more carrots from out of the bag there once. Johnny was off in school, doing better and better after being mediocre in high school. He banged through college in three years, then he went to that seminary in Indiana, and after that he had a congregation in Alaska, for God's sake, and when he wasn't fishing he was studying and writing scholarly articles on I don't know what, he sent me one and I tried to read it, put me to sleep in five minutes, and tending his flock, and pretty slim pickins as far as marriage prospects other than Eskimo squaws I guess, so he became this contented bachelor, and this goes on for ages it seems like, and we hardly ever see him, and then three years ago he jumps up and says he's going to Europe to study theology! Lord, have mercy! That meant we'd never see him. But that's the way he is. Just gets a notion, and off he goes, the little stinker.

There's a streak of that in the Mason family, though. Story is that his grandfather or great-grandfather or something went out West back in the frontier days and had some adventures. I think my mother knew about it, but I could never pry it out of her. Me, I always liked what Amundsen said: 'Adventure comes from a lack of planning.' Give me home and stability any day."

"Me, too," Rachel said. "Me, too. Security. That's what a woman wants. Men always want to go off on adventures and kill bears and fight wolves and it's us women who have to tie them down and civilize them for the sake of the children. Well, that helps explain some of it as far as John is concerned. TD seems just the opposite. Just a good, steady guy. He darn sure has been successful."

"I'll say," Millie replied with that same guarded expression. "Chop up some celery if you're done with those onions. He's been like that since he was little. Set his mind on something and just kept plowing ahead until he got it." Millie thought, but didn't say it, that Timmy also had a tendency to cut corners to accelerate acquisition, like the time he was selling peanut brittle for Boy Scouts and sold to the relatives of three other kids before anybody found out. Nothing technically illegal, but it made you a little uncomfortable when a kid was that ambitious.

"He's done well in real estate." Rachel was very curious to know exactly how well. TD had been showing definite interest in her lately. She liked the big Mercedes with its soft leather seats. She liked the good clothes he wore. But what kind of security did he have to offer? What kind of house did he have? Did he have anything in savings? What would they do with the farm if they were to marry?

"Well, I guess. After he took Ste. Genevieve High to the state championship in football he was about as famous as the president in these parts. That translates into business contacts, is what he always says, so just like a little kid selling stuff for a school fundraiser he got going in real estate even while he was going to college at Washington University—he graduated a few years before you went there for graduate school. Knocked out a degree in business and had enough money from selling that he graduated debt-free and was able to buy a good used Cadillac, which he says realtors need since they drive customers around to look at houses and you need to impress them with a good car."

"So he didn't play college ball?"

"Sure he did. All four years on a football scholarship. As the quarterback he was right out there in front of ten thousand people every Saturday afternoon. Again, the visibility translated into business contacts. To him, football was just a means to an end. It meant a lot more to Johnny, I think. Then there was that big game."

"When was that?"

"Both boys were quarterbacks for their teams, Timmy—around that time they started calling him 'TD' for 'touchdown' as well as for his name, Timothy David—for Ste. Gen and Johnny for Perryville, and Timmy was a senior and Johnny was a junior, you know, part of the old Clubhouse Gang—you remember, they grew up together here, throwing the football around and trying to put it through the old tire swing while it was moving. Timmy was always bigger and faster and more talented in sports than Johnny, but Johnny was pretty fair himself, and both teams were good that year, and it came down to a big game in the regional playoffs, and it was Johnny against Timmy. Johnny's team lost, of course, and that was that."

"I didn't know about that."

"Well, you were still pretty young."

"Yeah, and that's harvest time, too, in the fall, so we never paid any attention to football."

"Lord, those two guys sure did. John played the next year, but a couple of his key players were injured in that game and didn't try out again. So his senior year they went five and five, and John was just starting to find out he had brains and that school could be interesting if you applied yourself. That's when he got started with Latin. "

By now the meat was browned and sizzling in the pan, the aroma filling the house. Rachel dumped the beef into the stewpot, added the vegetables and some water and salt, threw a few more sticks of wood into the firebox, and put the pot on the back burner to simmer the rest of the day.

"Mm, boy, something smells good," said John, appearing at the kitchen door and leaning on his cane.

"Well look who's finally up," said Millie. "It's about time."

"I've been up. Ask Rachel. Such beautiful scenery early in the morning. Down by the lake."

Rachel shot him a dirty look.

"What's for lunch?" John asked.

"You sure have an appetite these days," said Millie.

"Here," Rachel said, tossing him a potato as she attempted a smile, "He that will not work, neither shall he eat. Get to work. Millie, we forgot the potatoes."

"Oh, well, it's not too late. That's what we get for talking while working. You and John peel potatoes while I make sandwiches. But put the potatoes in water for now. We'll add them later on or else they'll fall apart if they overcook."

John took the paring knife and deftly cut out the eyes of the first potato, then whittled away at the rough brown skin, letting the peelings fall into a bucket at his feet. As he looked down, he saw Doxie curled up at Rachel's feet. There were some meat scraps on the cutting board where Millie had trimmed the fat.

"Rachel, can I give these to Doxie?"

"Sure," she said as she chopped the potato she had peeled and tossed it into the bowl. "Big chunks."

"OK. Doxie!" John said to the sleeping dog as he held out his hand. "Doxie! Here, girl." The big shepherd sprang to her feet, took the two steps under the table, and eagerly gobbled up the meat from his hand. John patted her on the head and gave her the rest of the scraps. "Good girl. Good girl. That's a good dog. You're a good dog, yes, you are. Good dog, Doxie. Now don't attack me anymore, OK? See, Rachel? The way to a girl's heart is through her stomach."

"I think you may be right, John. You've made a friend for life now."

Doxie sat at John's feet. He scratched behind her ears. "Sorry, old gal, no more treats. Don't we have anything else I can give her?"

"Try this," Rachel said, handing John a piece of cheese from the table.

John gave Doxie the morsel, which she accepted with a canine grin. She put her right paw on his knee, a sign of peace and submission. John and Rachel finished the potatoes as Millie brought lunch and set it at their places. On each plate was a large slice of homemade bread, white, soft, and fresh, with a golden brown crust, and on the bread was spread a thick layer of soft, milky white *Kochkäse*[*] with caraway seeds, the kind old farm wives still make in Perry County, and John and Rachel and Millie each sprinkled a bit of pepper on their open-faced cheese sandwiches as was the custom of everyone in these parts. Then Millie poured them each a cup of black coffee.

"Come, Lord Jesus," John began, and Rachel and Millie joined in to say, "be our guest, and let these gifts to us be blest. Amen." It was the Common Table Prayer that all Lutherans say, except that at the end John made the Sign of the Cross. Rachel and Millie exchanged a glance with raised eyebrows.

"Well, I'm going to eat outside," said Millie, and went out the side door that led from the kitchen to the outside, leaving John and Rachel alone.

John took a big bite of his sandwich. "Oh, man. Fantastic. I'm starved. I can't seem to get enough to eat these days."

"Did you get some rest?" Rachel asked softly. "You must be tired from your trip."

"Thanks, but no, I was going over my notes and setting up my desk. I've got this dissertation to write. So I was just messing around mostly, doing preliminary stuff, unpacking books and whatnot, you know. I'd just thrown it all in a box rather hurriedly." John gulped down his coffee. He had said more than he had intended. They ate in silence for a few minutes. Doxie lay down under the table with her chin on John's booted foot. He looked up and smiled at Rachel. Their eyes met, she smiled back, then looked away quickly.

Finally John tried to start conversation. "I was sorry to hear about your dad and your brother. Millie told me a little about it, but not much. How did it happen?"

---

[*] Cooked cheese

Rachel nodded. "Thanks, John. A farm accident, you know. Just one of those things." The pain and shock of it were still fresh, even though it had happened two years before. But she had repeated it so many times to so many people she had it down pat by now. "It was in the spring. The fields were still muddy, the creek running high from spring rains. Dad and Bobby went out to disc the soil and prep it for planting. Maybe they should have waited a few days. Easy to say in retrospect. There's a section we have near the creek where the field slopes down at a pretty steep angle. Of course nobody was there to see what happened. But the policemen tried to reconstruct the chain of events, and they guessed that both men were on the tractor. Those things are top heavy anyway, you know. I came back from St. Louis right away. Mom took me out to the fields the next day and we looked at the scene of the accident. There were slide marks on the hill. The tractor had old tires. Dad meant to change them, but tractor tires are expensive, you know. So it looked like the tractor slid, the coupling jammed on the discer, then the tractor flipped and the discer went with it, and pinned my dad . . ."

Rachel choked up. John reached over and took her hand—an instinctive pastoral gesture—but Rachel withdrew her hand and dabbed her eyes and nose with a paper napkin. "They figure Bobby was thrown into the creek. They found his body the next day about a mile downstream." Then her mind raced through the blur of events that tumbled after. The funeral. The church crammed with everyone in the community. The burial in the churchyard. The rain. The water standing in the bottom of the graves. The enormous hole in her and her mother's lives. The impact on the farm with no men to run it. The decision to quit school and come back home. The guilt. The sense that God was punishing her for her sins. It was all such a jumble. She couldn't sort it out. But she would. She had to. She would carry on somehow. It was her duty as a farm woman to carry on. Not that her mother was making much of an effort. She looked at John again. His eyes were filled with genuine compassion. The big boy story teller. Now there was something else. There was a pastor in him. But not just a professional caregiver. Was there something authentic, something she could trust? Perhaps she could open up to him. Maybe she could risk it. Rachel gathered herself together. "You know, I still can't get through 'Abide With Me' without bawling," she said with a weak smile.

John became aware of the quality of her voice. There was a soft musicality about it that pulled you in and made you listen. What unbearable sorrow. She too had experienced anguish and grief. Should he tell her of his own? He should. Perhaps he would. She might understand. But not now. It was too fresh. Maybe someday. Some day a long ways away. He was still in shock himself. He needed time to think it all out, time to deal with it in his own way. "Let's go sit outside," he suggested.

"Sure," she said, and refilled their coffee cups. She carried both of them as John limped along on his cane.

They made their way to the green park bench that overlooked the lake. Millie had left her plate. Rachel set it on the ground, and Mr. and Mrs. Duck waddled over and picked at the crumbs, chatting companionably all the while. Millie herself was bent over by the side of the Clubhouse, deadheading the bright yellow chrysanthemums that had passed their first bloom. The lake was glassy and still, the air warm and southerly. Cicadas thrummed in the woods.

"So," Rachel began with a toss of her head as if to dispel the gloomy thoughts. She too would try to make talk. "The Third Use of the Law."

"Oh, yeah," John replied, raising his eyebrows. "My dull-as-dish-water dissertation."

Rachel looked at the two ducks. Such a contented old husband and wife. They probably had a hundred children by now. Why couldn't it be that simple for men and women? "OK, I remember this from confirmation. It's in the catechism. Let's see here, the First Use of the Law is as a curb, to, uh, wait wait, don't tell me . . . to restrain the coarse outbursts of sin in the world in general. Right?"

"Right."

"Like when everybody stops at stop signs whether they're saved or not. And the Second Use is as a mirror, to show us our sin and bring us to repentance so we'll believe in Jesus. And the Third Use is as a rule to guide us in our Christian life."

"Right. Good, Rachel."

"Well, Old Pastor Gottlieb drilled it into us."

"Yeah, me too."

"Didn't you take confirmation in town?"

"No, Pop insisted I come out here and get it from Gottlieb."

"But wait, I . . . "

"I know what you're thinking. Pastor Gottlieb had the church in Perryville—St. John's, right after he came back from being a missionary in Africa. But from what I heard Earl was too conservative for St. John's and they ousted him. So he took the call to serve Peace Church out here in the county. And Pop insisted I take my catechism from him."

"Earl?"

"Yeah, well, all us preachers are all on a first-name basis. Plus, we're related. He's my uncle."

"Oh, OK," Rachel said. "That figures. So tell me this. If the Third Use of the Law is in the catechism, why do you need a doctoral dissertation on the subject?"

"Because it's under attack. Do you know Pastor Kolding? He's attacking it, in a way. Here's the way I see it," John began like a fish rising to the bait. "The Third Use of the Law is in the catechism because it's in the Bible. Not in so many words, like the doctrine of the Trinity, but the idea is there, and theologians coined the term to sum up the teaching of the Bible." John looked at Rachel. Her face was a study of intense concentration. Could she be genuinely interested in this stuff? It seemed so. All the women John had met, like the outdoor types up North, were not the least bit interested in theology. They had brains, but not for thinking. Except for one. Except for Elizabeth, the one he had loved. He shook off the distraction and went on. "Luther was an exegete but Melanchthon was a systematician. So Luther had the idea of the Third Use of the Law, but Melanchthon coined the term and defined it."

This was fascinating to Rachel. She knew all the angles on the sixteenth century as far as England and Sidney and Spenser and

Shakespeare and the influence of Protestantism that led to the Elizabethan settlement, but she really had not had any religious instruction since confirmation in the seventh and eighth grade. She stopped her thoughts on that one. Maybe that was part of the problem: she had tried to handle adult problems with an eighth-grade religious education. But the thought passed and she continued: "OK, now, hold on. Melanchthon was Luther's friend, and he was a theologian too. I remember that. But what's a systematician and what's that other word you said?"

"Exegete. An exegete is basically a straight ahead Bible scholar, book by book, verse by verse. Luther taught mostly Hebrew and Old Testament."

"OK, got it. So then what happens?"

"So after Luther's death in 1546 things kind of fell apart in the areas of Germany where the Reformation had taken hold. Luther wasn't around to hold things together. Calvin had risen in Switzerland. Melancthon succumbed to their influence. The Pope was getting ready to send an army and wipe the Reformation out by force. There was a lot of wrangling and disputes among theologians about what the essential teachings of the Lutheran church were supposed to be. Finally some theologians assembled all the doctrinal writings that Lutherans agreed on and put them into the *Book of Concord* of 1580. Those are our 'confessions.' The *Small Catechism* that Earl—Pastor Gottlieb—taught us is one of them. That's what we subscribe to as being the true interpretation of the Bible. And that restored unity to the Lutheran churches."

"Hm," Rachel said, "we didn't have that in confirmation. So that settled it."

"Only for a time. The church is never at rest for long. There's always somebody who has a different idea of how the Bible should be interpreted. Like in the fourth century, Athanasius, who wrote the Nicene Creed, was banished five times. Theologians have to dive down deep into the Scriptures again and again, and swim around as it were and try to catch . . ." John faltered. " . . . what am I trying to say? It's that those truths are down there, waiting to be caught, and if you can get hold of them and bring them up... well, I suppose it's like fishing—and Peter and those men were fishermen—if you can catch hold of those truths they are good to eat."

Rachel looked out at the lake for a moment or two. "Oh, I meant to tell you. Your fishing pole is gone."

John stared at her blankly. "What do you mean, it's gone?"

"Just what I said. Gone. I went down to the dock after we talked this morning, just me and Doxie, and I was going to check your pole like you asked. And I saw where you had stuck the pole into the bank but I noticed that the whole thing was gone. There was just the hole in the mud bank where it had been."

John thought for a moment. "I know, Millie must have checked it and found that the bait was gone and brought it back inside."

"Oh, sure," Rachel replied. "That makes sense."

"Well, no catfish today. Too bad. I'm hungry for some, too. No catfish in Germany."

"Are you hungry again? You just ate two minutes ago. Speaking of Germany, you were in Heidelberg, right? What was that like?"

"A little snack wouldn't hurt. But yeah, Heidelberg. Oh, fantastic! Man, it's wonderful. Little winding streets and old crooked buildings with red tile roofs, and the river running past, and then on the hill across from town there is the *Philosophenweg*[*] where Kant used to take his daily stroll and think deep thoughts. And the musty little bookstores. And the coffeehouses, oh! And the real German *Kaffe und Küchen*[†]—straight from heaven. And the wine! Like the nectar of the gods, let me tell you. I stayed at this little place called the *Heumarkt*.[‡] Obviously because it had been a hay market in the past when Heidelberg was still something of a farming town. There was this courtyard surrounded by an old *Fachwerk*[§] inn, I guess it had been a century or two before, and I had a tiny little room up on the second story, and nothing was at right angles, and the floor creaked,

---

[*] Philosopher's Walk
[†] Coffee and pastries
[‡] Haymarket
[§] Half-timber

and I had books books books all over the place, and I'd go to lectures and meet with my *Doktorvater*[*] from time to time, not nearly as regimented as the American system. It was wonderful, Rachel. I absolutely loved it."

Rachel envied him his experience and drank it in. She herself had never had the opportunity to travel much except for the two week tour of Oxford when she was a junior at Cape. The ancient atmosphere of the place, the courtyard at Keble College, the learned tone of the Bodleian Library, the musty friendliness of the Eagle and Child pub where C. S. Lewis and J. R. R. Tolkein had read their works-in-progress to each other over dark ale and clouds of pipe smoke—all that had been enough to give her an infatuation with the Old World and old ways and old traditions. Then the day trip to Cambridge, listening to the choir at King's College sing Evensong . . . enchanting. And punting on the River Cam with its lazy fish in the shallows. "Wait a minute," she said, "I just had a thought. Millie was in town all morning. She couldn't have checked your line."

John paused. "You know, you're right. I can't figure it." Unless, the thought flicked through his mind, it was a fish. But it would take an awfully large fish to yank the pole right out of the mud . . . too large. "Probably a turtle," he said, settling the matter in his mind. "There's some snappers in there. Anyway, as I was saying, there was this remarkable unity that came about in the Lutheran church in the late sixteenth century, and it endured for a long time and Christ crucified was proclaimed at last in the pulpits of Germany. But the reason the Lord never sleeps is that the devil doesn't either, you know. Or maybe vice-versa. Anyway pretty soon you've got new intellectual currents rising among the learned class, and these are somehow always opposed to the Gospel. I guess the devil's college must have a department of philosophy."

Rachel chuckled grimly. "You want to find hell, try the English department at Wash U."

"Really?"

---

[*] Dissertation director, literally "doctor–father"

"God! I'll tell you about it sometime. You'll have to buy me a stiff drink, though. Maybe two."

"That might be nice." He looked at her with those penetrating eyes. She looked away. "So go on."

"OK. Here's where it gets a little complicated." John paused, took a deep breath, and let it out slowly. "You remember me talking about my uncle, Pastor JJ Kolding?"

"Yes."

"Well, he's kind of a big shot in the Missouri Synod. Pastor of a large church in St. Louis where a lot of the high muckety-mucks from headquarters attend."

"Is that the headquarters everybody calls 'The Purple Palace'?"

"Yes. So if you're pastor to the President of Synod, what does that make you?"

"I'd say an exceedingly big cheese."

"Bingo! So dear old Uncle JJ was not only a big shot in the LCMS, but a big influence on students he taught at the seminary, young pastors he mentored, but a formative influence on his clergy nephews, like Mark Brandon out in Arizona ... "

" ... and guess who?"

John nodded. He sipped his coffee, then continued. "There's this Modernist school of thought in Lutheran theology. Started in the eighteenth century with Rationalism, first questioning the authority of the Bible, then the divinity of Jesus, and in time the necessity of Christian morality."

"Are we back to the Third Use of the Law now?"

"Yeah—boy, you're quick, Rachel!"

She smiled.

"So by the twentieth century the idea was, 'Love God and do as you please.' The Ten Commandments are no longer in force. JJ really drew me into his circle, especially by ties of blood, and made me feel a part of this inner circle, the cognoscenti. Then one night after a very intense session of our group, during which I had made a few points that drew approving murmurs, JJ kept me afterwards, poured me a big slug of very fine scotch, and proceeded to tell me that I was anointed. Special. God had shown him that I would take his place as leader of the enlightened ones, and lead Missouri out of stultifying dogmatism into a new age of illumination."

Rachel was nodding her head vigorously. Had she not heard the same blandishments in her own little corner? She was so deep in thought she failed to notice that John was, too. Slowly she came back to the surface and looked at John.

"I can relate," she said softly and touched his arm.

John blushed, laughed nervously, and drew back his arm. "Oh! Where was I?"

"The guru and number-one disciple."

"Yes. Well." Another pause. "I took this all with me to Germany, and well, I, uh, I had some experiences, and, well, um, let's say I began to doubt some of the liberal verities I'd been schooled in by JJ and company."

"Oh, really!" Rachel returned, her inner red light flashing. "Such as . . . ?"

"Such as science, for one thing. The New Way we were exploring, with higher thought not tethered to out-of-date superstitions, was based on reason. Reason critiques faith, as we know. But faith can critique reason. Science boasts infallibility as does the Bible. Which holds up under scrutiny? Then Darwin comes along in the nineteenth century and seems to put a scientific basis under the idea of evolution, which had really been around since the ancient Egyptians . . ."

Just a darn minute, what was he talking about, Rachel thought, stiffening up inside. This was the kind of rigid, fundamentalist thinking she had encountered in students from the Missouri Bootheel during all-night bull sessions in the dorm.

"Wait wait wait, John, what do you mean, 'seemed to put'? Evolution is a scientific law. Any educated person knows that. You've been to college. This is Biology 101."

John rolled his eyes, and was immediately sorry he had done so. How many times had his mother told him not to do that when he disagreed with someone. It just infuriated them.

"Don't roll your eyes at me, John Mason! And don't give me this patronizing look. I mean, what kind of narrow-minded fundamentalist rejects Darwin, for God's sake."

"Jeez, Rachel. Calm down. Even Stephen Jay Gould—a *Hahvahd professah*—even Gould has admitted that there is no evidence in the fossil record for classic Darwinism. And now they've got this 'punctuated equilibrium' and all kinds of crackpot theories so they can teach Darwin on the basis of a lack of evidence."

"Crackpot? John!" Rachel was standing now. "Listen to yourself. You're sounding exactly like some backwoods Bible thumper. Next thing you'll say you believe in a literal six-day creation."

"Well, I might if you'd let me get a word in edgewise."

"It's you that's dominating the conversation. Besides, what does any of this have to do with your dumb thesis anyway?"

"Will you sit down and let me finish?"

Rachel threw herself back down on the bench, folded her arms, and glared ahead at nothing. This guy was supposed to be a brain. How could he reject established science?

"It's all of a piece, Rachel. That's the way I see it. I mean, I've been forced to do some serious rethinking. If Darwin is right, there is no historic Adam and Eve. If there is no Adam and Eve, there is no historic Fall. If there is no Fall, there is no sin. If there is no sin, there is no need for Christ. No first Adam, no Last Adam. The entire basis of the Christian faith is destroyed. The Second Article of the Creed is predicated on the First Article. And the Third Article is predicated on the first and second. No Creation, no Redemption. No Creation and Redemption, no Sanctification. And Sanctification is another word for the Third Use of the Law. OK?"

Rachel sat fuming and glaring at nothing and everything. She mumbled something. John barged ahead.

"So here comes modern theology claiming that all you needed was the Gospel. Just believe in Jesus, and that's all you need. You don't have to pay any attention to the Law anymore, because the Law always condemns. *Lex semper accusat.* So just love everybody. That's it, without any real morality." Again he felt the pain of his own transgressions in a fleeting moment, but then he was thrown back on the defensive as Rachel opened up with both barrels.

"Well, I agree with that," Rachel said firmly, both feet planted on solid ground. "I've had it up to here with fire and brimstone sermons: 'Do this and don't do that, or you're going to hell.' Forget it!" She recalled one hardshell Fundamentalist church she had visited with her friend Molly on a weekend. It was in the country outside of New Madrid, where the big earthquake had happened. The preacher was a young man with oily hair, fat and sweating, wearing a cheap black suit and a skinny tie, and he harangued the congregation for an hour on the evils of Evolution. She was the guest of a friend and couldn't storm out of the church. So she sat there and endured it, every blow hardening her heart against such mindless religiosity. It was unbelievable that such unenlightened minds could still exist in modern America. It was as if the 1925 Scopes Monkey Trial had never even happened.

Now John was fuming. "So I suppose you're a very open-minded person."

"Well, yes." Of course. She was a country girl, but like many farm people she was progressive, up on the latest developments in agribusiness, chemical research, grain futures, computer technology... and as an educated woman she was conversant with the contours of modern thought. Who was he to put her down as some dumb hick plowing behind a mule?

"Open to everything but the Bible?"

Rachel opened her mouth to speak but nothing came out. He had scored a point fairly, and her rage subsided for a moment. But he wasn't entirely right. She believed the Bible. She could quote it, if only facetiously. It was just in a different compartment than her intellectual life. Her mind critiqued her faith, but her faith did not critique her mind.

"Here's the problem," John continued. "Just let me say this one thing, then I'll shut up. The modern theologians were teaching in the seminaries that there was no Third Use of the Law, and what is taught in the seminaries finds its way into the pulpit, and what's taught in the pulpit finds its way into people's lives."

John flushed with the thought. The Sixties as a way of life had just rolled on through the decades. There were trendy campus pastors. They were cool. They were with it. They wore beards. They smoked pipes. They played the guitar. There were folk masses in the Christian coffeehouse—passé to the world, but still hip in the churches. Students flocked to them. There was pot in the dorms. They were students, and they were a long way from home. And for him there was Germany, a very long way from home, a place where nobody knew him, a place where he was invisible, at least to his fellow man if not to God, a place where he could dance on the edge of disaster if he wanted to. When you're in a place where nobody you know can see you, you begin to tell yourself that God can't see you either...

And Rachel on her part had troubling thoughts as well. She, like John, had left the county, gone away to school in a strange town, lived among strange people, taken up strange customs, tried new things that no one at home would ever know about. It was a time to be young and wild and free, heedless of the consequences, never imagining for a moment that what you sow you will one day reap. But the seed of a man when sown brings forth the fruit of the womb in woman... but he was a professor, so sophisticated, so worldly... it had to be handled discreetly, his career could be ruined... never mind Rachel's career...

BOOM! BOOM! John and Rachel started at the sound of shotguns going off, then echoing once, twice, between the cliffs and the hills. Looking toward the Clubhouse they saw Millie working the skeet-shooting apparatus and Ralph, John's father, with his .12 gauge, blazing away at the clay pigeons. Ralph reloaded. "Let 'er fly, Millie!" he shouted. Millie tripped the switch. Whirrr went the spring, flinging the target up and out over the lake. "Nigger in the woodpile!" he shouted again. *Blam-blam* went the shotgun again, hit one, missed one. Echo. Echo. Ralph and Millie waved at John and Rachel to come over. They did.

"How are you kids doing?" said John's father. Ralph Mason was a medium-sized man, an older edition of John but heavier around the middle, his face lined and creased, his hands brawny and hard from years of cranking wrenches and hoisting motors in the shop. He was wearing lace-up construction boots, khaki work clothes, both pants and shirt, and a green John Deere gimme cap. "Good to see you, Johnny, old man." He embraced his son heartily, pounding him on the back and tousling his hair as if he were a nine-year-old.

"Jeez, Pop," John said, "do you still have to say that?"

"Say what?"

"You know."

"Oh, 'nigger in the woodpile'? Hell, son, it's just an expression." Too much education, he said to himself. Got his head too big for his britches. Probably been around too many high-toned niggers, made friends with some. Probably votes Democrat, too. Why do we let our kids go off to college, anyway?

"Well, it kind of makes me uncomfortable."

"Well, all right, Johnny, if it'll make you feel better, I'll drop it. Now for some shooting," Ralph said. "Boys against the girls. One round. Loser does dishes tonight." He loaded the big gun with two Remington .12 gauge shells and said, "Let 'er go!"

"Democrat in the woodpile," he shouted. *Whizz, whirr*, two shots, two hits. Then turning he grinned at John.

"Great, Pop. Good shot," John said, shaking his head. "You nailed them Democrats good. Two to nothing, our favor. We can just relax tonight."

"OK, Millie," said Rachel, "show these guys how its done."

"Easy as pie," Millie replied as she loaded up. Rachel tripped the switch. Millie fired. One for two. "Two to one, still your favor," Millie said as she broke open the breach and handed the shotgun to John, then went back to the target house.

"Not bad," said John. "Where's Mom?" he said to his father as he loaded the gun.

"Back by the tire swing with Katie and Billy. You know how she hates guns anyways."

John glanced over and saw them. Katie, his brother Bill's six-year-old daughter, was in the swing under the big sycamore, being pushed by his mother. Billy, his sister Lou Ann's son, a husky ten-year-old, was heading toward them, fascinated by the sound of the guns.

"OK, Millie," John said. "Ready when you are."

The clay pigeons flew. John fired. Two shots. Two misses. Just like the tire swing. The big gun kicked hard. He wasn't braced right. Now his shoulder hurt in addition to his foot. And he had lost his touch.

"*Nya*, nya, nya, *nya*, nya," taunted Rachel.

"Watch it, Beezer," said John.

She made a face at him, and he made a face back. Then she shot him with a make-believe shotgun, and he clutched his bleeding heart, staggering on his cane.

"Rachel, you're up," said Ralph as he walked over to the target house.

"Ready?"

"Ready."

Ralph sprang the trap. Rachel snapped the gun to her shoulder and set it firmly. The birds flew, two clay pigeons trailing in a graceful arc over the lake. She led them with the gunsight, aiming just ahead of where they were going to be a moment after she pulled the trigger. She pulled the trigger slow, so as not to jar the muzzle. In a moment she saw in her mind's eye a certain professor. Take that, you s.o.b., she said under her breath. One shot. A hit. Take that! Another shot. Another hit. Clay shards like shattered dreams spattered on the water and sank without a trace.

"Ha-ha!" exclaimed Millie and Rachel at the same time. "Girls win!" Rachel was grinning but her face was fierce and grim.

John stood leaning on his cane. "Well, if you women are such good shots, go out in the woods and kill us something for supper. A little barbeque bear would be yummy."

"Don't you wish," said Millie. "Besides, we've got that big pot of stew."

Rachel said, "Yes, and I'm looking forward to putting my feet up and being waited on hand and foot."

By then Billy had come into the circle. "Can I have a turn?" he pleaded.

"No, not with the shotgun anyways," said Ralph.

"Please, Grampa? Please?"

"Can you reach over the top of your head and touch your ear?"

asked Ralph. It was a time-honored way of keeping young children away from guns.

Billy reached up and over. He was big for his age, with long arms, and had to stretch and stretch on his tip toes, making grimaces with his face, but he did it, just barely. "Well, OK," said Ralph. "But this shotgun will knock you on your butt. Take this one." And he handed the boy a small .22 caliber rifle, single-shot, bolt action.

"Coffee time," called Millie from the front screen door to everyone in general. Then she said to John's mother, "Betty, *kommst du noch!*"*

"*Was geht?*" Betty called back.

"*Kaffe und Küchen.*"

"Really? Great. *Was Uhr?*"

"It's three o'clock already," Millie said as she went in the side door to the kitchen. Betty called to Katie, who had gotten off the swing and gone down by the lake and was looking into the water. Katie returned, and the two of them walked toward the house, Katie's hand in Betty's. John on his cane and Rachel beside him were slowly going toward the porch, Doxie trailing along behind them, reading the ground with her nose.

"Look, I'm sorry if I popped off at you, John," said Rachel as they reached the porch steps. John sat down as Rachel stroked her horse's nose and made sweet little mouth noises. Doxie snuffled up to John, and he scratched behind her ear. She rolled over and he rubbed her pregnant belly. John looked up at Rachel, grinned and shrugged as their eyes met. She really did have the deepest brown eyes. Yet there was this hint of something under the clear surface, something down deep that he could only maybe fish for sometime when the time was right. Maybe a full moon. He could wait. Fishermen know how to wait. "That's OK," he said, "forget about it."

Then they became uncomfortable and looked away from each other, first at the animals, and then toward the lake where Ralph

---

* "Betty, are you coming?'
  "What's up?" Betty called back.
  "Coffee and pastries."
  "Really? Great. What time is it?'

was helping Billy shoulder the rifle. With quiet restored, Mr. and Mrs. Duck were paddling peacefully out toward the middle. Billy was swinging the rifle from side to side, saying bang-bang-bang as he annihilated an invasion of space aliens.

"Look, Billy," Ralph said, "this is a loaded gun, not a toy. You understand? You have to . . . wait, no, not at the ducks!"

Billy fired anyway. There was a confused squabble of quacks and flaps as the shot splashed harmlessly behind the ducks, who took off in a panic and flew squawking into the woods. John and Rachel looked at each other, smiling and shaking their heads, then erupted into laughter.

Rachel shook her head. "Once again," she said with a chuckle, "violence intrudes upon domestic bliss." She held the door for John, who limped up the stairs.

Inside on the porch, Millie had set out a coffee cake from the Hoffstetter bakery on the corner of the town square. It was the kind with a mild light buttery pastry laced throughout with faint hints of sugar and cinnamon, so sweet in counterpoint to the mellow bitterness of black coffee. John's mother Betty was serving the coffee. She was small and thin as teachers are, tidy and neat without being fussy, since she was used to helping messy little kids become tidy and neat, or at least moving them a step in the right direction while she had them.

Through the waning afternoon they visited, John telling his parents about Germany—the places he'd visited, the people he'd met, the topics of lectures, the outdoor cafes, the cathedrals, the wine, the forests, the mountains, the hikes, the coffee, the students, the theological arguments, his experiences, all the things a young man would want to tell his eager parents, a glowing report, carefully censored. Mixed feelings swirled in his mind. A man he knew but had a falling-out with. A woman he loved but left behind.

In the evening they ate the beef stew with homemade biscuits on tin plates, and John and his father—mostly his father, since John was still hobbling—served and cleaned up, and the women laughed and made fun of their bad shooting, though the score had been close.

And as evening gathered a chill descended from the hills and enveloped the Clubhouse, and Ralph gathered wood and made a fire in the fireplace. And the family gathered round the fire and the children climbed into John's lap and said, "Uncle Johnny, tell us a story." For in the Mason family evenings around the fireplace always meant story time.

"Oh," he said. "I don't know any stories. My mom dropped me on my head when I was a grownup, and all the stories fell out of my ear onto the sidewalk and scampered like mice down the street where they were eaten by a cat."

"Noooo," said Katie, making a face. John made a face right back at her, just as he had at Rachel that afternoon, the same kind of face he and Rachel had made at each other when they were children.

"Tell the one about the catfish," said Billy.

"Yes," said Katie, "the big, big catfish."

"Well," John began, "once upon a time there was this enormous catfish that lived in the Friedensee, and his name was Old Methuselah. He was ten feet long, and he had a great big mouth and big black glassy eyes."

"I saw that fish," said Katie.

"Oh, you did," said John. The grownups looked at each other with a wink and a knowing smile.

"Yes," she said emphatically. "It was today while everybody was shooting. I went down by the lake and looked in the water, and there he was. And he looked at me and said a word and then he swam away. And when he swam away, he had a hook in his mouth and a line and a whole fishing pole."

"Ha ha, no kidding," John went on absentmindedly. "Now Old Methuselah lived in a cave way down at the bottom of the lake. And he had a big pile of treasure down there, all the things he had found on the bottom and collected, bright shiny things like bottle caps and beer cans and a 1927 Hupmobile."

"What's a Hummable?" asked Billy.

"That's the greatest car that was ever made. Ask Pop."

John's father smiled and nodded his head. "That's right. Even greater than my mom's Hudson," he said. For his mother, Hilda Brunner Mason, at 93 was still driving around in the 1947 Hudson Hornet her husband Irving had bought for her after the war. Why get rid of it? She had a family of mechanics to keep it running.

"Well, all the mini-pirates that lived around the lake had great wars over the bottle caps they found, for bottle caps were considered great treasures, precious and beyond price."

"And they kept finding more and more, especially Falstaff caps after a Mason family reunion," interjected Millie to laughter and applause.

"But when they heard that Old Methuselah had a hoard of bottle caps they all united and built a submarine and sent an expedition down to the bottom to raid his lair. And then the pirates sent a delegation to the little girl who played at the side of the lake, and beseeched her to join them against Methuselah, promising to make her the Queen of the Barbary Coast. Being young and foolish like all little girls"—at this there was a chorus of protest from the women: Millie and Betty and Rachel—"well, at least young," John corrected himself, "she said yes, so they gave her a magic potion that made her only three inches tall like they were, and she got in their submarine and went with them down to the bottom of the lake. And there was Old Methuselah, smoking his pipe. Surrounding him was a vast treasure, heaps and heaps of it, glittering in the pale watery light. There was even a great big shiny 1911 silver dollar."

Katie scrunched up her nose quizzically. "How can a catfish smoke a pipe?"

"He smokes seaweed."

"Oh."

"All the pirates were trembling in their boots, but the little girl got out and walked right up to the old fish and smacked him in the nose. 'Why dost thou smite me?' he said with a great grumbly gravelly growly voice. 'I want those bottlecaps,' she said, and hit him again. 'Verily, verily, I say unto thee, the treasure is not mine,' Old Methuselah replied. 'It's not?' said the little girl, for now she was puzzled. 'No,' said the fish. 'Thou mayest have it if thou wishest.' Now the little girl was really puzzled. 'I can? OK, boys,' she said, turning to the quivering pirates, 'let's load up and get out of here.' 'Thou dost not yet understand, my child,' said Old Methuselah, 'In my cave are many rooms filled with treasure, free to all who will come and live with me in my kingdom.' 'Yuck,' said the little girl, 'I'd probably have to eat crawdads all the time.'"

"Eeeeuuuww!" said the children.

"So the little girl gathered the pirates and went back to the world. And she drank some magic potion upside down to restore her to her proper size, though after her experience she was always a little taller than she would have been otherwise."

Rachel was sitting off to the side, looking at John with the children in his lap. One second she wanted to cry with happiness, the next second she wanted to shout with rage. What in God's name is wrong with me, she asked herself, and got up abruptly and went into the kitchen to do nothing. Millie and Betty sensed something at the same moment and looked at each other. Betty got up and quietly walked into the kitchen after Rachel, who was standing at the sink and looking out the darkened window.

"What's the matter?" she said, and touched Rachel on the shoulder. Rachel's shoulders began to heave with sobs as she turned and melted into the old mother's soft bosom.

In the hall the fire was dying, the embers glowing and fading away, the children fading into sleep. "And what about the pirates?" asked Billy.

"Pirates are a pig-headed lot when it comes to bottlecaps," said John. "They tend to think solely in terms of material acquisition."

"Like realtors," Millie added with a chuckle.

"Precisely," said John. "And the Pirates' United Fearless Federation, or P.U.F.F., continued raiding up and down the lakeshore, to the consternation of the ducks. The End. To be continued."

"Awww."

"What's constirpation?" asked Katie.

"That's when you can't go Number Two," said Billy.

"OK," Ralph said, "time for beddy-bye. Betty," he called out, "you comin'?"

"Go ahead and start the car. *Ich komm vorbei,*"* Betty replied. She had been sitting with Rachel at the kitchen table. Just sitting and helping her cry. Nothing had been said, nor needed to.

"I'd better be going, too," Rachel said.

"You'll be all right?" Betty asked. "Do you need a ride?"

"Sure, I'll be fine. I rode over. Milton knows the way back in the dark." She whistled. "Doxie. Time to go." And she went out the side door of the kitchen without looking at John or anyone, mounted her horse, and went away at a canter.

Ralph carried Katie out to the car, Billy trailing along behind. Betty hugged her son and looked him full in the face. It was so good to have him home again. Too many side roads. Too many adventures. Time for stability and healing. Then she left, and John heard the car start as he sat back down in his chair by the fire and banked the coals. Just then the door squeaked and Ralph came back into the hall.

"Oh, Johnny," he said, handing him an envelope. "I almost forgot. This letter came for you." Then he left.

Millie had gone to her room. John pulled the coal-oil lamp a little closer and looked at the envelope. It was from the Ft. Wayne seminary. He opened it, and found inside another envelope, postmarked Germany, and addressed to him care of the seminary. This too he opened. The letter was painfully and awkwardly written, as if by a child with the wrong hand. But he could sense with a shudder that it was not a child. It was from a man he knew, a very large and very dangerous man. It read:

> John Mason—I will find you and I will find the child and I will have my revenge. I will make all of you pay in blood.
> Rafael von Päpinghausen.

A log shifted and a shower of sparks like the troubles of mankind flew upward to die in the cold night air. John Mason sat alone and shivered in the darkness and the gathering chill.

---

* I'm coming right away.

Chapter 3 ◉ Another Injured Man

Around the same time that John was arriving at the Clubhouse, another man was arriving at an exclusive, private hospital in London, England. His name was Rafael von Päpinghausen, a native German. He was a large man and tall, about six feet, four inches, 230 pounds, fair-haired, tanned, and good looking, given to expensive tastes in clothing and accessories, although on this day he was wearing pull-on sweats and running shoes with Velcro straps. As he got out of the cab, he tipped the driver well and exchanged a few words with him in fluent Arabic. This man was recovering from a fight in which the thumb and first two fingers of his right hand had been severed, a mark of shame in Islamic culture. The fight had been with John Mason, and they had fought with old, rusty Heidelberg dueling sabres. Rafael had lost a good deal of blood in the ordeal, and had required emergency surgery to cleanse and suture up the wound. Even so the doctors had found that an infection had set in, and they admonished Rafael that he must take particular care of the wound, and not neglect to apply the disinfectant and antibiotic ointment and change the bandages twice a day—a feat practically impossible to do with only one hand. Now with the right hand still bandaged he was taking daily physical therapy sessions to learn how to cope with only one hand and the remnant of another. Eating came first, a sloppy and messy affair that had ruined several good shirts, hence the workout clothes today. And dressing—how would he ever learn how to tie a tie? Or manage cufflinks? He was devoted to shirts of Egyptian cotton, well-starched and crisp, with French cuffs, and he had a favorite pair of cufflinks made of the gold of Ophir, where he had traveled during his time in the Orient, set with rubies, his birthstone. In former times when he would sit at dinner at an expensive restaurant—always alone, for he had forsworn marriage as a condition of membership in his military order—he would gaze into the depth of the gemstone, and the blood red color of the ruby set off a fire in his soul. He was slowly learning to write with his left hand, and as he learned to do so the first letter he wrote was to his enemy, John Mason. The heart of Rafael von Päpinghausen burned with a cold and analytical hatred, for it was John Mason who had cut off his fingers. No matter how long it took and no matter how much it cost, he would find Mason and exact his vengeance, every last drop of it, for he had a limitless supply of both time and money. He was one of the last of the Janissaries.

Across from the hospital was a cozy little English pub. English beer he could not stand. "Take Courage," indeed! Courage he already had in good measure. Courage coupled with a sense of daring. Risk seemed to attract him like a moth to flame.

Like the time he was out by himself, wandering the game trails and forests of his family estate in the *Schwarzwald*, near Freiburg am Breisgau. A happy stream went tumbling down the rocks, faster and faster, deeper and deeper. Suddenly the stream plunged down and the land shot up, until he was standing on the edge of a precipice with a waterfall far below. Across the chasm was a fallen tree, slender, covered with moss, and wet with mist. And in the middle of the log was a boy, clinging for dear life.

The child was as dark as Rafael was fair, his clothes as thin as Rafael's were rich, and he had no shoes. "*Es tut mir leid,*" the boy said without a trace of panic, "*aber können Sie mir hilfen?*"[*]

The boy looked to be about the same age as Rafael. In two clicks Rafael apprehended the situation. Germany was filling up with Turkish immigrants. The government was better, the benefits better, the schools better and the jobs better. This Rafael know from eavesdropping on his father. He would hide behind the couch as the men

---

[*] "Excuse me ... but can you help me?"

discussed the issues of the day over brandy and cigars. The Turks were glad to take the menial jobs that the Germans spurned—janitors and garbage men. Mosques had begun to appear. The Turks kept to themselves in the poor quarters of town. The boy on the bridge had apparently wandered off on his own.

"*Ich komm vorbei,*" Rafael called out over the pounding water. "*Aber ich glaube, dass wir beiden sind noch gestorben!*"*

"*Inshallah,*" the boy called back.

Rafael was puzzled. What language was that? Then without hesitation he set foot on the log, marched straight across, scooped up the boy—he was small and light while Rafael was big and strong for his age—and in a few long strides gained the other side.

They both collapsed on the mossy forest floor and began to laugh. Then they stopped. Then they started laughing again. Then they stopped. Then they looked at each other and erupted in laughter once again.

"I am an idiot," the boy said.

"And I'm an idiot for trying to save you!"

Then the laughter broke out again, but now it tapered off like a sudden mountain cloudburst.

"You saved my life."

Rafael waved his hand in dismissal.

"I'm Rafael."

"I am Sinan."

They shook hands.

"I owe you," said Sinan.

"Well," said Rafael, "I think I might just take you back to the house and shoot you for trespassing on my father's estate."

"I'd have been easier to hit on the log."

"Right you are. And the stream would have disposed of the body!"

They laughed again, but more soberly.

"I am serious, though, Rafael. You saved me. We are now bound together in true friendship for life." He fixed Rafael with penetrating

---

* "I'm coming right away... but I believe that we both will be killed!"

dark eyes.

Rafael started to protest, but caught himself. The heaviness of all this was beginning to press down upon him.

"What was that thing you said out there?"

"*Inshallah.*"

"Is that Turkish?"

"Arabic. It means, 'as God wills.' Like, I will take this job, if God wills it to be done. I am Muslim. You?"

"Oh, we don't go to church or anything. Like most people. Germans, I mean. Maybe Christmas. Or Easter."

"Hm. Well, I believe that there is no God but Allah, and Muhammad is his prophet."

"I think I heard about that in school."

"So God is in charge of everything. I decide to cross this stupid log. If it is God's will, I'll make it across. But then I slipped."

"This shows, I guess, that it was not God's will to let you cross."

"I don't know..."

"But since you fell, maybe it was God's will to let you fall off and get killed?"

"No, wait. God is merciful."

"Oh, OK."

"Then you came along, which means it was God's will for me to go across."

Rafael chuffed. "But you didn't make it across. So no *Inshallah.*"

"Not so fast, not so fast. I was just about to ask you to take me back across the log to the other side to prove that Allah is always right."

"Sure, Sinan, but I might take you halfway across, then throw you in, shouting '*Inshallah, inshallah!*'"

Sinan shook his head. "My friend, you are impossible."

They paused for a time, listening to the call of the birds, the voice of the waters.

"I suppose you live in Freiburg."

"Sort of."

Rafael shrugged. "Does your mom know you're up here?"

Sinan looked down.

"What? What?"

"I guess I'm kind of an orphan. My mom died last year. My dad was killed by the drug lords. He grew poppies."

"God! Where do you stay?"

"Here and there. Mostly I'm on the street. So are a lot of kids."

Rafael was gobsmacked. Here was an authentic poor person, the kind for whom his mother and father supported charities, but had never seen or met, much less brought into their home.

"How... I mean...?"

Again the big dark eyes shone out from the dirty, emaciated face. "*Inshallah,*" he said wryly. "I just have to trust in Allah the merciful."

"Well," said Rafael as he got up, "maybe Allah sent me along to rescue you. How about me and Allah take you back to the house and get you something to eat?"

And so it came to pass that the two boys became fast friends. The exception was that in the matter of religion, Sinan, who had faith, became master to Rafael, who had none. The poor Turkish boy explained the tenets of Islam, the Five Pillars, the Hejira, the Holy Qur'an, the life of Muhammad, the various branches—Sunni, Shia, Sufi—the history, the conquests, the wars, the battles, the Crusades, the glory of the Ottoman Empire, the learning, the science, the mathematics, the harems... all of which captivated the young German nobleman.

Rafael for his part provided food and clothing for his friend, along with books and money for education. Together they built a little hut deep in the forest where Sinan could find shelter and where the two boys could open their hearts to one another and recite passages from the Qur'an.

Finishing his glass of Macallan twelve-year single malt, Rafael walked out the door into bright sunshine. A good omen. Today, however, there was one more item on the agenda. Rafael needed to buy a car. Since he was right-handed and his right hand was maimed, he could no longer drive German cars with the gear shift on the right side of the driver. Even in his pain he would not consider an automatic transmission. It was just not good form. But a British car with a manual transmission to the left of the driver might do. He would be able to work the gear shift lever with his good hand while steadying the steering wheel with the palm of his bad hand, causing no pain. He was sure he could manage it.

Not far from the hospital was a car dealer. It was a high-end shop with all sorts of classics: a 1954 Jaguar XK 120 DHC with wire wheels, a 1955 Austin Healey BN4 100/6, red over black with a boot rack, a 1971 Triumph TR6 150 BHP with overdrive, a very nice 1986 Morgan +8 with low mileage, British racing green with tan leather interior. Not one of them carried a price tag.

"A very good day to you, sir," said the salesman, a slim, middle-aged man with a moustache clipped short in British Army style, wearing a navy blazer and rep tie. As he approached and extended his hand, Rafael could see that he walked with a stiff knee. "Geoffrey Windsor. How may I help you?"

Like a good German Rafael clicked his heels—not that the heels of his running shoes made a real click—and bowed slightly from the hip. "How do you do," he replied. "I am called Rafael. You will pardon me if I do not shake your hand. As you can see, I am somewhat inconvenienced."

"Bad luck," said the salesman in reply. "So sorry. What happened, if I may ask?"

"How do you British say? A bit of 'unpleasantness.'"

"I see, I see. You look a military man by the cut of you, if I may say so, sir."

"Even so," Rafael responded.

"Coldstream Guards, myself," the man said. "Got into a bit of a scrum a time or two myself in the way of duty. Rum thing, combat. Left me with a game leg and a dicky heart. But enough of that. Let's talk about cars. I suppose you'd want something in the way of an automatic transmission?"

"No, please," Rafael said. "I have always preferred manual transmission."

"Yes, of course. A man's car."

"You have it right."

"Automatic is for women. Might I interest you in a sport model? We have a very nice Morgan over here."

"Not so much, I think. I have some traveling to do, and I will have luggage to carry along with me. So I will need something with more room."

"Well, all right then. Let me see here. Perhaps that nice Jaguar sedan over there in the corner."

"What is this silver one?"

"Ah, yes. You'd like this one, sir. An Aston Martin DB4 Series 11."

"When was it manufactured?"

"1960, and very well cared-for."

"Once I am seeing this in a movie, I think."

"That you did, sir. Sean Connery drove a very similar model in one of his James Bond films."

"It has a... certain something."

"Right-o. That grill, don't you know. Most distinctive. And I might add that the transmission on this car is exceptionally smooth. Five-speed of course, with overdrive. The gears mesh quite smoothly. You won't have to fight it at all. And plenty of room in the boot for your grips."

"Motor?"

"Six cylinder, three-litre displacement. Plenty of pickup. Shall we take her for a spin?"

"Fuel?"

"Runs on regular unleaded petrol, that's the beauty of it. Thirty miles per gallon on the motorway. Quite economical, really."

"Very good. And the cost, please?"

"Thirty-eight, five. Reasonable terms if needed."

"I pay cash always."

"Quite right." The man didn't bat an eye. His clientele were of a class that often paid cash.

Rafael slid into the soft, supple leather seat. It welcomed him very comfortably and felt easy on his back. The ignition was on the left side of the column—another plus. He turned the key and the motor roared to life. He revved the motor a couple of times, then listened with satisfaction to the low, throaty burble as it idled. Geoffrey got in and they took off. Rafael had to concentrate very hard, for he was not used to driving on the wrong side of the street, but the car handled beautifully. He could steer quite easily with the palm of his right hand, even when not shifting gears. He popped it into third and stepped on the gas. It surged forward like a big cat. A stoplight was just ahead. He downshifted into second. There was that nice sound again from the muffler, a good masculine animal growl. This was a treat. He was hurt. He was angry. But with will and discipline he would regain his old form.

He would be able to eat.
He would be able to dress.
He would be able to write.
He would be able to drive.
He would be able to fight.
He would be able to kill.

◉ ◉ ◉

John went out and tried the ignition on his Jeep as he tried not to think about the wounded man in Germany who had written the letter of vengeance. The motor ground sluggishly. Easy does it. Don't drain the battery. "Come on, Annabelle," he muttered under his breath. "Be nice to Papa." He jiggled his foot on the accelerator. On the third try she grudgingly turned over, like a sleepy child awakened for school too early on a cold morning. John listened with learned ears to the motor. It was missing on one of the cylinders. Needed spark plugs, tune up, brake job, and who knows what else they might find once they started poking around. Muffler, too, if he could find one at a good price. The car itself, like John, needed help and healing. It was a plain red Jeep, the most basic model with no frills, no radio even, one he'd bought used years ago in Alaska for knocking around on back trails to the salmon streams. He had maintained it well, at least as well as a mechanic's son maintained an automobile, for mechanics tend to drive old jalopies that need work. Their life was keeping other people's cars in good shape, and as a result they let their own get run down. Besides, they knew all about cars and could get their own tuned up any time they wanted. It's just that they never got around to finding the time to schedule a day to work on their own car. The money was in fixing everybody else's car. John had left the Jeep with a seminary classmate when he went to Germany, a guy who was serving a church in New Jersey, and ministers let their cars run down even worse than mechanics do. So when John showed up unexpectedly they had to jump start the car, recharge the battery, and fix a flat to get it on the road, besides which a mouse had taken up residence in the upholstery of the back seat. So today John was going into town to work on the car. He had called ahead to Jasper to make sure there was a bay empty. Everything was set.

John pulled away from the Clubhouse. His left foot was a little better today, didn't hurt as much when he hit the clutch. A slight drizzle was flowing from the overcast sky. He took it slow. There was that sharp turn to the left and then to the right. Everyone agreed it was dangerously close to the ravine, but nobody wanted to be the one to have to make the decision to cut down the big old sycamore tree in order to straighten out the road. So everyone just drove carefully, knowing full well that someday somebody was going to take the curve too fast and end up in the ravine below.

After the curve the trail followed the tumbling stream down the hill to the place where they crossed each other at the low-water bridge. Then the stream said goodbye and turned to join the Saline Creek which flowed on toward the Mississippi River to the east, while the road continued through the fields and wound away toward town. John drove as if on automatic pilot, for he had gone this way so many times before. A car passed, going the other way. The driver was an old man wearing an old hat, gripping the wheel with both hands, and as he passed he lifted the index finger of his right hand, short for a full wave. John returned the salute. As he drove John remembered Grandma Hilda's story about how when she was a little girl she and the kids would come out and play at the Clubhouse all day, and when evening was come they would pile into the back of the wagon and go to sleep, and old Roscoe their horse would take them back to town, for he knew the way, and the children knew he knew, and they trusted him and were safe under his care.

The season was moving on toward harvest time. The corn was dry and standing in the fields, and when the wind blew it made a papery, rustling sound. Soon it would be time to gather it in. Swarming clouds of birds swirled overhead on their way south, and sometimes John could hear the honk of the Canada geese.

As he drove into town waves of memory wafted over him as they always did, for this was the town of his past, the town of memory, the town of imagination that he carried with him in all the far places he had traveled to and all the distant cities he had lived in. Here he could see the old Lutheran school he had attended as a child, across the street from it the old city library where he read Dr. Seuss books after school until his Mom called old Miss Lindeman to tell him that it was supper time. And here was the church. There was the park with the monkey bars he had fallen out of and broken his arm. Downtown was the drugstore where he and his brother Bill would sneak in and peek at the *Playboys* when no one was looking, or so they thought, until a call from Mr. Ahman and a spanking from their father had put an end to that. And finally there was the high school with its football field, the place where he had first known real success. And real failure.

But Perryville, Missouri was a town that also existed in the present, and this always came as a bit of a shock to John every time he returned. For his memory was fixed, and the past was constant and never changed; the contemporary Perryville was a real place and not a place of the imagination. The Interstate Highway had come through on the edge of town, and with it a McDonald's and a Walmart. Civic leaders—including some of his own classmates—had lured a Japanese automobile parts manufacturer to town, and they had built an enormous factory in the pasture that had belonged to farmer Wythe, who had taken the money and moved to Orlando, where he lived frugally even though he had plenty. The turn-of-the-century train station had been torn down, and with it the old Ross Hotel across the street. Nowadays the only trains that came through anymore carried freight, not passengers. In their place was a convenience store, where the men and women who worked ninety miles away in St. Louis could gas up and grab a coffee and a Little Debbie before hitting the road. They got on the highway early in the morning and they came back late at night, but for the most part the traffic on the big north-south highway just kept moving, half the people going one way, and the other half going the other way, nobody knew where, and perhaps they didn't know themselves. And they drove mass-produced cars and wore mass-produced clothes and when they were hungry they pulled off at the Perryville exit and grabbed a quick mass-produced hamburger from the drive-thru window and kept on going, back to their corporate jobs and their tract homes in the mass-produced suburbs.

But there was a reality here that continued somehow, despite the mass-market ephemera of interstates and progress. For underneath the surface in the small town there was a substrata of memory and heritage and tradition that regulated everything. And men who worked in the city during the week took their sons fishing on Saturday. And women who worked at the Walmart taught their daughters how to bake from scratch when the family gathered on Sunday after church. And sometimes the mothlike travelers on the highway had to stop and rest their wings for a time when their car broke down and the tow truck brought it in to Mason's Garage, just off the square.

It had been a several years since he'd been back, so as usual upon returning John took a turn around the square. There was the old courthouse in the middle, brick and stone, built in 1897, with a bell tower on top, and in front of the courthouse was the statue of a Union soldier and on the base a memorial plaque with the names of the men of Perry County who had died in the Civil War. None here had fought for the Confederacy, though Missouri had been a slave state. Even so, there had been few blacks in Perry County, the exception being the German-speaking Everett family that lived and farmed down by the river near Augsburg, and were members of St. John's Lutheran Church. Also there was a memorial to the fallen of World War One, World War Two, Korea, and Vietnam. The town square of Perryville, like those of all small towns, was surrounded by shops. There was Prevallet Jewelry, Rozier's Store, The Corner Tavern, Merle's Hardware, the Strand Theater, and Touchdown Realty, TD's branch office. His central office was to the north up Highway 61 in Ste. Genevieve. And there as it had been forever, right across from the county courthouse was the Square Meal Cafe. They always had the best homemade pie of any diner in the entire world, as John could attest, since he had been to diners everywhere and personally sampled the pie in most of them. None could compare. A cup of coffee and a nice piece of tart rhubarb pie would hit the spot about now. And there was a parking spot—not that there ever was a lack of parking in a town of 7,667.

As John entered the diner and walked toward the lunch counter where he usually sat, all faces turned to watch him like a herd of cows gawking at a passerby, then went back to their business. There were mostly old farmers in bib overalls and railroad caps at this hour, and retired folk who had chosen to remain here over mass-market options like Florida and Arizona. There in the corner booth was Old Man Roschke, his fourth grade teacher at St. John's Lutheran School, with his wife, Old Lady Roschke, who had been his first grade teacher, both ensconced in the newspaper and reading bits to each other, just as they had been three years before when last he had stopped in here. There was Emmanuel Hoffstetter, the jolly fat baker who was Santa Claus at the yearly town Christmas festival. One year he had reached into his sack and pulled out a little toy fire engine and given it to John. His favorite toy for a long time, it was still around somewhere. And there was Coach Hanewinkel, sitting with his brother Al who had the State Farm agency next to the cafe.

"Hey, Johnny," said the coach. "Back in town?"

"Yeah, for a little while. How you been, Wink?"

"Fair to middlin'. What happened to your foot?"

"Oh, that. Well, I've been in Germany for a couple of years, and tried out for soccer. My team won the World Cup on my last-second goal. So I was famous. Women, money, the works. Then I was contacted a few weeks ago by the Green Bay Packers since their kicker had been injured. They put me in a game against the Vikings. I tried to kick a sixty-five-yard field goal and broke my foot. Damn thing went wide right, too."

He nodded and grinned. "Yeah, I bet. Mason, you're still as fulla shit as a Christmas goose."

"How's the team this year?"

"One and two. Beat Farmington but lost to Jackson and Cape Central as per usual, but those were our two worst opponents and we had to play them early. Ste. Gen is not as strong this year. We play them tonight. You should come. Everybody would like to see you. I think things are looking pretty good for the rest of the season. We could run the table from here on out."

"How's the new coach working out?"

"Johnston? Not bad, not bad. He was my assistant for a couple of years, you know. New kid, played line at Mizzou, really drills the kids in the fundamentals. And you know, it all comes down to line play. So he's got these strong farm boys and beefed 'em up with weight training—something we never did much when you were playing—and he's running a pound-the-ground offense, right up the gut. Not much passing like you did."

"Not that I was much of a passer..."

"Oh, you did OK," brother Al said. "You got us to the regionals."

"How can I forget?" John said. Especially since everybody and everything reminded him of it. Perryville had never gone that far in state competition. It was the game of his life. The chance to shine. The big game against TD and his Ste. Gen Dragons. And he had blown it on a critical play.

Coach Hanewinkel went on. "But in the game with Cape Central we lost a fumble. They scored on us two plays later. The Cape squad was sucking wind by the third quarter, though. We almost had 'em. Good, old-fashioned, smash-mouth football. That's what I like." His eyes were gleaming. You could tell he missed the game, and regretted that the school had mandatory retirement at age sixty-five.

"Me, too," John said, though he really preferred the razzle-dazzle passing offensive style of play. Plus, he felt somehow uncomfortable speaking as an adult and as an equal to a man who had been an adult when he was a kid long ago. It was that irritating way that the past had of insinuating itself into the present but with a changed visage. And here was his old coach, thirty pounds heavier and with grey hair. "Well, see you around, Coach."

John sat down at the counter, said hello to Myrtle, then changed his mind and had banana cream pie instead with a cup of black coffee. After he finished he went back to his Jeep and drove around the corner to the garage. The big door was open, and he pulled in to the second bay and got out of his car. There was the old garage, unchanged, with its high ceilings and smell of grease and oil, a frame building, dingy with age, and lit here and there with naked light bulbs hanging from the ceiling. The place had been built by Irving Mason, John's grandfather, in 1920. Irving had taken over his father Godfrey's blacksmith shop as a young man, then gone naturally into automobile sales and repair. Things boomed for a few years and he expanded, bought land, and built a showroom for the classy Hupmobiles and a garage for general repair. He lost the car dealership not in the stock market crash of 1929 but in one of the many bank failures that were happening just before the crash. He managed to hang on to the garage, though, since like all Germans he had squirreled a little something away for a rainy day, and so it had remained in the Mason family ever since. The sooty high windows grudgingly let in a bit of sunlight. The floor was littered with old cans and car parts. In back was a tractor in for repair, and a couple of lawn mowers in various stages of disassembly, along with a rack of tires. The Young & Sons Funeral Home calendar hung in its usual spot on the wall. Only the year had changed. Next to the calendar was a dartboard with a picture of the recent Democratic candidate for president pinned onto it. There was the ancient cash register that jangled and rattled when you rang up a sale. The bay he had pulled into was the old-fashioned grease pit kind with a dugout for the mechanic to get down underneath the car. On the floor were grease guns and wrenches handy for the constant oil changes that were the mechanic's bread and butter. There was a tire machine and an air compressor in the corner, and the walls were lined with hoses and belts. Nearby was a fifty-five-gallon drum of Pennzoil, used by all country and small-town mechanics because they delivered. By the oil drum was the floor jack and jack stands, and a portable frame with a chain hoist for taking out 500-pound engines.

Over near the customer door was a pot-bellied stove surrounded by grimy chairs, and in the chairs were a couple of loafers shooting the breeze with Jasper, who was working at the bench. John could tell without listening that they were talking about baseball, football, politics, fishing, and how much rain fell in various parts of the county last week—a vital topic in a farming community—as well as the latest dirty joke that was making the rounds. Jasper was a wiry little man, about five-foot-six and 120 pounds, but strong and durable the way those little guys are who work from early till late. He had on steel-toed laceup boots and greasy overalls, but underneath a blue shirt and a bow tie, a holdover from the old days. On his head was a nondescript workman's cap turned sideways, for he had been under the hood of a big Mercedes in the first bay. His hands were dirty but wise. The workbench itself was a big old thing, made of white pine now black with age, grease, and shop dirt. There was a big vise on it and a little vise, ball-peen hammers in several sizes, and assorted tools littering the surface, picked up and set down many times in the course of a day's work, and a pegboard on the wall facing the workbench on which were hung a variety of pry bars, wrenches, screwdrivers, and pliers. Under the bench were drawers full of socket sets, metal screws, nuts, bolts, washers, tubes of grease, solvents, and the odds and ends needed in a shop that didn't just change parts but really fixed things.

John sauntered over to the workbench, nodding and murmuring a greeting to the loafers who looked up at him as he passed by. There was a fat one—Clarence, the unofficial mayor of the town idlers. There was a skinny one—Merle, Clarence's sidekick and factotum. Had John come an hour earlier, they would have been at the coffee shop. Now they were hanging out here, and later they would move over to the courthouse for checkers on their daily rounds before heading back to the coffee shop for lunch. Jasper of course had heard John pull in, and greeted him by sticking out his palm saying, "Hand me a thirteen millimeter," without looking up. John put the wrench in his hand and watched reverently as the master craftsman wove his magic on the fuel injector he had before him. Stationed in Germany with the Army years before and already knowing the language, Jasper had availed himself of some accrued leave time and taken the Mercedes mechanic's course. The big diesel engines, too, like they use on trucks and boats. He picked up the fuel injector, peered into an aperture, said "*Scheisse*" a couple of times, blew into a hole, smacked it with the flat of his hand, and then pronounced the verdict: "Dammit, that's good enough!" and turned to John with a big smile. He stuck out a grimy hand and they shook vigorously as Jasper said, "W-W-Well, there you are. *Wie geht's?*"*

"*Ganz gut,*" John replied.

"*Und Ich habe gehört, dass du hast in Heidelberg studiert, nicht war?*"

"*Ja. Es war sehr interessant. Liest du jetzt deine Triglot?*"

"*Dass tue Ich.*"

"*Sehr gut,* Uncle Jasper, *sehr gut.*"

"*Am was schreibst du?*"

"*An dem dritten Brauch des Gesetzes.*"

"*Ah, so. Wie im sechsten Artikel der Konkordienformel.*"

"*Spitze!* Excellent, Jasper. Still the lay theologian, I see. Well, I just fueled up on Myrtle's banana cream pie up at the coffee shop, so I'm ready to go on that brake job if you are. The clips are screeching."

"It's past due, then," Jasper said. One of the loafers spat tobacco juice into a coffee can by the stove while the other one put his nose back in the newspaper. "Let me just get this fuel injector b-back in first." Jasper worked swiftly and skillfully under the hood of the big car.

---

* "How goes it?"
"All good," John replied.
"And I've heard that you have studied in Heidelberg, right?"
"Yes. It was very interesting. Do you still read your *Concordia Triglotta* [an edition of the *Book of Concord* in German, Latin, and English]?"
"That I do."
"Very good, Uncle Jasper, very good."
"What are you writing on?"
"About the Third Use of the Law."
"Ah, yes. As in the Sixth Article of the Formula of Concord."
"You're right! Excellent, Jasper. . . ."

"What h-happened to your foot, there, J-Johnny?"

"Oh, that. Well, I was at the races at Monte Carlo just after winning a big pot of money at the casino. The cars were coming at full speed into a hairpin turn. There was this tremendous crash, screeching tires, twisted metal, fire and smoke. All of a sudden the severed head of one of the drivers came flying over the fence and hit me right on the foot."

Clarence and Merle hooted with laughter. This would go over great at the Legion later that night. Jasper just shook his head without looking up.

"A Mercedes," John observed. "Kind of high-toned vehicle for this neck of the woods, wouldn't you say?"

"Well, if you knew who the d-d-driver was, you'd understand," Jasper replied as they made their way to the second bay.

"Is that a fact. Who is it?"

"Touchdown Timmy Pope, the Real Estate King of These Here Parts and a Little B-B-Bit of Arkansas. Now we got to check the fluids first, John. The fluids in a car . . . " he began.

" . . . is like blood in the body," John finished. "I know, I know," he said, smiling. It was a family proverb, polished and passed on for generations. "I changed the oil before I left New York, so we should be OK there."

He popped the hood. Jasper removed the transmission dipstick, sniffed the fluid and rubbed a drop between his fingers. "Transmission OK," he said. "When's the last time you flushed the radiator?"

"Been a while," said John, "But let's not mess with that today."

Jasper unscrewed the top of the master cylinder and dipped his finger into the reservoir. "Brake fluid OK," he said. "Let's see here. This is a CJ5 model, so you got d-disc brakes on the front and drum on the back. Any squeak in the back?"

"No."

"I didn't think so. We'll just d-do the front, then." Jasper scrambled down into the grease pit as he said, "You been driving gravel roads out to the Clubhouse. I'm going to check for flying stone damage, might have dinged up the brake lines. Them stones can get in anywhere. Even jam the accelerator, and that's d-d-dangerous. You get the lug nuts off, Johnny."

John retrieved the floor jack and jacked the car up, pumping the long handle, then carefully placed the jack stands under the frame and released the jack. Then he took the air impact wrench, *brrp-brrp-brrp-brrp-brrp,* on each side, removed the wheels and set them on the floor. His bad foot was feeling better today, but he carefully favored the other foot and took pains not to let the unwieldy tires fall on him.

By then Jasper was by his side. He pulled up a squat little stool, scooted his toolbox over, sat down and squinted at the assembly. "Yeah, I think we can get by with p-p-pads," he said. "Hand me an eleven-sixteenths socket and a ratchet. We'll get these calipers off first here yet." Jasper looked at the brakes again, shifted on his stool, and cut a brisk fart.

"Damn, Jasper! Whew!" John exclaimed, fanning the air with his hand.

Clarence and Merle were laughing.

"Hey, b-boy," Jasper replied, "ain't you ever read in the B-Bible where it says, 'A mule that farts will n-never tire, and a man that f-f-farts is the one to hire'?"

"That ain't in any Bible I ever read."

"W-well, read it again. Plus, I read somewheres that you can beat the devil if you can manage to fart in his face."

"Actually you're right about that. It's not in the Bible but it was an old tradition in the Middle Ages. It's in Luther, too. Just don't fart in my face, OK? I ain't the devil. Leastways I'm trying not to be."

John fished around in the toolbox, found the wrench, and handed it to Jasper. "So TD is driving a Mercedes," he said.

"Yep," Jasper replied as he worked away, inserting the new brake pads. "He's done m-moved up in the world. Wears them nice suits he gets from a fancy store up in St. Louie."

"No off-the-rack stuff from Rozier's like the rest of us then," said John.

Jasper shook his head. "Rrrr, damn, this sucker is tight!" He took a breather, got off the stool and knelt to get more leverage, then cranked the wrench again. It gave, and he had the calipers off. "OK, gimme a pry bar." He took the pry bar and pushed the pistons back in, then removed the brake pads. "Yeah, old TD. Quite the ladies' man, too. Ever good lookin' gal in town, he gives her a tumble after him and Bonnie split up."

"She got custody of Danny, I assume."

"Oh, yeah. But TD takes him once ever so often. Everybody knew TD had been steppin' out on her. She got a big settlement, but what did he care, he's got money to b-b-burn these days. He made a killing on some big resort-type development by a lake in Arkansas." Jasper slapped in the new pads and secured them with rods and lock clips, then pushed the calipers back on. "I even seen him with Rachel McFadden the other d-day. You remember her, don't you?"

"Oh, sure," said John with deliberate nonchalance as he set the wheel back in place and Jasper moved to the other side of the car. "She was over at the Clubhouse the other day."

Merle, the skinny loafer, chimed in as he lit a cigarette. "She done turned out to be a purty one, didn't she? I seen her and TD at the football game together the other week, when we beat Farmington on that goal line stand."

Clarence, the fat loafer, nodded in affirmation, and spat into the can again. John looked over and nodded in reply. She had in fact kind of "done turned out to be a purty one." Not that he was interested. He had work to do. No time to get involved. No desire to.

"Alrighty," Jasper called out. "Get in and pump the b-brake pedal a few times, let's see how she's a-workin' here yet." John hopped in to the driver's seat and pumped the brake pedal while Jasper squinted at the calipers. "Lookin' good. OK, now hold it down ... hold ... hold ... " he said as he made a minute adjustment, "there! Done." He put the wheel back on, *brrp-brrp-brrp-brrp-brrp* with the air impact wrench, and the brake job was finished. "Jack her back up a ways, Johnny, and lemme git these jack stands out of here, and we'll check them spark plugs." John cranked the long handle a few times, and Jasper reached behind the wheels and removed the jack stands.

"Does TD still play his guitar?" John asked.

"D-Don't get me started," Jasper replied. John glanced over at the loafers, who were grinning and waiting for Jasper to get started. The fat one stood up and began to strum an air guitar and rock from side to side. "Gott dernit anyway. He's in that so-called Luthern church up in Ste. Gen, you know, the one that's doin' all that d-dern rock and roll worship. How you can take a Luthern church and turn it into a rock and roll w-worship service is beyond me, but there it is. If Bach was alive today, he'd be turning over in his grave. Gott dernit. I mean, they got one of these dang Baby Boomer pastors who wants to be 'hip' and 'cool' and all that crap, probably smoked too much of that d-damn LSD back in the Seventies, so he comes down here to Ste. Gen and gets this 'contemporary worship' going with a 'praise band' and all this crap, and of course Timmy, he's a b-big contributor and he's all for this progressive crap—gimme a spark plug socket there, John, should be one in the tool box... good, thanks—I mean, what the hell is wrong with good old familiar hymns like *O Haupt voll Blut und Wunden* and *Ein feste Burg ist unser Gott?** Instead they got Timmy and his praise band up there in front screeching into microphones and a drummer whanging away and some girl singer jiggling her ass around, and this is supposed to be w-worship in God's house? I ask you. Gott dern," he concluded as the storm blew itself out, "and Gott dern this stutter. If I could speak German with that pastor, I'd by Gott straighten him out. I don't stutter when I t-talk Dutch."

Jasper worked away for a few more minutes, adjusting the timing while still muttering under his breath. The two loafers were grinning at each other and nodding with raised eyebrows. They'd heard this rant before. "Well, that should take care of them spark plugs. Start her up once and let's give her a listen." John got back in and turned on the ignition. It turned over instantly. They both listened to the motor. The occasional faint *bup... bup* of the missing cylinder was gone. "Purrs like a kitten, d-don't she?" said Jasper with a smile. "Love it when I can take something broke and m-make it right."

Then he called to one of the loafers. "Clarence! Make yourself useful and git us some coffee."

---

* "O Sacred Head Now Wounded" and "A Mighty Fortress Is Our God"

The fat one groaned to his feet and went to the coffee pot in the office. Next to it was a German Bible and the *Concordia Triglotta*—the big green book with the Lutheran Confessions in German, Latin, and English in parallel columns. Both were well-thumbed. Clarence filled two grimy mugs with coffee and brought them back in. How coffee that had been on all day could taste that good was always a mystery to John. The secret, Jasper had always said, was never to wash the pot—it needed to be seasoned. And put in a few grains of salt to counteract the acidity of the coffee. That was the way he'd learned in the Army when he served his hitch long ago. He had come to the Army an experienced auto mechanic and they had of course made him a cook. "There's the right way, there's the wrong way, and there's the Army way," was another of Jasper's proverbs. At least the Army had taught him how to make coffee. They sat down with their coffee in the circle of chairs next to the stove.

"Cards beat Houston in twelve innings last night, two to one, finished on a double play," said Clarence, who had resumed his seat. "Jason Marquis pitched seven innings. Looks like the bullpen is finally getting its act together."

The skinny one stood up and stretched and yawned. "Perryville plays Ste. Gen tonight. Prob'ly get their butts kicked, I guess. You comin', Johnny?"

"I don't know. Maybe. Coach Wink said we're pretty good this year for being one-and-two."

"Yeah, well, maybe, Johnny, but not like when you led the team."

"Well, that was a good year. A lot of things came together."

"Tough luck about that there loss to Timmy's team."

John pursed his lips and nodded ever so slightly, then took another sip of coffee. It tasted bitter.

"Well, speak of the d-devil," said Jasper. For the office door had opened, and there was Timothy David Pope.

John cast a sidelong glance at Clarence and muttered under his breath, "Let's see if we can fart on him!"

TD was massive. Not big and fat, not at all. In fact, he was a little taller than John, though not much, but bigger, heavier, more muscular, powerful around the shoulders, and there was an intimidating presence about him. Standing still, he seemed to be coming at you like a train. In front of you, he seemed to be crowding in too close. In high school he had been able to throw the football fifty-plus yards downfield, unusual in a young player. It was that arm strength, no doubt, which he had amplified with weight training. He had excelled at all sports, of course, as had his father, Uncle Buddy, but particularly football, and so had been prized above all his peers. But as Aunt Millie had pointed out, Timmy had gone in a different direction than his upbringing would have indicated—the path of acquisition and success. He alone had taken that path; his younger siblings had not. The twins, Jane and James, were off in L.A., trying to break into the animation film business, and Joe, the eldest, was in New York City trying to make it as a sculptor. All three were happily living the bohemian life and washing dishes to keep body and soul together. But here was TD, the youngest, with all the trappings of worldly success—the 100% cotton Brooks Brothers shirt, starched and pressed by a good laundry, the Armani tie, the bespoke suit with a Rotary Club lapel pin, the Alden shoes professionally polished, the clean hands, beautifully manicured, the high school ring (the only one that counted in these parts) prominently displayed on the middle finger of the right hand, and the faint sweet ambience of Michael Jordan cologne surrounding all. He had stayed in shape with constant workouts at a pricey gym, but there were signs that age was taking its toll. His nose was redder and fleshier, perhaps as a result of too many of the Chopin vodka martinis he had acquired a taste for at posh realtor convention watering holes in Phoenix. His two front teeth, broken in a drunken car crash after his divorce, had been replaced with caps. Good caps from a high-priced St. Louis dentist, but fake nonetheless. His mouth, which curled up at the ends in a devilish grin, seemed larger and redder. And, most shockingly, he had gone bald, covering up the shame with a toupee. A good toupee from a high-priced St. Louis wig maker, but fake nonetheless.

"Hey, Tim," John said, sticking out his hand to shake automatically, but then drawing it back in view of the dirt on it and shrugging his shoulders instead while he wiped his hands on his jeans. "Good to see you. What's going on?"

"John-boy," TD replied, resurrecting the old childhood taunt that never failed to irritate him. "I'm just in town for the game tonight. I'm picking up Rachel after while. Thought I'd let Jasper poke around on my jalopy. I heard you were back on the block. Where is it you've been this time?"

"Europe," John said sheepishly.

"Europe! Fantastic place. I got to Paris a couple of times on the Concorde before they mothballed it. Fantastic. Maxim's. Mmmh!" John had been to Paris on a weekend trip. He had slept on the floor of a friend's apartment. One drizzly evening he and his friend had walked past Maxim's. The doorman had given them a fishy look. Inside were wealthy people at elegant tables with escargot and champagne. John and his friend had shared a loaf of cheap bread and a hunk of cheap cheese and a bottle of cheap wine. And he had slept again on the floor, and left the next day with a sore back on the train to Heidelberg, sitting in the cheap seats, with the leftover cheap bread and cheese in his backpack.

TD glanced at his watch, an ostentatious gold Rolex, then at his Mercedes. Every time he looked at them—which was often—his heart swelled with pride. He had worked hard. He had eliminated the competition. He was a Success. These constituted proof. "Well, John-boy, gotta go, gotta go, gotta make that next million by five o'clock." He laughed a big forced laugh. "Let's do lunch one of these days. What's Mom serving you out there, biscuits and beans?" He shook his head. "Maybe I'll take a day off and we'll buzz up to St. Louis, grab a bite at Tony's. How's that sound?"

"Sounds great," John replied with a sinking heart. He'd heard of Tony's and walked by it once. Like Maxim's. It was a real place, but for him it existed only in the imagination. And his imagination, at age thirty, fed only on bits and scraps. The die was cast for him: suits from Rozier's, Thom McAnn shoes with vinyl soles, poly-and-cotton shirts, 60/40, a ten-dollar Casio watch, and an old Jeep that he worked on himself. Of course he knew that Timmy was not really serious about taking him to lunch. Or if he were, it would be to build himself up at John's expense, belittling him with a display of worldly goods.

TD was by then backing his big black Mercedes out of the bay when he was almost clipped by a passing car. There was a screech of brakes and TD in a panic threw his car into drive and lurched forward to get out of the way. There was a look of sheer terror on his face, for fear that one of his prized material possessions was in immanent danger of being hurt. He jumped out of the driver's seat, his face red with rage, and was about to let loose a stream of manly invective at . . . his grandmother.

For there was Hilda Brunner Mason, aged ninety-three, the matriarch of the family, in high dudgeon, getting out of her pale green 1947 Hudson Hornet. The Hornet had been the hottest car on the road in the days after the war, when Detroit was swinging back into production of domestic vehicles. The Hudson had those flowing lines and that unibody construction. It was innovative in two dozen ways, and anybody who knew anything about cars wanted one; only the lucky few got one. Irving Mason, the blacksmith-cum-auto mechanic, had connections at the factory and bought it for her as an expression of pure love and devotion, and Hilda had driven it every day since. With a family of mechanics to keep it in tip-top condition, the car was a moving dream.

Not so Hilda. In a moment she was out of the car, her hat knocked forward over her brow, and bawling out her grandson: "Dammit, Timmy, why in tarnation don't you watch where you're going? You ain't got the sense God gave a goose. You and that no-good fancy foreign car. Why can't you be like the rest of us and get a plain old American car. What are you, trying to show off, think you're better than the rest of us? You almost plowed right into me. Dammit. Dammit!"

"God, sorry, Grandma. Sorry," TD said, two or three times.

"Hey, Grams," John said as he moved quickly to her side and put his arm around her, "are you OK? Take it easy. Nobody got hurt. It's OK now." And Jasper was there in an instant, looking over the car.

TD had successfully backed out of the garage by now, and his pedigreed car was slinking away with its tail between its legs. Hilda meanwhile had slid back into her car, gripping the wheel with both hands as old ladies do, and peering over the enormous hood. "Dammit," she muttered three or four more times as she pulled herself together, then said, "Hop in, Johnny, we'll go for a spin. It's about lunch time anyway, ain't it?" John waved a signal at Jasper, who gave him the thumbs-up and waved him off. The two loafers were making their way up the hill toward the courthouse, laughing and rehearsing the incident they had just witnessed and which they would embellish and repeat for the next week to all the other loafers from all the other loafing circuits in town, until at last the story would take a permanent place in the mythology of the town, another illustration of the motif in which the Big Shot Gets Put in His Place. "Damn little idiot," she sputtered, "thinks he owns the road. Always did. Doesn't watch out for anybody but himself. Just barges ahead and everybody else has to get out of the way."

This she said while driving down the exact middle of the street, as if on a one-lane country road in a Model T Ford. Indeed, that was where Grandfather Irving had taught her to drive in 1925. Her driving habits, once fixed, had never changed. Everybody in town, including the cops, knew her and knew the big Hudson, and just pulled over to the curb when they saw her coming. Hilda on her part knew every nuance and detail of the little town and could have driven it blindfolded, though she had a fixed daily circuit from her house to the post office to the beauty parlor to the Square Meal—which took her past the garage—and back home again for an afternoon nap. So it was Timmy's fault for getting in her way. Dammit!

John and his grandmother drove around, with the Hudson like old Roscoe, the children's horse of long ago, plodding along like it knew the way so that the passengers could rest and talk and enjoy the ride and the passing view. The old car led them around the courthouse a few times and took them to lunch at the Square Meal, then around the courthouse again and off toward the city park where Grams told again about the pond that was drained and how everyone in town gathered to catch the fish that were being stranded and the grand fish fry they all had afterwards with a baseball game between the Perryville Nine and the Altenburg Saxons, then a band concert under the gas lights in a little park in a little town of long ago when she was a young girl and America seemed somehow a more innocent place, though she knew now as an adult that even then in the Twenties there was evil loose in the world and in this country, and that the soul-scarred boys that had come back from World War One had a cynicism about them that jarred on the ear of those who had stayed home, and they drank too much and listened to strange music, jazz, and there were loose girls who found them exciting and wanted to sleep with them, and to her old mind they didn't seem so different from the jaded young people and strange music and loose morals of those who came along a generation later in the Sixties. And now yet another generation had passed, and the world was passing into the hands of young people yet again, and who knew what they would become and what they would make of their lives.

They lapsed in and out of German (John had picked up much of his *Sprachgefühl** at his grandmother's knee, though she spoke with an East Perry County accent and a Saxon dialect in which the language had evolved to accommodate neologisms like *der Tractor* and *das Combine*). He told her about living in Germany and how he thought he would assimilate to the culture but didn't. He thought he was a German-American when he went over, but quickly learned that he was just an American of German heritage, and finally, just an American. Germany was a foreign country to him, and he missed hot dogs and baseball and had to stay up half the night with some friendly American soldiers at a nearby post to watch the Super Bowl, and the German pizza they ate was the godawfullest *Scheisse* you ever had in your life, at which Grams roared with laughter and the Hudson bucked forward.

They had gone down Highway 61 through Longtown and Uniontown (formerly Paitzdorf but renamed during the Civil War) and had turned east on County Road A toward the villages that

---

* Feeling for the language, fluency

remained of the original Saxon Lutheran colonies of 1839. Only three were left now, Frohna and Altenburg, and Augsburg down by the river, but they hung on despite poor soil and hard times. They stopped at the West End Tavern in Frohna for a beer and said hello to a half-dozen old-timers Hilda had known all her life, or rather, all their lives, since she was older than they, while the young men scrambled outside to get a closer look at the legendary automobile. Then they continued on through the rolling hills and fields and woods until the road went down and down and down in the long descent to the old river road to Augsburg and past the old Gottlieb farm, now in possession of The Children of Abimelech, then back to the place that once was Wittenberg, now only the shells and foundations of a few buildings, the rest having been swept away by floods, and they drove through the ruins and then stopped. There was the great river, the Mississippi, flowing past, wide and strong and brown, flowing from north to south. Upstream were austere frozen places like Davenport and Minneapolis, downstream cities of warmth and luxury and sin like New Orleans. But here there was nothing, no city, no culture. Only history. Only memory. Only the ghosts of ancestors. Or so it appeared to the naked eye. For the spirits of the past live on in words and thoughts and ideas and traditions, and the push of the past is as powerful as the pull of the future.

At last John said, "It just gets me down sometimes, Grams. I mean, here's Timmy with all his money and nice clothes and a good car. And it makes me feel bad in comparison. I know preachers aren't supposed to make much money, but if I'd work the system like other guys do I could get a big church and go from there to being a district president or synodical big shot and probably do all right financially. But I keep shooting off on these crazy adventures, taking these out-of-the-way churches in places like Alaska, for God's sake, and now I've been in Germany without *zwei Pfennig** to rub together . . . it just gets me down sometimes."

Hilda pinned him with a look. Even at her advanced age, her

---

* Two pennies

eyes were clear and bright. "Runs in the family, John. Don't give it a thought. It's your nature. Things will work out. Don't fret."

She took a deep breath, settled back in the car seat, and looked out at the river. "It was your great-grandfather, Gottfried Meissen, the one customs renamed Godfrey Mason. He had the *Wanderlust,* too. He come over from Germany in 1870 and settled in these hills. But he was restless with farming, though he was running a smithy at the same time and made pretty good money, too, at least in comparison to the other hardscrabble farmers. All them horseshoes add up, I guess."

John said, "Don't we have one of his horseshoes?"

"Well, yes," she replied. "That one that's framed in the hallway along with the family pictures, that was one he made. In fact, as far as I know, it's the one he had to make out of a plain bar of iron to pass his blacksmith's apprentice test. Anyway, he got to thinking about things out West, all these wild stories that were in the papers and magazines, cowboys and Indians and so forth. So he started making knives, real shiny fancy ones with big blades, beautiful things . . . "

"Do we have one?"

"No, I'm getting to that. Godfrey made all these knives, each one with a deer antler handle and a nice leather sheath, and put them on a pack horse and saddled up his own horse and lit out for the West. He was gone two whole years. Just traded his way along the river route all the way up into the Dakota territory and back again, and danged if he didn't bring back an Assiniboine squaw with him."

She paused. John stared at her. "Really!" he exclaimed. "I knew from family stories that he'd gone west, but I didn't know about the squaw."

Hilda nodded her head with pursed lips. "Well, people around here are prejudiced. 'If you ain't Dutch, you ain't much,' that sort of thing, you know. Anybody that wasn't German and Lutheran—or Catholic, for that matter—was just an outsider. Pretty closed community. And everybody fought for the Union in the Civil War, but I guess you've noticed that there ain't hardly no colored in Perry County. They know when they're not wanted. Except for the Everett family. They stuck it out. Where was I?"

"The Indian woman."

"Oh, yes. Well, apparently old Godfrey had made this fantastic battle-axe, just a piece of whimsy that he took along with him, though it had been his prize. It was modeled on these things that the Medieval knights would hack people up with when they went to war. And they say Godfrey would come riding into the Indian villages carrying this awesome looking thing, and the Indians would fall all over themselves trying to get a look at it, and word spread along the trail that a white trader was coming with this great tomahawk. So finally he ended up in the Assiniboine nation way out around Montana, and they rolled out the red carpet and he had a heck of a time, went hunting with them, taught them to play baseball—he was a young man, you have to remember—and anyway the upshot of it all is that he ended up trading the battle-axe for one of the chief's daughters. Her name was Laughing Brook. A striking woman, by all accounts, though why there's no photograph of her, nobody seems to know. But that, young man, is why all you Masons have that very distinctive Indian schnozzola."

John absentmindedly stroked his nose. It was a very fine nose, keen to things carried on the wind, new movements in the air, changes in the atmosphere. So he had Indian blood. Assiniboine! He'd have to look that up. And he had the *Wanderlust* of his ancestors. He was not a bad boy. He was true to his nature. And he himself had gone on an adventure, not to the Wild West but to settled Europe. And he himself had loved a woman. She was a singer: "I am black, but comely, O ye daughters of Jerusalem, as the tents of Kedar, as the curtains of Solomon..." and John would answer, "Rise up, my love, my fair one, and come away..." And what would be the end of it? Lost in thought, he was momentarily deaf, slowly coming to when he realized that his grandmother was still speaking.

"... and so like most Indians she was very practical-minded, learned German to get along just like all us Germans learned English after World War One, took an American name—well, a biblical name, Ruth, but an ordinary name—and got baptized Lutheran and just became one of us, you know. And as I hear if anybody gave her any crap about being an Indian she gave it right back to them, cause as the wife of a blacksmith she knew all the German cuss words, and the spectacle of a white man being cussed out in German by an Indian squaw was so funny—*du bist eine Gott-verdammtes dumme Esel*[*]—after a while everybody gave up and just accepted her. Besides, she'd threaten to sic her father on them with that battle-axe of his that old Godfrey had made. So that was that."

By now the gray skies had parted and patches of sunlight were moving across the landscape, lighting up the forests on the Illinois side of the river. They sat in silence for a time, the young man and the old woman, and watched the river go by, the old river with its great fish and deep secrets, and the river imparted to them a sense of wonder and peace as it always did to those who took time to sit and watch and listen to its voice, the voice as of many waters. At last the old woman got chilly from the late afternoon air creeping in, and she asked John to drive back to town, and she retrieved an afghan from the back seat and pulled it around her shoulders and went to sleep as he drove back through the hills, back through Altenburg and Frohna and Uniontown and Longtown, through the hills that imparted a peace and blessing of their own, with their own voice, a voice unlike that of the river, for it did not change, but stayed the same from generation to generation.

---

[*] You're a goddam stupid ass.

Chapter 4 ◉ Conflict on and off the Gridiron

Timothy David Pope and his magnificent precision German driving machine sped out of town. Objective: Rachel McFadden. Of course he was going to pick her up and take her to the game. Of course he found her attractive. Of course he liked her quick mind and musical interests. But Rachel represented something else in his mind. She represented opportunity. It had been in the back of his mind for some time, but now it was growing like a vine in his heart of hearts. The McFadden spread adjoined the Friedensee Hunting and Fishing Club. They had a hundred acres plus. More than half of the lakeshore was theirs. TD's imagination leaped ahead. He envisioned a resort development on the lake. High-end condos. There was a certain something about the lake. He couldn't quite put his finger on it. But something. Something that felt good somehow.

There were scads of stressed-out businessmen in St. Louis. He knew a lot of them personally. They had means. They had discretionary income. They would pay well—top dollar—for a place near town where they could get away for a day or two and relax. The gently rolling hills of the farm would be ideal for a golf course. A five-star restaurant overlooking the lake. A spa. He snapped his fingers. Yes! A luxury train ride from Union Station, then a horse-and-buggy ride out to the resort.

TD had done very well on the resort in Arkansas, even though it was in an out-of-the-way location and he was leveraged to the hilt. But here was a perfect setting near St. Louis, a metro area of three million! In his imagination, TD had it built. All he needed was a bit of venture capital. All he needed was a few men with vision to bankroll it. That was his M.O. for success: visualize, then actualize. And this resort was clearly visualized in his mind. Just think what a benefit it would be for Rachel—and her mother, too. They were strapped. This would give them financial security for the rest of their lives. TD's heart swelled with religious feeling. He would be able to do a good deed, an act of charity for the needy . . . and turn a tidy little profit on the deal at the same time. He smiled, and stepped on the gas. The big car surged forward smoothly. Jasper had fixed it well. TD drove the car and gave no more thought to Jasper than he would a shoeshine boy.

Rachel was getting ready for her date with TD. She showered and washed her hair, combing it back and letting it air dry as swimmers do. She paused and looked at herself in the mirror. At twenty-five she was still in good shape, but like all women she thought she was too fat. Hips too big, breasts too small. And not married. And not likely to. Slim pickins down here in the boonies. Worse, she was a farm girl. On a failing farm. And worse yet, she was an intellectual. She pulled on her undies and jeans. The jeans felt tight. Better eat nothing but salads for a few days. She peered closely at her face in the mirror. God, was that a wrinkle? Why was she so odd? Most girls get desperate in their senior year of college. They turn up the pressure on their boyfriends. They Want To Talk. What Is Our Relationship? Where Is This Going? Spring is coming. Graduation is looming. He might escape. I have to nail down a Commitment. But no, not Rachel. She was a brain. She was fired up by ideas. She wanted more study, more books. She went to graduate school. She got more books. She got more study. She got more trouble.

She'd like to take her Mensa IQ and flush it down the toilet. Now here she was, feeling fat and over the hill, getting ready for a date with a balding divorcé. But TD was a well-to-do balding divorcé. And he was stable. And he was steady. He was hard-working. He was successful. He drove a luxury car. Those things count to a woman. Especially a woman like Rachel who went skinny-dipping and did other impulsive things. They count for a lot. TD wasn't like John. John was too unpredictable. Who knew what he was going to do or where he was going to go next? Not so with TD. He had built up a good business. He was dependable. He would be a good provider. When a woman gets to a certain point in life, stability equals love.

Rachel threw on a sweatshirt and picked up her guitar. It was an old Martin D-28 her father had bought cheap from a folding bluegrass band a long time ago. He had intended to learn to play but never got around to it, but Rachel did, and so the guitar went to her. It was beat up and scratched but sang like a bird. She noodled around for a minute or so, random chords, E minor, A minor seventh, the lonesome, bluesy chords her fingers often strayed to, then found her way into an old Eagles song: "Desperado." Her voice, a sultry alto, rang out clear and strong and as she sang she looked out the window and saw the sun going down behind the far hill, and she sang to the dying ember.

After a while she went downstairs. The old house was a shambles. Her mother had fallen into another depression and had let things go again. She was sitting in a chair and staring out the window toward the fields, as if waiting for her lost husband and son to come walking back over the fields laughing, and come into the house with muddy boots, and she would fuss at them lovingly, and bustle about in the kitchen and make them a big meal of pot roast with potatoes and carrots and onions, and homemade bread, and home-churned butter, and schnippel beans, and blackberry cobbler with vanilla ice cream, and coffee. But now it was all gone, and the dust was settling, settling on her silent life.

But there was no time for Rachel to deal with her mother just now. TD's car was pulling in. She heard the *bumpety-bumpety-bumpety* as the tires went over the cattle grate. Now he was in front of the house and getting out. Rachel grabbed a down vest for later when the night became cool. Where would they go after the game? Would he try to kiss her? Would he try to cop a feel?

But Rachel felt anything but sexy. Not with worry over her mother. What if she came home and found Mom swinging from a rope in the barn? She thought about it all the time. But if she stayed around, she'd go crazy herself. Sick people make other people sick. Depression is contagious. Here was Timmy walking up to the door like a gentleman.

He would hold the door for her. Not John. He'd sit out there in his old rusty Jeep and lay on the horn. No, John would not do at all.

Then came the polite knock on the door. Rachel went to her mother and stroked her matted hair and kissed her on the cheek. "Bye-bye, Mom," she said. "I'm going out with TD. We're going to the football game." She laid her hand on her mother's shoulder. "Will you be OK? Try to eat something, OK?"

Rachel's mother looked up and smiled and patted her daughter's hand. Reassured, Rachel walked to the door, then turned back and flipped on the lights. She did not want to come home and find her mother sitting alone in a darkened room.

Rachel opened the door and looked at TD. You could tell he'd been working out. And boy, what nice cologne. Really nice. He had changed clothes at his branch office and was wearing Dockers, tailored to fit perfectly, and expensive tan loafers with a tassel and no socks, like the preppies in Clayton and Ladue, and his 100% cotton light-blue Brooks Brothers button-down dress shirt with the TD monogram, sleeves rolled up three-quarters. Then Doxie was there by Rachel's side, muttering a low growl in the back of her throat. "Doxie," Rachel said, "mind your manners!"

"Hey, kiddo," TD said with an easy grin as he gave Doxie a sidelong dirty look, "all ready?"

"I suppose so," Rachel said as she glanced back at her mother.

"Well, let's blast off, then."

He held open the car door, for her, gently touching her arm as she got in. He helped her with the seat belt, and closed the door ever so quietly, as if she were an egg that might break if jostled.

But I'm not fragile, Rachel thought as the big man walked around in front of the car and she saw his upside-down reflection pass smoothly over the polished hood. I'm a woman, she said to herself with rising anger. Dammit, sometimes I'd like a man to just grab me and kiss me. Hard. With no apologies. Or I'll kiss him, just like that, on impulse. And an image of John flitted across her mind, but she brushed it away like a pesky fly, and it was gone, and she was herself again, collecting her thoughts. Self-control, that's what was needed.

Self-control and restraint.

And there was TD in the driver's seat, shutting the door with authority and revving up the big strong motor: in command, in charge, in control, a master with his horse and chariot. He turned to her as he dropped it into gear.

"You look great, kiddo."

She blushed a little. God, those penetrating blue eyes. Like he could see right through her clothes.

"Oh, no," she said, "just some old rags I threw on..."

He looked at her again, closing the sale. "I said, you look great," then added with another professional smile, "don't argue with me. Say, where are we going to sit, anyway? I'm a Dragon and you're a Pirate. The Ste. Gen fans will be on one side of the field, and Perryville on the other."

An absurd idea popped into her head. "I know, right in the middle of the field."

TD laughed. "Yeah! In folding chairs with helmets on, and the game going on around us." He laughed again. "Well, neither of us have our colors on, so we'll be safe." He drove for a few more yards, then said in a practiced offhand way, "Oh, this is off the subject, but I was wondering if you'd like to come sit in with our praise band sometime."

As they cruised away at a slow, majestic pace, TD glanced out the window. There was the sand trap, there was the seventh fairway, there was the quaint bridge over the creek for the golf carts to drive across.

Rachel, too, looked out the window. There was the bush under which she and her brother had played as children, there was the tree in which her father had built her a clubhouse, there was the porch swing where the Arizona hippie Aunt Jane had proselytized her into the world of literature, there was the trail that led toward the Clubhouse and John, there was the field in which her father and brother had died, forever holy and sanctified by their blood.

"I ran into John at the garage today," began TD. "He was working on that rattletrap Jeep of his."

"Yes," Rachel answered. "I've seen him, too. He's staying at the Clubhouse."

"Oh, really? Not with his Mom and Dad?"

"No, not enough room, he says. Plus, he needs a quiet place to work on his dissertation."

"No computer?"

"Funny, I haven't asked about that. I suppose he prefers to do the first draft in longhand."

"So he'll be here for a while, then." This could mean trouble, TD thought. John was a potential suitor for Rachel. And just when things were going his way. TD liked it when things were going his way. He generally tried to make sure things went his way so that he could maintain a favorable negotiating position.

"Yes, I suppose so." Why hadn't it sunk in till just now? Of course. John would be here at least through the winter for a large writing project like a dissertation. Here was her opportunity to reconnect with this significant person in her past, someone who had been away for a long time and now returned unexpectedly, someone she had obviously been infatuated with as a little girl but now was a man, an equal. TD had always been around. He was a known quantity. But there was this touch of mystery about John. Something she'd look forward to solving.

TD chuckled. "Old John-boy!" He chuckled again.

"What?" Rachel asked. What was TD thinking?

"Oh, nothing," TD said, smiling and shaking his head.

"No, what? I want to know." Was there something TD knew about John? Rachel needed all the clues if she were to solve the mystery.

"Well, I hesitate to say anything . . ."

Now her curiosity was piqued. "Go on."

He shrugged. "It's just that . . . well, I guess since I'm a close relative I hear more things. I don't like to knock my own cousin. He's a great guy and all that. Man of the cloth, you know. But there's this thing about John, I'm trying to put my finger on it . . ."

"I'm not sure I follow you. He's been off in Europe for several years."

"Maybe that's part of it. He just seems, I don't know, unpredictable, unsettled."

"Unsettled?"

"Yeah. You know, a couple years here, a couple years there, here today, gone tomorrow, like a rabbit, pops up over here, then goes down another hole, and pops up over there, who knows where or when. Yeah. Unsettled. That's the word." Yes, that was the word. The word to put doubts in Rachel's mind. TD knew enough street-level female psychology to know that stability was number one with most women. They'd have a fling with the big jock or the crazy poet just for the thrill of it, but when it came down to the nuts and bolts of a steady relationship, they'd go for the accountant every time. Or, more to the point, the realtor.

"Unsettled." Rachel repeated the word. It tasted sour in her mouth, like milk that had gone bad. She'd seen things in John she liked. Really liked. The way he was with the children the other night, when they climbed into his lap and he told them stories. And the way he had put Doxie at ease—something TD had never managed to do. And the ineffable something, a sadness in the corner of his eye, and his hurt foot. She had sympathy for him. Something in her wanted to mend him. But no, he was unsettled. That was a fact. He bounced around too much. What was he looking for? Why was he so restless? She couldn't say. Whatever the case, he'd have to find himself a female rolling stone. Let Millie mend him, then send him rolling along.

◉ ◉ ◉

John pulled into town and dropped his grandmother off at her little efficiency apartment at the senior center. It was assisted living, though she didn't need it. But the assistance was there just in case—people to check in and make sure everything was all right, give help as needed with clothes, medicine, food. Hilda had been there for ten years and not needed a thing. But her clock was winding down, ticking slower and slower. Her afternoon naps were longer. Her skin was papery and transparent. Her sleep was light. Her dreams were vivid, her memories strong. And the grip she held on this world was tenuous and weakening day by day. The prospect of eternal life was much in her mind,

and she saw death less as an enemy than a friend. *Komm, süsser Tod.**
She had her set routine. She would read *Good Housekeeping,* watch the six o'clock news on TV, eat a bowl of corn flakes, then go to bed, and bed would feel so good, so warm and dry.

Jasper had had Clarence or one of the other loafers park John's Jeep in front of the apartment. After putting the Hudson in the garage, John limped over to the Jeep, got in, and turned the ignition. It roared to life, feeling frisky and full of fun. Jasper must have tinkered with the carburetor, making the fuel mixture a little richer. Good deal. In time he'd give it a radiator flush. Check the hoses. Evict the mouse from the upholstery. Let the city mouse see what it's like being a country mouse. Maybe even give the old heap a new coat of paint. John checked his watch. Five o'clock. Time to hustle. His parents were expecting him for dinner, and the game started at seven. Back through the square, down St. Joseph, and left on Kiefner Street past Fred's Flower Shop and Johnnie's Poultry to the plain little white house with asbestos siding. It was a nondescript thing, one of those barracks-like houses that had sprung up like mushrooms after World War Two. There were dozens like it all over town, and thousands more in every other little town in America. It was a two-bedroom house with a small kitchen and a small living room and a carport on the side, and his parents had placed lawn ornaments in the front yard—a birdbath and a shiny globe. The interior was likewise unremarkable, with wall-to-wall carpeting in earth tones and plain wooden furniture. But down the main hallway there was a photo gallery. Here was a pictorial history of the Mason family from the earliest times to the present. The patriarch was there at the beginning, Godfrey Mason in his blacksmith shop, with his enormous bushy nineteenth-century moustache, burly arms and big grimy hands gripping a hammer as he stood by his anvil. His Assiniboine wife, Ruth Laughing Brook, refused to have her picture taken. Then came Irving Mason, his son and only child. Irving was wearing a white suit and sporting a crisp boater hat, looking jaunty at the wheel of one of his Hupmobiles at the height of his prosperity. He

---

* "Come, Sweet Death" (title of an old Lutheran hymn)

had married late in life to a much younger woman, and that woman was Grams, Hilda Brunner, and there she was as a girl in her confirmation dress and prim white shoes, looking like she had just recited Luther's *Small Catechism* in German, which she had.

Irving and Hilda begat four children: Jasper, Walter, Mildred, and Ralph. There was an old photo of the family—mother, father, and four children, all dressed up and posed and looking serious, which in real life they hardly ever were. Then Walter had died as a child of a bee sting. He and Jasper had been very close, and Jasper always said that when his time came he wanted to be cremated and his ashes interred with Walter so that at the Last Day they could greet the Lord together in the resurrection of the body. There was a picture of Jasper in his Army uniform. There was a picture of Mildred "Millie" and Herbert "Buddy" Pope, dressed in sloppy clothes and holding a string of panfish on the shores of the Friedensee, young and carefree, as if the happiness would continue and the fish would keep biting forever. Ralph had married Betty Reinhardt, and there was a picture of them in wedding clothes. Betty, who came from a long line of Lutheran pastors going back to the eighteenth century, was the daughter of Ernst and Alma Reinhardt. Ernst had been pastor in Farrar, and when his car broke down one day Ralph was sent out to fix it. It was only a loose battery cable, so the story goes, and Ralph tightened it up in five minutes and was going to go when Pastor Reinhardt invited him to stay for dinner, for of course the Mason's Garage never charged the pastors for car repair, even though all the pastors in town drove old cars that needed repair. Dinner was the least courtesy that could be shown.

It was a small party, as the Reinhardts' other children were away. So it was Pastor and Mrs. Reinhardt and Ralph Mason at the table, and directly across from Ralph they put their daughter Betty, who had just graduated from the LCMS teacher's college in Seward, Nebraska. And she looked at him with those big brown eyes. And he looked at her. *Dass ist alles. Der war Kaput.*[*] So they were married at the church in

---

[*] That was it. He was a goner.

Farrar, with her father officiating. Of course both families had known each other for years, just as everybody in Perryville and Farrar had known each other for years, for they were in bowling and softball and dartball together, and Walther League and Lutheran Laymen's League and Lutheran Women's Missionary League together, and some had lived in Farrar and moved to Perryville, and others had lived in Perryville and moved to Farrar, and all had cousins who had married into Farrar or Perryville families, or had gone to Lutheran school together, which was as good as being related, or had been confirmed by the same pastor, which was the next best thing, and so constituted one small unit of a two-million-member Lutheran denomination in which everybody knew everybody. The wedding reception was held under the oak trees in the picnic grove behind the church, and there was fried chicken and homemade pie, and a beer wagon and an oompah band, and relatives who had moved away long ago came back and within ten minutes were able to establish a personal connection with someone they'd never met in their life. In the Missouri Synod, the six degrees of separation had been reduced to one.

So Ralph Mason and Betty Reinhardt were wed, and a year or so later their firstborn came along, a son, and they named him John, after Betty's much-admired brother-in-law John "JJ" Kolding, who had married Betty's older sister Joan and was now in his first call, a large, important church in St. Louis. There was a high school picture of John Mason, trying to look debonair in a white jacket with a boutonnière and a bow tie, and another of him in his green and white Perryville Pirates football uniform, posed as if ready to pass the ball but with his helmet off. And a couple of years after John, William was born, and they called him Bill for short. It took a while for Bill to get started in the insurance business, but once he did, he married Judy Brickman, and their daughter was little Katie, the one who said she had seen and talked to the big fish at the lake, which nobody believed. There was a standard Walmart family photo of them, showing Bill as a big straightforward guy, Judy with cascading red hair, and baby screaming its head off, but they took that shot just for laughs. A few years after Bill, Lou Ann came along, a little tomboy in jeans and pigtails. There was a snapshot of her hanging upside down like a possum from a tree next to the Clubhouse. Now she was an unwed mother. She named her son Billy—that's the one who took a potshot at the ducks—after her brother, and she and her son were living with her parents while she worked at the bakery and looked for a husband. And that is why the younger daughter had the older child, and why there was no room at the inn for John when he came back, and he had to stay at the Clubhouse, which he preferred anyway.

So that was the dinner party that night: Ralph and Betty, Bill and Judy and Katie, Lou Ann and Billy, and John. And Millie, who had driven in separately. When he walked in everybody was crammed into the dining room, seated at table, everybody talking at once with their mouth full, "Pass this, pass that, how are you doing, what's been happening, did you hear about, no kidding, what do you think about, is that so," and so forth and so on.

"Hey, Johnny," everybody yelled when they saw him, "it's about time. Come on, sit down here and put on the feedbag."

"Yeah," Bill said, "we waited and waited 'cause we can't eat without a prayer and we can't pray unless the preacher in the family says the prayer."

"But the food was getting cold so we just said *Komm, Herr Jesu* and dove in," added Ralph.

"Right," Lou Ann said, "the heck with the darn preacher, we're hungry. So Pappy led the prayer and the roof didn't fall in, can you believe it?"

"Who's got the mashed potatoes?"

"Uncle Johnny, come sit by me."

"Pass the salt."

"No. Me."

"No. Me. Me me me."

"I need some more chicken."

"The new coach is doing good with the team."

"Coming up," said Betty with a smile as she grabbed the platter and went back into the kitchen. She had made fried chicken, fresh killed that day at Johnnie's Poultry down the street. Good chicken, too, grown on the ground, not factory chicken raised in cages. You could always taste the difference. And mashed potatoes from scratch, lumpy, with loads of butter. And gravy that the children put into a duck pond in their potatoes. And corn that the grownups mixed in with the potatoes and put salt and lots of pepper on top. Betty was a good cook, and proud of it. She liked cooking, and liked to see men eat. She had learned from her mother, and she had taught her daughter Lou Ann, and worried as she was for Lou Ann's future she knew if she could get a man to the table, she could set the hook. It's just that eligible guys kept moving away, looking for something better than Perryville had to offer. Something new. But one of these days a good solid Lutheran boy would come along. It was just a matter of time. Keep going to church. Keep going to the singles group. It would happen. Lou Ann was in the game. John was another problem, though. Bill had married and settled down, so she could cross him off her list. But what of John? John the wanderer. John the dreamer. John the theologian with his mind on heavenly things. He needed a sensible woman to ground him, put his hand to the plow, get him into the harness. But who? All his high school girlfriends were married, though a few were divorced and back on the market. Bonnie Petzold. Martha Eifert. Then there was Rachel. She was unattached, well, technically unattached. Everybody knew she had been seeing TD, but no formal engagement had been announced yet. So let's say she's available. She might be a possibility, even though Millie said she was impulsive. Like Johnny.

Betty loaded up the platter with chicken and brought it back in and set it on the table. One pass around the table, and the chicken was gone. Ralph as always took the neck and the livers and the gizzards. The kids got the drumsticks. They left the wings for John. After coffee, the men, as was the custom in the family, did the dishes while the women sat and visited in the living room. But there was room for only two men at the sink, Ralph washing and Bill drying and putting away. So after John had cleared the table his mother drew him aside.

"How is your foot? Do you need to see the doctor?"

"I think it's coming along OK, Mom. This boot thing really takes the pressure off. It was just a hairline fracture anyway. Nothing serious. But it hurts like the dickens. A few more weeks and I'll be out of this thing altogether."

"What happened, John?"

He paused and looked into his mother's eyes. "I was attacked by a vicious dog. It broke the metatarsal bone. There's no infection."

"I worry about you, John."

"Well, I'm fine."

"It's my job to worry. I'm your mother."

"Well, don't. I'm fine."

"You're thirty years old. It's time you married and settled down."

"Please!"

"Did you meet any nice girls in Germany?"

In fact, he had. He had fallen deeply and hopelessly in love. With the wrong woman.

"You should take Rachel out sometime, John," Betty continued. "She really is a good girl. She has a heart of gold."

"I'm sure she does, Mom. It's just that I'm not interested in getting involved with anyone just now. Maybe sometime later. I don't know." Sure. Maybe later, John thought. Rachel was OK. A nice kid from his childhood. A memory from his past. Better to keep her there, safe and secure, not let her invade his present. Plus she and TD were an item. Don't interfere. Don't want to get tangled up with TD again. Definitely not.

There was a commotion near the front door as Ralph called out, "Loading up! Everybody pile in!" Betty was staying home with the kids. Ralph was in the cab of the Mason's Garage pickup, beeping the horn. Judy sat beside him. John and his brother and sister jumped into the bed of the pickup and they took off. Down the street they rolled, going slow and honking the horn like all the other vehicles that were moving through the town toward the football field. Round and round the square they went, bawling out the Perryville fight song at the top of their lungs and yelling "Go, Pirates, Go Pirates, Fight! Fight! Fight!" over and over and cranking themselves up to a frenzy, arms around each other and rocking back and forth. At last they reached the parking lot and Ralph was cruising slow, looking for an empty space. In the distance they could see the lights of the field and hear the drums and horns as the band assembled and began to warm up. Just as Ralph was parking the truck—as luck would have it right next to Millie who had just pulled in—Bill and Lou Ann looked at each other and read each other's mind. "Get him!" they both yelled simultaneously as they pounced on their older brother as they had done so often when they were little. John yelled, "No, no, help, police, murder, help!" as Bill, now 245 pounds, held him down and Lou Ann tickled him without mercy, knowing all his good spots from long childhood experience, and Bill and Lou Ann were yelling, "Hah, got you now, buddy. Think you're tough, don't you? You wanna play hardball? We'll play hardball," and John was yelling in mock agony, "Mercy! Mercy!" and struggling not too hard as the torture continued. Just as the mayhem was at its height Rachel walked by and peered into the bed of the truck.

"What the heck is going on in here?" she said grinning.

"Oh, Rachel," John said. "Thank God. Save me! I'm being murdered by these miscreants."

"Forsooth!" she exclaimed. "Unhand him, thou varlet!" she said, laughing and giving Bill a shove and dumping him over and socking Lou Ann in the arm and enjoying the fraternal laughter and fun on top of John and digging her fingers into his ribs. But just as she did a sudden shock hit her bang in the chest. She had no brother to wrestle with. She stuffed it and came back to the present mayhem. For here were John and Bill and Lou Ann, part of the old Clubhouse Gang that she too had been a part of, and she was as close to them as if they were brothers and sisters. And as Lou Ann got off her brother and Bill fell over panting, John was under Rachel, laughing, and he looked up at her and she looked down at him and their eyes met as his laugh evaporated. And then their eyes fused for a long breath, then two, then three. And something happened, some kind of knowledge was exchanged, one soul to another, some inexpressible penetration of hearts . . . but then just as quickly they looked away as John remembered Elizabeth and Rachel remembered TD who was coming up just then and they laughed an embarrassed laugh and said something trivial as John sat up and brushed himself off. But Bill and Lou Ann had seen it, and they looked at each other again, and again read each other's thoughts. And Millie too had seen.

So they all trooped into the little stadium, arm in arm, laughing and joking and shoving and punching each other: Ralph and his sister Millie, John and his sister Lou Ann, Bill and his wife Judy, and Rachel and her boyfriend TD. They sat together on the Perryville side, high up by the announcer's booth at midfield where they always sat. As they came in they all were greeted by friends. John especially was welcomed by many old pals and schoolmates and teammates, as well as by Coach Wink and Old Man Roschke, who always sat together; Old Man Roschke had not only taught John when he was in grade school, he had taught Coach Wink, who now looked after him.

TD took orders and went to the snack bar—black coffee for Ralph, Millie, and John, Coke and two hot dogs for Bill, a Moon Pie for Lou Ann, a Diet Sprite for Judy, and nothing for Rachel, who was really determined to lose weight this time. At the snack bar fans from both sides were mingling, and a familiar voice called out, "TD! Praise the Lord!"

TD turned toward the voice. It was the Reverend Dave Henderson, a dapper little man with a blow-dry hairstyle. "Hey, Pastor Dave! Thought I might see you here."

"I reckon so, since the entire Ste. Gen backfield is in my youth group. Say, buddy, who's that good-lookin' girl I saw you come in with?"

"Oh, that's Rachel McFadden. We've been seeing a good bit of each other lately."

"Is that the one you told me about that sings and plays the guitar?"

"Yeah. Fingerstyle, too."

"We should get her involved in the praise band."

"I've already mentioned it to her."

The minister looked at him. "That's what I like about you, TD, always thinking ahead, anticipating. Well, listen, some of us are going to Pio's for pizza after the game. Bring her by and let me meet her.

I'll save a table."

They looked at each other square in the eye, two salesmen who thought alike. "I'll do it," TD said, and paying for his order took off as the crowd roared and cheered at the kickoff.

John was watching the game with an intensity possible only in those who had experienced combat in the arena. His muscles twitched and his body reacted with every play as if he himself were on the field. And in a sense he was, for as the battle raged onfield John was reliving in his own mind the battle he had fought fourteen years before in the State Regionals between Perryville and Ste. Genevieve.

It had been a close game, hard fought by kids who knew each other from having nearby farms and mutual activities in 4-H and FFA and Luther League. But the Ste. Gen coach was a hard-ass, win-or-die type who had played pro ball for a couple of seasons, and he had taught his boys how to get away with holding and how to deliver the cheap shot when the ref wasn't looking. TD because of his size and speed played in the secondary on defense. In the third quarter he had thrown a cross-body block on Louie Oswald, the Perryville left tackle and taken him out of the game with a knee injury. John's brother Bill, only a freshman at the time but big and strong, was at right tackle. John argued with the coach to move him over, but Wink decided to throw in another kid at the critical position that protected the quarterback's blind side. So it came down to the last play of the game, Perryville trailing by three points. But they had driven to the Ste. Gen eight yard line with ten seconds on the clock. Third and goal. Time to run one more play. The hell with a field goal. Go for the win. Wink sent in wideout Billy Vogel with the play, a buttonhook pass to the left corner of the end zone. Hut one! Hut two! Vaughan Brunke, the center, gave him a weak snap. John juggled the ball but got control as he took a five-step drop, freezing the Ste. Gen secondary with a look and a pump fake to the right. He cocked his arm again to throw, but just at that moment TD, who had moved up for the blitz and bowled over the left tackle, speared him in the back with his helmet. John felt a spasm of pain go through him and he went down hard with a yell, letting go of the ball, which Ste. Gen recovered as time ran out.

And so John's football season had ended with a bitter loss. TD had gone on to the State Championship. And glory. And success. And a Mercedes. And John had gone on to a crummy old Jeep that needed a radiator flush and a paint job.

◉ ◉ ◉

After the game, TD and Rachel went to Pio's. It was the usual after-the-game hangout for everybody, and both Rachel and TD saw people they knew, and chatted briefly with them as they made their way to the Hendersons' table in the back. TD seemed to know everybody, for he had been in business in the area for almost ten years, and was one of the movers and shakers of the community, making things happen that were profitable to everyone right down the business food chain. Kenny Dreyer, the mayor of Perryville, was sitting with Tony Petzold, the mayor of Ste. Gen, and their wives were with them, along with Jim Johnston, the Perryville coach, and Albert Phipps, coach of the Dragons, and Kenny was grousing about having to pick up the tab since his team had lost. He made a wisecrack about recruiting TD to play for Perryville. TD thought with satisfaction: he'd never say that to John.

By the time TD and Rachel reached their table Pastor Dave and his wife Barb were already there. She was tall—taller than Dave—and had a big Alabama smile with big white teeth, which she used to dazzling effect when singing a solo in the spotlight just before the sermon. Her big number was "He Touched Me" by Bill Gaither, and she caressed the microphone and closed her eyes as she sang and moved her hands sensuously, and it never failed to generate tremendous applause. She made Rachel feel at home, asking her about her life, her interests, her church background, her studies—Barb, too, had been an English major at U.S.A., the University of South Alabama, school colors red, white, and blue. Barb carried the conversation as Dave and TD glanced around, working the room from their seats, making eye contact with a short upward nod of the head to the VIPs.

At last the pizza came, a thin-crust, St. Louis style combo with bacon, cut square. They dug in. Rachel was dying for a beer, but Pastor Dave ordered a pitcher of root beer. Even though as a Lutheran pastor he was permitted to drink, he never did so in public for fear of offending the Baptists he was trying to emulate (and attract to) his church. At last he leaned forward and smiled at Rachel.

"TD tells me you're quite the guitar player."

"Oh, I don't know, just a few simple things . . . "

"Come on, kiddo," TD said. "Stop putting yourself down."

"Well," she said, "I do OK, I guess. I have a few numbers worked up. Old folk-rock numbers, mostly. Eagles. Crosby, Stills & Nash. That sort of thing."

Dave brightened and clapped his hands one time. "That's exactly the musical style we have at our church. We're trying to appeal to the unchurched Baby Boomers by offering a worship format that's in a familiar musical style."

"Really," she said, becoming interested. She'd heard something about this new thing in worship, mostly bits and pieces from TD.

"Yes," Pastor Dave went on enthusiastically, "To attract the unchurched, you have to have worship that is vibrant and entertaining. You have to have music that is in the same style they listen to on the radio every day so they can relate to it. Like Seventies folk rock. And sermons have to relate to their felt needs—corporate stress, family relationships, those kinds of things."

TD nodded and said, "That's where Pastor Dave is so great. He's young and dynamic and progressive, drives a Corvette, really relates to ordinary people. He always says that the Bible is the manufacturer's handbook . . . how does that go?" TD said, setting up the play.

Pastor Dave caught the ball and ran. "The Bible is the manufacturer's handbook, and to be a success in life you have to study it and apply its principles."

"His teaching has certainly helped me maximize potential," TD said. "And the music is just so great."

Pastor Dave held up his hands in the "please, no applause" gesture.

"It's nothing," he demurred. "Just a few ideas I picked up at one of JJ Kolding's workshops."

Rachel thought for a moment. She'd been in Pastor Gottlieb's church all her life, except for when she had been away at school, and then she hadn't attended any place regularly. Of course there was that anti-evolution fundamentalist service she'd been to that really antagonized her. Worship at home was the same every Sunday. She knew the service by heart: Confession and Absolution, Kyrie, Gloria, Creed, Sanctus, Agnus Dei, Nunc Dimittis. She knew it so well that often her mind wandered during church. But then during the week after she would find herself humming bits and pieces of it: "Create in me a clean heart, O God, and renew a right spirit within me. Cast me not away from Thy presence, and take not Thy Holy Spirit from me." She had heard of these "seeker services." Maybe an inspiring, success-oriented sermon would help her out of these doldrums. Give her some energy, some direction. Maybe she needed a change, like new clothes and a new hairdo. Maybe a new church.

"So what's involved, Pastor?"

"Please, just Dave."

"Oh, OK."

"It's a commitment," he replied. "We rehearse on Wednesday nights, seven to nine P.M. Then we have two services on Sunday, and we have to be there early for warm up and sound check."

Barb reached over and touched her arm. "To be honest with you, Rachel, we really need another guitar and voice in the praise band. We need your help."

Rachel was sold. She didn't have another commitment on Wednesday nights. Or any other night for that matter. "Well, all right. I'll give it a try."

Dave and TD looked at each other with the businessman's smile of success. Ka-ching!

☙ ☙ ☙

When John got back to the Clubhouse after visiting an hour with his parents, he found Millie, who had left after the third quarter, still up, sitting in her favorite chair on the porch and reading a book. It was Hemingway's *The Old Man and the Sea*. She had a plate of cold cuts set out for him and a bottle of Bud, ice cold from having been in the spring all day.

"What a game," John said as he laid into the meat, cheese, and crackers. "I thought we had a good game plan, pound it out on the ground, grind down the opposition, wear 'em out and kill 'em in the fourth quarter. Strength and domination. Good, old-fashioned, smash-mouth football. But the mistakes!" He threw up his hands. "Fumble in the end zone. Interception and run back. That cost us nine points right there. Put us in a hole we never could dig out of." He shook his head. "Dang!"

He ate in silence for a few minutes. The tree frogs were chirping loudly. A lone bullfrog boomed from the far side of the lake. But autumn was gathering. Soon they would be digging in to hibernate. Millie smiled to herself as she continued to read. Finally she put a bookmark at her page and set the book aside.

"You know, John, I'm surprised to hear that you saw any of the game."

"What do you mean, Millie? I was there. I saw the whole game. Every play."

"Is that a fact?"

"What are you getting at?"

"You mean you don't know?"

"No!" Women were so darned aggravating, expecting you to read their minds all the time. "What are you talking about?"

"John." She leveled her sights at him and pulled the trigger. "Half the time you were making goo-goo eyes at Rachel."

"What?! No!" John said with rising panic. "No. You're making this up. She was sitting right in front of us with TD. So I suppose I might have glanced her way a couple of times . . . couldn't be helped."

Millie smiled again as she picked up her book to end the argument. "I saw what I saw." She opened the book and took out the bookmark, then went back to reading as she shook her head and added softly, "And they say women don't know their own mind!"

Chapter 5 ◉ An Unexpected Guest

And so the season trailed away into autumn, the days growing shorter, the nights longer and colder, the leaves dying away in the deep, russet, mourning shades of old oak. The sun hung lower in the sky, and on clear days shone through to the forest floor as more and more leaves fell. The frogs burrowed down into the mud and ceased their singing. The birds found their way south, except for the lone heron who like an old bachelor kept his dwelling way high up in the sycamore by the lake. Deep down in the water Old Methuselah settled into his nest beneath a pile of fallen timber next to a snapping turtle that had been his neighbor for generations. By the Clubhouse the woodpile was high with split oak, replenished every few weeks by another rank or two from local farmers who cut Millie a special deal because of the quantities she used. The other families that had shares in the Clubhouse had come out for their annual deer hunting parties. Henry Schuttenberg, a teenager, had bagged his first deer, a ten-point buck. Pretty impressive for a kid. The family had the head mounted and hung in the hall, and gave Millie a big supply of deer sausage. The mayor, who wasn't in the club but was invited anyway as a friend of the families, came out to try his luck with the wild turkey. God was good to him this year, and he came away smiling with a large tom. This hunting prize virtually assured him of re-election.

John had set up his writing desk and was beginning to work, writing longhand with a black fine point Cross pen on college ruled notebook paper. He had all his notes in order, the primary and secondary sources, the quotes from German and Latin, the outline—these things he had all completed under the guidance of his *Doktorvater* while in Germany. Professor Klaus Otto von Günther, who was tops in his field, had a cluttered office overlooking the Neckar River with a cable TV on which there was always a soccer game playing with the volume turned down so he could listen to his Django Reinhardt records while chain-smoking Gauloises. Professor Günther had a highly ordered mind despite his eccentricities. He insisted that the essence of all good writing, whether academic or creative, was thinking. He was fond of repeating the story of the playwright, perhaps it was Feydeau, who burst into the coffeehouse one day and exclaimed, "I have finished my play! Now all that remains is to write it." In other words, he had thought it through. He had created the structure first. Last he would hang words on the frame. This was a new approach to John, who had always written his way into things and then had to go back and overhaul and change and rewrite before handing in a paper. But the first commandment of graduate study was, "Obey your *Doktorvater*." So he obeyed, and had gotten a couple of published articles out of it, including one in the prestigious *Lutheran Quarterly*.

So he sat down to work in the quiet of the old Clubhouse, and the juices were flowing, the pages were mounting up, there were no distractions, and when he needed a break, there was Millie in the kitchen with hot coffee on the stove, and they would chat for a few minutes, and then he would go back to work. His foot was healing, too, and he took a walk every day to strengthen it. Doxie had dropped her litter, and often trotted over of her own accord and accompanied John on his rambles. The days were generally clear, and he enjoyed going down to the low water bridge and watching the squirrels bustling about preparing for winter. All around he could hear combines bringing in the harvest of corn. Rachel was busy overseeing the work at her farm and didn't come over very often, which to John was just as well. He liked to be around her but felt uncomfortable at the same time. He had his work. She had hers. Best keep it that way.

On Fridays John would go into town with his pages and key them into the computer. He had a laptop that he kept at the city library with the permission of Miss Lindemann. She kept his favorite table and his favorite chair in his favorite corner reserved for him as a kind of personal study carrel, and made sure nobody touched the computer when he was away. God bless Miss Lindemann. She had been a little old lady it seemed when John was a kid, and here she was at the same library twenty years later, even littler and older but still as genial and helpful as could be. Librarians live forever; good books preserve them. John had an old but reliable printer set up at his table and would print out drafts as he went along. In the intervening week Miss Lindemann would look them over and find the inevitable typos and punctuation errors. She was a stickler for semicolons, and read his work for clarity and cogency of argument. In another life she might have been a top New York editor. But here she was living contentedly as a small town librarian, shaping the minds of grubby little kids who smelled of barnyard chores, and tutoring their parents in worthy, character-building books to read to the little ones before bedtime.

So the work progressed in a satisfactory rhythm of creation and analysis, Clubhouse and library, back and forth, back and forth, while in England Rafael von Päpinghausen continued his physical therapy at the hospital. He took a flat in Highgate across from the cemetery. One day he took a stroll through the cemetery and saw the tomb where Karl Marx is buried. He paused in reverent meditation. Here was a great man. Here was one man who changed the world with revolutionary ideas. He did in the nineteenth century what Muhammad had done in the seventh. Somehow there was a common thread between the two. What difference did it make whether revolution came out of the barrel of a gun or religious conquest advanced at the point of a sword?

Rafael made great progress as he learned to drive again; he went into town to take in shows and museums, enjoying the great city. As he watched action movies he dreamed of blood vengeance. Rafael would find John somehow and even the score for his mutilated right hand. He tried a people search on his computer, but there were scores of John Masons all over the United States. So he would have to take his British car and go to America, and enjoy the trip, and look in this place and that for his quarry, and patiently track him down, and then have the pleasure of killing him. Today Rafael was pure, full of righteous wrath. Other days, doubt would creep in as he remembered John with fondness.

How had it come about? he asked himself. How had he become—what do the American gangster movies call it—a "hit man"? An assassin. A professional murderer. How did it come down to this, not only that he must, but that he *wanted* to kill a man, a man he had loved as a dear friend, and over and above this, the friend's son, an innocent child? It all went so against his nature.

Rafael knew the Qur'an. He knew the Suras. Allah the merciful. Allah the forgiving. All those beautiful appelations.

He also knew the others, the Suras that called for vengeance, wrath, and punishement

How had it come about?

He knew, of course.

It was Sinan. It began when they were young men. They had been meeting for a long time, and, in addition to the stupid things that young men do, had been discussing Islam. Rafael had also discussed it with his mother and father. His mother, still clinging to Catholicism, was opposed. But she deferred to her husband, who was not religious but was nonetheless open-minded. He had even gone so far as to set up a trust fund to provide for Sinan's education, had visited the local mosque with the two boys, and had been present when Rafael stood up in the assembly and confessed his belief in Allah and the Prophet.

Then one spring day, when the cuckoo was heard amongst the fir trees, and the two boys' trust for one another had grown and settled, Sinan began to tell Rafael about the Janissaries—how they were formed in the fourteenth century, how they were an elite infantry corps comprised of captured Christian children made Muslim, how they took vows of chastity and moral rigor according to the inner jihad, how they were the purest and most consecrated of all Muslims, how they protected the sultan . . . and sadly, how they began to decline, demanding more and more women, money, and power, how they began to threaten the sultan they were supposed to protect, how in 1826 they were destroyed by the "Auspicious Incident" in which six thousand Janissaries were beheaded.

And how a determined remnant escaped and fled to the wilderness, how they survived despite the bitterest privations—hunger, cold, persecution, how little by little they increased their ranks, how they became attached to a wealthy Saudi oil sheik, of the Wahhabi sect of Islam. This man gave the funding and a support network while redirecting their focus to precision assassinations of infidels who opposed the Crescent. Moreover he maintained the secrecy of the restored Janissaries over against the outside world, while discreetly informing the higher-ups that here was a clandestine cadre of black ops fighters that could go anywhere and do anything, so fierce was their zeal for the Crescent.

"But Sinan," he said, "this secret order of Janissaries, it seems like the highest and purest form of Islam. I'm not cut out for that sort of thing. And even if I were and wanted to join, how would I find them? How would I become one?"

Sinan nodded his head with sympathy and understanding. "You start with one of these," he said, and drew from within his tunic an object that Rafael had never seen, nor had he ever seen the like of it. It was a knife—a deadly thing of beauty, an Ottoman *yatagan*, of Damascus steel, wickedly curved, with an ornate, bejeweled handle and sheath, shorter than the common *yatagan* but better for close-in hand-to-hand combat. Or stealth and assassination.

"It was my father's," Sinan explained. "It has been handed down for generations. My father killed a heroin kingpin. They got him him in return. I was hiding close by. They saw me when I ran out and retrieved the knife. They know I can recognize them. They will find me and kill me some day. But this sacred knife they will not get."

"How?"

"Because I give it to you."

Rafael drew in a sharp breath.

"Here is a contact person in Berlin," Sinan said as he scribbled a note. "Find an excuse to go there. Call him. He knows me and knew my father. He will take you in."

Still more time passed, as Rafael continued his undergraduate studies. He had embraced Islam, but still he hesitated. He kept the knife and the contact information in a hidden place. He had heard what military training did to your soul. They took you from an ordinary, peace-loving person and turned you into a killing machine. They taught you to hate. They filled you with rage. They made you so angry and vicious that you could go against nature and kill your fellow man. Some men cracked under the strain. He had read a book in American literature class about a young man this happened to in the Sixties. PTSD. These were quietly discharged. Ruined and unfit for life in the ordinary world, they became the lost souls, the wanderers, the beggars, the drifters, the homeless, the dharma bums.

Most men adapted to military life for a short term. But the Janissaries, a lifelong commitment to an elite corps—my God, what must their training be like.

Then came the day when Rafael went to the shack to meet Sinan. It was a holiday. Sinan by Rafael's father's benevolence and influence had gotten into a top medical school and was making good progress. Rafael, a bit younger, was still an undergraduate but making plans for graduate study at Heidelberg. The two young men had gone their separate ways but kept in touch not only by phone calls, but also by old-fashioned letters. Rafael had bought two sets of fine stationery and two Mont Blanc Meisterstück fountain pens. Both men used them often.

Perhaps the drug lords had intercepted their correspondence. Who could say? They probably had some kind of Janissaries of their own, some elite cadre of trained professional assassins.

As he came down the trail approaching the cabin, Rafael sensed something wrong. It was too quiet. The birds were not singing. Plus, Sinan had turned out to be an excellent musician. He enjoyed playing old Mississippi Delta blues songs on his guitar. Always in the past Sinan arrived early and began strumming and singing as Rafael drew near. Today there was nothing.

As he rounded the corner of the path, he could see why. He fell to his knees and vomited. There was his friend, his true friend, his faithful and beloved Muslim brother. Sinan, or what was left of Sinan, was hanging from a tree, naked and eviscerated. His eyeballs had been gouged out. His fingers had been cut off.

With deep reverence Rafael took the body of his friend down from the tree, covered his nakedness with a blanket, and laid him down on a narrow cot. He recited holy words of mourning from the Qur'an. He knelt before the body and swore vengeance against these monsters who had shed innocent blood. He gathered kindling, and burned the cabin down to the ground. As the flames waxed greater and greater and hotter and hotter, Rafael's heart turned to cold stone. He retrieved his *yatagan,* went to Berlin, and called the number Sinan had given him.

And so began the long, arduous training of Rafael von Päpinghausen into the secret order of Janissaries. Now it had come down to this, his last field mission before assuming command of the academy hidden in the Afghan mountains.

John for his part thought of Rafael often, accompanied by a dark chord of fear as he remembered the threatening letter, though he thought it unlikely that Rafael would be able to locate him. They had struck up an instant friendship, the way you do in Europe where everybody is open to new experiences and new people. They had met in fencing class—both had decided that as long as they were in Heidelberg they may as well get in a little dueling—and went out afterwards to a nearby *kneipe** for beer, and the conversation had continued long into the night. They exchanged a lot of philosophy but very little personal information in the days they had hung around with each other, and about all Rafael knew about John was that he was from the States—the town of Perry-something, somewhere—and had gone to the Ft. Wayne seminary. And at long last, to his great surprise, he had learned that John was involved—quite seriously involved—with Elizabeth. And that, of course, was the fatal piece of information that Rafael had been seeking.

As autumn gathered about the Clubhouse, the season was also waning in the church. The numbers of the Sundays after Pentecost

---

* tavern

had advanced into the Twenties, and the appointed Scripture lessons were becoming increasingly apocalyptic, as they did every year. On Sundays John and Millie drove the short distance to Peace Lutheran Church. It was a small, white frame church building surrounded by cornfields, and next to it was a small, rural white frame parsonage and a small, white frame parish school. It looked pretty much like all country churches except for the German inscription on the cornerstone: EV. LUTH. FRIEDENSKIRCHE, 1841, U.A.C. Though John knew from his seminary studies what U.A.C. stood for now, he remembered being puzzled as a child and asking his father, who explained that it meant "Unaltered Augsburg Confession" (the other being the altered vesion that Melanchthon published under pressure from Calvinists and that opened the door to a symbolic view of the Sacrament). These were the conservative Lutherans. These were the hardheaded Lutherans. These were the Lutherans who chose to leave their beloved *Vaterland* rather than compromise their religious beliefs. These were the Lutherans who in America refused to be assimilated to the surrounding Protestant culture, knowing that if they did their pure Lutheran doctrine would gradually become diluted. Except that it would have come about incrementally and painlessly over a long period of time rather than suddenly and traumatically. So here in America they became known as the different Lutherans, the obstinate Lutherans, the fundamentalist Lutherans, the backward Lutherans, the "other" Lutherans. The Catholics hated them because they were too Protestant; the Protestants hated them because they were too Catholic. And the mainstream Lutherans, the ones who had assimilated to American liberal Protestantism or conservative Evangelicalism, were too pious to hate them, so they patronized them as if they were a quaint anachronism like the Amish. They were the people of the Lutheran Church–Missouri Synod.

The Reverend Earl Gottlieb, former missionary in Africa, was more or less typical of the older generation of Missouri Synod pastors. A tall, spindly man with a perpetual smile and thick, Coke-bottle glasses, he wore a cassock and surplice to celebrate worship. He had candles for all services and sometimes incense on high festival days.

There was a crucifix on the altar. All very "Catholic." When he got up in the pulpit, though, he proclaimed nothing but salvation by grace through faith in Jesus Christ alone, apart from works. All very Protestant, and worse yet he condemned the pope in no uncertain terms on Reformation Day and whenever else the mood struck him. Yet for all the fervency of his Gospel preaching he laughed at the Lutherans who were trying to be like Billy Graham, and he refused to allow "Amazing Grace" to be sung in his church. He walked the lonely way between Geneva and Rome, and those who followed were few.

But those few included John and Millie, and on holidays it included the larger Mason clan. This particular Thanksgiving they all attended church together, filling up two whole pews. Everybody came: Ralph and Betty, Lou Ann and Billy, Bill and Judy and Katie, besides John, and Millie, Millie's son TD and his son Danny, and Hilda. Jasper for some reason didn't turn up for church, but nobody gave it a thought, figuring somebody's car had broken down and he was at the shop. He'd come by later for dinner at the Clubhouse. Rachel and her mother normally sat with them, but lately they had been going to TD's church in Ste. Genevieve. That was the Lutheran church that was trying to be Protestant, and Gottlieb worried about it and worried about Rachel while keeping on a game face, for he was a true shepherd, and that's what shepherds do. They worry and they keep unceasing vigil.

The service that day was the same old, well-worn service they did all the time at Peace, and the people droned the familiar liturgy, and when they sang the hymns they slid into notes from lower to higher, and from higher to lower, nobody knew why, it's just the way country people sang Lutheran hymns. They sang "Now Thank We All Our God" before the sermon just like always and concluded with "We Gather Together to Ask the Lord's Blessing" at the end just like always, and the sermon was on Jesus' healing of the ten lepers from Luke's Gospel and where are the nine? Just like always. And just like always the family invited Pastor Gottlieb to join them for Thanksgiving dinner at the Clubhouse, and just like always Pastor and his wife Ann accepted.

In addition, a number of relatives from East Perry County usually came. The normal rotation was Thanksgiving and football at the Clubhouse, and Easter and baseball at the Old Gottlieb family farm near Augsburg. So Paul and Lori Gottlieb were expected, and their son, Kurt.

But this year would not be like always, for Betty's brother-in-law and John's godfather and namesake, Reverend John Kolding, was coming. A trim, good-looking man with a full head of wavy white hair, he had served a silk-stocking congregation and built up enough in his pension plan to take early retirement, and so was now free to join the family for holidays, which of course he had never been able to do while in the parish. He and his wife Joan had driven down from St. Louis and arrived late, and sat in the back of the church during the service, fuming the whole time, for though no longer young and hip like Pastor Dave in Ste. Genevieve, Kolding was one of the progressives among the clergy of the Missouri Synod, and believed in innovation for the sake of missions. Fossil ministry like this was to him like fingernails on the blackboard. So after church amidst the pleasantries and "hi-how-are-ya" to old friends from long ago and old schoolmates and neighbors there was a note of gathering tension ratcheting up steadily as the day went on.

The weather was clear and crisp, a beautiful autumn day with a nip in the air, the kind of day that made you want to run around outside and play football. And indeed, that's what the kids were doing, Billy and Katie and their cousins. For TD had custody of his son Danny that day, and Kolding's son Louis and his wife Janet had also come with their two children Bobby and Mary. So the kids all played a loose, chaotic game of football in the yard with a lot of arguing about boundaries and rules while the women took over the kitchen and began to prepare the meal—John and Millie had put the turkey in the oven before church—and the men were sent outside to have a beer and keep an eye on the kids. Bill and TD supervised the football game.

Ralph, Paul, and Kurt were sitting on the park benches.

"Hey, Doofus," said Paul to Ralph.

"Hey, Mugwump," said Ralph to Paul. "How's life with 'Mr. Ka-ching'?"

Paul made a face, then brightened. "Hey! I knew if I stuck with it, being a feckless, irresponsible, dirty hippie guitar bum would pay off some day."

"While I get to change the oil on your BMW," Ralph snorted.

"I give you a good tip, don't I?"

"Sure. Pie at the cafe."

Kurt was grinning and nodding his head. Here it comes, he said to himself.

"Can I help it if the royalties keep rolling in?"

"From the book and the record. Sheesh!" said Ralph.

"I suffer for my art. Sensitive soul that I am," Paul said with a grand gesture. "Can you imagine the pain I feel when I hear my song in a Lawrence Welk arrangement?"

"You're breakin' my heart."

"Or see *The Pilgrim* in the remainders bin at Walmart?"

Ralph started playing the air violin.

Kurt interjected, "So what'd you finally get for the attic jackpot?"

"The what?" asked Paul.

"Oh, you know, all the old books and pictures that went to you after the farm was sold to that weird commune—"

"The Children of Abimelech? Yeah, well, after World War One Opa stayed in Paris and hung out with Hemingway and Gertrude Stein, and got some signed first editions of Fitzgerald. And little things by Picasso and Renoir. Yes, indeedy. A tidy little sum. Rather not say how much."

Ralph turned to Kurt, now twenty-seven. "I hear you've got a new handle."

"Yeah," Kurt said, "they started calling me 'Dutch.'"

"I can't imagine why," said Paul. "Just because he's been to Germany and learned the language and established a sister-city relationship between Augsburg, Missouri, and Augsburg, Germany."

"And got him a cute little German Fräulein, too," said Ralph, punching Kurt in the arm.

Kurt raised his hands and eyebrows as he shrugged. "What can I say? Guess I inherited the charm from my Old Man here."

"How did you meet her?" asked Ralph.

"Well, I went over to learn German at the Goethe Institute in Augsburg. One night our class went to a local vintners for a *Weinprobieren*, where we sampled all the grades of white wine from *Tafelwein* to *Eiswein*. I got to talking with Herr Schneider about winemaking, since Perry County used to be a big wine-producing area."

"Sure was," said Paul. "Like the August Lueders winery in Frohna."

"Right. So he invited me to stay the night, and lo and behold next morning over *Früstuck* there was his daughter Lisle. One thing led to another. Herr Schneider gave me some cuttings when I returned to the States..."

"...leaving a budding romance behind..." added Paul.

"...which I cultivated with long, mushy letters," Kurt concluded. "The grapes are coming along nicely on my little ten-acre plot. I've fixed up the old cabin and added some amenities, and I'm saving up for a press and barrels and things. As soon as I'm ready, I'll go back and we'll be married, then come back here and try our luck."

"Too bad we had to let the farm go," said Paul. "All those prime acres."

"Yeah," said Kurt. "But I'd be overwhelmed with an operation that big."

"Hey," said Ralph, "maybe you could lease a few acres from what's-his-name."

"Parcell," said Kurt with a look as if he'd bitten into a green persimmon. "I don't think so. He's got that Children of Abimelech church or commune or whatever it is up and running now, with fences all around, and security guards. And they've made a lot of changes."

"But the old barnyard ballfield is still there, isn't it?" asked Ralph.

"Yeah, but you wouldn't recognize it except for the old sycamore behind home plate. They've put in bleachers and dugouts. Our baseball club from Augsburg plays them once a year and gets stomped. Their guys have long hair and beards, but wow! can they ever play the game."

"Speaking of which . . . " said Ralph.

"*We wuz robbed!*" all three men said simultaneously, then laughed a rueful, bitter laugh as they shook their heads.

"Tell me about it," Paul said. "Here we had the best team in baseball. This rookie Pujols. Unbelievable. Edmonds. Rolen. How could we get swept?"

"And by Boston. Boston!" said Ralph. "The Cubs of the East Coast."

"Tell me about it," said Kurt. "Down three games to zero against the Yankees. Then they win four straight, then come here and sweep us."

"The baseball gods are angry," said Paul.

Ralph nodded. "Time to toss another virgin into the volcano."

The three baseball philosophers shook their heads and looked at their shoes, then took a swig of beer.

Meanwhile, the three pastors—Mason and Gottlieb and Kolding—sat down at the picnic table by the lake, and the rest of the family kept a respectful distance while the men of God discussed Holy Things.

"Still the same old same old, I see, Earl," said Kolding with a sarcastic smile on one side of his mouth and a shake of his head.

John cringed, for he knew what was coming. Gottlieb lowered his gaze and rolled an acorn around on the table. He too knew what was coming, but he sat unperturbed. He and Kolding had been having this argument for years. Whenever they got together they beat each other up, yet the old friendship continued.

"I guess things never change down here in the boonies," Kolding went on. "At least in St. Louis County we have a chance to try new things. People are more modern, more open to innovation and outreach."

"Yes, I heard about your ecumenical service," Gottlieb said.

"Absolutely. I know some narrow-minded ultraconservatives yelled and screamed about it, but who pays any attention to those dinosaurs? I mean when there's a national emergency like we had with that terrorist attack, the local clergy have to show some leadership and bring people together."

"You mean the local Christian clergy? I saw a picture in the paper, and you had Jews, Hindus, Sikhs, and Muslims. What on earth were you thinking, JJ?"

"Of course we did. I'd do it again, too. Proudly. We're all Americans, Earl. We can't afford to be fighting amongst ourselves and splitting hairs about obscure points of doctrine while people are dying all around us."

"Well, I agree that we need to come together as Americans in a time of crisis. But why not have a patriotic rally instead of a worship service? Most people have the impression that there is just one God and many different paths to him, and it doesn't matter what you believe as long as you're sincere. Your worship service just reinforced that."

Kolding looked down his nose at his colleague. "There's that narrow-minded fundamentalism again. Listen, Earl, I've become good friends with these men. We're in Rotary together. They are good religious leaders. We have to be open to their ideas. Religious truth is religious truth, whatever the source. I find it hard to believe that God doesn't hear the prayer of my rabbi friend or the imam just because they don't subscribe to some narrow set of dogmas about Jesus."

John cringed again. This was rank heresy. He needed to say something, but in intense debates like this he was never any good. His mind always went blank when someone confronted him with a challenge. But he tried anyway. "Uncle John, didn't Jesus say, 'I am the way, the truth, and the life. No man cometh unto the Father except through me'?"

"Egad, Johnny, don't tell me you've become one of them!" He laughed confidently. He really was a striking figure with his tanned face and white hair. He had done graduate work with the old, liberal seminary faculty in the days before the denominational split of 1974. He knew his theology. He had studied at Cambridge. Even though his side had lost in the church fight, he retained that assured air of someone who was in the right and flowing with the main stream of liberal American Protestantism. Like the Marxists, he knew that history was on his side. "We went through all this before you entered seminary. Do I need to give you a refresher course?" He sighed and rolled his eyes. "Certain sayings of Jesus are authentic and others are not. You need to look at the assured results of higher criticism. You need to rely on the work of Schleiermacher and Wellhausen and Bultmann. Their scholarship is impeccable. The Jesus Seminar has continued their work. Come on, you know all this. The verse you just quoted is not authentic according to the findings of the best theologians. It was added in the second century by a Fundamentalist redactor."

There it was, John said to himself. Stumped again. He had no snappy rejoinder. His mind had blanked out on him, just like a carburetor that was clogged and getting no fuel to the piston. But Gottlieb came back in to the fray. "Now you listen to me, JJ. Let me remind you that what you are saying has only limited currency. It may fly in sophisticated St. Louis, but not in the rest of the world. I started my ministry as a missionary in Africa."

"I know that, Earl. You've told me this a hundred times."

"Well, listen to it again, JJ. I don't think it's sunk into your thick skull yet. The Muslims were strong over there. The threat of persecution was real. If you converted to Christianity, you could be killed. And some were. I was working with the king of the country, a fine leader and a good man with a wife and a large family. His tribe had been animists, you know, worshipping the spirits in rocks and trees. And he was listening to the Muslims and he was listening to me, for he felt his people needed the guidance of an advanced religion. The Muslims had all that oil money, and were building big mosques, and giving scholarships away like business cards to young people. And there was little old me, and what did I have but a beat-up old Bible. And the truth. And a local man that worked with me, Shadrach Teseney, a man of the king's own tribe, a young fellow just my age and his wife Miriam, who was maidservant to the queen. But the truth convinced him, and he was baptized along with his family, and we had great success for a few years. Those good people needed the simple teachings of Christ, not the ethereal speculations of ivory-tower theologians who never had to face mutilation with a machete."

Gottlieb paused and looked out at the lake, still rolling the acorn around absentmindedly with his fingers. In the yard the kids were squabbling because someone had thrown the football into the lake, and TD was trying to reach it with a cane pole. From the kitchen there came a peal of women's laughter, and Millie's high-pitched *hoo-hoo-hoo* trumpeted out over the rest. Gottlieb flicked his finger and sent the acorn sailing across the yard, where a squirrel pounced on the unexpected treasure and scurried up a tree.

Then he began to speak again, but his perpetual smile was gone. "JJ, Muslims know down deep that Jesus Christ is their mortal enemy. They react to him the same way the Jews used to. With force. They know they can't win people's hearts, so they resort to intimidation and fear. When they saw that they were losing in Mayangala, they sent a death squad and killed the king and his wife and set up their own government by military coup. They got about half of the children, too. They wanted to kill them all lest there survive a legitimate Christian heir to the throne. But the king had faithful servants who managed to get some of the kids out of the country. They'd be grown now. I've no idea what's become of them."

Kolding looked thoughtful. "I didn't know that. You never told me that last part."

"Well, it hurts to talk about it. But there it is." Gottlieb's smile came back, but it was wistful and faraway, as if searching across the miles and through the years for traces of lost brothers and sisters in the faith. John felt like he'd been hit over the head with a hammer. Gottlieb's story had striking similarities to things that Elizabeth had told him. The pieces were tumbling together. Could she have been one of those children? And Miriam ... it was the same name ... John began to ask, but just then a wet football landed in his lap, and the thought vanished.

John looked up. TD was calling him. "Hey, John-boy, let's do the tire swing drill."

John shook his head. "Not this again!"

"Sure," TD said. "Come on. Best two out of three. Or three out of five. Or whatever it takes for me to beat you."

John got up with a groan and walked across the yard as the women called the children to come in for a snack. John and TD had been doing this since they were kids, putting the tire swing in motion and trying to throw the football through the moving target. It was difficult, and only a hard throw with extreme accuracy could hit it. When they were younger, John would usually win, for he had the better natural arm. But TD had practiced and practiced and practiced when he had gotten into high school, and even after, and now was the better man. So it had become an annual ritual at Thankgiving get-togethers to go through this and let TD have his moment of cheap victory. Except this time John noticed that Rachel and her mother were just arriving and walking across the yard carrying covered dishes. Why did that bother him? He couldn't say, tried not to think about it, tried to focus on the competition, tried to put her out of his mind.

"OK, here we go," TD called out as he held the swing. "You go first." He let it go and it swung in a long slow arc across the yard. How long had it been since John had thrown a football? It was just not something theological students in Europe frequently did for recreation. He gripped the football, fingers on the seam, stretched back and threw, cursing himself for flicking his wrist the wrong way. The ball wobbled in mid-air like a dying duck and missed the target entirely. "Two more tries, then my turn," TD said with a laugh as he tossed the ball back to John. He threw again. This time he managed to put a good tight spiral on the ball, but bonked it off the side of the tire. John heard a chattering up in the tree and looked up to see the squirrel with the acorn laughing at him. Then the screen door twanged and there was Rachel looking at him. Or TD. He couldn't tell which. She had on a wool skirt and sweater combination that somehow concealed but at the same time revealed the curves of her womanly figure. "Last chance to impress the ladies," TD called out mockingly as he threw the ball back to John. "OK," John said, "let her fly." TD gave the swing a big shove and as it swung out wide John cocked and threw in anger, drilling the ball right through the center of the target as it paused on the apogee of its arc. John heard Rachel's small hands clapping. "Wow, John! Great throw!" He turned to her and grinned and shrugged and felt good about himself for a moment until TD went three for three and then walked off toward the dock hand in hand with Rachel.

So John was left by himself for the moment, tossing the football up in the air and catching it himself, when his uncle John Kolding came up to him. "Well, Johnny," he said with that elegant smile, "let's sit down and chat a bit. I'm dying to hear all about your studies and your experiences abroad." John cringed again as they strolled over to the park bench overlooking the lake, the same bench where he had told Rachel about his travels, at least some things about his travels. John cringed because he had had to sort out for himself a lot of the things his uncle had taught him, and he had slowly, painfully come to a more conservative point of view. And here at last came the confrontation he'd been dreading. Maybe he could get around it by sticking to trivial details. John glanced down the shore toward the dock. TD had his arm around Rachel and she had her arm around him and he was pointing to something.

"It was three years ago when I went over, JJ. Flew from Chicago to Luxembourg with a stopover in Reykjavik—what a desolate spot that is! Not a tree in sight—and got the train in Luxembourg to the Frankfurt Hauptbahnhof. Do you know it?"

"Yes! Enormous barn of a place. Pigeons flying around inside. A kind of shopping mall in there, too."

"Right. And a little bookstore with a good selection of English language titles. That's where I got started reading the Father Brown mysteries by G. K. Chesterton."

"I must have missed that. But we were only there on a group tour."

"Well, I was in and out of Frankfurt pretty often, because I made a number of trips up to the little seminary in Oberursel, just twenty kilometers north of Frankfurt, that we have an exchange program with. I had gotten to know Professor Roensch when he taught for a semester at Ft. Wayne and I had him for a class in the Lutheran Confessions. I'd go up and visit him and his wife. We'd grill sausages. He had Sheboygan bratwurst flown in, as if there wasn't any good sausage in Germany, and then we'd smoke cigars afterwards in his study. Actually he's the one that encouraged me to go on to graduate school in Europe. He had studied in Heidelberg and gave me a recommendation. So between coming and going and waiting for trains I spent a lot of time in the Frankfurt Hauptbahnhof."

Kolding gave John a sly look. "But there's one thing I remember about that place: Dr. Kraemer's Sex Shoppe. Do you know what I mean?"

"Well, yes, Uncle John. I went by it. You can't miss it with that big red sign. There's one in every train station in Germany, I think. It's like McDonald's."

Kolding wasn't satisfied. "But did you go in?"

Here it was, John said to himself. The difficult question the master poses to the disciple. Or rather, the former disciple. "No!" John said, and immediately reproached himself for lying. His evil nature had gotten the better of him. Uncle JJ's theological appeals to his sin nature had gotten to him. He was far from home. Nobody knew him like in Perryville. He could go in and come out and not be recognized. So he went in. He was horrified but fascinated by the things he saw in there. It stimulated him, it excited him. It had opened him up to new sensations and in time led him to new experiences.

Kolding pursed his lips and knit his brow, tilting his head back ever so slightly. "And why would that be?"

He was probing. He wouldn't stop until he had John nailed to a tree. It was like this when he was younger, during long conversations in college and seminary when he would visit his uncle, and JJ was always so confident, always so persuasive, always so theological. And here again John's mind was blanking out as he felt his face flush and his body shrink to a child's size again. He rested his elbows on his knees and looked down at the ground. In an even lower voice he said, "Thou shalt not commit adultery."

Kolding clapped his hands once. The echo bounced off the cliff and back, then died. "There you have it!" he exclaimed with a note of triumph. "The tyranny of traditional mores. Society is making progress, Johnny. That's the golden word: Progress. Things are evolving into a better world. It's been developing slowly for centuries. Every once in a while you see things move forward more rapidly, things break out in a kind of cultural revolution, like there was in the Sixties, when an entire generation shakes off the shackles of outmoded, hidebound old traditions and breaks free, tries new things, experiments with new lifestyles."

"Yes, but..."

"No, let me finish, Johnny. What I've been trying to tell you all these years is that this is tied directly to the Gospel. This is Christ at work in the world, getting people to live on the basis of love instead of sin. And guilt. And laws. Even among people that don't formally acknowledge Christ..."

"Like Jews and Muslims?"

"Yes! Especially Jews and Muslims, with whom we share a common heritage from Abraham. When people who don't formally acknowledge Christ love one another and try to live in peace with one another, then they are unconsciously following the teachings of Christ. Jesus came to teach us a higher way, the way of love. When people love each other, it's clear evidence that they have the Christ-spirit in their hearts, no matter what the external trappings of their religious tradition may be.

"And that's where Dr. Kraemer's comes in. Because when you follow the spirit of love, it may take you into unusual places. You may find your mind being opened to all kinds of new experiences, just as when you have the spirit of God's love in your heart, you might find yourself loving all kinds of strange people that traditionally you might have thought were your enemies. That's why the church has to support the gay rights agenda. That's why all this legalism has got to go. Law, law, law! It comes from an angry, Old Testament demiurge, and just teaches people to hate each other. The way of the Gospel is to love God and do what you like. What feels good."

Down on the dock TD and Rachel were kissing. He put his hand in his pocket, drew something out, and gave it to her. She threw her arms around him and kissed him again. They were in love. John felt like going down and pushing both of them into the lake. He looked at his uncle. He was so serene, so confident. He'd like to push him into the lake, too. Why couldn't he get the words out? It all seemed so easy when he was talking to Rachel about things that mattered. She seemed to draw it out of him. Besides, this was the subject of his dissertation: that even though we're saved, we are not freed from the demands of the Law. Because we are both saints and sinners, we are subject to both the Law and the Gospel. If he couldn't defend this to his own relatives, how on earth was he going to defend it to the theological faculty at *Universität Heidelberg*. And how on earth could he defend his own behavior before God on Judgment Day.

Millie came outside, rang the dinner bell and yelled, "Come and get it!" in that loud fishwife voice of hers. The bell had been at the old Ross Hotel for years and years. According to family tradition it had been salvaged from a train wreck some time back in the mid-nineteenth century, when locomotives still had bells and steam whistles, whistles that echoed for miles in the hills and made farm boys plodding behind a mule in the hot sun want to hop into a box car and light out for parts unknown and find the landscape of their dreams, a place where there were mountains and the sea. But those days were gone, and now what few trains there were had irritating air horns that stood your hair on end with their blast of noise. But this was an old train bell, a real one, and it called with a clear voice.

Slowly the Clubhouse began to gather her chicks under her wings as the children of all ages who had grown up in her shelter got up from where they were sitting here and there in the yard and one by one made their way inside. A long table had been set up in the central hallway with the deer trophies looking down, and the table was groaning with food. The turkey—a twenty pounder—had been yard raised at the Schuttenberg farm and killed that morning. There was a steaming bowl of schnippel beans, and another enormous bowl of mashed potatoes, made from scratch with loads of hand-churned butter, and a tray of home grown sweet potatoes, mashed and cooked with brown sugar and crusted over with big fat marshmallows, and a big bowl of five-cup salad with coconut and pineapple and mandarin oranges and sour cream and teeny tiny marshmallows, and tart cranberry sauce from an old family recipe, ground up coarse with orange rind and pecans and sugar, and Millie's apple pie with the cinnamon sugar crust on top, and pumpkin pie that Rachel and her mother had made from pumpkins they had grown in their own garden. So the family gathered and stood by their places at the table, Grams Hilda at the head as matriarch of the family, then to her right Millie at the seat nearest the kitchen so she could jump up and get anything that might be needed, then Ralph and Betty, then John, then Bill and Judy and Katie, then Lou Ann and Billy, then JJ Kolding and his wife Joan, and their son Louis, a pastor in nearby Kentucky, and his wife Janet and their children Bobby and Mary, then TD and Rachel with TD's son Danny between them, Rachel's mother Eileen, who was looking at the ring on Rachel's left hand, then Pastor Gottlieb and his wife Ann, then Paul and Lori and Kurt, and finally an empty seat for Jasper, who would certainly show up later. And under the table was Doxie, alert for any crumbs that might fall, or scraps that might be offered from the children.

Hilda took her spoon and tinked the side of her coffee cup. "*Sollen wir beten,*"* she said in a clear voice. And all joined in, saying, "*Komm, Herr Jesu, sei unser Gast, und segne was du uns aus Gnaden bescheret hast. Amen.*"

And all sat down and fell to with gusto, heaping their plates full and talking and passing things and laughing and eating and eating and eating. And for a long time there was peace and stillness in the midst of the bustle and activity, for heritage and tradition had reasserted its right and held sway as the extended Mason family held its feast as it had for generations. And as the pile of turkey went down and down, and the bowls were passed and passed again, and the coffee was brought out and cups were filled, and the pies sliced and pieces distributed, first to the children, then to the grown-ups, they heard a car drive up, then the motor cut off, then doors slam: one, two. There's Jasper, everyone thought, ignoring the fact that they had heard two car doors slam, not one.

The screen door squeaked and banged, and footsteps and low voices approached. Everyone looked toward the porch. The door opened, and there was Jasper, and with him an old woman. She was black-skinned, indigo black, short and stout, her face fleshy, with laugh crinkles around her eyes, and as she smiled she flashed a

---

* Let us pray . . . Come, Lord Jesus, be our guest, and let thy gifts to us be blessed.

gold-capped tooth. She was wearing a brilliant garment made of red and gold cloth, and she had on a headdress of the same material. She looked African, as indeed she was, and she was so exotic that she seemed twice as large and twice as colorful as she really was, and the rest of the room and the people in it seemed pale and drab by comparison. Riding on her hip was a small child, a little boy by the look of him, about a year-and-a-half old. The child was also black, though not as dark as the woman, more coffee-with-cream, and his hair was dark and curly, seemingly of mixed race. He was dressed in a pair of new denim overalls and sneakers that looked like they had just been bought at Walmart, and in his hand was a professional wrestler action figure. His right ear was pierced, and in it was an earring of unusual design. He looked around the room once, then put his thumb in his mouth and laid his head sleepily on the woman's shoulder.

Jasper stepped forward and began to speak. "This is M-M-M-... this is M-M-..."

"Miriam Seyoum!" called out someone.

Miriam looked over. "Pastor Earl! My God, is it you?" she said with a British accent.

By now everyone was murmuring in wonderment as John stood to his feet and walked over to Miriam and embraced her. The child held out its arms to John and he picked it up and it patted his face as if it knew him.

"And this," John said with a lump in his throat as he looked at all the astonished faces in the room, "is my son. His name is Josiah."

Chapter 6 ◉ The History of Mayangala

John looked at the members of his family and tried to read their faces. He was stunned yet at the same time joyful at this totally unexpected development, for here was his son, his own flesh and blood, the child of his beloved, the lost child, the child he thought he'd never see again, now restored to him against all odds. He loved Josiah. But would they? His skin was dark. This was southeast Missouri. Besides the Everett family, there were almost no black people in this area. And even if his family by some miracle took him to their heart, what about the community? Where would he go to school? How would other children treat him? None of these things had ever crossed his mind when he was flinging himself headlong into an affair with Elizabeth in Germany. They were in love, consequences be damned.

Grandmother Hilda looked at John and the child. Now here was a highly interesting development, and completely in character with the latent wild side of the Mason boys, that John like his great-grandfather Godfrey would run off somewhere and come back home with a wife—or a child in this case—that would force the community to change.

Ralph looked at John and the child. He was a respected member of the business community. He had worked hard all his life. He was in Kiwanis. He was an elder at church. He had achieved respectability. And here was his own son with a colored child.

Betty looked at John and the child. My God, a grandchild! He had John's grey eyes, she could see that. He was one of the family. So what if he was black. He was her grandson. She wanted to scoop him up and not let go.

Millie looked at John and the child. Then she sprang up and went to the kitchen to get another place setting for the African woman and a high chair and a bowl and little spoon for the child. This explained a lot, she thought. No wonder John was so tight-lipped about his experiences abroad. But now he'd have to tell the whole story.

Lou Ann looked at John and the child. This was astonishing. Now she was not the only member of the family to have gotten in trouble and caused embarrassment to everyone. Her love for John doubled in the blink of an eye.

JJ looked at John and the child. Aha! He was lying to me when he said he didn't go into the sex shop. He did go in. He opened himself up to new experiences of sensuality. He got involved with some nigger woman, probably in a Heidelberg whorehouse, and this was the result. Good for him! This will teach him from experience how life is for the oppressed and downtrodden, and why we should fight for peace and justice.

TD looked at John and the child. How satisfactory this was! The great, brilliant John Mason was humiliated in the eyes of his family and, when word got around—and he would personally see to it that it did—to the entire community. The Masons of Perryville would be knocked back on their heels, and his own stock would go up.

Rachel looked at John and the child. The baby was so little and sweet, and its cappuccino skin was just right for it. Did it need a diaper change? Did the woman need any help? Was the baby hungry? Was it thirsty? Could she hold it? Would it like her?

Paul and Lori Gottlieb looked at John and the child. Here it was again, the wild streak in the family. John had done what he had done. But thank God, the baby had not been destroyed.

Pastor Gottlieb looked at John and the child. His mind was spinning. Here was Miriam Seyoum, his dear old friend from the past. This child was John's, but who was the mother? Could she be one of the lost children of the king? And why was Miriam here and not the mother? And what could he do for them? And how could he help John in this crisis?

Billy and Katie looked at John and the child. Oh, boy, a new kid.

Let's go show him our bucket of army guys.

Doxie looked at John and the child. Her tail began to wag happily as she trotted over and sniffed the little boy.

"Gog-gie!" exclaimed Josiah with a huge smile and wrenched himself around until John set him on the floor. Doxie licked the boy's face, anointing it with dog slobber. Josiah laughed big peals of laughter that started everyone else laughing as the child pulled the dog's ears and tried to climb on its back and ride it. Ralph Mason shrugged as he helped Josiah onto the dog's back. Pickaninny or not, it was his grandson.

Just then Millie came back in with the plates and said, "Somebody get another chair and everybody move down so this lady can sit down and eat."

"Thanks ever so much," Miriam said with a proper British accent. "I'm famished!" The two old women looked at each other and smiled and took an instant liking to each other.

A general hubbub ensued in which men and women and children, having finished their meal, were moving about and clearing the table and talking and murmuring about the new visitors—though at some level they knew the visitors were here to stay—and John sat down with Josiah in his lap as Miriam cut up turkey into tiny bits and put it into a bowl, along with the sweet potatoes, which the child had never tasted and consumed huge quantities of, expressing his satisfaction after the meal with a smile and a grunt and a big poopy diaper. Miriam jumped up to change him, but Betty and Millie wanted in on the action too, while John insisted that he as father should do the honors. So all four of them trooped into the kitchen—Doxie was following close behind, fascinated by this wonderful new smell—and spread out some newspaper and Miriam got the stuff out of the baby bag and Betty took the wet wipes and began to clean his bottom while Millie made goo-goo noises at him, and when the child was clean John strapped him in to the Pampers. And that was that. Meanwhile the men were doing dishes while the kids were in a corner playing Army guys, and Jasper was making a fire in the big fireplace. The sun had gone down and the Koldings—JJ and Joan, and Louis and his wife and children—who had to drive to St. Louis, said their goodbyes and took off. With the table cleared and the dishes cleaned, the family began to move toward the fireplace for the annual tradition of storytelling. It was an unusual aspect about Jasper that when he told stories, as when he spoke German, he did not stutter. There were old stories he told that were traditional Missouri yarns, like Old John Barleycorn, and stories that Jasper had made up to entertain John and Bill and Lou Ann and the kids in the Clubhouse Gang when they were little, like Witchy-Witchy. As the Clubhouse Gang grew up the mantle of family storyteller had fallen upon John. But tonight there was new expectation for stories, not only because John had returned after a long absence, but because he would tell a new story—his own.

So the coal-oil lamps were lit, and pipes were filled and fired, and fragrant tobacco smoke drifted up to the rafters, and mellow corn whiskey was passed around, and Josiah toddled off with Billy and Katie and TD's son Danny, and the men and women settled into their chairs and looked at John. He opened his mouth and began to speak.

"Well, I have to be honest with you. There are parts of this story I'm not particularly proud of. But here is Miriam and here is my son, and I owe you an explanation.

"I had gone to Germany as you know. I was a long way from home. I didn't know anybody. I was struggling with the language. It's hard to explain unless you've been through something like that. I was lonely, desperate for friendship." It was a hint the men would understand. This was a story, not a confessional. In a story you proceed often by hints and suggestions. So he left out explicit details like his moral unraveling under the influence of JJ.

"One night a group of us in the Goethe Institute language school—I was the only American, and there was a Japanese and a couple of Russians and an Israeli—went out for beer after school let out for the day, and we were fumbling along in German, which was the only language we had in common, when all of a sudden I heard someone speaking English. It fell like music on my ears. I looked down the table and saw the most beautiful woman I had ever seen in my life. She was tall and slender, with a long, graceful neck, and big doe eyes. She had just been speaking in English—with an upper-class British accent—to Miriam here, and when Miriam left to do something for her, she resumed the conversation she was having in French with a woman sitting next to her. At first I thought she was African-American and had picked up the accent on a Rhodes Scholarship or something. But it turned out she was African, pure and simple. Pure, though not so simple, as I soon found out. A couple of people left, opening up a seat next to her, and like a man in a trance I went over and introduced myself. I don't know what I said, but she smiled at me with this brilliant smile of hers and I was a goner.

"I guess she must have liked me, too, though I can't imagine why, perhaps she was lonely and desperate, too, but we got to talking about all kinds of things and ended up walking around Heidelberg half the night, through the narrow, winding streets, and past the little shops, and across the bridge, just the two of us—Miriam had long since gone back to their apartment—and I don't know, it was just love at first sight I guess, though I can't imagine a more unlikely couple. For you all know me, a plain, small-town American boy, plays football, works on cars. And here she was, Elizabeth of Mayangala, a genuine, by-God African princess."

A single handclap rang out like a shot, and Pastor Gottlieb exclaimed, "Yes! I knew it. I knew it! She's the baby that got away when the Muslims took over. Miriam, help me out here. Fill in the blanks."

"With pleasure," Miriam said, then, with a sarcastic face and inflection, "Islam is a 'religion of peace,' don't you know. When they saw that you were having success with the Gospel and that the king of Mayangala had converted and had his household baptized, they began to be concerned. Peaceful relations with Muslim neighbors were in jeopardy, and further strained by rumors of uranium in the mountains. An ambassador came on a formal diplomatic mission, bringing gifts—along with an armed guard. Negotiations began to break down. Concern was expressed on both sides. The ambassador grew more insistent, the king more resistant. At a hidden signal, the foreign guards quickly took control.

The king and queen had been expecting something like this and were prepared to die, but as a precaution they made sure that the children were not all in the palace at the same time. On that night my husband and I were away with three of the younger boys—there were ten children in all—and Elizabeth, the baby, since I was not only maidservant to the queen but wet nurse to the children. We made it out of the country by a back way, and went to Ethiopia where we stayed for a short time, and then to England where the king had set up a trust fund for the support and education of the children. So there we were as exiles for a long time. The boys went to Eton and Cambridge as their father had, and became jolly good rugby players, and grew up and carved out lives for themselves in England, but Elizabeth had private tutors. Then one day when she was about sixteen we were in London and she was spotted by a photographer. One thing led to another, and before you could say Jack Robinson she was flitting off here and there for fashion shoots and runway shows. She became restless, though, and in time wanted to get back to her Lutheran roots and find some stability. So she decided on a whim that we would go to Germany and learn the language so she could take a course in Reformation history. And that's how we ended up in Heidelberg."

"And what about the boys?" asked Gottlieb. "I remember them. Peter was one, and Jacob."

"Peter is an airline pilot. Jacob is a barrister at the Old Bailey. And Isaac is teaching at a tiny little school in Cornwall. Peter gets them free passes, and they all fly off somewhere at moment's notice. You never know where they're going to turn up next. Wouldn't surprise me in the least to see them walk right through that door."

Everyone's head turned in the direction she was pointing, but there were no boisterous African men bursting through the door.

"I never had the chance to meet them," John said, "but Elizabeth would buzz off to England to visit them and then come back full of wild stories about all their escapades. It seems that all three of them drove Morgan Plus 8s . . ."

"Whew!" whistled Jasper, "would I love to get under the h-h-hood of one of them!" Ralph nodded his head reverently.

"Yeah, me too," said John, nodding his head, "and Elizabeth said they'd go tooling around the country just like you and I would do if we were young and had plenty of money and a sports car."

"Back to Heidelberg," Millie put in.

"Heidelberg!" John continued. "Well, there we were, mooning over each other. We stayed up all night that first night we met, just walking and talking. And I kissed her under a streetlight and she kissed me back. She was just the most wonderful, sweet, beautiful, exotic thing I'd ever met in my entire life. Not just physical beauty, which she had plenty of, believe me, but a spiritual beauty also. We could talk about the Bible and the things of God and the Reformation and Lutheran theology..."

"In between making goo-goo eyes," Miriam said to everyone with a wink, sighing and imitating the face of a lovesick kid, and everyone chuckled as John hung his head and smiled.

"Now come on, give me a break, guys," he continued. "Here I am pouring out my heart..."

"Yeah, yeah," Ralph said, "we have to kid you because we've all been there. But eventually we got over it." Betty punched her husband in the arm saying "Ralph!" and shooshed him.

"I was just captivated by her. I don't know what she saw in me."

"I'll tell you what," Miriam said. "You had roots. Stability. You were from someplace. You had a home. Elizabeth was like a vine, trailing this way and that, looking for something solid to cling to. She'd been exiled from her own country as a baby—she'd never even seen Mayangala—and grown up as a black woman in lily-white England, always felt an outsider, a stranger in a strange land. And in the international fashion set, everybody was the same. Rootless. So when you came along, she felt grounded for the first time. It was so good for her. I could see it, John. Plus when you fixed her car, that cinched it. Very manly thing to do, you know. Very sexy." She winked.

"It wasn't a big problem. I just changed the fuel filter. Something Jasper showed me to do when a Mercedes starts to cough on cold mornings."

Miriam continued, "Well, my good man, to us women cars are

these mysterious, threatening dragons. We drive them, but we're really afraid of them. And when we find a man that is not afraid and even can tame one, it melts our heart."

Ralph and Jasper looked at each other with amazement and pride. Nobody had ever put it quite like that before. Maybe this black woman was OK. Just then there was a ruckus in the corner where the children were playing Army guys. Josiah was crying and Billy and Danny, TD's son, were yelling at each other and shoving each other back and forth. Betty rushed over and said as she picked up Josiah, "All right, break it up! What's going on here?"

"Grammy," Katie said, "Danny took the baby's toy soldier and pushed him down just to be mean."

"Tattletale!" Danny said to Katie, and stuck out his tongue at her.

TD was there in an instant and swatted his son on the butt. Danny absorbed the blow but didn't cry. "You come over here and sit by me for a while, son." Sulkily, the child obeyed. Rachel looked at the two of them with a feeling of dismay and bewilderment. She had a relationship with TD, but what about his kid? And she had some kind of relationship with John, but what about his kid? Why was she surrounded with all these single fathers all of a sudden? She needed to get her horse Milton out of the barn and go on a good fast gallop to clear her head.

Betty had scooped up the baby as her own and was walking him back and forth, patting him on the back and saying comforting things to him, and as she did she soon had him calmed down. She looked at her son with a beatific smile.

"I forgot to ask," Ralph said, "Miriam, how did you find us?"

"A bit of luck, that," she replied. "I knew all about Perryville, Missouri, from John's blathering on and on about it, how it was the best little town in the States and all that rot. So when the dust settled down after the unpleasantness I talked to Elizabeth's brothers about what to do, and they held a kind of tribal council and decided the child should be with his next of kin, namely John here. So we flew from Heathrow to New York to St. Louis, then caught the bus down here." She paused and laughed. "You should have seen some of the stares I got as I walked around the town square asking about Mason's Garage. But I guess it isn't every day they see an old black woman with a baby in her arms and toting a suitcase on top of her head. Fortunately someone pointed me in the right direction. It was a couple of characters loafing near the courthouse steps."

"A fat one and a skinny one?" asked John.

"Why, yes. They knew right where it was, and I went there and found this good man in the shop changing a tire."

"Betty," said old grandmother Hilda, "quit hogging the baby and pass him over to me." Betty complied as Rachel looked at the child with a mixture of fear and longing. There was a lull in the conversation as the child looked with fascination at his great-grandmother's wrinkles and everyone looked at the child and the old lady. Jasper refilled his pipe and lit it up. Millie asked who needed more coffee. Ralph poked the fire, banked the coals, and threw on another log. The old Clubhouse creaked and stretched its bones as cold night descended outside.

"And then there was her singing," John went on as he stared dreamily into the blazing hearth. "She had picked up all these English ballads and folk songs and used to sing them to me. My favorite one was 'The Water Is Wide.'"

"Oh, I know that one!" Rachel blurted out, and immediately wished she hadn't, for now she'd be asked to sing like always, and she was, and she put up a mild protest like always, but gave in like always. So she fetched her guitar, tuned it up, and with her fingers plucked a melodic introduction to the old song, as Paul, who had brought a harmonica in his pocket, played along. Then she opened her mouth and began to sing:

> The water is wide, I cannot see o'er,
> Nor have I light wings to fly.
> Build me a boat that can carry two,
> And both shall row, my love and I.

Then to her surprise John began to sing with a firm, manly baritone voice she'd never heard before:

> Now love is handsome, and love is kind,
> Just like a jewel, when first it's new.
> But love grows old, and waxes cold,
> And fades away, like the morning dew.

And they sang the refrain again, and this time she and John were singing in harmony, and she was surprised, for they sounded good together. And then he sang another verse as if his heart were breaking:

> There is a ship that sails the sea,
> It's laden deep as deep can be,
> But not as deep as the love I'm in.
> I know not ere I sink or swim.

And for that moment it was as if the eaves of the old house were leaning down close to listen to the music, and resonate sympathetically with all the echoes and harmonics of all the songs that had been sung there for many generations past, for then John and Rachel began to sing the refrain again and their notes rang out in the hall, and some of the folks began to sing along, and they all sang the refrain one last time, and Rachel added a lovely flourish on the guitar to close the song as Paul trailed away on the harmonica, and then there was stillness, and in the stillness John and Rachel looked at each other full in the eye and smiled at each other as everyone applauded quietly, but then looked away just as quickly lest anyone see. For there was that same something again that had happened between them at the football game back in September, and it made the both of them extremely uncomfortable. TD shot a jealous glance at his fiancée.

Rachel put her guitar away and John settled back into his chair and looked at the fire with a faraway look in his eyes. In the shimmering coals he saw pillars and columns ablaze, cities and civilizations all burning, burning, burning away to dust and ashes, leaving men destitute, and women bereft of their men, and children motherless and alone in the world.

"She often sang that song to me," John continued, "and sometimes we would sing it together. And things were just so magical for such a long time." He looked at Miriam, who looked back with a glow of happiness yet a hint of sorrow in the corner of her eye. "But now comes the hard part. I'm afraid, we . . . well, I don't quite know how to say it except to say it. We went too far. And one day we learned that Elizabeth was pregnant."

That much was obvious to everyone in the room as they glanced at little Josiah, curled up on Hilda's breast and sucking his thumb. "So you got married?" asked Earl.

John laughed ruefully. "No. We wanted to. We really really wanted to. But we hesitated. Can you understand why? What would I do back here in Perry County with a black wife?" And what am I going to do with a black child, he said to himself.

"But here's the real kicker," John said. "The one with the biggest scruples was Elizabeth. Part of it was family considerations. I was, well, the wrong color. How would she explain to her brothers that she had taken a white husband? In their tradition you just didn't cross the color line. Whites were *Ausländer*. And the other part of it was political. Or cultural, call it what you will. For she was of noble birth—and I have to tell you that there was always something royal about her that never went away no matter what the situation or circumstance. I don't know if you've ever met a real live princess before. Or a king or queen. But if you had, you'd never forget it. It makes you stand up straighter when you're around them. And watch your tongue, and be careful to use proper English as they do so naturally. So here we were, crazy in love. But I was a commoner. How could she marry me? There was always the welfare of her country to think of. She was heir to the throne. Someday things might change. Someday she might be able to go back home. And what would the people think of a princess who had a white commoner for a husband? And what would I do in Mayangala? Work in the royal garage?" With a rueful grin John shook his head and tossed a stray twig onto the fire.

"So I kept my little room in the *Heumarkt* and she kept her apartment with Miriam, and I went on with my studies and she with hers, and we went on with our love affair, but things were more difficult now for us, knowing that a new life was coming into the world not as a result of a blessed conjugal union, but an ugly carnal mistake. Difficult as it was, abortion was out of the question. We had both strayed from the teachings of the Lord, but we at least remembered enough of our catechism to eliminate that choice. Things would be hard for us and hard for the baby, but just because we made a mistake didn't mean we could correct it by killing the baby. So we waited and waited, and then the baby was born, just a year and a half ago, and we named him Josiah, for the Mayangalans had taken to giving their children biblical names since Pastor Gottlieb converted them years ago. And we were happy about the baby of course, but there was this pall of regret hanging over everything.

"Meanwhile I was finishing my courses in theology. And to tell the truth, my mistake ... no dammit, I'm going to call it by its name ... my *sin* had driven me into a complete re-evaluation of the liberal ethics I had come over there with, and I began to pour myself into the dissertation, which I won't bore you with, but basically about how the Ten Commandments remain in force for us after we're saved, but we approach them on the basis of love, not fear."

Hilda spoke up as Josiah squirmed out of her lap and rejoined Billy and Katie—minus Danny, who was sulking next to his father—in the corner with the Army guys. "Oh, sure, you mean the Third Use of the Law." Pastor Gottlieb smiled and nodded his head. John shrugged and threw up his hands. "There you go, Grams. They should put you on the theological faculty at the University of Heidelberg."

"But has the child been baptized?" asked Gottlieb.

John shook his head. "No. When we screw up, we go all the way, don't we? We talked about it a lot. But we were thinking that somehow things might work out for us against all odds, that maybe we could get married and have Josiah baptized at the same time, maybe stay in Heidelberg and make a life there, or live in France where blacks are more accepted, and just be expatriates for the rest of our lives. But the princess had the pull of her people on her. And so did the mechanic. So we kept talking and putting it off." John paused for a long moment. Then he took a deep breath. "And then Rafael entered the picture."

John looked hard at Miriam and she looked back. Both of them had that look of grief in the corner of their eyes, but now it came forth and dominated the very center. The story was reaching its grim climax. Everyone could sense it. People shifted in their chairs. Ralph tended the fire. Millie came round with more coffee. John relit his pipe. In the corner the kids were playing nicely, and Katie was saying to Josiah, "... and down in the lake there's a big big fish, and when you're real quiet he comes up by the shore and talks to children, but grown ups aren't allowed..." Doxie was lying on the floor near the children, thumping her tail lazily, and Josiah was draped over the top of the dog as if it were his mother.

"The symbol of Heidelberg is the crossed swords. You've probably seen it on travel brochures and such. That's because of the tradition of dueling that goes back hundreds of years. Nobody knows when it started or why. But it became part of the culture, and if a student came away from his Heidelberg years with a dueling scar on his face it was considered a real badge of honor and something the man was proud of for the rest of his life. I had met some guys in one of my classes who were in one of these dueling clubs—this is strictly outlawed, you understand, but the constabulary by common consent just looks the other way—and they invited me to join. So I did. What the heck, I thought, I'll get in some fencing lessons, might be fun, but avoid dueling. I had all the scars I needed from football. So I'd go to the club—it was one of these wonderful old half-timber buildings with a large hall upstairs where we had fencing lessons, and dances. Meeting rooms and offices on the ground floor. A *Rathskeller* in the basement, and a passageway leading to a cave where they kept the beer and wine. Which of course was the main thing, because nobody took the fencing very seriously; the club was an excuse to sing good old German drinking songs and knock down some beer after the meeting.

"So it went for quite a while, just good clean fun, and every couple of months or so one of our guys would be challenged by somebody from one of the other dueling clubs in town, and they'd go off to the country and hack away at each other for a while, accompanied by their respective seconds and members of their clubs, and then come back with their cuts and after they were stitched up we'd sing and drink some more beer and it was all quite jolly.

"Then last Spring a new guy joined the club. His name was Rafael von Päpinghausen and supposedly came from some very old vaguely upper-crust German family. He quickly became active in the club and was elected secretary when a vacancy opened up, so then he had the keys to the building and everything. A big guy, blonde hair, typical German, you know, full of fun, loved to pull pranks on people. He had this enormous Rottweiler he called Cerberus for laughs. But there was a little something exotic about him, as if he'd spent time in the Orient. And there was something a little scary about that dog. It never threatened me, but you sensed that it was well trained and could attack you if given the command. Rafael and I hit it off and spent time together talking about all sorts of things, current events, German culture versus American culture, baseball versus football, Shakespeare versus Goethe, Heidelberg versus Harvard, theology versus philosophy, on and on, in the afternoons on the *Philosophenweg,* in the evenings at the *kneipe,* and doing things together, hiking in the forest, playing tennis, drinking beer, singing songs, just doing things that young men do, and all the while getting a private tutorial in German as Rafael corrected me as we went along.

"As our friendship deepened one night I opened up and confided in him about Elizabeth and the baby. He seemed interested in an objective way but at the same time very sympathetic, asked about Elizabeth, her background, the normal questions one would ask, and I told him all I could, trusting that he would keep it confidential. I just needed to talk, you know. I'd had this bottled up inside of me, and it all came pouring out. Like a confession, almost." He and Earl exchanged glances.

"And that was that. I appreciated his friendship and discretion and the chance to get this off my chest at last. Then one night in late August, after I'd been out of town for a couple of days at a conference at the Institute for Reformation Studies in Mainz, I came by the apartment . . . " John looked at Miriam.

She said, "And Elizabeth wasn't there, and you asked where she was, and I said somebody called and said you wanted her to meet you at the club. So she went, and I stayed home with the baby."

"Yes," John said, "and this seemed strange to me because it was a Sunday night when the club wasn't open. So I went over to the club. Elizabeth's car was parked in front. But it was dark inside. Something gave me a bad feeling. I tried the door. It was locked. So was the back door. I thought of calling Rafael, since I knew he had the key. But I changed my mind. Elizabeth might be in trouble. I needed to find out first if she was OK.

"So I pried open a ground floor window and got in. Nothing creepier than an empty building at night. I was looking in the meeting rooms and calling out her name. Then I thought I heard a cry, very faint, coming from somewhere down below. I ran down to the Rathskeller. No one was there. But the door to the passageway that led to the cave was open. I sprang to the door and ran down the passageway. I had only been in there once before. The light was very dim. I could hear a commotion up ahead, Elizabeth's voice pleading, a man's voice threatening.

"I ran faster, then burst into the cave. A few candles had been lit. In the faint light I saw Elizabeth tied up against a support beam with her hands behind her back. Her blouse had been ripped open. And there with this fierce knife at her breast was Rafael, saying, 'because you are an infidel, because you are the daughter of that wicked king who opposed Allah and His Prophet Muhammad...'

"'What the hell is going on here!' I shouted. 'Rafael, what are you doing?'

"He turned and looked at me with a grimace of hate. His dog was by his side, growling. 'Put down that knife,' I yelled, 'Now! Put it down.' There was a brace of old rusty swords on the wall. I took one down and threatened him with it. He plunged the knife into Elizabeth, then drew it out. She screamed and slumped over.

"I thrust the sword at Rafael but he parried with the knife and knocked me down with a sweep of his left hand. In an instant he had retrieved the other sword from the wall and was coming at me. I was on my feet again and thrusting and parrying as best I could, but he was bigger and heavier and he pressed me hard. The fight was a clumsy, blundering affair, not like you see in the movies, just two men hacking away at each other in anger and fear in a dark, small space, ignoring all fencing rules in a desperate attempt to kill each other. I was backing up when he called to his dog: 'Cerberus! Attack!' I kicked at the dog but it gripped my left foot in its maw and clamped down. I screamed in agony as I felt bones breaking. In a desperate final effort I lashed out wildly and knocked the sword out of Rafael's right hand. I must have cut his hand—it was hard to see in the dim light—because he fell to the floor crying in pain. The dog was still mangling my foot. I felt myself close to passing out, but I gripped the hilt with both hands and brought the blade down on the dog and cut off its head. I fought off the wave of nausea and struggled against the urge to faint. Rafael had passed out. I limped over to Elizabeth and cut the ropes. 'John, take me outside. Please. I don't have much time.' The pain in my foot was excruciating. But I picked her up somehow and brought her outside and laid her down on the lawn. 'What happened?' I asked.

"Her breathing was heavy and labored and irregular. She slipped out of consciousness, then came back. 'Rafael . . .' she said, 'he's . . . a Janissary.'

"'What the hell is that?' I replied.

"'A Muslim . . . assassin. He . . . was sent . . . to kill me.'

"'Well, I wounded him and killed his dog. There's nothing to worry about for the moment. Come on, let's get you to the hospital.' My mind was still whirring at triple speed from the battle, still in crisis mode, adrenaline pumping, reacting and deciding and acting. My emotions hadn't caught up with me yet.

"'No,' she said, ' . . . too late . . . too late . . . save . . . the baby . . . ' And then she was gone. With great effort I got her into the back of the car and drove to the apartment. But I must have passed out myself. I'm not sure what happened next."

"Yes, you were unconscious," Miriam said, "but when you passed out you fell forward and set off the horn. I heard it and came out and there I saw you and my dear girl. I thought you both were dead. Bringing the baby with me I pushed you aside and drove to the hospital."

John said, "That's where I came to later on. And they kept me several days and treated my foot. But when I was released, you were gone and the apartment was closed and empty and I didn't know where you were. To tell the truth I was afraid of running into Rafael, or I thought maybe he might have some accomplices. So I threw my books into some boxes and bought a one-way ticket to New York, picked up my Jeep, and drove back to Missouri, and here I am. And you, Miriam?"

She paused and sipped her coffee.

Miriam drew a deep breath. "It had always been in the back of my mind that we had enemies. The people that killed the king and queen would try to kill the rest of us. As long as there was a living Christian heir to the throne of Mayangala, there existed a real threat to their power and reign of terror. Tyrants are always insecure, don't you know. That's why they have to kill off the competition. Like Herod."

John raised his finger and asked, "Elizabeth said Rafael was a Janissary. What is that exactly?"

"Ah, yes," she replied, "you Westerners wouldn't know, would you now. Let me see . . . short version: Muslim assassins. Long version: centuries ago in the Ottoman empire Christians were tolerated as 'People of the Book'—the book being the Bible of course—but they had to pay a special tax that Muslims were exempt from. This tax became heavier and heavier. In time—around the fourteenth century, I think—the Muslims also exempted Christians who would turn over to them one of their male children. These Christian boys were raised Muslim, thoroughly indoctrinated in Islam, given the best education, and trained in the finest military academies by the foremost experts. Thus they were formed into an elite fighting force that was called in Turkish *Yeniceri*, which has been Anglicized as 'Janissary.' This young man you knew, John—what did you say his name was?"

"Rafael."

"Just so. The avenging angel. I never saw him, though I'm sure he saw me and marked our whereabouts and comings and goings. He was clearly one of them."

"I see," John said. "It all makes sense. He'd learned from his sources that Elizabeth was somewhere in Heidelberg, but he didn't know exactly where. But he guessed that she'd be attending lectures at the university, and so with his upper-class German background he blended in easily and went to class, looking in the crowds for her. Then by a stroke of luck he met me at the fencing club. God! To think I opened my heart to that sonofabitch. And he killed my . . . " But, choking up, John couldn't finish. He couldn't say, "my wife," though, for she wasn't. All she was was the only woman he had ever loved. And now she was gone, and he hadn't even been able to go to her funeral and say goodbye. So there was no closure. There never would be.

Some of John's family members felt the impulse to go embrace him. His mother especially. And Millie. But before they could, something happened. First, Miriam reached over and took his hand in hers and patted his shoulder. And then the children—Katie and Billy and Josiah—hearing John sobbing, got up as a little group and came over and stood before the man and little Josiah climbed into his father's lap and embraced him and Katie hugged him too and said, "Don't cry," and Billy stood by with an expression of sorrow as Doxie too came and licked his hand. And by then everyone was quietly weeping.

At last the cloud passed over and as people sniffled Millie got a box of Kleenex and passed it around. Miriam resumed the narrative.

"There I was with an immense practical problem on my hands. What was I to do with the body of my mistress? The proper thing to do, of course, would be to call the authorities. But then there'd be an investigation and police procedures and a thousand layers of German bureaucracy to hack through. So I called Peter, who as luck would have it was at Gatwick having his private plane serviced. He filed a flight plan, took on petrol, and was in Heidelberg before dawn. We took Elizabeth back to England and buried her at Peter's estate in Cornwall according to tribal custom and the Lutheran funeral rite, which my husband Shadrach read at the grave. It was at this makeshift, hurried-up funeral of ours that Peter stood up to sing, which was his duty as eldest son. You knew Elizabeth as a singer, didn't you, John?"

"Yes," he said quietly. "She enchanted me with her songs."

Rachel leaned in closer to listen as Miriam went on. "Our people are a singing people. That's one reason we became such natural

Lutherans. And quite happily so. Those sturdy chorale tunes. And the sung liturgy! When the king heard it—oh! You should have seen the look on his face. Pastor Gottlieb, do you remember when you put on the record of Bach's *St. Matthew Passion?*"

"I do indeed," Earl said. "He stood up regally as only a true king can do, and he exclaimed, 'That's the church for me!'"

"So it was," Miriam said softly, "and though we had nothing comparable in our own culture, we had a musical tradition of our own, a body of inherited songs that went back centuries, some say even to biblical times. None of them written down, an oral tradition passed down from father to son, a vast body of literature, really. I suppose it would fill a very big book if all the songs were to be written down. But on that gray, chilly day in Cornwall, on a hill overlooking the sea, there we were, five African expatriates in tribal dress with spears and shields. And a baby. And bumbershoots, of course. And Peter lifted up his voice and began one of the funeral lamentations, all of which we had of course heard many times, but for some reason on this day he also chose a song that was the least often sung because of its difficult sayings. It was full of threats and warnings and prophecies. But Peter was moved by the Spirit that day and he sang loud and his voice echoed off the cliffs below and his words skipped across the water far out to sea, perhaps as far as Mayangala, where I hope they struck fear in the heart of the tyrant that had usurped the throne. And in this song was a dark verse no one had ever understood, just memorized and repeated for generations. So Peter sang it faithfully and true:

> And there will arise a princess
> From the loins of the slain king.
> And though she fall like David,
> From her womb shall spring forth
> He of Fair Skin
> Who shall come out of the West
> To rule as Solomon.
> And he shall be a shepherd to his people.

"And when Peter sang those words he stopped and we all stared at each other in amazement, for suddenly we understood, and realized that those ancient words had come to pass, that Elizabeth was the princess who had sinned, and Josiah was the fair-skinned child of the prophecy. Was he to be King of Mayangala, or one of Elizabeth's brothers? In our tribal lore our wise men had always thought that the West meant Ghana or Mali or somewhere in the continent of Africa. But now it seemed to us that the West might possibly mean America, which of course is where his father was from.

"So we stayed with Peter for a time. I had to go back to Heidelberg to close the apartment and get the car. That's when I learned that you had come here. So one day the men built a fire outside and sat down cross-legged around it and took counsel. The decision was up to the brothers, but my husband Shadrach as eldest man was carefully heeded. So it was decided that I should come here with the child and bring him to you."

"So you packed up and left," John said.

"No," she said with a smile, "we all went in and had a nice cup of tea and a lovely trifle I'd just made that day, and the men all watched the football match between Man U and Birmingham. Sadly my husband passed away shortly afterward, so I was delayed yet once again."

"Dear Shadrach," Earl said. "I would so much have liked to see him again."

"And he you," said Miriam. "He spoke of you so often. You were an apostle to us, my dear."

"So here we are," John said. "What do we do now? And what happened to Rafael, I wonder?"

☉ ☉ ☉

Rafael had come to in the small cave. He was a bloody, filthy mess—most distressing for an orderly man of fastidious taste. He was wet with beer—a keg had spilled—and his own blood. The pain in his right hand was excruciating. Half of it was gone. In the dim candlelight he looked at his wound. His thumb and first two fingers were missing. He moaned out loud, but gritted his teeth with sheer willpower to keep from crying. After all, he had a military code to honor, and it imposed its discipline on him even when he was alone. Especially when he was alone. For he normally operated alone, though his Saudi prince had created a support network he could access if needed. The one remaining candle was guttering low. By its dim, flickering light he could see the remains of his dog: the lifeless body, the severed head. Seeing this he moaned in sorrow, for he loved his dog as a comrade-in-arms. Besides which, it was inconceivable that he should be bested in combat and his attack dog killed by some common American. And that thought added salt to his wounds. Yet despite his physical and emotional pain he forced himself to think and act. He had been well-trained. There were protocols for everything, procedures to follow even when things went wrong. His pager was in his right pocket—damned hard to get out with his left hand, but somehow he managed. Squinting in the failing light he punched in the number of his contact cell, giving them the address with the words, "Code 5. Repeat. Code 5."

By the time Rafael had made his way outside there was an SUV on the curb. Two men jumped out and helped him into the back, where they laid him down on a stretcher and began emergency medical treatment. Meanwhile a third man went in to retrieve the dog's carcass and the severed digits. A fourth drove, and they all sped to a remote place deep in the forest outside Heidelberg where they had their operations compound. There they chanted prayers for healing in Arabic, along with prayers for revenge. And they called Riyadh for instructions. It was decided that a doctor would be sent immediately. Rafael would remain in Germany for initial treatment, then go on to a hospital in England for therapy, and finally proceed to America to finish his job. Spies had already reported that John had survived and was being treated at the hospital in Heidelberg. Surely he would return to America. The child was still at large. Where John Mason was, there the child would be. It was the stupid emotional way Christians typically went about things. But action must be taken. For reports from Mayangala were not at all encouraging. Despite the imposition of Sharia, Christianity continued to flourish and spread, and as long as any descendant of the king remained alive there was the possibility that the people would rise up and throw off Islamic rule. John Mason and the child must be killed. How satisfactory it would all be when concluded.

◎ ◎ ◎

"As to the second question," Miriam said, "I'm sure we'll never know. But you didn't kill him, more's the pity. My guess is that he'll come after you." She paused. "And Josiah."

"Well, if he tries, he'll have a helluva time finding us back here in the woods."

Miriam nodded. "As to the first question, we've got a tired little teddy bear on our hands here, and we need to change his nappie and send him off to the Featherbed Ball."

At this there were murmurs of assent, and family members began to arise and stretch and yawn and say yes it's time to be going and milling around looking for purses and glasses and car keys and rounding up the kids.

Rachel meanwhile had come up to John and asked to hold the baby. And he said, "Yes, of course," and she cradled the sleeping child in her arms and hummed the tune of "The Water Is Wide," at which Josiah half-opened his eyelids and looked at her, then closed his eyes, then woke up and looked around, and shifted round so that he was riding on her hip.

Just as all this was happening TD called out, "Don't run off yet. Rachel and I have an announcement!"

"Oh, yes," Rachel said, and moved over next to TD, who gave the baby a fishy sidelong glance.

TD cleared his throat officiously. "I have the distinct pleasure of announcing that Rachel and I are en-"—and just as he was speaking Josiah reached up and snatched off TD's toupee—"-gaged." Everyone began laughing as TD put his right hand on top of his bald head to cover his shame and with his left hand tugged at the toupee to try and get it back from Josiah. But the child had a strong grip and pulled back hard. TD lost his grip. Josiah then amazed everyone, for he seemed to have a natural arm. He flung the wig across the room. As it skidded across the floor, Doxie, barking and thinking it was a rat, pounced on it with glee and ran off with it, TD running after her and yelling, "Stop, stop!" while everyone was holding their sides and leaning against each other, they were laughing so hard.

Finally Doxie stopped in a corner to chew on her prize. TD caught up with her and took back his toupee. As he put the shredded thing back on his head he muttered under his breath, "I'll not be made a fool of by some goddam little pickaninny."

Chapter 7 ◉ Chortazo

Millie and Miriam settled in to the tasks of housekeeping together, and together cared for the young child Josiah as his father John continued to work on his dissertation. For Millie, who to tell the truth had been pretty lonely since Herbert died, Miriam was a godsend. Their personalities—both oriented to serving—meshed perfectly despite their cultural differences, and they seemed to know instinctively from long years' experience running kitchens what the other needed, handing over the paring knife, sweeping up the cuttings, building up the fire, fetching the flour, and all the hundred things women do together in the joy of feeding their men. Millie had one—John, and Miriam had one—Josiah. Now they were brought together. And both loved them and cared for them, and now John and his son were reunited and the two old mothers were happy looking after them. Besides, they just plain liked each other. Both liked to read, and Miriam had brought with her a stack of British mysteries like P. D. James that Millie had never read, and Millie for her part had a pile of Midwestern writers like Larry Woiwode that Miriam had never heard of. Plus the kind of down-home plain cooking that Millie excelled at was a wonder to Miriam, and she saw with satisfaction that John had gained a few pounds under her care. But when Miriam took some day old white cake and whipped cream and jam and threw together a good English trifle Millie was enthralled and begged for the recipe. Plus Miriam brought in the African touch to the cooking—some spices she always brought along on travels, some traditional lamb dishes, even couscous on occasion, with little white Muscat raisins tossed in, that Josiah loved to hunt for with his pudgy little fingers and pop into his mouth first before eating the rest of his meal.

Josiah for his part loved being in the country—what kid doesn't?—and spent all day every day outside, playing in the yard, finding bugs and beetles, poking around in the mud, getting filthy dirty, and screaming in outrage when it was time to come in and take a bath in the old tin washtub, which he enjoyed thoroughly once he was put into it. Doxie would ramble over from the farm to visit Josiah, and look after him when he played, and curl up with him in bed and keep him warm when it was nappy time in the afternoon. The child was constantly picking up rocks and shying them at anything and everything. At lakeside he threw sidearm, skipping rocks over the surface five and ten times before they sank. His fastball was reserved for game: squirrels and rabbit. Then one day he hit a big sow groundhog, which turned and started to come after him. He ran in terror until Doxie chased it off.

Even though it was by now December the weather was not intolerably cold, with a tendril of Southern air sometimes coming up the Mississippi Valley as so often happens in Missouri in winter, and on pleasant days John, his broken foot healing well, would take his son down a hundred yards or so through the cane brake to the Saline Creek, with Doxie tagging along, and sit on the sandbar and catch panfish—bluegill and crappie and smallmouth bass—then bring them back and clean them and the women would fry them up in the old black cast-iron skillet and serve them with biscuits and black coffee, a meal fit for a king as they say, and indeed, who knows? Perhaps with God's help the grubby little kid in a high chair surrounded by crumbs might one day sit on the high throne of Mayangala surrounded by princes. For below the peaceful scenes of country living at the old Clubhouse there ran deep underground a current of tension that must somehow someday be resolved.

One of these was the tension of John's guilt. It was not just that he felt guilty. He *was* guilty. He had sinned. He had broken the commandment, "Thou shalt not commit adultery." The Bible was very clear. John knew it. He knew it and the truth of it ate away at his soul like an acid. He had been led astray by his feelings, and the feelings were wonderful the brief moment that they lasted, but he and Elizabeth both had let their feelings for each other carry them away, and in the stress and bewilderment of being strangers in a strange land they had forgotten their childhood catechism and had succumbed to the lust of the moment. The result: a bastard son, the death of the mother, the guilt of the father. And though externally things were peaceful and he was making good progress on his dissertation John kept asking himself how in all honesty he could write on the Third Use of the Law when he himself had so flagrantly violated it. And now in his own soul the Second Use of the Law was coming into play. For the Law was a Mirror that showed him his sin. He would wake in the night sweating and afraid. The few pounds he had gained began to melt away. He tried to read Scripture but found no comfort. Instead he heard God shouting at him in wrath. He found a verse in Psalm 38, one of the Seven Penitential Psalms:

> O Lord, rebuke me not in thy wrath: neither chasten me in thy hot displeasure. For thine arrows stick fast in me, and thy hand presseth me sore. There is no soundness in my flesh because of thine anger; neither is there any rest in my bones because of my sin. For mine iniquities are gone over mine head: as an heavy burden they are too heavy for me.

These were the words of David. David knew full well what it was like to be saved then fall into sin because of the weakness of the flesh. David knew what it was like to know the terror of damnation from the God he once had loved. David knew what it was like to smell the smoke and sulfur and stench of hell. And now John knew it too. There was only one way out. David had confessed to Nathan the prophet. John would confess to Earl the pastor.

It was one of those raw days. The weather changed—the sky overcast and low, a surly mist over the ground, swirling around and dripping from the trees, and the temperature in the twenties with a damp chill in the air that seeped through your clothes and chilled your bones no matter how much clothing you had on. John wrote his pages in the morning, finding it difficult to concentrate knowing what he was going to do. He had called Pastor Gottlieb on the old crank telephone and made an appointment, even though he knew full well that the old man never strayed far from the parsonage, especially on miserable days like this when his arthritis nagged him and reminded him of his mortality.

From outside where he was gathering kindling, John could hear Millie and Miriam in the kitchen. Men work together in silence but women talk. And these two were talking, talking, talking, about cooking, about books, about church gossip, and of course mostly about those mysterious creatures they had to look after all the time—men. At last Millie yelled out for lunch and when he came in she licked her fingers and smoothed down his cowlick like she'd always done when he was a kid, and like he'd always done when he was a kid he made a face and tried to squirm away as Miriam smiled to herself and set out blue ceramic bowls on the red checked tablecloth. One of the club members, a bowhunter, had shot a deer and left them a good piece of venison. This they had made into a hearty beer roast with thick brown gravy, hot and savory, and big chunks of good plain homegrown potatoes and onions and carrots. Its aroma wafted through the kitchen and the warmth was most welcoming to John after the chill of the outdoors. He shivered a little as he began to warm up. Wan winter light filtered in through the steamy windows.

John scooped up his son and put him squirming into the old wooden high chair. After saying grace they dug into the venison, but after three mouthfuls Millie jumped up and exclaimed, "Oh! The cornbread!" banging open the oven door and with thick oven mitts on both hands hauling out the big black cast iron skillet full of the hot golden cornbread. She made it sweet, as was the tradition in Missouri, and they sliced it open and with the steam rising put on thick dabs of real butter and rich dark homemade molasses that poured slow from the cold. And they ate and were satisfied, and the venison was savory and good, though different than of old for Miriam had put her touch to it and added a hint of some spice they used in Africa when roasting lion for the king and his men after a hunt. And John too ate and was warmed and fed in his body, but not his soul.

Lunch finished. It was time for Josiah's nap. Millie had found Theodore, John's ratty old teddy bear, in the attic, and given it to Josiah, who dragged it around and loved it and abused it as John had done when he was little. She tucked him into his crib with his blankie and Theodore and sang him a little soft song while Miriam had coffee and read at the kitchen table and John cleaned up the kitchen. "Be a dear and bring in some more firewood," said Miriam. John nodded his head as he wiped the last dish and put it away and went toward the door. "And put on a hat and coat or you'll catch your death," she fussed as he laid his hand on the doorknob. This he ignored with a wave of his hand. Striding quickly toward the woodpile he threw back the tarp and loaded his left arm with split oak, as much as he could carry, then came quickly back to the house and dumped it into the woodbox by the kitchen door. By this time Millie was at the kitchen table with her mug of coffee and her book and Josiah in his crib was singing and cooing softly to himself and Theodore before drifting off to sleep.

"I'll be back in a bit," John said with affected nonchalance. Neither woman looked up from her book nor gave it a thought. In recent days John had been going in to town to help Jasper in the shop and earn some extra money. Sometimes he would visit his grandmother or his parents or an old high school chum and not be back until the evening. So John threw on his old letter jacket—green wool with white leather sleeves—and walked outside. A thin drizzly mist was drifting through the woods and a low cold wind rattled the dry brown leaves that still clung to the oak trees. With a shiver he hopped into the Jeep. It was running well now. Jasper and he had given it proper care: oil change, grease gun on the joints, valve job, radiator flush, points, plugs, condenser, and tune-up. He drove slowly and carefully around the bend, thinking as did everyone who passed that way that one day they were going to have to cut down that big sycamore tree, especially since in recent years the ravine below had eroded the creek bank little by little until it was a tight squeeze between the tree and the drop-off. If they didn't someday somebody was going to come around that curve too fast or the bank would crumble and down they'd go. But it was such a magnificent tree with its huge white trunk, etched with initials of generations of Clubhouse members, and towering eighty feet high and providing good shade all summer long. So they kept putting it off.

In a few minutes he was at the church. The yard had been seeded with winter rye and presented a welcome blaze of living green over against the dreary greys and browns of surrounding winter. Likewise the church building stood out strong from the dull winter, white and shining as if lit from some unknown source, for the members, few though they were, kept the place in top condition and freshly painted at all times. It was a humble, unpretentious little country church which the members had built themselves from wood they had hewn on the premises a hundred and fifty years before. The same family names that appeared in the charter were still active and in the pews today—good old solid German names that smelled like honest labor and hearty sausage and dark beer, names with multiple syllables you had to work to say, like Schultheiss and Hebermueller and Oberklingenberg. These were the quiet, dependable, unpretentious yeomen that constituted the strong backbone of church and society. Unlike the tongue, they did not speak. Unlike the hand, they did not show. Like the spine, they just stayed in the background and held everything else together. They kept their farms neat and clean and tidy, and mowed their lawns meticulously, and planted marigolds along the borders of their gardens to keep away bugs but also to give passersby a splash of color to enjoy. They never bothered anybody and hoped nobody would bother them so that they could live a quiet and peaceable life in all godliness and honesty. These were John's people. He was of them and for them and to them he returned when he needed wholeness and healing.

Walking up the worn stone steps he swung open the red door and entered. He hung his jacket on the coat rack in the narthex and stepped quietly into the nave and looked around. Quiet empty churches have a certain tension, as if filled with fierce angels fully armed and waiting for the physical people to appear and enact rituals like an infant baptism that would change the world forever and usher in the Kingdom of God. There was Peter in one window, sinking into the sea but clinging to the hand of his Savior. There was Jesus in another window, carrying the poor lost sheep in his strong and merciful arms. Past the ornate wood-carved pulpit and through the little door, and there was Pastor Earl Gottlieb, puffing on a cigar and poring over a pile of New Testament commentaries and lexicons.

"*Ach, du Johannes,*" he said, glancing up. "*Wie geht's heute?*"[*]

"*Ganz gut. Du auch?*"

"*Immer besser.* Look here a second. What do you think of this word?"

"What have you got?" John asked.

"*Chortazo,*" Gottlieb replied. "Right here in Matthew 14, where Jesus feeds the five thousand. 'And they all ate and were filled.'"

"Yes, I remember."

"Well, *chortazo,* which means 'to be filled,' is derived from *chortos,* which means, 'grass.' The picture here in this word is of cattle grazing and grazing and grazing until they are so full in both stomachs they can't possibly eat another bite. So when it says they all ate and were filled, I mean to tell you, they really ate a whole lot, like you would expect of people living in a land where famine was always just around the corner and they often didn't know where their next meal might be coming from. So when they had the opportunity to eat without restraint, they really packed it in."

"Kind of like we all did at Thanksgiving at the Clubhouse."

"Exactly. But more so. We were full, but nothing like this word describes. It's a wonder the people didn't all fall asleep during Jesus' sermon."

"So how are you going to develop this homiletically?"

Gottlieb leaned back in his chair and drew on his cigar and looked up at the scrolls and patterns on the old tin ceiling. The old wooden office chair creaked softly as he gently rocked back and forth. "This word tells us a lot about God. He sends the rain on the just and the

---

[*] "Ah, John," he said, glancing up. "How are you today?"
"Very good. You, too?"
"Better and better. Look here a second..."

unjust. He gives food and clothing and shelter to everyone, even those who ignore him entirely. So that's part of it. Jesus fed the people and they all ate and were filled and most of them walked away with the same unbelief they had before dinner. The meal did them no good spiritually. So there's the Law in this passage. Where's the Gospel? You tell me."

John crossed his legs and folded his arms. "I'd connect it with Paul's word in Romans 12, where he says, 'Oh, the depth of the riches of the wisdom and knowledge of God!'"

"Good."

"And in Colossians, 'For in him all the fullness of God was pleased to dwell.'"

"Good."

"So when you put it all together you see that we have a God in Christ who has an inexhaustible supply of grace and mercy and forgiveness that he offers to us through his death on the cross and his resurrection. And we come to him starving and hungry."

"Good."

"And he is glad to feed us. 'Blessed are those who hunger and thirst after righteousness.' And no matter how much we stuff ourselves with his grace there is plenty left over."

"Excellent. You've written my sermon for me. Now I can loaf the rest of the week!"

They laughed together, then John grew serious. "Well, Earl, I think I need a bite or two of those loaves and fishes."

"Oh?" Gottlieb swung forward in his chair and leaned over the desk with his face closer to John. His features softened with compassion.

"Do you do private confession very often?"

"No," Gottlieb cracked, "everybody around here is pretty darn righteous." John smiled and nodded his head as Gottlieb stood slowly, went to the closet, and slipped on his cassock, surplice, and stole. "But occasionally a stray cat wanders in that needs it."

"I guess that would be me," John said.

"Well, come on in to the chancel. We'll see what God will do for you. Like we just was saying, there's plenty of mercy."

They went though the little door and John knelt on the prie-dieu as Gottlieb sat to the side. Both opened their hymnals to the Order of Private Confession. John looked up at the altar, the old, ornately-carved German altar, the altar with the statue of Jesus on the Cross looking down at John and Mary. This was the altar he had seen all through his childhood, the statue he had contemplated through many sermons, the image of home he had carried with him in his imagination in travels through faraway lands. Jesus in his loneliness and agony was caring for his loved ones. But now John was a man and now he was here in truth and now he needed the rock-hard reality of God's mercy. *Father, forgive me,* he thought to himself, *for I know not what I do.*

"Dear pastor," John began, "please hear my confession."

Then Gottlieb said softly, "You have come to make confession before God. In Christ you are free to confess before me, a pastor in his Church, the sins which trouble you."

John took a deep breath and let it out. Then another. At last he began, slowly and quietly telling his pastor the things he had told the family, but with more detail about his moral unraveling, the influence of Kolding and his antinomianism, the dark corners of Europe he had wandered into, and his breaking the Sixth Commandment with Elizabeth. As he confessed he thought he might do something dramatic like weep and wail. But he did not. There was no more emotion than if he had gotten dirty and was taking a bath. At last he was through. Then they said the words of the Psalm together, the Psalm David had written after his sin with Bathsheba:

> Have mercy upon me, O God, according to thy lovingkindness: according unto the multitude of thy tender mercies blot out my transgressions.... Create in me a clean heart, O God, and renew a right spirit within me. Cast me not away from thy presence; and take not thy holy spirit from me. Restore unto me the joy of thy salvation; and uphold me with thy free spirit.

Then Pastor Gottlieb said, "Do you believe that the word of

forgiveness I speak to you comes from God himself?"

"Yes, I believe."

Then Pastor Gottlieb arose in the full dignity and authority of his office and, laying both hands upon the head of the penitent, said, "In the stead and by the command of my Lord Jesus Christ, I, a called and ordained servant of the Word, announce the grace of God to you, John Mason, and I forgive you all your sins in the name of the Father, and of the Son"—and with this he made the sign of the Holy Cross on John's forehead—"and of the Holy Spirit. Amen."

Then they prayed together, and standing up shook hands and then embraced. A car drove by outside, tires crunching on the gravel road. The afternoon was waning and the light through the stained glass windows was growing dim. In silence they walked down the aisle, through the narthex, and out the door as John slipped into his jacket. There was a barren cornfield next to the church. In it was a flock of black crows, cackling complacently and feeding on something stinking and dead they had found. As the men walked to John's car, Gottlieb still in his robes of office waved his arms once and the black, unholy crows flapped away in panic, cawing and cursing until they were far away and out of sight and sound.

◉ ◉ ◉

The car that John had heard pass by the church was TD's big Mercedes. What a car! It had supple leather upholstery, a state-of-the-art sound system, a solid burl walnut dashboard, and understated Berber carpet. As he swept through the entrance to the farm and up the road he felt like a king in his chariot surveying his domain with satisfaction, for he had found his queen and sealed the deal with an engagement, and in due time they would be wed and this property, this very valuable and developable property would be his to exploit. It was all coming together. A few weeks before, he had gone up to St. Louis and met with his potential business partners Frank and Ben Laclede. The brothers had been his classmates in the Olin School of Business at Washington University and they had kept up with each other through marriages, divorces, football games, class reunions and so forth, though they had been more acquaintances than close friends. TD was a self-made man. Frank and Ben were from a line of landed old-money people that were descended from the first families of St. Louis. The old homes their ancestors had built in the city and in the Central West End were now on the National Register of Historic Places, and the Lacledes now lived in Ladue without ostentation, as is always the case with the truly wealthy. Their Jaguars—bought with cash, not credit—were a tasteful and understated brown. The boys continued the successful real estate company their great-grandfather had established, and added law degrees from Yale to their Harvard MBAs—something TD had been unable to manage. But they seemed to accept him as one of their own and had agreed to meet him for lunch in the revolving restaurant at the top of the Millennium hotel downtown. TD had arrived as always right on time, but Ben and Frank were late by half an hour. TD fidgeted and paced and glanced at his watch. Perhaps they had forgotten. Things like this had happened to him in the past. Important people he had tried to connect with had stood him up. At last the elevator dinged softly and elegantly as if it were an English butler and the two young men stepped out. They were both of average height and average build and average looks—that kind of nondescript appearance a lot of really rich people have—with the bit of weight around the middle that comes from success in business. Frank had on a standard business suit, dark blue with a subtle pinstripe, cut to fit perfectly, and if you knew clothes you could discern the tasteful, understated elegance of Brooks Brothers above the Alden shoes. Ben by contrast had on Weejuns and no socks, wrinkled 100% cotton khakis, a wrinkled 100% cotton white button down dress shirt, and a navy blazer with his prep school crest.

"Hey, TD," said Frank as he shot out his right hand and with his left loosened his rep tie. "Sorry to keep you waiting. I had this thing with the mayor all morning at the Missouri Athletic Club. God how these politicians do drone on and on. Nobody should be allowed to go into politics until they've been in business at least ten years. That way they'd learn how to make their point in five minutes or less and move on to the next item on the agenda. Jeez!"

"Yeah," echoed Ben, "I was out there double-parked for half an hour getting dirty looks from the cops. I'm starving. Let's put on the old feed bag."

"Which reminds me," Frank said, "Did you check on the horses this morning?"

"No, I thought you were going to do that."

"Well remind me to call the stable right after lunch. The mare was getting close to dropping her colt. I wanted to be there for it." He looked at TD with a grin. "Thoroughbreds!" he said with a laugh and a shake of his head with his eyebrows raised.

The waiter, dignified in black slacks, bow tie and white jacket, ushered them to their usual table next to the window. They were in one of the tallest buildings in St. Louis, and from their perch they could look down on everybody else. There was the Arch, there was the river, and as he looked at them TD suddenly felt a bit queasy and disoriented, for this was a revolving restaurant, and they were moving, moving ever so slowly, and the cityscape was going past while they sat still. The waiter came by again and bowed imperceptibly. "The usual, gentlemen?"

"Oh, sure, what the hell. It's five o'clock somewhere, as the song says," Ben said.

"And for you, sir?" he said, looking at TD.

With a slight blush which he hoped they wouldn't notice, he said, "Um, yeah, I guess so."

There was the Old Cathedral.

"Yeah, these politicians!" Frank went on. "Jeez! They scream about how big business is ruining the country, then they pump us for donations to their campaign."

The waiter appeared with the drinks, very large Bombay gin martinis, straight up with olive. "Mud in your eye," said Ben, raising his glass. TD took a sip. It was mighty strong. Beer was more his speed. But he had to keep pace to save face. "And can they ever put away the hooch! Yikes!"

Frank cackled. "Remember the time we were at that Christmas

thing for the President at the country club?"

Ben laughed. "You mean when the stripper popped out of the cake?"

"Yeah, and that thing she did with the whipped cream?" They both laughed uproariously and gulped big swallows of their martinis. TD of course tried to chuckle along and be part of the fun, but he had not been there at the country club bash for the President of the United States, nor would he ever have been invited, nor would he ever have been asked to join the country club in the first place, nor did he even play golf, for he was a self-made man, or was trying to become one, from little old Ste. Gen.

There was the Eads Bridge.

The waiter surreptitiously appeared, and Frank lifted one finger for another round. For TD, who had skipped breakfast and was finding that that martini was going straight to his head, the room was spinning in more ways than one.

There was the Old Courthouse.

The waiter was back with the drinks. "And for lunch, gentlemen? The usual?"

"Oh, sure, what the hell," Frank replied. TD had glanced at the menu. Prices were listed in whole numbers or none at all: 20, 50, market price. He of course would be obligated to pick up the tab since he had proposed this meeting. The drinks were probably ten bucks a pop. How many had they had? "Ah, uh, sure," he said, "likewise me also," then mentally slapped himself for the grammatical error. But nobody seemed to notice.

There was Busch Stadium.

In a moment the waiter was back with the pate foie gras and yet another round of drinks. TD dug in and ate a lot of the pate, hoping to take the edge off the alcohol. No such luck. Then came trout almondine with Minnesota wild rice and honey glazed carrots, and to finish a crème brulee with fresh raspberry garnish. Then the waiter discreetly set before them snifters of brandy, Courvoisier of course, and held out a tray with a selection of cigars. Frank took a huge Cohiba Churchill, Ben a Fuente Opus X, and TD in wild confusion, for he hardly ever smoked, picked the smallest one he could find, a Macanudo Portofino. The waiter clipped the cigar ends and the men lit up. TD with an enormous effort kept from coughing. He was beginning to feel sick to his stomach.

There was Ralston Purina.

Frank slumped back in his chair and took a big drag off his Cohiba. "So what have you got for us, Champ?"

TD was as jumpy as an American pianist backstage before the Rachmaninoff Competition in Moscow. With an effort to look nonchalant he pulled a sheaf of papers from his coat pocket.

"Well, let's review these details on the proposal I outlined to you a couple of weeks ago. My fiancée has this farm in Perry County, about ninety minutes south of here... make a dandy resort close to St. Louis. Once we're married I'll have joint ownership of the property. It would be ideal for a golf course. Those gently rolling hills, you know. You mentioned horseback riding. I hadn't thought of that, but sure, why not? Plus the property is right on this beautiful lake, peaceful and quiet, gives a good feeling just being there, you know. We build a first-class resort hotel on the hill overlooking the lake. Four-star restaurant, spa, the works. And one idea I had since we met last time is to have the parking by the main entrance and take people up to the lodge in a horse-drawn carriage, goes over the creek on a covered bridge, down the shaded woodland path, so the consumer is in a relaxed mood even before he checks in."

The two brothers pursed their lips and nodded their heads, then exchanged quick glances.

There was the Poplar Street Bridge.

Ben drilled TD with a shrewd look. He seemed to be affected not at all by the drinks. "So basically the same deal you described before, right?" TD nodded apprehensively. A hell of a lot was riding on this negotiation—nothing less than his entire future. Frank spoke up. "We did some checking around on our own. Never hurts to be on the side of caution when considering a business venture. You put your money in, but can you get your money out? Plus a little extra to sweeten the pot."

Oh, shit, thought TD, they've decided not to invest.

"You've done pretty well in business, champ," Frank continued. "Not too shabby. We flew down and looked over your development in Arkansas. Very nice. We've been pals and classmates and all that, but on the other hand we're talking about business partners here. That entails risk." At this Frank reached into his jacket and produced his own sheaf of papers. "That's why we have a counterproposal of our own." He unfolded the packet and set it in front of TD, who put his cigar into the ashtray and tried to focus on the print that was swimming around on the table in front of him. "Our best estimate is that this development will cost about three mil—using local contractors to keep construction costs down, and then you and your wife own the property so there's no overhead for the purchase of land. That's attractive. At the same time, while we of course have no way of looking into your piggy bank, we feel certain that with your real estate business and the Arkansas development you'll be able to go halvsies with us." He looked at TD for a response.

TD was stunned. He was strapped for cash. He was hoping that if he offered the land, they would provide the venture capital. This proposal meant $1.5 million from him up front.

"Of course," Ben put in, "in business sometimes cash flow is a problem." To TD at that moment it was as if Ben were reading his mind. "But borrowing shouldn't be a problem since you can put up your business as collateral. In fact, we tossed the idea out to our old man and he hinted that he might be able to offer favorable terms on a bridging loan. The old boy network, you know. Oh, incidentally, you do play golf, don't you?"

God, were they hinting at a membership in a country club? "Oh. Yeah. Sure." He was lying, but he was a jock. How hard could it be to pick up golf?

"Anyway," Frank said, "I think we can go with this, don't you, Ben?" Ben nodded in affirmation. They had worked out the details with their corporate attorney a week ago. This was a show of force, to put the two brothers on the power side of the negotiating table. "We'd just need your name on the line with the X there," Frank said. "Do you have a pen?" TD had a nice gold Cross ballpoint he wore on dressy occasions, but deferred to the more expensive, more elegant, more understated Mont Blanc fountain pen Frank held out to him. In a daze, he signed. Then they all shook hands. "Great! Great! Then it's a deal," the brothers said, each one tumbling over the other with a different sentence.

"You won't need to pony up before the first of the year."
"Besides, you're not even married yet."
"Yeah, what if that falls through?"
"Ha, ha, then you'd be screwed, blued, and tattooed."
"But old Touchdown Timmy is too shrewd to let that happen. Ain't that right, champ?"
"Did you say 'pony up'? Jeez, the horses!"
"Go call the stable, you moron."
There was the Arch, there was the river.

The unctuous waiter brought the bill, which TD took like a bullet from a firing squad. He had just signed for a million and a half. What difference did a hundred bucks for lunch make? They made their way toward the elevator.

Ben was speaking. "No colt yet, but we ought to head on over. Remember the time the governor's daughter..."
"You mean Muffy? What a little slut..."
"Jeez! and right there in the tack room..."
"And her old man knocking down the scotch with Pop right in the next room..."
"Politicians! Jeez!"
There was the Old Cathedral again.

TD weaved his way out through the lobby, found his Mercedes, fumbled the keys, got in, sat down, and puked all over the supple leather upholstery, the state-of-the-art sound system, the solid burl walnut dashboard, and the understated Berber carpet.

But that was weeks ago. Today he was back on top of his game. Sometimes in life, as in football, you got sacked and lost yardage. So what? You got up, dusted yourself off, and tried to do better on the next play. He had analyzed his assets and found that he could in fact cover a loan of $1.5 million with his businesses as collateral. Plus his house and his car. And his savings and investments. He was going way, way, way out on a limb here, and he knew in the back of his mind that if anything went wrong and the deal collapsed he would be wiped out. But what could go wrong? He had clinched the deal with Ben and Frank. He had talked to their father and clinched the deal on the loan. And most importantly he had clinched the deal with Rachel. He had taken a hit, but now he was on his feet. He had thrown the long bomb. The ball was in the air, spiraling perfectly. His man was wide open downfield, the goal line in sight. Damn, it was good to be alive!

Rachel came bouncing down the sidewalk and hopped into the car, tossing her guitar into the back seat, before TD could get out and hold the door for her. Their familiarity was growing. And Lordy, didn't she look good in those tight jeans! They gave each other a quick hug and a kiss and sped off. Rachel was in high spirits like all engaged women are, full of mischief and fun. She, too, had clinched the deal.

"How are you, buddy boy," she said as she biffed his arm. "So tell me more about this music deal we're going to do."

"I'm good good good, sweetie." They were starting to develop pet names for each other, a positive sign. "OK, well, today is just warm-ups, a bit of practicing, getting to know each other. Pastor Dave is putting together a new praise band." TD didn't mention that the old praise band had quit. They had been hired by the newest, fastest-growing community church across town. As a result, Pastor Dave's church had lost market share.

"And you know," TD went on, "Christmas is coming up, and we want to do something special to attract the unchurched in the area. The Christmas market is as big or bigger for churches than it is for retail outlets, it's a prime selling time for our product, which is salvation, of course, but the marketing data has shown that the average consumer who is shopping for a church just doesn't feel comfortable in these big imposing piles of cold old stone with boring sermons and draggy hymns played on the organ. They need a place where they don't feel under pressure to convert or put money in the plate. They need a place where the culture inside the church is like the culture outside the church, where the music is familiar, where the sound is like what they hear on the radio, where the sermons are funny and relevant to their felt needs, where they can drop their kids off in a Sunday school that's fun and safe and entertaining. And where they can kick back and have a cup of coffee while listening to the band right in church. This has been Pastor Dave's formula for success, and I'll tell you, he's been successful."

"He sure seems the successful type, the few times I've met him," Rachel said. "What's his background?"

"I don't know a whole lot," TD replied. "He plays his cards pretty close to the vest. Fantastic in front of a crowd, you know, but one-on-one somewhat guarded. Perhaps shy, I don't know. Which is fine, many people are like that. But from what I've been able to gather he comes from a long line of Lutheran pastors from up in Minnesota or Wisconsin. But he wasn't at all interested in the ministry, and majored in business in college and played in a weekend rock band. Like I did. Probably why we click so well—similar background, similar interests. And for a number of years he worked in the marketing department for some big corporations like General Motors and General Electric, something like that. Of course like a good Lutheran boy he would go to church on Sunday. But somehow he got restless with the big stone church building and the slow draggy hymns and the boring sermons. One day he was on a business trip to Los Angeles and he went to this Baptist church out in Orange County that was doing a 'contemporary service' led by a 'praise band.' This was a revelation to him. He's often spoken about this, so the life path is pretty clear from here on out. It's like he had this vague idea in his head about how church might possibly be done differently, and lo and behold, here was a church that was already doing it. He was blown away. He got an extension on his trip, visited the staff on Monday, learned about their marketing strategies and everything—really they were combining the teachings of Jesus with the latest American business practices. A dynamite combination. They had conducted polls of their target demographic group and ascertained the radio stations they listened to and the kind of music they liked. So they created a praise band that did Christian songs in the same soft-rock style that appealed to the broadest cross-section of their consumer base. The church took off like a rocket: two hundred worshippers per weekend, then five hundred, then a thousand, then two thousand... it just kept building. That's when Pastor Dave decided to go into the ministry.

"He saw that he could bring all his marketing savvy right into the work of the Lord, and be successful in the work of the Kingdom. So he went through Concordia Seminary in St. Louis like his father and grandfather had, and he was assigned to do his internship under JJ Kolding in St. Louis County. You know him, he was there at Thanksgiving at the Clubhouse. JJ was very open to Pastor Dave's new ideas, and let him experiment with a freer, more open, non-liturgical worship style. JJ was older than Dave, of course, but he was very open-minded and affirming and nonjudgmental. People criticized him for being liberal, but I don't understand all this theological hair-splitting. All I could see was that he was a wonderful person. He always said that God is love and Jesus didn't come into this world to condemn people but to love them and lift them up and show them the right way, and that if we are followers of Jesus we should just love one another. It was all so positive with JJ, and Pastor Dave really absorbed that. It really comes through in his sermons. He doesn't go into all this boring dogma and he doesn't condemn other people who have different beliefs, he just uses the Bible as the 'manufacturer's handbook' so to speak, and gives us practical guidance for successful living in our daily lives. He sure helped me, I'll tell you that."

TD thought about the pain—the agony—he had gone through with his divorce. Pastor Dave was right there to pray with him and comfort him. And during the worst of it when TD fell into the arms of an old girlfriend and started sleeping with her, Dave was so understanding. A man had physical needs that had to be satisfied, he had said. These come from God. They can't be denied. People are made to love each other. That's the way God made them. Love casts out all sin, the Bible says. Dave said he had learned this from Kolding. It was a newer, freer, more advanced way of looking at morality. The stodgy old conservatives condemned it as 'Gospel reductionism,' Dave had said, but who ever paid any attention to those old birds. The world was changing. The world was changing and the church had to change with it: new ways of preaching, new ways of worshipping, new ways of living.

By now they were at the church. At first Rachel thought it was a shopping mall or corporate center. The first thing that met you was a large, well-groomed parking lot. The building itself was low and wide and painted in a neutral color. They passed through glass double doors into a carpeted reception area, decorated inoffensively in earth tones, with soft chairs and potted plants tastefully arranged. She felt immediately comfortable, for she had been in any number of doctor's offices and business suites that were decorated in exactly the same way. Soft inoffensive music was playing though the overhead sound system. To one side was the nursery—a clean, well-lighted place. Next to it were the church offices, where attractive, tastefully dressed young ladies were filing and answering the phone and working the copy machine. To the other side was the entrance to the 'celebration center,' which is what this congregation called the sanctuary. A receptionist, also an attractive young lady at a desk in the lobby, was on the phone when they came in and was peering into her desk calendar. "Yes," she said, "eight and ten-thirty, and when you come in to the lobby just look to the right and there will be someone there to take care of your children while you enjoy the show ... yes ... see you on Sunday."

She glanced up. "May I help ... oh, TD! Great to see you. Praise the Lord. And this must be Rachel," she said as she approached them, giving Rachel a hug. She was slender and blonde, just like the girls in the office, and dressed tastefully in a beige dress, hose and heels. "We've all heard so much about you. TD has just gushed about you, haven't you, TD." She winked at him with a certain familiarity, and he shrugged his shoulders and looked the other way. She ushered them in to the auditorium. There were no windows. There was no stained glass, no saints, no cross. There were plush theater seats, no pews. There was a stage, no chancel. There was a podium, no pulpit. There was no organ, but to one side of the stage was the setup for the band: a trap set in a plexiglass box, a bass and some electric guitars on stands, a Fender Rhodes keyboard, big black boxy Marshall amps stacked high, a forest of gleaming chrome microphones, and on the floor a profusion of black cables slithering every which way. Pastor Dave was already there doing a sound check, running a few riffs on the keyboard, and speaking into the microphones one by one and giving instructions—pot it up on number six, a little more reverb on the keyboard—to the little man in the sound booth in the back of the auditorium. Pastor Dave was dressed casually, St. Louis preppy style: beef-roll Weejuns with no socks, a pair of Dockers, a Madras shirt, and a navy blazer.

"Hey, you guys," he called out. "Come on up. We've been expecting you." He looked at Rachel with an extremely friendly smile and said, "Can I give you a hug?" then gave her one, long and tight.

Rachel McFadden was an intelligent and independent-minded woman. She was happy to be in love and engaged, though like all women she had that little reservoir of doubt that she could dip into in case things didn't work out. So as regards TD she wanted things to work out, she really did, especially since he represented financial and emotional security, but there were still these little nagging questions that she would try to suppress, but that nibbled away quietly like mice, and that she could hear only late at night when the house was quiet. Like why was he so harsh with his son? Didn't he like being a father? And would he want to have children with her? And was he really as financially secure as he seemed to be? And why was he into this progressive, contemporary church? And who was that smirky bimbo at the reception desk? Those were the restless things that squirmed around in the little reservoir, but like all women about to clinch a marriage deal she kept a tight lid on it.

The drummer took his seat, the bass player strapped on his axe and began to noodle a few scales, TD and Rachel took their guitars out of their cases, and the stagehand adjusted the mikes for them. They took a minute to tune, the drummer made some adjustments on his snare, and they were ready to begin.

"OK," said Pastor Dave, taking the center mike. "We're getting ready for the Christmas program in a couple of weeks. The women are getting the kids ready with their little costumes and everything, and we need to work up these musical numbers, OK? So I've written some new songs just for the occasion. Let me run through this first one by myself so you can see how it goes, then we'll work up an arrangement, OK?" He closed his eyes and leaned in close over the keyboard, stroking the keys like a lover, giving the chords a steady rhythmic pulse with a gentle but sensuous backbeat, and the drums and bass came in—he had gone over it with them previously—and when the beat was established he began to sing in a beautiful clear tenor voice:

> You are mine and I am yours.
> You are mine and I am yours.
> Lord, I love you so much, and I know that you love me.
> You are mine, mine, mine, and I am yours.

This was not too difficult, three chords and a repeated chorus. TD and Rachel were to add rhythm with their acoustic guitars and put in harmony on the echo-line: *You are mine (you are mine) and I am yours (I am yours),* and so forth. They just kept repeating this little chorus until the arrangement just sort of evolved in that mysterious way musicians have of reading each others' minds and anticipating what the other is going to do. They repeated it and repeated it and repeated it until they were almost in a trance with the love, love, love of the Lord, Lord, Lord. Then Pastor Dave gave a glance to everyone and a slight nod of the head the way leaders of the band always do when it's time to wrap it up, and they repeated the last line twice and with an instrumental flourish brought the number to a close. And so they did throughout the rest of the afternoon with the other songs, each one tender and enticing, each one with a good backbeat, each one full of love. The beat was sensuous and loving, the love was pulsing with sensuous energy, the senses were beating with feelings and love. Rachel was getting into it; she'd never experienced anything like this before. She'd always played solo. Now she was in a group, and the group dynamics were reaching out and pulling her in, making her part of something larger and different than herself, and she was getting lost in the sound, embracing the feel of the music, eyes closed, moving her body with it. Then in the middle of a song she opened her eyes. There in the back of the auditorium, leaning against a doorway, in deep shadow but lit from behind, was the silhouette of JJ Kolding.

◎ ◎ ◎

The 747 was circling New York City on its final approach to La Guardia. A large, impeccably dressed man sat at a window seat and looked down. The tall straight buildings directly below him were like the tall straight trees of his native *Schwarzwald,* but nothing like the wide empty spaces of the Arabian desert where he been trained in religion and war. The plane continued its route down Manhattan toward Battery Park, and looking down the man could see where the World Trade Center had been destroyed. How satisfying it all was. The Great Satan had been brought to its knees. The great tradition of Muslim caravan raiders lived on, sweeping in unexpectedly from the desert, wreaking unbelievable havoc, then melting away again into the darkness. This was real jihad for the modern era. The martyrs had been successful in their quest for destruction and glory. And now he, Rafael von Päpinghausen, would bring glory to the Crescent. He would destroy the child of John and Elizabeth, a possible heir to the throne of Mayangala, and secure the future of Islam in that tidy little kingdom with uranium in its mountains.

The plane landed and the people crowded the aisles to disembark. He reached into the overhead to retrieve his overcoat and attaché case. By mistake he reached in with his right hand—he still was not accustomed to his handicap—and bumped the place where his thumb and forefinger had been. He winced and uttered a little curse as the pain shot up his arm. He had taken too many pain pills and now he was running low—even when he had plenty they weren't helping much and he absolutely must find a doctor right away—and had to cut back. He had gotten behind the pain curve and it was a constant nagging thing, the physical pain plus the emotional pain of his defeat.

He had killed Elizabeth, but that clumsy infidel John, untrained in the art of war, had hurt him. And so he must not only kill the child but John as well. He liked John, and Rafael might have been willing to let him go at some time in the past. But John had interfered, and now he must pay the price with his blood. He hailed a cab and went to his hotel, the Waldorf Astoria on Park Avenue. In his room he took out a pocket compass and determined the direction of Mecca, then unfurled his prayer rug and on it bowed down in devotion. He missed his dog very much and choked up at the thought of that brave companion. His oblations complete, Rafael changed clothes—the cufflinks were still a considerable problem, especially with French cuffs on a starched shirt—and went down to the restaurant for dinner.

As a Janissary he was accorded certain dispensations not allowed to other, more ordinary Muslims. In addition to a dog, he was permitted alcoholic beverages, for example, and for this he was glad as the drink helped assuage the pain. He downed a martini, then another, and as the welcome haze descended upon him he relaxed a little and looked around. The dining room was decorated with understated elegance, gilt trim and crystal chandeliers. The other diners were sitting up straight in their chairs and conversing in low, cultivated tones. He ordered oysters Rockefeller for an appetizer, and a bottle of 1971 Rhinehessen Trockenbeerenauslese to go with his medallions of pork. To finish, he had a latte and a crème brulee, then retired to the bar for brandy and a cigar—Rémy Martin and a Partagás. He mulled over his plans. Tomorrow he would get his automobile and then set out on his quest for vengeance. And he must find a doctor and get more pain pills. But tonight he was feeling good. For the moment. The pain was there, but in the background. But there was another discomfort he was feeling that needed to be taken care of. He caught the waiter's eye. He came to Rafael's table, the model of discretion, and leaned over to hear a few whispered words. He nodded with understanding as he palmed the fifty. It would be no problem. Room 379. Everything will be arranged to your satisfaction.

Rafael took a bottle of brandy and a snifter with him up to his room and sat down in the easy chair. He turned on the TV. A lascivious American sitcom was on. He watched for a time. Soon there came a soft knock on the door. He opened the door and a stunning blonde came in, trailing a faint whisper of very expensive perfume. He looked at her with satisfaction and said, "I need someone to help me with these cufflinks."

Chapter 8 ◉ Old Methuselah

It was the week before Christmas, and the weather was clear and cold with a stiff north wind blowing as Rachel made her solitary way around the Perryville town square. TD was off in St. Louis on another of his business trips—something about some partners he had to see regarding a real estate development, he'd explain the whole thing to her as soon as he got a chance, it's just that he was so busy and had so many irons in the fire, one thing and then another, phone calls, emails, people waiting to see him, deals to clinch, arrangements to be made, you know how it is, honey.... Frankly, she didn't. Things on the old farm moved as slow as molasses in January, with just her and her mother, and Doxie curled up on the rug. The fastest thing around was her horse Milton, who had grown his winter coat and was ever eager for a good canter over to the Clubhouse where Miriam always slipped him carrots and sugar cubes when nobody was looking. And besides, Doxie was at the Clubhouse half the time anyway looking after little Josiah out of a sense of canine responsibility, but also because Millie always saved her a good hambone which she could gnaw to her heart's content and while away the hours until nap time with the baby. With her mother at the hairdresser's all afternoon for a permanent and Doxie at the Clubhouse and TD away on business, it was up to Rachel to make the rounds of the merchants, her letter jacket zipped up tight and the wind freezing her buns. There was the baker to see about a wedding cake, and the printer to see about announcements, and the bridal shop to see about a dress, and the jeweler to see about the rings, and the florist to see about corsages and bouquets, and the organist, who lived in town, to see about music, and the caterer to see about the reception, and the travel agent to see about the honeymoon, and a million other details that went into one, nerve-wracking, thirty-minute ceremony. Though Rachel had not settled on a date, TD wanted a June wedding, and it wasn't a minute too soon to begin preparations. Plus, TD had made it clear that he wanted to use all Perryville merchants in order to shore up his business relationships in the county seat.

So she started at Fred's Flower Shop on Kiefner street. She wanted orange blossoms in the bridal bouquet, that was certain, for it had been a tradition in her family going back generations. And gardenias. Jack, the tall, bearded florist, assured her it would be no problem, for these were southern flowers and would be available in June. Then it was on to the travel agency, the jeweler, the print shop, and the bridal department at Rozier's. By this time her feet were screaming at her but like a good, hard-working farm girl she was determined to get through this shopping list. When she opened the door to Hoffstetter's Bakery, there was Lou Ann Mason behind the counter.

"Hey, Rache," she said with a grin as she smacked on her chewing gum, "how the heck are ya? Man, you look whipped."

"Tell me about it. It's these wedding arrangements. I'm about ready to just elope and get it over with."

"Sounds like a plan," Lou Ann said as she put donuts in a sack for a customer.

"But TD wants this big church wedding and plans to invite everybody he ever sold a house to, or wants to sell to, which is everybody in town, so we're going the whole nine yards." She raised her eyebrows and puffed her cheeks and blew. "So just give me Cake A and decorate it however you want."

"No, no, you don't want to do that. Look, Rache, I have to take these pies over to the coffee shop. Let's go have coffee and take a break. I'll show you our brochure. It'll be painless."

"Anything you say. It's about lunchtime anyway."

"Good. Hey, Alma!" Lou Ann yelled into the back of the store.

"Yeah," came the faint reply.

"Watch the counter for a few minutes, OK?"

"OK," came the faint reply.

"Here, you take these, Rachel," Lou Ann said, handing her four big white boxes marked "custard/apple/banana cream/rhubarb" respectively, while she herself picked up the other boxes marked "coconut cream/cherry/pumpkin/chocolate." A gust of wind hit them as they hurried down the sidewalk past Prevallet Jewelers to the coffee shop. Two or three people they knew greeted them as they hustled along.

"Hi, Lou Ann," said the lady behind the counter. "It's about time."

"Hey, Myrtle," Lou Ann replied. "We were out of cherry filling and I had to run to Walmart."

"Well, that's fine. The lunch rush will be starting in about a half an hour, and you know how these men have to have their pie."

All three women rolled their eyes and gave each other The Look. They took a seat at a small table by the front window next to Old Man and Old Lady Roschke, who greeted them with raised eyebrows and an upward nod of the head and a brief glance up from their newspapers. Coach Wink across the room waved to them. Clarence and Merle were on their usual stools at the lunch counter. They had made the mistake of making a wisecrack about "jigaboos" a few weeks before when Millie and Miriam and Hilda had come in for lunch with little Josie. A few people sniggered. Hilda had heard it, marched right up to Clarence, who towered over her like a bear, and reduced him to a sniveling puppy with its tail between its legs by cussing him out in German and English, just like Ruth Laughing Brook had done a generation ago, while the rest of the crowd listened in awed silence. Ralph, who had just come in from the garage and joined the group, saw and heard the whole skirmish from up close. He had gone over and stood behind Hilda. With Hilda on the warpath, criticism of the Mason family would be subdued, if not extinguished. Besides, he was learning that in this post-Sixties day and age, more and more, nobody much gave mixed-race romance a second thought. The times, they had a-changed.

Lou Ann had her back to the door and Rachel was sitting across from her. Myrtle came over and gave them each a cup of coffee without asking. For one thing, she knew them. For another, everybody in Perryville drank coffee. Lou Ann took out her gum and wrapped it in the corner of a paper napkin as she looked at Myrtle. "It's Wednesday, so the special is meat loaf, right?"

"Right," Myrtle said. "You want gravy on the mash potatoes?"

"Works for me."

"How 'bout you, Rachel?" asked Myrtle.

"I'll just have the house salad." The bride-to-be was trying to lose weight.

"OK," Myrtle replied, "be up in a minute."

Both women sipped their coffee and looked at each other, shaking their heads. The window was steamed up. An icy draft trailed down and tickled their bare ankles. The door swung open, bringing in a couple of businessmen and another puff of cold air. Rachel could see them take a seat at the counter.

"So what else is on your list?"

"I need to go by Prevallet's and look at rings."

"How come TD isn't helping with this?"

"Oh, he's got some big business deal cooking in St. Louis. Mum's the word, but he's all excited about it. Besides, what else do I have to do? I'm not needed that much at the Clubhouse since Miriam came. So besides babysitting my mother and seeing that she gets her meds, I'm kind of a fifth wheel. At least I'm catching up on my reading."

"Shakespeare and all that crap?"

Rachel smiled and nodded her head. "Crap, mostly. A lot of feminist literary theory I had in grad school, all about how us gals have been oppressed since the dawn of time by all these nasty evil men."

"So that's what them plays are about. I always wondered."

"Well, its not what's in the plays, it's what's *not* in the plays."

"Huh?"

"Well, at the end of *Measure for Measure* the main female character, Isabella, doesn't have any lines."

"OK?"

"So Dollimore and these other critics deduce that she has been oppressed and silenced by a repressive male patriarchal society."

"That's a crock."

"I think so, too."

"I rather like men."

"Me, too."

"They're big and loud and hairy, but if you get one that loves you he'll work himself to death to provide for you."

"Yep."

"I wish I had one. You're lucky. Here, let me show you this catalog."

Lou Ann plopped the big book onto the small table. Rachel opened to page one. There was a beautiful three-layered cake with fancy details on top and around the sides, and on top under a floral bower stood a little bride in a white gown and a little groom in a black tuxedo. As Rachel stared at it, she felt a puff of cold air on her face. Glancing up she saw that John Mason, dressed in his grimy garage overalls, had come in to the cafe and was taking a seat on one of the red vinyl stools at the counter near Clarence and Merle. Rachel felt that vague uncomfortable twinge of something she always felt when John was around, that she had felt ever since she was a little girl, that she had felt when they were talking by the lake, that she had felt when they sang together at Thanksgiving. She stuffed the feeling down and nailed a lid on it.

"... and this is our most expensive one here, but it's ideal for a big wedding like you're plan-..." Lou Ann was going on when Rachel snapped back into consciousness.

"M-hm. OK. Go back a couple pages. I got distracted."

"What are you..." Lou Ann twisted around in her chair and looked over at the counter, instantly recognizing her brother from the back of his head. "Oh, it's Johnny! I'll go get him."

Rachel touched her arm. "No, let's keep going with this."

"You sure?"

"Sure. I liked that model A-5. Show me that one again."

"Right. That's the one with pink bunting around the edges," Lou Ann said. And she continued to flip through the pages of the cake catalog and describe the virtues of the various models, but she saw that every so often Rachel would cast a sidelong glance toward John at the counter. She pursed her lips and nodded her head. Lou Ann was a woman. She had eyes to see, and she saw.

☙ ☙ ☙

That night was the annual Sunday School Program at church. Clouds had moved in and snow had begun to fall. As people came to church, they could see the light from inside shining through the stained glass windows and making blurry and beautiful colored patterns on the new-fallen snow. John and Millie came as was their custom, and Rachel too, with her mother, since their farm was close by. As it happened, the church was very full so latecomers had to sit in the balcony—it was one of those old-fashioned horseshoe balconies that went around three sides of the church—and by the time church started John and Rachel were squeezed in tight and seated right next to each other. They smiled and nodded awkwardly, but there was no other place to go except to stand. John helped her with her coat, and as he removed it from her shoulders caught a breath of perfume from between her breasts, and he liked the smell of it and he breathed a deep draft and held it in, then breathed another before slapping himself in the face mentally and snapping out of it.

The old church was decorated with freshly cut pine bunting trimmed with red ribbons and little white lights, and in front was a very large cedar tree, decorated and shining. The air in the church was filled with the fresh pine and cedar smell. When John was a child, he, like every other child, would marvel at the size of the Christmas tree, for it stood from floor to ceiling, and he never could figure how they got it through the tiny front door of the church. But there it was, festooned with chrismons in white and gold, symbols of the faith, the Holy Trinity, the Anchor of Faith, the Dove of the Holy Spirit, the Holy Cross of Our Savior, and red apples to remind us of the Fall, and white lights to remind us that Jesus Christ is the light of the world, and at the very tip-top a beautiful angel in white robes with flowing white hair, announcing peace on earth, goodwill toward men. Best of all, at least as far as the children were concerned, were dozens of brown paper bags filled with candy and nuts. After the program the children would file forward one by one and an elder of the church would give them their bag of candy. Oh, the agony of sitting through the last ten minutes of the service and not being allowed to root around in the bag. John's favorite when he was little were those little orange slices encrusted with granulated sugar that were all chewy when you bit into them and made a big gloppy mess in your mouth but tasted wonderful and fresh. Every single person in church had been a child here once and had gone up for his bag of Christmas candy, and now would watch with the deep satisfaction that only comes with long tradition as his own child, or grandchild, or great-grandchild would now go up for his.

People rustled their bulletins and talked quietly as Myrtle played pre-service music—no fancy prelude, just old familiar hymns. Then the lights dimmed, the congregation hushed, and Melvin Huffnagle's boy Jerry, aged nine, sang from the back of the church in his clear high voice, "Once in royal David's city, stood a lowly cattle shed." With the congregation singing the rest of the carol, the crucifer led the procession, followed by the torchbearers and the thurifer, then the children, each one dressed in red cassock and white surplice, and lastly old Pastor Gottlieb, his body stooped and slow, his face beaming with joy, vested in alb and chasuble, and carrying as the sign of his episcopal office a crosier—not a manufactured piece of ecclesiastical art from a catalog, but a real shepherd's crook he had been given by a real shepherd in the land of Mayangala. It was old and weathered and polished smooth from his hand, and he carried it with the authority of a shepherd who tenderly leads and cares for his flock, but also fiercely drives off any predator that lurks in the near shadows.

The pastor took his seat and nodded to old Mrs. Graumann, the Sunday School Superintendent, who directed the recitation as she had done for the past thirty-seven years. The children, who had been practicing for weeks, would stand up and recite Bible passages in their piping little voices. Again, according to long tradition, this was done in the King James Version (since the German language had been abolished after the First World War). First came the messianic prophecies from the Old Testament. Then the annunciation to the Virgin Mary. And finally Bobby Mestad, the sausage-maker's son, stood up and exclaimed, "And it came to pass in those days, that there went out a decree from Caesar Augustus, that all the world should be taxed," and so on to the end of the passage in Luke chapter two, while other children in bathrobes with towels on their heads would portray the nativity scene. This year they had a real live baby in the manger, for Don and Nancy Vogelsang had had their fifth right before Thanksgiving, and their oldest daughter Lucy was playing the part of Mary and kept the child mollified throughout the service. Not one single woman in the church heard a word of what went on in the service, so focused were they on the baby every time it gurgled or cooed. And Rachel was one of these.

Josiah was among the small children dressed as angels, gathered in adoration around the manger, his dark eyes filled with wonder at the lights and the costumes and the pageant. His eyes were also filled with wonder at the animals, for the farmers had brought in a live donkey and a calf and a sheep and a goat to stand by in the manger scene.

So it went through the sermon and the celebration of the holy Eucharist, and at last came the close of service, the benediction, the lighting of the small, handheld candles, one in each person's hand, and the singing of "Silent Night." Everyone knew it by heart, of course, in both English and German, and by old tradition still sang the first stanza in German. "*Stille nacht, heilige nacht,*" they all began, and as soon as everyone had the pitch the organ dropped off, leaving the congregation singing a capella. Each person's face was aglow from the little candle. The overhead lights were dimmed, and the only light in church was the candlelight and the lights on the Christmas tree, suffusing the little church with a warm glow as the people sang. Then the harmony began, for the Germans are a singing people, and many could read the notes in the hymnal and sing the harmony, and others would just improvise. Among these were John and Rachel in the balcony, his deep, warm voice lifting other voices with support on the rich, low tones, while Rachel's clear alto soared over John in close harmony and a high descant like a glad angel flying in midheaven, and though the two of them were caught up in the moment and unaware, others could hear and would marvel at the sound, and in the nave below, even though they weren't supposed to, some children and even adults turned and looked up to see where this music was coming from. It was coming from a man and a woman who had their eyes closed and no idea what they were doing.

It became warmer a few days later as happens from time to time in Missouri, a state that is not entirely northern, southern, eastern, or western, but borders on all four regions of America in culture and climate. St. Louis looks east with its settled, red-brick German culture and is in many respects very much like Philadelphia, while at the same time being the Gateway to the West by virtue of its place near the great Missouri River, and all St. Louisans have that westerner's itch to see what's over the next hill. Some winters get so cold you can see the northern lights, which you never do in Arkansas or Louisiana to the south. Then in the same winter you can get a breath of warm air coming up from the Gulf of Mexico and you can go outside in your shirtsleeves, which you never do in Iowa or Minnesota to the north. This particular day John was able to go outside wearing a light jacket, Josiah toddling after him. John set up a folding chair on the shore near the dock, baited his hook with a doughball laced with bacon grease, and waited as the ripples slowly widened on the glassy surface and faded away. The heron that was wintering over sailed silently over the water, then up to its ramshackle nest. The woods were still, the squirrels and groundhogs in hibernation. On the far side of the lake a doe tiptoed quietly to the water and drank. Josiah climbed into his lap to watch and wait, and John began to teach him the old nursery rhyme, "Fishy, fishy in the brook, papa caught him with a hook, mama cooked him in the pan, baby ate him like a man." From far away came the sound of an axe. Some good man was gathering wood so that his house would be warm for his wife and children. As always the oak trees retained their leaves. A small breeze came through and rustled the leaves, then passed along, going wherever the wind goes, for the wind has a mind of its own. In the middle of the lake a fish splashed. Then the ripples were gone. After a while the cork bobbed as something nibbled his bait. Then it swam away. Fish are easily distractible. Fish get nervous when they feel tremors coming from the land. That is why fishermen speak quietly and walk softly, so as not to break the fish's naturally weak concentration on the task at hand, namely getting caught. John and his son were keeping the ancient, long-agreed-upon rules between fish and man. But before long John could hear what the fish could sense. Someone was coming up the trail on horseback. Then Doxie came bounding into view, full of excitement and adventure as all dogs are when they're outside. "Gog-gie," squealed Josiah as he squirmed out of John's lap. Doxie trotted up and began to lick Josiah's face, knocking the small child down and making him laugh and laugh. The laughter echoed off the cliff at the far side of the lake as Rachel came into view, sitting erect in the saddle and riding Milton at an easy canter.

"Hi, John," she said as she dismounted and dropped the reins so Milton could graze freely. The horse walked down to the shore and drank as John set the drag on his reel and secured the tackle.

"Hi," he returned. "What brings you by?"

"Oh, you know. Milton needed exercise, and besides the girls needed help getting ahead in the cooking."

"Right. I'd forgotten. That group of coon hunters is coming out this weekend."

"Yes. So there's meat to cut and vegetables to dice and this and that."

"Yes. I guess so," John replied.

"Yes," she said.

"Yes," he said.

They stood for a moment in each other's presence.

"Any luck?" Rachel asked.

"What?" John said, for his mind like a fish's had been wandering.

"Fishing," she said.

"Oh! Oh, no. No. Just a nibble."

"Oh."

"Yes."

They stood for another moment in each other's presence.

"Well, I'd better . . ."/"That was a nice . . . " they both began at the same time, then laughed and each said, "You go ahead, no, you, no, you . . ."

"I was saying, that was a nice service last night," John said.

"Yes."

"Um, you have a really nice voice, Rachel."

"Oh, thanks."

"Yes."

They stood for yet another moment in each other's presence. Doxie was lying down in the grass. Milton was looking at Josiah, who was looking into the water. Both the man and the woman turned away from facing each other and side by side looked toward the lake. Josiah was murmuring to himself as he watched the water.

"I'm singing in the praise band at TD's church now."

"Oh, really," John said. "That's great. I'd like to hear you some time."

"Yes, you should come to our Christmas program."

"When is it?"

"Saturday night. Seven o'clock."

"I'm scheduled to work at the shop that day. Maybe Jasper and I could come together. If you don't mind a couple of grease monkeys."

"No, not at all. We could all go out for pizza afterwards."

"Sure. That would be great," John lied, not overjoyed at the thought of spending any more time than he absolutely had to with TD. He glanced at the dazzling engagement ring on Rachel's finger.

"Well, I'd better get to work. Millie might dock my pay."

"Right," John chuckled. "She's a taskmaster. What in the world is Josiah looking at?"

"Crawdads, probably," Rachel said as they walked down to get him.

"Pishy book, pishy book," they could hear the child saying. As John and Rachel drew near they saw a ripple on the surface of the water as if a fish had turned and swum away back to the deep, but this was a very large ripple, and when they looked into the lake they could see a great cloud in the water where the muddy bottom had been roiled as if by huge fins. But they could see nothing and thought nothing of it, for their mind was on other things. Rachel scooped Josiah into her arms.

"What are you up to, you little stinker?"

The child looked at the woman square in the eye and said, "Mama cook 'im."

"Oh, ha-ha," Rachel laughed. "What a silly boy. I'm not mama..." but the little small boy riding on her hip threw his arms around her and lay his head down upon her shoulder, and something inside of her began to break and weep. But she fought it off as they went inside.

Millie and Miriam were in full swing in the kitchen, yakking away merrily as they banged the pots and pans around and bustled to and fro. The big cookpot was on the stove, full of water and coming to a boil. They had made cornbread muffins, and the cornmeal sack was on the table, along with a brick of butter and the big jar of blackstrap molasses. Rachel set Josiah down in a corner with his toys and went to work on a pile of potatoes that needed peeling. Miriam was at the sink cleaning some utensils that had accumulated, and Millie was cutting meat and browning it in the skillet. It was the old Clubhouse stew recipe they'd made a hundred times, and everyone knew the drill by heart. John went out to the woodpile to fetch more kindling, then remembered his fishing pole. Reeling it in he felt the resistance of a fish on the line, but it was only a small bluegill, too little to fool with. So he removed the hook from its mouth and tossed it back in. As he walked back to the woodpile he cast an idle glance out across the lake. Some movement had caught his eye. He looked again more closely. There was a "V" on the surface of something swimming. At first he thought it was a muskrat, for that is the way they swim, low in the water with their snout sticking out. But this was larger than a muskrat. John stopped and stared. Finally it reached the far shore and clambered out. It was a beaver. As far as he or anyone knew, there had never been one in the Friedensee. He walked rapidly and quietly to the kitchen door, opened it, and called in in a stage whisper, "Hey, guys, come and see this. There's a beaver in the lake!"

Chattering excitely the three women came out, wiping their hands on their aprons, and walked the thirty feet to the lakeshore. Sure enough, there was the beaver at the inlet on the far side where a little stream trickled in, gnawing on a sapling. They watched in awe for a few minutes. Then someone said, "Oh, jeez, what's the baby doing?"

"He was playing in the corner with his toys."

"Yeah, but the hot stove..."

"Right! We'd better get back in there..."

"Yes..."

"Right, let's go..." And off they marched like a small platoon of mothers.

If you had timed it, the women would have only been gone ninety seconds from the time they left the kitchen till the time they returned. But as all parents know, it is truly astonishing what a determined and resourceful child can accomplish in ninety seconds when no grownup is looking. Josiah had squished the butter in his hands, tried to drink molasses out of the jar, spilled it all over his face and down his clothes, then covered the entire mess with a thick layer of fine, powdery cornmeal. It was truly a sight to behold.

Rachel was first in the door.

"Hey, you little..." she yelled in shock and anger, startling the child. "What have you done? Look at this mess!" She grabbed the child and jerked him away from the table, giving him a swat on the behind. The spanking did little material damage, the child's bottom protected as it was by denim overalls with a diaper underneath. But Josiah reacted instinctively to a large angry woman being upset with him and began to cry. Millie and Miriam of course had been in this situation scores of times with numerous children over many years, and began rapidly to take things in hand, pouring water for a bath in the sink. John, who like Rachel was young and unused to children, also reacted in anger. But he was angry at Rachel.

"Hey, listen! Lay off! What the... what are you doing, yelling at the kid and making him cry."

"Well, look what he did," she replied sharply.

"I don't care what he did. That doesn't give you the right to blow your stack like that."

"Look, we had everything organized, nice and neat," Rachel shot back. "And he comes along and makes this huge mess."

"He's just a little kid, for God's sake. That's what kids do."

"Well, he shouldn't have done it. Why weren't you watching him?"

"I was getting firewood. Why weren't you watching him?"

"You made me look at that stupid beaver in the lake."

"So?"

"Well?"

Then Miriam was at their side. "Stop squabbling, you two," she said in a matter-of-fact way, and handed Rachel a broom and John a mop. The young man and the young woman worked at their tasks in fuming silence. Millie and Miriam were at the sink, cleaning up the baby, and as they worked they shot each other a sidelong glance like women do when they are reading each other's minds, and shook their heads ever so slightly. After a while John, still in his anger, went outside and threw the football at the tire swing, again and again and again.

Chapter 9 ◉ O Tannenbaum

New York City in winter is the most marvelous place. Night falls early but it makes no difference; the city is filled with light. It is filled with light even more than at other times, for to the glare and dazzle of Broadway are added the glitter of festooned Christmas decorations. Evergreen bunting is draped from buildings, light poles are wrapped in ribbon to look like candy canes, and all the great stores—Macy's, Saks Fifth Avenue—have their windows decorated with Christmas displays. Parents bring children to marvel, as they marveled when they were children, at the tableaux. In one window is Santa's work shop complete with little elves raising and lowering their hammers, in another is a winter scene with an elaborate toy train set running all through it. Good old New York. At this time of the year you see that it never forgot its Dutch Protestant roots. No American can help falling in love with the town.

But Rafael von Päpinghausen was not American and certainly not Christian. To his mind and as he had been taught, New York represented the distilled essence of everything that was evil about the West. The place was controlled by Jews, and there were more of them here than in Israel. Jews—they were the ones who had resisted the Prophet (peace be upon him) when he fled Mecca and established an Islamic government in Medina. Muhammad (peace be upon him) was right to put them to death and sell their women and children into slavery. And the Christians—they were the ones who in the Crusades had plundered Muslim lands. And here was this abomination of New York City with all its wealth, a place where Christians and Jews worked side by side to oppress the Muslims of the world, extracting the oil while injecting in its place Western ideas like women's liberation. And what hypocrites these Christians were! They build these skyscrapers as monuments to commerce but then they tolerate such filth as XXX porno shops. Every good Muslim looking at this excess and dissipation felt the wrath of Allah rise up in him and with it the passionate desire to smash it all to the ground. How satisfying it was to see what the martyrs had achieved at the World Trade Center. They had destroyed like avenging angels. They had brought the Great Satan to its knees.

And here am I, said Rafael to himself, one of the last of the ancient order of the Janissaries, on a mission for the faith. Nothing so dramatic as flying airplanes into buildings, but important to the world triumph of Islam nonetheless. For as long as an heir to the throne of Mayangala lives, the stability of the Islamic government there is in jeopardy, and Mayangala was strategically located, politically critical, and rich in natural resources. If it overthrew Sharia and went Western, other nations would be inspired to do the same. Moreover, there were rumors of uranium in the mountains. He was just one man working alone. In his mind he was like the righteous warriors that King Herod sent out to kill the presumptive heir to the throne of Israel. It's the least I can do to kill the child of Elizabeth and his father, the infidel John Mason.

But first Rafael needed help. His wounded hand was excruciatingly painful and slow to heal. It was not just constant pain; one could bear that. It was not just severe pain; one could endure that. This was constant severe pain, and it was driving him crazy. He needed medicine and plenty of it. He was taking more and more of the Darvocet. The increased dosage would work for a while, then level off. And the pain came back. The pain was dreadful, and when the medicine was working even the thought of the pain that he had experienced and the pain that would come back if he didn't get more medicine obsessed him day and night. So he contacted one of the Prince's support groups. They put him in contact with a Wahhabist doctor who gave him the pills he needed. The doctor was surprised to see a big strapping blonde German come in to the office after speaking perfect Arabic with him over the phone. They talked for a long time. All Muslims are brothers and equals, no matter what their race or country. The doctor invited him over to his apartment for dinner along with the men in his group. Together they prayed. Together they recited. Together they broke bread.

One of the men brought some powerful hashish, laced with Afghani opium. They all smoked and reveled in the glories of the old Muslim world, where hashish-smoking men would go forth and secretly kill their enemies: the *hashishim*, the assassins. Hashish was wonderful. It gave a man confidence and courage. This, combined with the chronic overdose of pain medicine, gave Rafael a whole new lease on life. He felt like he could jump out the window and fly. Instead he suggested they go for a drive in his Aston Martin, the sleek, silver sedan he had picked up from the docks the day before. The four of them trooped down the stairs and tumbled into the car. As Rafael started up the car he gunned the engine and the throaty roar shouted and echoed in the parking garage. The men all shouted in approval as well. Rafael dropped it into reverse, gunned the engine, and backed out, straight into the side door of a big black Mercedes.

"Camel excrement!" said Rafael in Arabic.

The boys began to laugh.

"What do we do now?" one of the men asked.

"Forget it," said the doctor. "I know that car. It belongs to a Jew."

Then they all laughed hysterically and drove off into the night in Rafael's car with its crumpled rear fender and broken taillight. They drove all around Manhattan, in their imaginations blowing up everything they saw. They blew up the Statue of Liberty. They blew up Wall Street. They blew up the Brooklyn Bridge. They blew some more hashish, and then some more. And at last they blew into an all-night sex club and sat in the front row, drinking scotch and stuffing dollar bills into the panties of the dancers. Ordinary good Muslims were not supposed to do this, of course, but these men were special, entitled to privileges just like Muhammad Atta and the heroes of September 11, who had gone to the strip clubs the night before their deaths.

There was a hotel. It was in Dubai, where even the beggars wear Armani suits and Gucci shoes, or so it seemed, at an exclusive resort hotel that catered to Islamic military men and their guests. Rafael had graduated top of his class at the academy in Riyadh, and was rewarded with a weeks' R&R. On the ground floor, in a very small room. But the opulence of Dubai, the finest foods, the extravagance of the hotel, the swimming pool, the golf course, the polo grounds, plus the congenial company of fellow Muslim brothers from all over the world, from big black Somalis to tiny Thai kickboxers who were reputed to be the toughest of the tough, as one Arabian black belt karate expert found out to his shame and regret. (The hotel covered the orthodontist's bill.)

It was a heady time, a time of pure devotion. He was young, he was filled with fire and passion for the Crescent. Soon he would go on his first Hajj. He fought the inner jihad for purity of mind and body. He fought the outer jihad and completed assignments with finesse during his undergraduate days on weekends and holidays when others were rowing or playing rugby. Big and blonde, charming and disarming, he could go anywhere in Western Europe or Great Britain and fit right in. No one suspected; everyone trusted.

Word got back to him through the grapevine that the higher-ups, those who occupied the upper floors, maybe even the penthouse, were talking about him with approval. He was marked. He was anointed. Bigger and better things were expected of him. A shot of 100-proof vanity went straight to his head, but he placed it with all his other faults in the struggle of inner jihad.

◎ ◎ ◎

TD was back in St. Louis to meet with Ben and Frank Laclede. He had worked out a loan with their father at Laclede Savings and Loan for the $1.5 million, but with everything he had on the line as collateral, now he was having trouble making the loan payments. It was the classic cash-flow problem: plenty of tangible assets, but no ready cash. Even with a 4 percent ARM, the payment was pretty stiff.

And it was going to be at least a year until the construction could be completed and they'd get some income flowing from the resort. Plus, Rachel had not given him a definite date for the wedding yet. He needed to nail that down, as well as negotiate for more favorable repayment terms. Never let 'em see you sweat, was the old business mantra. But TD was getting just a little moist on the brow.

The winter warm spell that had allowed John to go fishing with his son had brought out all the golfers in St. Louis for a winter round. The Lacledes were charter members of the Algonquin Golf Club, one of the area's oldest and toniest clubs, located on Berry Road between upscale Glendale and exclusive Webster Groves. Like all things associated with the rich and powerful, it was understated. There were no gilt chandeliers in the lobby, no liveried servants, no ostentation. The men and women who golfed there drove their own cars and toted their own bags, using the caddies mostly for advice on the lay of the fairway and green, club selection, that sort of thing. They all knew each other, as had their parents and grandparents, and, in the case of the Lacledes, for generations past going back to the founding of St. Louis in the eighteenth century. They had gone to school together at Clayton or Ladue high, or private schools like Country Day or Burroughs, and college at Princeton or Yale. They were Episcopalians and Presbyterians. They knew Lutherans like TD, but only as employees, not as equals and colleagues. They had an easy camaraderie in the locker room and the clubhouse, and made deals over drinks in the bar after nine or eighteen holes. Their daughters were debutantes, presented yearly at the Veiled Prophet Ball, and after college these girls married the sons of these approved families, and the closed circle continued, generation after generation, assuring the long-term stability of St. Louis society.

TD was an outsider trying to break in, and he must not under any circumstances let them see him sweat. Frank and Ben had suggested a round of golf when he had called to say he needed to talk to them as soon as possible. TD was in a hurry, because he was rapidly becoming strapped for cash, but they never were. Like all moneyed people, there was never any rush, for time is money and when there is plenty of money there is plenty of time. Time even for golf, which costs a lot of money and takes a lot of time. TD had bought a set of Pings, which he couldn't afford, and a box of Titleist balls, and Allen Edmonds golf shoes, and a Tiger Woods golf shirt and slacks, only to find Frank and Ben in jeans and tennis shoes, wearing ratty old Izod shirts, and dragging around crummy bags of Wilson clubs they'd bought cheap at a re-sale shop in Maplewood. TD had been practicing for a week, trying to get ready for this thing. How hard could this be, he had told himself. The ball is sitting still right on the ground. It's not like trying to hit a fastball, or connect with a receiver downfield who is running as fast as he can while you have two linebackers coming at you on a blitz package. On the driving range he felt like he was getting the hang of it pretty well. But nerves can do funny things to you. TD didn't care about golf, but he cared about money. Really cared. And he had to have some concessions from old man Laclede on the loan repayment. The first hole was a par three. On the tee, Frank and Ben hit decent but mediocre drives about a hundred yards down the fairway. TD sliced his first shot into the rough. The boys said call it a mulligan. Then TD sliced his second shot into the rough. They gave him another mulligan. On the third try he jerked his head up and lofted a high shot into the water hazard. Yet another mulligan. This was getting serious. The damn ball was just sitting there on its little white stool, mocking him, and he was piling up more mulligans than Bill Clinton. Bringing all his concentration to bear, TD uttered a desperate prayer and swung at the stupid ball. This time he topped it and launched a worm-burner. Thank God it was on the fairway and the game was on. But when would he be able to broach the subject of the loan?

First he had to suffer through this aggravating game. Frank and Ben were way ahead of him and he was left to his own devices on club selection. How the hell were you supposed to hit it when it was lying on the ground? Why couldn't you tee it up for a long fairway shot? With no idea whatsoever what he was doing he pulled a 3-wood out of his bag and took a hack at the ball. He topped it again. He swore again. By this time he was even with Frank and Ben. He watched them. They swung easily, as easily as if they'd been doing this their whole lives, which in fact they had. Their club head went through the lie and let the angle loft the ball as it sliced up a divot ahead of where the ball had lain. So that was it.

"I'm new at this," said TD.

"So I see," said Frank.

"What club should I use?"

"It's still a long way to the green. Try a three-iron."

"OK."

There was a hill in front of them, but they could just see the flag of the first green. TD pulled out the 3-iron and took a practice swing or two.

"Keep your head down," said Ben. "We'll spot the ball for you."

"OK." TD swung, aiming for a spot ahead of the ball, and followed through. Then he looked up. The stupid ball was arcing beautifully up into the air and straight for the pin. A surge of joy went through him, from toe to crown, and he exclaimed to himself, by God, this is a wonderful game. I can do this. I feel like a million bucks.

"Good shot, TD," Frank called to him as they walked ahead.

"You're getting the hang of it," added Ben.

"Thanks, guys," TD replied, striding on with his chest out and his chin high. Yes, sir, golf was a great game. A game for men.

As they approached the green they scanned the ground for their balls. Frank and Ben of course had an assortment of odd balls they had bought in a grocery bag from the skin diver who fished them out of the water hazard. It was easy to spot them, for Frank put a red "X" on his ball and Ben put a blue "X" on his. Ben was on the green, about twenty feet from the cup. Frank had overshot the green but not by much. He was just on the lip, and decided to go with his putter.

"Anybody see my ball?" TD asked.

"It's the Titleist, right? Look in the bunker," said Ben.

"OK."

TD looked. There it was, smirking at him.

"Use your pitching wedge," Ben said, and stood back for TD to make his shot. Now what did the book say? Were you supposed to shoot off your front foot or back foot? Now his forehead was moist again. He tried the front foot. No luck. Back foot. No luck. Center. The ball struggled up to the lip of the sand trap, then rolled back down to exactly where it was before.

"Just toss it up and charge yourself a shot," Ben said.

"OK." Embarrassed, TD pitched the ball out and onto the green.

"Go ahead, Frank," Ben said. "You're the farthest from the pin."

Frank tapped the ball with his putter. It bobbled its way over the grass onto the green, then took a smooth trajectory toward the pin, stopping about four feet short.

"Good!" said Ben, as he squared up to his ball. He looked up, looked down, looked up, looked down, took a practice swing, looked up, looked down ... waited ... waited ... took a breath ... waited ... then swung. TD watched with satisfaction as the ball swung way off to the right, then watched with dismay as the shape of the green guided the ball back again and brought it right down into the cup with an arrogant rattle.

"Good shot," said Frank and TD. Ben just nodded smugly and confidently. Par. He'd been doing this all his life.

Frank tapped in for a four. Now it was TD's turn. He had noted the lie of the green, though his ball was further to the left of Ben's. He had a beautiful putter, not that it did him any good. He hit too hard, and the ball ran way over to the far side of the green. He swore. Ben and Frank waited patiently as TD stomped over to address the ball again. This time he hit short, but only three feet from the pin. Easy, he said to himself. We'll see about that, said the ball. He squared up ... waited ... took a breath ... then swung gently. The ball dribbled forward straight toward the hole, then gleefully swung round the lip of the cup and out away to the side. TD swore.

"Tough luck," said Frank, who was keeping score. "We'll call it a gimme. What do you have, TD?"

"Six," he lied. He wasn't sure, but it was probably closer to twelve.

And so it went for the rest of the day. Hit the ball. Swear. Hit the ball. Swear. Hit the ball. Swear. Up and down the hills, round and round the course. The trio would be together for a few minutes on the tee and later on the green, but in between TD was all over the fairway or in the rough, hacking away and swearing. TD became more and more distraught, for there never seemed to be a propitious time for him to advance his plea for clemency on the loan. So with each stroke and each swear word the tension mounted. At last they were in the clubhouse. Loser picks up the tab, the boys said, so once again TD was going to be stuck with the bill. They had a beer to slake their thirst, then Ben and Frank transitioned to martinis. TD had learned his lesson the last time, though, and stuck with beer, sipping slowly to keep his head. To keep the cost down for himself he ordered a burger with onion rings. Frank had the cordon bleu, and Ben, who as usual had won, enjoyed the beef Wellington, a house specialty, washing it down with a bottle of very good and very expensive Alexander Valley Cabernet Sauvignon. The boys wore cheap clothes and swung cheap clubs, but they spared no expense at the table. TD was mentally toting up the tab. It was going to be over a hundred once again. Plus gas had gone up again and that Mercedes really went through it, especially running back and forth between Ste. Gen and St. Louis. Maybe he could sell that set of Pings. He'd only used them once.

"Listen, guys," TD said at last, cursing the moisture that had once again broken out on his brow, "I was wondering if we could talk about my loan with your father."

Ben took out his victory cigar, a Cuban H. Upmann. He had taken his private plane up to Canada, bought a whole box of them, and smuggled them back in. It was easy. He had an understanding with the mechanic at the hangar. He slipped the mechanic a few hundred bucks, the mechanic got the cigars and stashed them under the plane with duct tape, kept the change, and Ben's immaculate hands never touched the contraband. If customs found them, he had no idea where they came from. No fingerprints. *No problemo.* Ben clipped the end, removed the band, moistened the cigar with his tongue, and lit it, carefully keeping the flame an inch below the tip of the cigar. He took a big drag, then let it out. The smoke swirled round his head, TD thought for an instant, as if it were the sulfurous fumes of Hades that enveloped the devil. But in this case it was the benign face of an old college chum, and the aroma of the cigar was wonderful. Ben nodded his head and smiled at TD, surely a good sign.

"Yes, we're concerned about that, too," Ben said as he glanced at Frank. "We talked to Pop about that yesterday. Your last payment was fifteen days overdue. That's why we wanted to get together and iron things out."

"Right," TD responded, his hopes rising, "the real estate market has been a bit slow lately, and the cash flow isn't where it should be. This is just seasonal, though," he lied, as easily and fluently as he did about his golf score. "It always picks up after the first of the year." The truth was that since the Japanese auto parts factory in Perryville shut down two months ago, there was a glut of homes on the market, and the few that sold went for rock-bottom prices. But Frank and Ben and old man Laclede wouldn't know this. This was poker. He had been dealt a lousy hand. But he could bluff his way out of it.

Frank and Ben gazed at him steadily. Damn that moisture on my brow, TD thought. Too much exertion on the golf course. Swing more easily next time. If there was a next time. Then Frank spoke up. "You have to make those payments, TD. This is business. No hard feelings, you understand. Nothing personal. Just like in sports. You play by the rules. When you get hit, you get up and try again. You know how it is."

"Yes, yes," TD said weakly, the bluff gone out of him.

"However," Ben put in with a smile, "Pop was very understanding and offered a bridging loan to tide you over until things pick up again for you. Same rate of interest, which I have to say is very generous on his part, and of course the amount will be added to the principal. How's that sound?"

How did it sound? It sounded like a death knell. He was in debt. They were offering him increased debt to help him make payments on the existing debt. He couldn't make payments on the loan he had, and now they were oh-so-kindly helping him to take out yet another loan. But he had no choice. He had wanted a ninety-day grace period on loan repayment, to be made up on the back end. But no soap. These were college chums, but when it came to business, they were heartless. So he agreed to the bridging loan—they'd fax him the forms—and he shook hands and dragged himself back to his car, paying the bill on the way out. He slumped into the leather seat and sat for a moment, staring straight ahead. He didn't puke this time, but he felt sick all over nonetheless.

That night was the community interfaith Christmas service, and this year it was being hosted by Pastor Dave's church. After driving back from St. Louis, TD went directly over to the farm and picked up Rachel. They needed to get to church early for sound check and to run through their pieces one last time.

"Honey," he said to her as they stopped at McDonald's for a quick bite, "I hope you don't mind me bringing this up again, but I sure wish we could settle on a date for our wedding. I don't want to pressure you or anything, but here it is Christmas already and my calendar is getting filled up. There's the national realtor's conference in Phoenix in February, and in March is the Elks Club convention in Orlando. Each of those takes me out a whole week, and I have to rearrange everything here at home to make room on my calendar, and when I get back from these deals I'm swamped with paperwork and phone calls and . . . well, it just gets crazy. And the only thing I want to be crazy about right now is you."

He fixed her with those penetrating blue eyes of his. She looked him over. What a good-looking guy. His new toupee was really nice. Who knows what he must have paid for it? Unless you already knew you could hardly tell it was fake. Plus here it was winter and he was still tan. Must be the golf he's taken up. He'd said that he was going up to St. Louis for a golf date with some business partners. How impressive it all was. The Mercedes. The Pings—even she knew enough to know they were the best. The classy golf clothes. TD was just a good solid guy on top of his game, successful in every imaginable way. She wasn't head over heels for him, but at her age and with her experiences, well, women took a more analytical approach to these things, more like sizing up a business opportunity. He would do nicely. Plus, they had a lot in common. Music, for one thing. He really did play pretty good guitar in the praise band. And she enjoyed the new kind of music. Even though for some vague reason she felt a little uncomfortable around Pastor Dave. He had a way of looking at you, a kind of leer ... it was hard to perceive, but you just caught a glimpse of it once in a while out of the corner of your eye. And sports, for another. TD was a football player. She was a swimmer. Neither did either competitively any more, but there were lots of physical things they could try together. Golf. Tennis. Racquetball. He was in good shape. He worked out. There was an aggressive, animal presence about him. She could smell it underneath the expensive cologne. She liked it. It turned her on. They had made out a few times at his place. She was careful not to let it go too far. She had made that mistake in the past. She didn't want to repeat it. Still, it felt good to feel good, to be sexually aroused, to get that female motor turned on, to see that she still had what it takes to drive a man crazy. This guy would be amazing in bed. She liked his size, the hardness of him, the flat stomach, the narrow waist, the tight buns. She thought about it and stroked her chin. Sure, why not? Mother would just have to cope, that's all.

"OK, big boy," Rachel said, looking him square in the eye. "Let's do it. Some time in Spring. Maybe around Easter time. I always like it in early Spring when the redbuds and the dogwoods are in bloom."

"Terrific," TD said, then stretched across the table to kiss her. Oh, thank God, he thought, this solves a million problems. I can start lining up contractors and architects. It will take at least four months to arrange all that, plus the wedding, the guest list, the reception, a million details to look after. He whipped out his PDA. "Let's see ... how does the Saturday before Easter sound?"

"Works for me," she said. "Sounds good." Of course it was good. Any day was good. That was the whole problem. She'd ended up in one of life's little dead ends, babysitting her depressed mother, and doing odd jobs at the Clubhouse just to have something to do. At least when she and TD were married she'd be involved in the whirl of his business interests.

"OK," TD said, marking the date with his stylus, "Let's go with it." Then he glanced at his watch. "Yikes, we need to get a move on. Dave gets cranky when the band doesn't show up on time."

They walked out to the car with their arms around each other. He held the door for her as he always did. But before she got in he swept her into his arms and kissed her hard and passionately. She liked it. She kissed him back. They kissed a long time. They were getting turned on.

"Oh, baby," TD panted, "I love you so much."

"I love you too, big boy. Whew! Now drive me to church before I rip your clothes off right here in the parking lot."

He stood there a moment longer.

"Come on, let's go," she said.

Then he said, "I think I'd rather stay and get my clothes ripped off."

She laughed and biffed him on the arm, then jumped in. The sun was going down as they sped off.

They needn't have worried. They arrived in plenty of time. Though already dark outside, it was only 6 P.M., and the service didn't start until 7:30. The wide, clean, well-lighted parking lot was open and inviting. In half an hour it would start to fill, but now there were plenty of spaces. TD and Rachel parked in the back of the lot as instructed, for the first twenty-five spots right next to the entrance were reserved for visitors. They were always taken, for the Community Church had a steady stream of visitors. Visitors were its lifeblood, for the church had a specific growth goal of 15 percent per annum. Like any well-run business the church had a marketing strategy. Billboards along Interstate 55, radio spots, TV commercials, print media . . . the Community Church used them all, and to good effect. For they had a system, and the system was built on proven theories of mass marketing and the sociology of group dynamics. Pastor Dave had a D. Min. in Church Marketing from the Fuller Seminary in Pasadena, where he had actually studied with Win Arn and Donald McGavran and C. Peter Wagner and Lyle Schaller, the gurus of the Church Growth Movement. He had learned from guest lectures by Joel Osteen and Bill Hybels and Rick Warren, pastors of megachurches that were drawing five, ten, even fifteen thousand attendees to services per weekend. These were the men who had written the book on attracting large numbers of worshippers. And what they all stressed was the importance of the parking lot to the prospective worshipper. Put yourself in the consumer's shoes, they would say, or rather car. His first real experience of your church begins with the parking lot. What if it's too small and he can't find a space? What if he has to park way in the back and it's raining? What if it's dirty and unswept and the pavement is cracked and chipped? He's going to drive right away from there, and you'll never have a chance to reach out to him because he didn't even come in the door. In fact, you'll never even know he was a prospect. The first-time visitor has absolutely got to find a good parking spot within fifty feet of the entrance. Parking, parking, parking. The Gospel begins with parking.

Of course Hybels was in suburban Chicago and Warren was in suburban L.A. and Osteen was in suburban Houston, while Pastor Dave was in little old Ste. Genevieve, Missouri, population 4,476. A weekend church attendance of even 2,000 would take away all the attendees from all the other churches in town. It was statistically impossible. But Pastor Dave was committed to Church Growth Principles, and he was transforming this historically Lutheran parish right before your eyes. He had staffed for growth, adding a youth pastor and a small groups coordinator. He had built in anticipation of growth, adding the new worship center with the attractive parking lot. A lot of the older members had been upset when he tore down the old brick church building they had grown up in. But Church Growth Principles dictated that in order to grow, a certain percentage of hidebound traditionalists had to go. And tearing down a traditional building was a sure-fire way of antagonizing them and forcing them out. A group of them had made the exodus together two years before. Some of them were even driving all the way to Gottlieb's church, where the old ways continued. But that was fine. They had to be leveraged out in order to make way for progress. Besides, they always parked close to the entrance and even took up visitors' parking spaces in open defiance of Church Growth Principles. So Community Church was well rid of them.

The only concern was that this bunch of traditionalists were generous givers. The weekly offering had really taken a hit when they left. Cash flow was an ongoing problem on a month-to-month basis. How were they going to make budget and meet payroll? All that advertising was costing a mint. And the mortgage! They had missed a couple of payments. Even though they had taken a loan on very favorable terms with the denomination's own internal lending program, they were finding that the powers-that-be in St. Louis could get pretty stern when it looked like you were going to default. Although Pastor Dave was having success—he had doubled church attendance from what it had been, and it was now averaging over 500 per weekend—he was seriously overextended, since all those new visitors he was attracting were coming for the free coffee and donuts (there was yet another expense) and were putting a dollar in the offering plate or nothing at all.

TD and Rachel grabbed their guitars and entered the lobby. It was decorated with a Christmas tree and sprigs of holly everywhere, ribbons and bows all green and red, and pleasant Christmas music—the kind you hear piped through the sound system at the mall—played unobtrusively in the background. Rachel caught a refrain of "Frosty, the Snowman" with lush strings and glockenspiel. She felt immediately comfortable as she always did when she came to Community Church, and just now it began to dawn on her why she did. Community Church felt like the mall. It was neutral. It was bland. It was inoffensive. It was appealing. It was welcoming. It was a place where the consumer was catered to, and never challenged with either sin or grace. And with that realization a flicker of doubt crossed her brow like a mosquito, but she brushed it away.

Inside the worship center, a big Christmas tree with false presents underneath was set up on stage right. Onstage there was no altar and no cross, but a lectern in the center with a potted plant on either side from which Pastor Dave delivered his messages, or rather began to deliver his messages, for he paced to and fro like a tiger when he preached, and often leaped off the stage and went up the aisle like a TV talk show host. Indeed, it was Pastor Dave's messages that drove the engine of Community Church, for he told people what they needed to know about life. He had learned from St. Louis's own Joyce Meyer—an ex-Lutheran—that people don't want doctrine, they want somebody to tell them how to live. And so his messages were relevant. He addressed people's felt needs: how to manage your money, how to get along with your kids, how to get over a bumpy spot in your marriage, how to be successful. Visualize and Actualize. Plan Your Work and Work Your Plan. If It Is To Be, It Is Up to Me. And as a result, he was successful. People were flocking to hear his messages. Even successful people like TD. And people like Rachel who were failures but wanted desperately to succeed.

At stage left was the setup for the praise band. The members were just arriving, unpacking instruments, tuning up, running through riffs, singing into the microphones, doing the messy, chaotic, yet purposeful things that musicians do before producing wonderful things in performance. Pastor Dave was already there with them, giving last-minute instructions to the lead singer. TD and Rachel joined them. As she bent over to get her guitar out of its case, she had that intuition that you get when you sense that someone is looking at you. She glanced quickly around. It was Pastor Dave, admiring her behind. This time the flicker of doubt was stronger, for she had felt this before. But it got lost in the flurry of activity as the band set up and tuned up and stood up and ran through its numbers quickly. For people were beginning to arrive, and among the first who came and who sat on the front row were John and Josiah and Miriam and Millie. Rachel smiled and waved, and they returned the greeting.

Finally everything was ready, and the band went into its uptempo pre-service music, a peppy chorus to get the consumers into the mood to buy the product, the product being increased attendance at Community Church, for the business plan for that year had the goal of exceeding six hundred in worship per weekend. Pastor Dave had written new songs for the Community Christmas Service, and this one had only one word: "Jesus," repeated by the girl singers over and over again to a thumping back beat from the drums and bass, above which the lead guitar wailed, smashing power chords right with the beat. They had hired a professional from a St. Louis blues band, and when he whipped out the bottleneck slide and began doing blues licks, the audience went nuts. They were clapping and stomping and whistling and standing and dancing and waving their arms.

After about fifteen minutes of this it was time to turn the temperature down to a simmer. The sociology of Church Growth had ascertained through scientific study of audience response that the unchurched consumer was more receptive to spiritual things if he was first aroused through heavy rock music, then sedated with a soft Seventies rock sound. So now the band turned down the volume and shut off the overdrive on the amps, and began vamping on some nice major seventh chords. Here is where Rachel had her solo. She stepped up to the mike and closed her eyes and began to sing:

> I love you so.
> You're my everything.
> I'd do anything for you.
> You make me so happy.
> I just want to be with you all the time.
> You're the world to me.
> I love you so.

Rachel was praising God, she was in the Spirit, she was singing to the Lord with her eyes closed. The audience was on its feet, singing along to the lyrics on the overhead screen and gently rocking to and fro. She sang the chorus three or four times and was really feeling it, when for some reason she opened her eyes and looked at the audience, and there she saw John on the front row as she sang, "I love you so." And she squirmed inside and tried to get away for she had said something accidentally true, even though John was sitting and glaring at the neutral carpet in front of him.

John for his part was fuming and trying to burn a hole in the carpet with his eyes, for to him this was not church, this was ... what was it? A rock concert? And not even a genuine rock concert at that. Rock music was about sex. And drugs. And rebellion. And here this music was being imported into the house of God. Except this place didn't seem like the house of God. It was more of an entertainment center. It was all so ... so worldly. If a man from Mars walked in he'd never know it was supposed to be a church. John was feeling more and more agitated. He felt like walking out, but he had Josiah in his lap and the two women with him, so he hesitated a moment, then a moment longer, and just when he was about to make up his mind to leave, Pastor Dave stepped up to the microphone.

"Good evening, ladies and gentlemen!" he said with that professional smile. His teeth were white and perfect. Dave was smiling, but inside he was tied up in knots. Attendance was down. He had expected the house to be packed tonight, but while attendance was respectable there were big gaps in the seating, and lots of people were way in the back—typical Lutherans—and the place didn't have the energy a large crowd created. It was next to impossible to really get people whipped up when attendance was down. Plus the mortgage was overdue again, St. Louis was getting hostile, and the elders and he had been counting on a large offering from this service to help meet their budget goals. But Dave was a trouper. Like all good thespians, he knew that whatever the circumstances, the show must go on. So he grinned even bigger. "Welcome to our Community Church Christmas Special! We're so glad to be hosting here at our church this year, in the ecumenical spirit of the times, for we know that whatever our differences we all worship the same God, ain't that right?" He began to clap his hands, and the audience began clapping as well. Dave was gratified by the response, for the applause was strong and warm. He looked around. There was John Mason, scowling. But behind him was Jason Silverstein, the Reformed rabbi, and next to him was Brooks Abernathy, the Unitarian minister—a Harvard man, too—and next to him was Muhammad al Fayid, the imam from the new mosque, and next to him was Abimelech Parcell, leader of the commune on the old Gottlieb place, and they all were beaming, as was JJ Kolding, who was sitting with them. They had brought members of their congregations. They were all active members of the local clergy association. They were all committed to the principle of brotherly love and mutual understanding that Jesus came into this world to teach. This gave Pastor Dave that shot of energy he needed.

"In the spirit of this festive occasion," he said, "I'd like the children to come forward to hear the Christmas message."

So the kids began trooping forward up to and onto the stage while

Pastor Dave sat down on a low stool next to the Christmas tree. Next to him was a big box, wrapped in gold foil and tied with an enormous red ribbon. Josiah had wriggled free from John's lap and joined the throng of children sitting in a big semicircle in front of Pastor Dave. One child began to cry and had to be fetched by his mother. Another stood to the side and made faces at the audience.

"Hi, kids!" said Pastor Dave. "What do you think I have in this box?"

"Presents, presents!" they all chimed in.

"That's right," said Pastor Dave. "I have presents in this box. But I have a very special present in here. Can you guess what it is?"

"Candy!" said one child.

"Toys!" said another.

"No," said Pastor Dave. "It's not candy." The children moaned.

"And it's not toys." The children moaned again.

"Its something far better than toys or candy."

The children went "Oooo."

"Can anybody think what it might be?"

There was a long pause. Then a six-year-old boy blurted out, "A .38 caliber Smith and Wesson semi-automatic!" The audience laughed loud and long. Excellent, Dave thought, just the thing to bring them into it. Now he had them.

He smiled a professional smile and laughed a professional laugh. "No, kids, it's not candy. And it's not toys. And it's not a gun. It's something far better, OK?" And at this he began to tear off the paper and remove the lid from the box. He reached inside and pulled out a Christmas tree ornament. But instead of a common, ordinary globe, this one was made in the shape of a heart and had the word "LOVE" painted on it in big letters. "In this box we have the gift of love. For here is what I want you to remember. The Bible says that God is love, OK? And in this Christmas season we need to remember that we should love one another, as Jesus told us to do. But when we receive love, we must pass it on. So I'm going to give each of you one of these ornaments, and I want you to go hang it on the Christmas tree, and then go back to your seats, OK?"

And he gave an ornament to the child nearest him, a little girl, and she hung it on the tree and went back to her mother. And then he gave an ornament to the next child, and the next, and the next, and so on down the line, and each child hung his ornament on the tree. And as luck would have it the last child was little Josiah, his eyes filled with wonder. And he received the ornament with great joy, and walked reverently over to the tree, which by now was festooned with ornaments of love. Except for one problem. All the children were small, as children are, and they had all hung their ornaments low on the tree, and they had all hung them on the same side of the tree. So when Josiah hung his ornament on a branch of the tree and stepped back to take a look at his handiwork, and as Pastor Dave looked on, helpless and aghast, the tree from the weight of all the ornaments began slowly to list over to its left, then wobble, then creak, and finally come crashing to the ground, breaking every single ornament as Josiah and all the children began to cry at the top of their lungs in shock and horror at the Christmas debacle, for all the love had been smashed to pieces.

That was it for John. All the parents of small children went to the clean, well-lighted cry room to settle down their children and John went with them. But the other parents went back in to hear Pastor Dave's sermon, leaving the kids in the nursery. John stayed in the lobby and let Josiah toddle around. But John could hear every word of the sermon, for it was piped in to the lobby over the speaker system. The sermon was the same as the children's message. Love, love, love. After the sermon Miriam and Millie, seeing that he had not come back in, slipped out and joined him, and they all went home.

The next day Rachel came over and sat with the women, drinking coffee and making small talk. When John came in for a refill he gave Rachel an awkward hello. Millie and Miriam gave each other another one of those looks and conveniently remembered that they had to take Josiah into town and get some more diapers at Walmart. That left the man and the woman alone with each other, sitting across from each other at the old kitchen table, staring into their coffee mugs. John had been up early that day to chop wood. Rachel could tell by the way he smelled. The top button of his flannel shirt was open. She could see the hair on his chest. She could smell the musky odor of man-sweat and wood smoke and the outdoors. He had not shaved, and there was a manly stubble on his chin. She envisioned him swinging that big axe, splitting those pieces of wood with power and masculine authority. She touched her engagement ring and held on to it. John could smell Rachel. A womanly fragrance wafted over to him. Though she was dressed in jeans and a turtleneck, she may as well have had on an evening gown, for she had showered and shampooed, and those faint pleasant smells combined elegantly with a little touch of perfume she had dabbed on without thinking, though normally she wouldn't have for a trip to the Clubhouse. Her hair looked soft and inviting. She was letting it grow out. It would be so nice to bury his face in it . . . but he snapped himself out of it. He was still fuming about last night.

"More coffee?" she asked.

"Thanks," he replied.

She fetched the old porcelain coffee pot from the stove and poured them both another cup.

"Biscuit?"

"Mm."

She brought him the last leftover biscuit from breakfast. He pried it open ever so gently and spread the soft creamy butter all around its soft insides, then dribbled on sweet dark molasses, then picked it up ever so gently in his strong hands. Then so quickly and ravenously it startled her he wolfed it down in two bites. He took a sip or two of the strong black coffee and looked at her with those penetrating eyes of his. Her lips were parted as she looked back at him . . . then she caught herself and looked away.

"So how'd you like the service last night?"

He shook his head. "God!" he said, then shook his head again.

"What do you mean, 'God'?"

"OK, Rachel, let me put it this way: where was God in that service?"

She bristled. She had worked hard on that service. "I don't know what you're talking about. God was all over the place. He was in the music. He was in the sermon. God was everywhere. I don't know what you're talking about."

He threw up his hands. "Well, if you can't see it, there's no use trying to explain."

"What kind of answer is that? I ask you a decent, honest question, and you come back at me with all this hostility, John. What's going on? What are you upset about, really?"

"Listen, Rachel, that so-called worship service was a travesty from beginning to end."

"How would you know? You walked out in the middle of it."

"I saw enough and heard enough to form an opinion."

"Right. An opinion. A personal, subjective opinion. Big deal."

"Well?"

"Well?"

They glared at each other. She was breathing rapidly, her heart beating faster.

"Listen, Rachel. A worship service is supposed to be centered on God, not man."

"You're telling me we weren't focused on God?"

"Yes, that's what I'm trying to say. There's no cross in that church—if you can call it a church—no religious art, no hymnal, no liturgy, no stained glass windows, nothing there to point you to Jesus Christ. No Sacrament. And the sermon—nothing about what Jesus did for us on the cross. Nothing about the forgiveness of sins. Just moral teaching about how we should love one another."

"Well, we should love one another. That's what Christmas is all about. That's why Jesus came into this world."

"I'm not denying that. But I can get that message at the Baha'i temple. If I go to a Christian church, I have a right to expect Christian worship."

"That was Christian worship. It's just a more contemporary style than you're used to. Our church is trying to reach people with the Gospel, we're not just sitting there catering to a dying generation of old folks like Pastor Gottlieb's church. We're trying to save lost souls. Don't you care about evangelism?"

"Save them with what, Rachel? Morality never saved anybody. Love, love, love, that's all Dave talked about. Where did he bring down the hammer of the law? Where did he point them to Christ on the cross?"

"You just don't understand, John. You're just a hidebound traditionalist."

"Well, the tradition has served the church well for a couple of thousand years, if you don't mind my saying so."

"I do mind. You can say what you want, but times are changing, and if the church doesn't change with them, it's going to be left behind." She looked at her watch. It was a Lady Rolex that her fiancée had given her. "I have to go. TD is taking me to lunch. See you."

"Yeah, see you around," John said sullenly.

She banged out the door and was gone. John looked down at his coffee mug. It was half empty. He took a sip. It was cold. He opened the door and threw it out. He saw the football lying in the yard. Going outside he picked it up and threw it angry and hard at the tire swing. With a perfect spiral it went right through the hole.

Chapter 10 ◉ Two Kinds of Confession

There is a real winter in Missouri, and therefore also a real spring. In winter it gets cold and the ground gets hard. Sometimes piles and piles of snow will fall, and the bears—what few there are in the woods any more—go into hibernation, as do the squirrels and groundhogs. On rare occasions the northern lights can be seen. But then again there comes an occasional warm spell, especially in southern Missouri close to the great river. But for all intents and purposes you can call it winter. Then spring comes. Mark Twain, who had traveled the world, was once asked what the most beautiful place was that he had ever seen. Without a moment's hesitation he said, "Missouri in springtime." And who could argue with him?

In late February the crocuses start to push up through the snow, brightening the soil with their royal purple and pure white, the colors of approaching Lent and Easter. In March, winter really starts to loosen its grip. At this time you begin to see the first returning robins. The winds in March are wonderfully strong and cold, and the parks and schoolyards and playgrounds are filled with bundled-up children, and the skies are filled with the children's kites, blue ones and red ones and green ones, sailing and bobbing and falling and rising and dipping and dancing, their tails happily wagging behind like joy-filled puppy dogs.

In April the trees begin to leaf out. For months and months everything has been drab, the earth brown, the forests grey and dead. Then one day you wake up and find grass growing on the ground and it is stricken and barren no longer, but fertile and green. And right at the same time the leaves begin to bud on the trees, but slowly and not all at once, and the new leaves are very small and light pale green in hue, delicate and tender, wonderful and fresh against the pale blue of the sky, and as you drive along out in the country it seems like there is a mist over the hills, a pale green vapor cloaking the rolls and folds of the earth, and then you look again, and sprinkled through the pale green are sprinkles of white and pink where the dogwoods are blooming and dashes of rose where the redbuds are coming into flower. Now you begin to hear the mockingbirds singing, and at the same time the great blue herons come up from the south and go back to their nests, back to the ancestral homes that they have lived in for generation after generation, time out of mind. They call to each other from high in the great forest trees, and they find mates and they breed, as do all the birds, for springtime is the time for love and fertility, a time to be fruitful and replenish the earth.

    Not so for John Mason and Rachel McFadden of course, for every time they got together they seemed to end up in an argument and go away fuming at each other. Besides, the time for Rachel's wedding was getting close. She had her trousseau put together, the dress bought, the cake selected, the invitations engraved, the reception hall booked. It was too late to stop it now, even if she'd wanted to, even if she'd had doubts or misgivings, for Missouri people keep their word and stand by their commitments, even if it leads to hardship and suffering. John meanwhile was putting the ball in play. He had finished a draft of his dissertation and emailed it to his *Doktorvater* for critique before turning it in. At the same time he was "putting in for a call"—letting it be known to church officials that he was now available to serve, whether in the parish or one of the Lutheran church-owned colleges. Of course he would like to go back to teach at his alma mater, the Ft. Wayne seminary, but getting a call there was something of a labyrinthine process, cloaked in mystery, wheels within wheels, known but to a few initiates, and even the men who had gotten calls there were completely mystified as to how their names were chosen, nominated, and elected. So John dreamed, but tried to put it out of his mind. Most likely, he'd end up somewhere remote like Minnesota. But the walleye fishing was good up there, and if he had a small congregation he could continue his research and writing.

So it was a time for new things and new beginnings—Rachel with her marriage and John with a fresh start in ministry. There was the question of what to do about Josiah, of course. Miriam was formally attached to him by edict of his grandfather, the king. Since John had no wife and the child needed to be cared for, it was a relief to know that Miriam would go with him to look after the boy. And there was a trust fund for his education, as there had been for the sons of the king and it provided an annuity to defray living expenses for Miriam. Still, with no wife and an illegitimate child it seemed unlikely that any self-respecting congregation would even be willing to take a look at him, and the Lutheran sections of the country are as white as white can be. Maybe if he got a congregation down south, where there are fewer Lutherans and more black people. But no, de facto segregation is still well-established there, by mutual consent of both black and white communities. The whites go to white churches and schools, and the blacks go to black churches and schools. And John had an integrated family, such as it was, with a mulatto child and an African housekeeper. Probably the only place they'd fit in would be somewhere like Hawaii, where all the races are different and equal in number, and whites do not predominate, nor any other race, and people of different races intermarry all the time. Calls to Hawaii were few, however, and coveted, and district presidents guarded them jealously and handed them out only to close friends or men to whom they owed political favors. So, like a call to the seminary, he tried to put it out of his mind.

But for now there was a pause in the rush of activities, and on a warm day in March everyone was relaxed and in a good mood, Josiah was running around in the yard, throwing rocks at critters, finding treasures and putting them into his little bucket, which he would forget completely as soon as the next activity came along, and Miriam was napping in the hammock, and Millie was on the porch reading, and Rachel was exercising her horse Milton and jumping him over the woodpile, and John, having thrown his quota of footballs through the tire swing, was out on the dock under the shelter he had built, daydreaming while looking at the herons and paying no attention to the line he had in the water. Not that he needed to, for the hook had been nibbled clean by the aggressive little fingerling bass that abounded in springtime. Just then he came to attention, for he smelled rain and knew that the fish always get hungry right before a shower. He re-baited his hook with a fresh juicy worm and cast it back in.

 It was a simple thing, this shelter he had built out at the end of the dock. John had made a frame of two-by-fours secured with elbow joints to the dock. It was open at the sides so you could cast in any direction, and it had plenty of hooks for hanging the kinds of things that fishermen toted along, baskets and jackets and hats and knives and nets and paraphernalia of all sorts. Out on the end facing the wide expanse of water was an old park bench he had scrounged, and that is where he liked to sit. On the side nearest shore he had made a small table for cleaning the fish. You cut off the head and throw it in the water. Same with the guts and scales, and the next day the mess is all gone, having fed the next fish you were going to catch. The frame had extra two-bys and shelving up under the roof, and there he had stowed cane poles and a net and a big old tackle box he'd found, a heavy grey metal thing that had been up in the attic for fifty years, full of old hooks and weights and lures and bobbers made of real cork. The roof of the shelter was simple half-inch plywood shingled over, just something to keep off the sun and the rain, but it had an unusual feature, a touch of whimsy like country boys come up with in winter when they have too much time on their hands. John had built a miniature steeple on the roof of the shelter. It was painted white and even had a little bell in the belfry, a dinner bell he'd bought for five dollars at an auction. So from a distance the shelter looked like a makeshift roadside chapel, and indeed in a way it functioned as such, for when John went out to the dock to fish, he would sit under the shelter and read his Bible as he waited for a bite. On this particular day he had been reading 2 Samuel 11 and 12, as part of his regular course of Old Testament reading, and Romans 7 in the New Testament.

 Rachel watered Milton at the lake, then curried him and put on his feedbag as she tied him to the handrail next to the porch. She waved and said hello to Millie, who had dozed off over her book. Millie lifted her head momentarily and returned the greeting, then went back to sleep. Rachel decided to check on Josiah, and saw him poking around in the sand bar next to the dock. Doxie was close by, lying in the cool grass and watching Josiah. The big dog as usual was pregnant again, and her belly was swelling. As Rachel walked toward the dock the wind began to pick up and a few splatters of rain came down. Miriam woke up, gave a little yelp, and bustled into the house. Josiah ran to the shelter and sat down gloating like a pirate over his bucket of swag. The storm was coming on fast. Rachel had to make a quick decision. She would have preferred to be inside the Clubhouse with the women and coffee and magazines and chit-chat, but she was closer to the dock so on impulse ran for it and made it into the shelter just as the shower cut loose, the rain whispering loudly on the lake, tracing patterns in the water as it fell. She shook her head and wiped her hand across her face. Doxie ran in to the shelter and shook her body, then plopped down next to Josiah. Rachel's t-shirt was wet and clinging. She crossed her arms across her chest in an attempt at modesty, for she had neglected to put on a bra. "Idiot!" she said to herself. She shivered a little as the wind blew in. Her nipples perked up. John saw, and gave her his fishing jacket.

"Hi, Rachel," John said.

"Hey. Any luck?"

"I probably would earlier if I'd kept bait on the hook. The little ones kept nibbling it off, though, and I finally gave up and just sat and read for a while. Do me a favor, will you?" he said as he handed her his Bible. It was an old Thompson Chain Reference Bible, covered with black morocco leather, and worn and shiny from much handling. She opened it up at random and flipped the pages. Every page was covered with notes and underlines in different colors, red and green and blue and black, and yellow and orange highlights. "See if you can put this up on the shelf so it won't get wet."

"OK. Let me just step up on the bench here once."

She stood on the bench. It wobbled.

"Hold me steady, John."

He stood up, shifting the fishing rod to his left hand, reached over and put his right arm around her waist. It was the first time he had ever done so. Her body was round and soft and firm.

Rachel reached up to put the Bible on the shelf as John touched her. It was the first time she had ever felt his arm around her. A shiver raced up her spine. Then he helped her down from the bench, and she felt the quiet strength in his hand. They both sat down on the bench, on opposite sides, and looked into the water.

Just then the bobber on John's line dipped, then dipped again, then went under. John yanked back hard to set the hook, and the fish in response went straight for the bottom, the line singing as it whizzed out from the reel. "Let him run," shouted Rachel.

"No, I can't," John yelled back, "its a big one, and this line is only five-pound test. If I let him go he'll snap it. I've got to play him."

The fish ran to the right, then ran to the left, then to the right again. Every time it turned John reeled him in a few feet. "Man, this thing is fighting like the devil," he said. "I hope this line holds. Rachel, look up in the rafters, there should be a net up there somewhere."

She looked. There were cane poles, strung and ready to go. On the shelf was the old tackle box. And there was a scoop-net with a long handle. John was bringing the fish in with knowledge and skill. As it came near the dock, the fish broke water.

"Daggone, it's a cat," John yelled in his excitement, "a big one, too. Look at that baby fight."

"Don't lose him, John, don't lose him!"

Josiah was in on the action by now. "Pishy, pishy, pishy!" he was saying excitedly as he jumped up and down, "Daddy caught 'im!"

"Get that net ready, Rache!"

"I got it! I got it!"

"A little more, a little more, come on baby, don't break on me."

"Pishy, pishy!"

"Get him in a little closer, John!"

"I'm trying, believe me. This damn thing is strong!"

Rachel reached down with the net, tried to scoop up the fish, and missed.

"Oh, no, he got away!"

"He's still on the line. Try again."

The water was roiling as the big fish thrashed for its life. John's heart was pounding, as was Rachel's. Josiah was jumping up and down, shrieking with delight.

"OK, Rache, try again, he's tiring. I think we can . . . "

She swung the net down hard just as the catfish turned and she caught its big, heavy head. She pulled up, and the rest of the fish slid right in.

"God, it's heavy!"

"Here, you take the rod. Gimme the net!"

"No, I can do it, I can do it!"

"Heave-ho, then."

"OK, here we go."

She grunted and heaved, almost lost her grip, then heaved again. And there it was on the dock, a magnificent catfish, brown and glistening, gasping in the net. The man and the woman and child all looked at it in wonder for a moment, then in jubilation John and Rachel whooped and gave each other a high five and looked at each other with an expression of wide-eyed wonder and hugged each other and when Josiah whined they picked him up and hugged tight, the three of them together.

"Oh, man, we did it! We did it!"

"John, you did great, reeling him in like that."

"First he ran to the right," he said.

"Then he ran to the left," she said.

"Then he went straight for the bottom," he said.

"Then you reeled him in," she said.

"Well, maybe, but I had my hands full. I'd never have been able to land him. You done good, Beezer." He biffed her on the shoulder.

She biffed him back. His shoulder was lean and hard. "And don't call me Beezer, John-boy."

He biffed her again. "Beezer, Beezer, Beezer!"

"You asked for it, buddy." And she tickled him in just the spot she had seen Lou Ann tickle him in the back of the truck at the football game. "No more Mr. Nice Guy. You wanna play hardball, we'll play hardball."

John fell down laughing, and she tickled him some more, and then Josiah jumped on top of his father, laughing and trying to tickle him, and John said, "No fair, two against one," and he began to tickle Josiah, who squealed and laughed.

Just then Millie poked her head out the kitchen door and yelled good-naturedly, "Can you keep it down out there? Us old ladies are trying to take a nap."

Rachel called back, "Get ready to make biscuits, Millie. We're having catfish tonight!"

"Really? OK, great!" Then the door banged and she was gone. At last Rachel relented and let John get up. They gazed upon the big fish. "Wow, will you look at the size of that thing," she said. "It must be two feet long."

"We'll put it in a tub of cistern water for a few hours before we clean it," John said. "That will get rid of that muddy taste the big ones have."

Quiet returned to the scene, the soft sussurance of rain on water, the occasional flap of the fish's tail, the panting of the man and the woman slowing down, returning to normal, the soft voice of the little boy looking at the fish, touching it and talking to it in a low voice. After a while John put the fish on a stringer and lowered it into the water. The man and the woman sat down on the park bench. They sat at opposite ends of the bench, now feeling a little shy and self-conscious after the happy chaos and spontaneous joy of landing the fish. And they went within themselves and were silent with their thoughts for a time.

"That's the biggest catfish I ever caught," said John.

"Unbelievable," said Rachel.

Then they were silent for a while.

"The big ones like this are the dickens to clean."

"Really?"

"Yes. You have to nail them to a tree and strip the skin off."

"Oh."

There was another long pause.

"It'll feed all five of us."

"Yes," she said softly.

"We can't fry the whole thing," he said. "have to cut it into steaks. Or maybe fillets."

She nodded her head.

Then they were silent for a while longer, sitting on the bench and looking out at the wide water. The rain kept coming down. He looked at her. Their eyes met, then they quickly looked away and kept within their thoughts. Soon she would be married. Soon he would be leaving.

Then unexpectedly Josiah came over to Rachel and crawled up into her lap. And he looked at her with his innocent grey eyes, eyes like John's that spoke truth, and he looked at her and said as he had once before, "Mama cook 'im."

And then Rachel began to weep. As the rain came down and whispered on the lake she pressed the little boy to her bosom and wept quietly, and he put his arms around her neck and laid his head down on her shoulder, and she cried and cried and cried. John moved over and sat next to her and put his hand on her shoulder. She reached up and grasped the man's hand and clung to it as she wept.

"What's wrong?" he asked in a low, kind voice.

"I don't know. I'm being silly, I guess. I . . . " and the tears came again.

John waited and held her hand. Josiah fell asleep in her arms, and her tears fell down as she looked at him. His mouth was open, and before too long he began to snore a tiny, high-pitched baby snore. She sniffled and laughed softly and blew her nose.

"Snores just like his old man, I bet."

"Not a chance," John replied. He waited a moment as she gathered herself together, then said, "Do you need to talk?"

"Yes," she said quietly. "It's children. I react to them. I must be crazy. Sometimes I love them to death and other times they just drive me up the wall."

"Well, me too. Like at your church when he knocked over the Christmas tree."

Rachel laughed. "Yeah, that was a classic." She bent over and kissed him. "You little stinker." He opened his eyes halfway then closed them again. Then her tears welled up again. "There's a lot you don't know about me, John."

The rain was coming down harder and the temperature was dropping. She shivered. He put his arm around her. She nestled in tight.

"What I do know impresses me a great deal."

She turned looked up at him. "No," she said, "I'm a lousy piece of dirt."

He looked at her steadily as he waited.

She looked down at her feet, then out at the water. The far shore was shrouded in rain and mist. White dogwood petals were drifting down like snow and landing in the lake.

"It was when I went up to Washington University to go for my master's in English lit," she began.

"That was right after you graduated from Cape, right?"

"Yes," she said, easing into the narrative. "I couldn't believe my good luck, getting admitted to the program at Wash U. I mean, this was where Tennessee Williams had gone to school, and Howard Nemerov was in residence, and Stanley Fish was there as guest lecturer . . . "

"Tennessee Williams I know, but who . . . "

"Oh, big names in literary studies. Fish had been at Yale when the whole deconstructionist thing was coming in from France—Derrida, Lacan, you know."

"Well, no, I don't know, but go on."

"It was just a radical departure from the traditional approach to literary criticism. Very exciting. The idea was that words have no intrinsic meaning, that words are only defined by other words, and so forth, and at the end of they day there is no absolute truth, just the value you impose on words and concepts from your own subjective frame of reference. Postmodernism and all that. And that behind all knowledge lies the will to power."

"Sounds like a dollop of Nietzsche mixed in with some of the developments in hermeneutics after Schleiermacher."

"Nietzsche I know, but . . . "

"Oh, well, you know, Schleiermacher put forth the idea that the Bible had more than one interpretation, and you had to ask what the text means to you, rather than looking for some single, privileged reading."

"Yes, I see. Yes, of course." She stopped and thought for a moment. And her thought at that moment was that she had never had this kind of conversation with TD. And she never would. He was obsessed not with ideas, but with money. "Well there I was, starry-eyed little grad student, among all these giants who were revolutionizing the profession. And there were all these other intellectual currents at the same time, radical feminism in the Women's Studies area, not to mention the traditional Marxists. The after-class discussions were unbelievably intense. I was just absolutely blown away. We'd talk and talk till late at night, then go listen to jazz at one of the clubs on the Delmar Loop, you know, Riddle's and Brandt's and places like that."

"Yes, I know the Loop. We used to go there after baseball games at the Sem when I came over from Ft. Wayne."

"You played ball?"

"Shortstop."

"Right, the Sem is not far from Wash U and the Loop. But I mean, fantastic music. One guitarist I heard, Dave Black—St. Louis guy, unbelievable. That was the good part." She paused, in pain at what she had to say next.

"There was this one professor, Jacob Goldfarb. He was short, stumpy, pudgy, homely. Nothing physically attractive about him at all. Yet the girls all swarmed around him. How can you explain it? Like Cyrano de Bergerac, I guess. He was a wizard with words. Dazzling. Brilliant. And in a world of talkers like we had in the English department, it was like he was seven feet tall and handsome and athletic. He had a wife and children somewhere, but he spent just gobs of time with us grad students, taking us around to little hole-in-the-wall jazz clubs he knew of in run-down neighborhoods in the Loop and Laclede's Landing and Soulard. There was this little group of us, mostly girls, and we joked about being 'Jake's Harem' when we were gossiping together and he wasn't around. Then one of the group, a tall, dark-haired girl from Connecticut that had seemed to be his favorite, suddenly dropped out of the program. The buzz was that she had been seeing a little too much of Jake privately and his wife swooped in and ran her off. But none of us could verify that, and none of us wanted to confront Jake because with the vacancy we were all politely scratching each other's eyes out to be the next favorite. And guess whose stock went up."

John stroked his chin. "Let me see . . . how about Little Miss Rachel McFadden, Rural Route 2, Perryville, Missouri."

"You got it. Now I was the one basking in the glow of his approval and the other gals were green with envy. He was taking me into his confidence, telling me about how miserable he was with his shrew of a wife, giving me plum research assignments, letting me work with him on his new book—where I'd get credit in the acknowledgments, of course—and giving strong hints that he could get me into a prestige school for doctoral work. Harvard, Yale, one of the Ivies. In the world of academe, he had power and influence. And that, John, is an aphrodisiac for an ambitious girl."

"An ambitious girl like Rachel McFadden," John said.

"A very aggressive and very ambitious girl like Rachel McFadden," she replied. "Then one day he surprised me by inviting me to go with him to an upcoming MLA convention. He was delivering a plenary address and asked me to do a sectional. He wanted me to revise a paper I had written on Shakespeare's *Measure for Measure,* the same thing I was developing for my M.A. thesis. I don't know what would be parallel in your profession, John . . ."

"I get the picture. It would be like preaching at the national church convention, something that would put you on the map."

"Exactly. It would put me on the map. The convention was to be held in Boston, and all the Harvards and the Yales and the Princetons and the East Coast bigwigs would be there, and who knows, some of them might drop in and hear my lecture, especially if their old pal Jake gave them a nudge. So we flew out together, dropped into Logan International, went to the hotel, checked in, went to the bar, had a few drinks, then a few more, all on an empty stomach, went up to his room where I slept with him, woke up hung over, gave my paper in a fog, repeated the debauch every night the rest of the week, came back, and soon found out I was pregnant, just like promiscuous old Doxie here." The dog looked up at the invocation of her name.

Rachel sighed and looked down. John nodded his head in silent acknowledgment.

"Oh, I forgot to mention. When I was reading my paper I stopped for a moment to take a sip of water. I looked out at the audience and got a shock. There was the tall, dark-haired girl from Connecticut, just staring at me as if she were a ghost. Or as if I were about to become a ghost."

Then Rachel continued. "Well, this just wouldn't do at all, would it? What would the shrewish wife do if she found out? What effect would it have on his career? We had to handle things quietly. Everything had to be hush-hush. Everything had to be discreet. There was a Planned Parenthood clinic Jake knew of. He could cover the expense. Not to worry." The tears welled up again. "I didn't have to worry about a thing, did I? Except what happened to the soul of that little baby I destroyed!" And she began again to weep, Rachel mourning for her lost child, because it was no more.

She turned to him and wept into his strong shoulder as he held her tight, and she cried for a long, long time as the rain came down all around the little chapel on the dock over the lake. Then as she blew her nose she said, "God forgive me."

And John said softly, "Rachel, I'm a sinner, too. Except in my case the baby lived and the mother died." And tears came to him as well, and Rachel looked at him with compassion, for she had heard the story. There were the two of them in the shelter, vulnerable and exposed, their souls naked before each other, and yet they were not ashamed. "God does forgive you. You know that, don't you?"

"Yes, but I need somebody to tell me."

"I went to Pastor Gottlieb, and he . . ."

"No." She stated it flatly. "I need you to tell me. You: Pastor John Mason."

He hesitated. He was a poor, miserable sinner like herself. He had fallen from grace. He was out of office. Probably no congregation would have him after what he had done. Nevertheless he struggled to his feet and faced her, hesitated once again, then placed both hands on her head.

"Upon this your confession," he said through tears, "I as a called and ordained Servant of the Word announce the grace of God to you, Rachel McFadden, and by the authority vested in me I forgive you all your sins, particularly the ones you have confessed this day, in the name of the Father, and of the Son"—and here he traced the Sign of the Cross upon her forehead, and as she did so she could smell his hands, and they smelled like the hands of a fisherman—"and of the Holy Ghost. Amen."

"Thanks, John." And somewhere in her soul the darkness fled away like a flock of black crows over the horizon. She stood up and faced him. "I needed to hear it. I needed you to tell me out loud."

She was near to him. She was looking up at him. Her mouth was slightly parted. He could smell the sweetness from that soft and tender place between her breasts. His mouth was dry. He said hoarsely, "There's something else I need to tell you, Rachel. I need to speak these words to you. I need to speak the truth that is in my heart."

Then she knew—as all women know at these moments—what he was about to say. She had made her confession. Now he was about to make a confession of his own. And if he said what he was about to say, even though she knew at that moment that she longed to hear him say those true words more than anything else in the whole world, it would wreck everything. It would turn her world inside out and upside down. She had made a promise to TD, a promise she now knew she had made in desperation for security. And she wanted that security, oh, God, how she wanted it! And cursing herself for being so damned practical when the only man she had ever longed for since she was a little girl was right in front of her and about to speak true words, a confession of love, she put her hand over his mouth, then pushed him away, shaking her head and saying, "No. No. Don't say it, John. Don't say it."

That stopped him. He stepped back from her, back from the precipice. He had stood on the brink. He had looked down into the mouth of the volcano. He wanted to fling himself down and be burned up with incandescent love. But what was he thinking? Where was his commitment to Elizabeth? Where was that sacred shrine to her memory that he had sworn he would always keep in his memory? He cast his gaze to the far shore. The rain had stopped. A heron was doing its slow dance in the shallow water, picking up its feet high and setting them down slowly, and looking intently into the lake for sustenance. As the heron studied the water, there was a movement in the brush nearby. Something was stalking the heron. John looked intently. He had heard from hunters that a cougar had been spotted. He thought he saw the twitch of a long tail.

◉ ◉ ◉

The trouble Rafael was encountering meanwhile was that there were dozens of Perryvilles—every state seemed to have one, Commodore Perry having been such a huge military hero in the nineteenth century as the country was being settled—and hundreds of John Masons. His Internet search had tossed up too much information to be of any use. So he collated a list of Perryvilles with John Masons and shoved off from New York. It would take time, but it was a chance to see the country he hated. Before he left he had one last night on the town with his friends. The doctor fussed at him because he was not tending properly to his wound. An infection could set in unless he looked after it. But Rafael didn't care. The doctor had given him a big supply of the Darvocet. It was as easy for him as it was for an A-list entertainer who was touring. Like Johnny Cash. The Darvocet made him feel wonderful all the time, especially in combination with liquor. He was discovering that he had a taste for American bourbon. He bought a case of whiskey and put it in the trunk of the Aston Martin. So it was off to see America, looking for a man named John Mason in a town called Perryville, or something like that. His mind was fuzzy, and try as he might he couldn't remember the exact name of the town or the state it was in. He would just have to take his time and visit each one, looking for a town with a garage that contained his lawful prey.

Perryville, Alaska, population 107, he felt he could safely scratch off the list. Likewise Perryville, Arizona. There was Perry, New York. May as well give it a try, along with Perry, Rhode Island, population 50, and Perry, Pennsylvania, population 180. Besides this there were two Perryvilles in Pennsylvania, both quite small, but he visited them anyway, getting stares from the locals who had never seen an Aston Martin. Perryville, Maryland seemed more promising with a population of 3,672. There were a couple of John Masons there but they were not the one he was after. On to Ohio, with the town of Perry, population 1,195, Perry Heights, population 8,900, Perrysburg, population 16,945, and two Perrysvilles, both quite small like their near-relation cities in Pennsylvania. Oh, yes, and Perryton, population 60. After Perry, Michigan, population 2,065, it was on to Perrysville, Indiana, population 502, then down to Perryville, Kentucky, population 763. Still no John Mason for him to kill.

Continuing south, Rafael stopped in Perryville, Alabama; Perry, Georgia; Perry, Florida; Perryville, Louisiana; and Perryville, Arkansas. No success yet, but like the scientist or detective eliminating possibilities one by one, he knew with each failure that he was getting closer to the end of his quest. Further north was Perry, Iowa, and further west was Perry, Kansas; Perry, Oklahoma; and Perry and Perryton, Texas. But something told him he was getting close. Due north was Perryville, Missouri. It was a hunch. It was a soldier's intuition that gave him a sense of what bush his enemy might be hiding under.

Winter in New York had given way to spring in the south as Rafael traveled around. As often happens to foreign visitors to America, he gradually developed a sense of awe at the sheer size of this country. One could drive across Germany in a day. Same with Iraq, one of the largest Muslim states. But this was a nation the size of a continent. You could fit all of Europe into it with room left over. And the miles and miles and miles of fields and forest... there was room enough for everyone. And the places where he stopped had an effect on him. He was a killer and he was after blood. But he was a human being. And in Pennsylvania when he stopped in Lancaster County the men in the Amish country store struck up a conversation with him a*lles auf Deutsch.* Every Perry, and Perryton, and Perryville, and Perrysville had a little cafe. And every cafe had homemade pie. And every cafe had a talkative waitress that chewed gum. And every cafe had a couple of old-timers sitting on stools at the lunch counter, reading the local paper and waiting for something to happen that they could talk about that evening over beer with their buddies at the American Legion. And in every little town Rafael brought that something that they were waiting for—a well-dressed stranger in a fancy car. So as he traveled he learned to talk to the loafers and the old-timers, easing information out of them about the population of John Masons in the area. But at the same time Rafael was developing a taste for custard pie, especially if the crust was crispy and the filling had a little nutmeg sprinkled on top.

And as he traveled he listened to the radio, and on a back road somewhere between Perryville, Kentucky, and Perry, Tennessee, he heard a Hank Williams song on a weak AM station just after the weather report and tobacco and hog prices, and something in him said, "That's my music!" And he cruised the channels on the back roads, listening for the elusive sounds of the old music, Jimmie Rodgers and the Carter Family and Hank Snow and Johnny Cash and Willie Nelson and Merle Haggard. In Perry, Florida, he bought a pair of western boots, and was amazed at how comfortable they were. "As comfortable as an old shoe," as the American idiom puts it. That also described his relationship with John Mason. As a German Rafael put great store by real friendship. That's what he had with John, and he esteemed it highly. Their personalities meshed. Though American, there was enough German in Mason to facilitate compatibility. They both liked to do things that all Germans like to do: hiking, talking, smoking, drinking beer, and talking. They talked and joked and argued, they drank *Doppelbock* in ancient taverns, they heard lectures, they went to the opera. John was a likeable guy: Rafael liked him, even his dog liked him. Good, wholesome things. Then John wrecked it all by telling him about Elizabeth. Elizabeth and the child.

In Perryville, Alabama he bought a John B. Stetson hat. And after Perryville, Arkansas, he decided to take a detour and visit Memphis, Tennessee, where Carl Perkins and Johnny Cash and Elvis Presley and Jerry Lee Lewis had all gotten their start at Sun Studios. He walked down Beale Street. He heard B. B. King. He visited Graceland. He had a good time. He took more pain medicine, and then a little more, for his wound was red and inflamed, and if he hit it on something a pain shot all the way up to his elbow. He had a few drinks at the hotel bar. He asked the concierge to recommend a discreet escort service, palming him a fifty. The concierge was only too happy to oblige.

The woman he sent up to Rafael was very large and very black. When she was done with her business she sashayed around the hotel room with nothing on but Rafael's cowboy hat and cowboy boots as she brought him brandy and a cigar. Rafael enjoyed the spectacle as he reclined luxuriously in the king-sized bed, humming a tune to himself. He started out with an old country song, "Your Cheatin' Heart," and at last when he got tired of that he began to sing a new song he had heard. For the station he had been listening to the past few days in Memphis had a program that featured new praise and worship songs that were being written in the churches of the area. This was fascinating to Rafael, since all the church music in his native Germany came out of the Reformation almost five hundred years before. And of course there was no church music in Islam. No instruments, no singing, no choir, no organ, nothing to stimulate the senses when you went to the mosque. It was just the recitation of the prayers and a sermon by the imam. And if Rafael was Muslim, he was also German, and had to have music to live. So he listened to this new music with fascination. There was one song he particularly liked. The announcer said the new CD came from a church up in Missouri. The lyrics were:

> I love you so.
> You're my everything.
> I'd do anything for you.

You make me so happy.
I just want to be with you all the time.
You're the world to me.
I love you so.

Rafael sang the song over and over again as he looked at the big black naked whore, half his mind on her and half on Allah, then mixing the two like a martini while singing the song to her and Him alone.

In the cold grey dawn he awoke feeling like shit in both body and soul. What the hell had happened to him? Where was the religious purity of life he had so desired? Where was the moral jihad? Where was the military discipline?

He knew, of course.

He remembered the moment when everything changed for him, a moment like a blast of sound after a long crescendo. It was at that hotel in Dubai. He had heard the jaded waiters hinting with a wink and a nod at "interesting" goings-on up top in the penthouse, where high-ranking officers with their aides-de-camp relaxed with their wives. Their *Nika mut'ah* wives. Their legal, temporary wives.

Rafael's rapid rise in rank corresponded to his admission on return trips to higher-status accommodations on the upper floors, with a discrete and gradual relaxation of Sharia law— first a fifth-floor larger room, then a twelfth-floor efficiency, followed by a twenty-third-floor apartment with a balcony and a view, and at last, as aide to a certain general whose name was a household word throughout Islam, the top-floor penthouse.

There was an open bar, an endless buffet, a balcony spa, a massage room, a sauna, a luxury bathroom with a roomy tub, and a young *mut'ah* wife for him during his month-long stay. She was a Persian beauty, a faithful Twelver Shia Muslim, and from a famous family. Shy and chaste she was, and always dressed modestly in a burka—a burka made of rare, fine, sheer silk that both concealed and revealed at the same time.

One night there was a party. In the spirit of true brotherhood it was share and share alike. Many of the ladies, it seemed, were interested in the strapping blonde German fellow. The festivities went on and on and on, in the balcony spa, in the massage room, in the sauna, in the luxury bathroom... on and on and on.

Very late or very early, he knew not which, Rafael awoke with a *mut'ah*—not his own—in his arms. Somehow they had ended up behind the couch. He was untangling himself and looking for his bathrobe when he smelled cigar smoke and heard low voices. He froze. It was like in his childhood when he would hide behind the big brown leather sofa and listen to the grownups discuss the affairs of the day.

Rafael did not recognize the voices of the two men. One was deep and resonant, the other high and nasal.

"Yes, yes, yes," said Deep, "we've been through this a hundred times before, and at least ten times so far this evening."

"Well, my dear general," said High, "let me try once more to get it through your thick Pakistani skull. Islam is a religion of peace. These wacko terrorists are giving us all a bad name."

"Oh, come off it. You may be a big-shot imam, but your malnourished childhood in Bangladesh must have lowered your IQ by half."

High squealed with laughter. "Ha-ha-ha! Better watch out, my friend, or I'll issue a *fatwah* against you."

"Just try it," said Deep. "See if I don't sic young Rafael on you. He'll slit your throat while you are asleep in bed with your wife. Have some more of this American whiskey."

"Don't mind if I do. What is it?"

"It's called Jack Daniel's. It's become quite popular among the officers. A fellow in Mayangala got us all started."

"Is that so. Not bad, not bad," answered High. "But young Rafael had better be advised that when I'm in bed with my wife, I don't get much sleep. She keeps me very busy."

A booming laugh from Deep, then, "Back to the matter at hand. Of course we are a religion of peace. Once everyone in the world is Muslim, we will have peace. And of course the terrorists are giving us a bad name. But when in the name of Allah are you going to wake up and realize that *Islam has nothing to do with it!*"

Rafael gasped.

"Say, did you just hear something?"

"I did."

Rafael could feel his heart knocking like a loose piston rod. There was an excruciatingly long pause.

"Probably just the wind."

"Sure, that's it. That ocean breeze is nice this time of night."

"But hear me out," said High. "Look at all the Suras that enjoin vengeance and death to our enemies. These are the verses by which we conquered the Near East, and Constantinople, and North Africa, and Spain."

"OK, OK, I grant you that. But in those days Muslim raiders attacked openly in massed, coordinated armies with uniforms and standard weapons."

Rafael heard the *glug-glug* of the bottle and the *clink-clink* of the ice cubes.

"We're out of ice. I'll call room service."

"That's all right. This is last call for me."

"Me, too. The sound of your droning voice is putting me right to sleep."

"Har-de-har-har," said Deep.

"But listen," High began...

"No, dammit, you listen to me!" exclaimed Deep. "The terror tactics we employ today come right out of Adolf Hitler!"

"Now, really! You've gone too far this time."

"I have not. Read *Mein Kampf* some time. Look at the tactics of the Brown Shirts. You castrate a few Jew-boys, word gets around. A few old war heroes who spoke out about Hitler mysteriously disappear. Pretty soon a pall of fear descends like black ugly smoke. Except Hitler was confined to Germany. We operate on a global scale. Saddam Hussein figured this out. Use mustard gas on a few Kurdish villages. Fear! Throw a couple of stubborn old generals into the dog pit. Fear! Get some dumb kids to fly airplanes into the World Trade Towers. Fear!" The couch began to shake as Deep laughed. "Look at the long security lines at every airport in the world. Fear! Its really too much."

By now High was laughing as well.

Rafael was not. What kind of cynicism was this? He had felt uneasy about the liberties accorded to residents of the higher floors. But this—what was it? Nazi jihad? And here he had been questing for holiness, for purity. Where was it to be found? Perhaps among the simple folk like Sinan, who just believed and went about their business and took care of their families.

Sinan! It was upon the sacred altar of his dead body that Rafael had sworn to become a Janissary in a holy cause. And now this. Rafael had taken a course in Reformation history. He learned how Luther had traveled to Rome on monastery business, and came back disillusioned by the flagrant corruption of the priests. How could he, a lone soldier of the Crescent, cope with a profound disillusionment such as this? Disillusionment, like mold, grows slowly in the dark; like acid, it eats away from inside.

The conversation drifted to a close. The lights went out. Rafael waited. Then he waited some more. He found his robe, and placed it over the sleeping girl. He tiptoed back to his room, where he found his wife asleep in the arms of another man. Rafael gently walked him out the door, got into bed, and turned his back on the woman when she reached for him.

He slept deep and long.

In the late morning he showered deep and long.

He dressed and looked around. The penthouse was empty. All the people were gone. A maid was vacuuming the living room. The party was over.

On the bedside table was an envelope. He opened it. Inside were orders. He was to find and kill Princess Elizabeth of Mayangala, the rightful heir to the throne.

His heart was a cold stone at the bottom of the sea. But he was a soldier. He would do his duty. He would follow orders. He would kill the woman.

Chapter 11 ◉ The Argument

The day everything came to a head began like any other. John got up early as usual and went down to the dock with his coffee and his Bible to say his morning prayers, then put on his overalls and went in to town to help out at the garage. Josiah had a doctor's appointment, but it wasn't till mid-morning, so Millie and Miriam were going to bring him in and get in a bit of shopping and get their hair done and meet Hilda at the coffee shop. Except that it had been raining all the previous week and Josiah was begging his daddy to take him fishing again. The kid couldn't get enough of it, and expected to catch a great big catfish every single time like they had once before. So Hilda was going to bring Josiah back out to the Clubhouse while the other women finished their errands, so that Daddy could take his boy to the lake later on.

It was a routine day at the shop, a couple of oil changes, a blade to be sharpened and replaced on a lawn mower, a tune-up on the Baptist preacher's Ford Escort (at no charge). But Jasper had one bay tied up with an engine replacement on a stock car that had blown a rod on the racetrack and needed to be back in action for the weekend, so he needed John to handle the normal stuff while he worked on the hot rod.

"Well, J-J-Johnny," Jasper began as he bent over the radiator of the stock car and disconnected the battery cables, "did you see the p-p-paper this morning?"

"No, I didn't. *Was geht?*"*

"*Veil spass,*" Jasper replied. "Seems like a couple of kids, nobody knows who, went up to Ste. Gen last night."

"Yeah?" John said as he stood in the well and clapped a socket wrench onto the drain plug of a venerable Chevy.

"You know that statue of a dragon they have in front of the high school?"

"Yeah, that's the school mascot. We always tried to spit on it whenever we went up there and played."

"Well, them damn kids went up there and painted the whole thing green and white."

"The Perryville colors?"

"Yep. Ain't dat somp'n?"

John laughed out loud. "That's great! Why didn't I think of that when I was in school?"

"*Ja,* me too," Jasper said.

John deftly removed the drain plug and let the oil dribble out into the basin. "A green dragon! Ha-ha, I bet TD is fit to be tied."

"*Ja,* you betcha," said Jasper as he grunted and heaved the heavy battery out of its frame and set it on the floor with a thump. "That is, if he don't get himself hung first."

John's ears pricked up. "What on earth are you talking about?" He replaced the drain plug and began to unscrew the oil filter.

"You know Clarence and M-M-M-M . . . M-Merle, don'tcha?"

"The fat one and the skinny one."

"*Ja,* the 'mayor' and the 'sheriff.' Well, they was down at the Legion, you know . . ."

"Yes, Tuesday is fried chicken night."

"Sure, everybody goes, even folks from Ste. Gen, and everybody was t-t-talking and visiting b-back and forth, and some of the b-b-boys from the Legion in Ste. Gen was saying what they heard about TD." Jasper was reaching down and taking the serpentine belt off.

---

* "What happened?"
  "Lots of fun," Jasper replied . . .

"Yeah? Go on." John took a new oil filter out of the box and screwed it into place.

Now Jasper had the fan off and was detaching the water pump from the front of the motor. "He's gonna tear down all the trees at *d-d-der Friedensee* and bulldoze everything and put up high-rise condominiums!"

John stopped cold. "Are you kidding?"

"As they say in the N-N-N- . . . N-N-Navy, 'No shit!'" He cranked the bolt four or five times and had the water pump off and laid it to the side. "Got dern this s-s-stutter. I never h-h-have it when I talk D-dutch."

"*Dass ist schade,*"* John replied, both to Jasper's speech impediment and the news about TD. "I can't believe he'd do something like that. I mean, how could he? He only has a share in the Clubhouse like the rest of us, and as long as his mother Millie is alive she has the controlling interest. She'd never give him permission." John was up top now, where he tapped the oil drums.

"You m-moron," Jasper replied. "You don't know nothin'. You never seen the plat maps, have you?"

"No," John said as he poured the oil into the crankcase, *glug-a-glug-a-glug.*

"All the north shore of the lake is M-M-McFadden property."

The light bulb went on over John's head. He replaced the oil cap, put the oil can back in its place, and wiped his hands on a red shop cloth. "So when he and Rachel get married he can develop that property."

"You got it."

"I can't believe she'd let him do that, Jasper. God, it would ruin . . . it would just ruin everything. It would destroy the place. The spirit would depart from it and never come back." He unscrewed the wing nut over the air filter. The filter was dirty with county road dust and needed changing. He fetched a new one and plopped it in. "I'm calling her up."

---

* "That's too bad," John replied . . .

Jasper was detaching the hoses as he said, "If I were you, I'd s-s-stay out of it. Ain't none of your business."

"The hell it ain't," John shot back. "It's all of our business. I know you can't reason with TD, but maybe Rachel can get through to him."

Jasper stood up and looked at his nephew. He shook his head and muttered to the carburetor, "It's your funeral."

John went into the cluttered office and picked up the receiver of the grimy old black rotary-dial telephone. Mrs. McFadden picked up at the other end.

"Hello?"

"Hi, Mrs. McFadden, this is John Mason. How are you?" John was instantly sorry he'd asked, for he knew from pastoral experience with depressives that they always took the question literally, and then launched into a long recital of their problems.

He was surprised to hear her say, with a bit of a lift in her voice, "Pretty good, for an old lady. Thanks for asking. The cobwebs kind of got cleared out of my head. But you don't want to listen to me complain. I'll get Rachel." She called for her daughter. John heard a faint "Coming!" through the line.

"Is that so," John said absentmindedly as he waited for Rachel, impatient to get on with business. "That's really great."

"Yes, it is great," she continued, oblivious to John's impatience. "It was a couple of months ago, and Rachel had to go over to the Clubhouse to help Millie get food prepared for a big hunting party or something, and she just grabbed me and said, 'Come on, Mom, quit moping around. We need you to help peel potatoes.' And just like that she had me bundled up and out the door and put me behind her on that damn horse of hers, and you know, it's hard to feel depressed when you're bouncing along through the woods trying to hang on and keep from falling off the back of a horse. And by the time we got to the Clubhouse we were laughing and joking just like old times. And then we got inside and Millie and that black woman were cracking each other up with stories about their men, and don't you know, I started telling stories about Peter and Bobby. Lord, I'd been so depressed about their . . . their deaths"—and here she paused, took a breath, and then went on—"that I don't know, I had shut myself off from their lives. The bad memories had pushed out the good. So anyway, there we all were, a kitchen full of women, all yakking away and having a jolly old time, and then somebody said we needed firewood, so I threw on my coat and went outside to the woodpile, and then I stopped. Something just stopped me in my tracks. The lake was frozen over, all clear and white and still. And the woods were white with the snow that had fallen the day before. And the sky was that clear blue like it gets after a storm. And everything was so quiet and peaceful, you know. On the far shore I could see a rabbit hopping along, foraging for a snack. A beaver had built a dam. And some cedar waxwings were chattering away and arguing over the berries in the holly tree. And all of a sudden this peace just came into my soul, and . . . oh, here's Rachel."

At last, thought John, irritably.

"Hi, it's me," said Rachel.

"I'm at the shop. Can you talk?"

"I don't think I can come in. Mom needs the car to go to the beauty shop. What's up?"

"It's important, but I don't want to go into it over the phone."

"You want to just meet at the Clubhouse in an hour or two? I have to go over anyway. TD wanted me to meet him there."

"That's good. I told Josie I'd take him fishing. So, yeah, sure, let me see if I can wrap things up here and I'll see you at the Clubhouse in about an hour."

"OK, bye."

"Bye."

John hung up the grimy phone and slumped back into the shop. It would be just like TD to leverage his marriage into a business deal. Of course Rachel was desirable and would make any man an excellent wife. But how despicable could you be? Some men married for money. Looks like old Touchdown Timmy was marrying for property. Jasper had been working with his usual speed and efficiency and was getting down to the last few parts to be taken off the old engine.

"*Was geht,* Johnny?"

"I need to see Rachel about this thing, Jasper. I have to find out the truth."

"Did you get the oil change done on the Chevy?"

"I just need to lube the joints, but . . . "

"I'll do it. Go on, b-b-beat it."

"Thanks, Jasper. I'm just going to grab a quick cup of coffee, then go."

John threw on his light jacket and walked up the hill. He had parked his Jeep in front of the courthouse to show off its new paint job, fire engine red. It was gleaming in the sunlight. Not a bad looking old flivver, John thought as he passed the cafe. And as he turned the corner, a rare automobile pulled up in front of the garage. It was a classic but had a lot of dirt over the silver paint, it was scratched and dented with parking lot dings, and the left rear taillight was missing. It was an Aston Martin.

Rafael got out and sauntered into the garage, looking from side to side like a pacing lion on the hunt. He saw only Jasper, bent over the car he was working on.

"Good morning," he said.

"And a g-g-good morning to you, sir," Jasper replied. And detecting the accent he asked, "*Sind sie Deutscher?*"*

---

* "Are you German?"

"Yes," Rafael returned . . .

Jasper . . . said, "I'm called Mason. What's your name?"

"Rafael von Päpinghausen. Hello, Mr. Mason."

"You are very welcome. Where do you come from, Mr. von Päpinghausen?"

"I have come from Heidelberg."

"A beautiful city! And what brings you to the USA?"

"My car is a bit sick" . . . "Can you help me? And also, I'm looking for a friend from Heidelberg, Mr. John Mason."

"Oh, Johnny!' Jasper said. "I'm sorry. He's not here. He went to our Clubhouse."

"The Clubhouse in the woods, near a lake?"

"That's right."

"John often spoke of this place. Perhaps I can meet him there."

"Yes, very good. But first, we'll get your car fixed."

. . .

But he stood tall and answered, "Thank you."

"You're welcome," Jasper replied, and then said, "Would you like to drink some coffee?"

"*Ja,*" Rafael returned, clicking his heels and bowing.

Jasper bowed also and said, "*Ich heisse* Mason. *Wie heissen sie?*"

"Rafael von Päpinghausen. *Grüss Gott, Herr* Mason."

"*Sie sind herzliche willkommen. Woher kommen sie, Herr von* Päpinghausen?"

"*Ich bin aus Heidelberg gefahren.*"

"*Eine schöne Stadt! Und was machen Sie im* USA*?*"

"*Mein Auto ist ein bischen krank,*" Rafael answered evasively. And indeed it was, for he had totally neglected it, and it desperately needed an oil change. Plus, the accelerator was sticking. "*Können Sie mir hilfen? Und auch, ich suche einen Freund von Heidelberg, Herr* John Mason."

"*Ach,* Johnny!" Jasper said. "*Es tut mir Leid. Der ist weg. Er ist nach unsere Clubhouse gegangen.*"

"*Der Clubhouse in dem Wald, in die nähe von einem See?*"

"*Sie haben recht.*"

"John *hat manchmals von diesem Ort gesprochen. Vielleicht kann Ich ihn dort treffen.*"

"*Ja, sehr gut. Aber erstmals, wir wollen ihre Auto gefixen.*"

Rafael winced at the American bastardization. "*Gefixen?*" It hurt the ears. One of those horrors like he'd heard when he was among the Pennsylvania Dutch: "*der Truck,*" "*das Tractor.*" But he stood tall and answered, "*Danke sehr.*"

"*Bitte sehr,*" Jasper replied, and then said, "*Möchten Sie gerne Kaffee zu trinken?*"

"OK, sure," said Rafael, lapsing back into English.

"Well, there's a little coffee shop up the hill and around the corner."

"Do they have custard pie?" asked Rafael.

"The b-b-b-best in all the land," answered Jasper. "Come back in ha-half an hour, I should have you back on the road. And you might catch John. He often stops in there."

"OK. See you," said Rafael and walked out the garage door and up the hill.

John meanwhile had been at the coffee shop. He had been walking toward his Jeep when he heard a tap on the window. Looking in, he saw Millie, Miriam, and Hilda sitting with Josiah at a table next to the window, motioning for him to come in. So in he went, ready for a second cup of coffee. Myrtle had spotted him while he was still outside and had his coffee at the table by the time he arrived, along with a piece of rhubarb pie with a slice of cheddar cheese on the side. John sat down and dug into the pie. The women were buzzing.

"You'll never guess what we heard," said Millie.

"Hilda overheard it while she was in the restroom," added Miriam.

"That's right," said Hilda, "those walls are thin as paper. There were a couple of guys in the men's room—I'm sure I recognized Clarence's voice—and they were going on about how TD was going to tear down the Clubhouse and put in an amusement park as soon as he marries Rachel. There's going to be a water slide that goes into the lake, and a Tilt-a-Whirl, and a Penny Arcade, and a steam Calliope, and a Ferris wheel, and a rolly-coaster, and you name it. The works."

"Is that so?" said John as he finished the pie and slurped his coffee. Now he was beginning to have doubts about the whole thing, since obviously the Perryville rumor mill was now working overtime and cranking out increasingly fantastic fiction at full speed. "What does Rachel have to say about all this? Has anybody talked to her?"

The women looked at each other like the thought had never occurred to them. "Oh, I think she's so bamboozled with the wedding she's blinded by love," said Millie.

"Yes," added Miriam, "you know how women get when they're getting ready to tie the knot."

"No, I don't," said John. "Perhaps you could explain."

They all looked at each other again like, who is this moron. They all started to talk at once but Hilda came out on top. "Let me put it this way. A woman starts to plan her wedding when she is about five years old. She dreams about the wedding, the music, the ceremony, the cake, the reception, and most of all, the dress. Finally she snags a man. Now she's got the blinders on, like a racehorse. All she can see is the finish line. It's just up ahead. She's galloping for all she's worth. She is completely deaf to any distractions from the outside world. Somehow that weasel TD has figured this out. He could tell Rachel that after they get married she has to paint herself blue and go around stark naked and she'd say OK, fine, whatever you say, dear. It's worse than when a woman is trying to tell something to a man when he's reading the sports page. I'm tellin' ya."

She shook her head. John laughed and sipped his coffee. "OK, Grams, I get the picture. Well, I'm supposed to meet Rachel at the Clubhouse in about..." he glanced at his watch, "yikes! I need to blast off. She said she had to meet TD there anyway. Maybe I can knock some sense into her. Or at least find out the truth about this deal." While I'm at it, John thought, I'd like to knock something out of TD, the dirty bastard. "Let me take Josie with me. I promised to take him fishing after while anyway."

"Well, I'm coming with you," Hilda said. "Just let me get my hands on that little weasel Timmy. I'll give him what for."

Miriam and Millie nodded assent and began rummaging in their purses in preparation for leaving. "Sure," Millie said, "you go on with Johnny and Josiah. Miriam and I have to go to Rozier's grocery. They have *Kochkäse* today and I want to pick some up. Plus a couple of other errands. We'll see you later."

So they paid their bill, John leaving the tip, and went out into the morning air. It was a beautiful day, warming up from the sunshine beaming through a clear sky, and the fragrance of springtime surrounded them. The courthouse lawn was brilliant with banks of tulips and daffodils, and the azaleas were just beginning to blossom. John picked up his grandmother and set her gently into the passenger seat, and put his son in her lap. It was a fifteen-minute drive at low speed, and nobody who was going out to the country ever bothered with seat belts, any more than they would if they were riding on *das Tractor*.

No sooner had John rounded the corner of the courthouse square than Rafael came up the hill and entered the coffee shop. He immediately turned heads, not only because he was a stranger, but because he was big and strikingly good looking, and had on a nicely tailored suit along with his hat and boots. In Germany men remove their hats upon entering a building, but as he had learned in America, men keep their hats on. So Rafael kept his big Stetson square on his head as he straddled a stool at the counter. Looking in the pie safe he saw that yes, indeed, they did have custard pie. He ordered a slice to go with his coffee. American coffee was wretched in comparison with the good German *kaffee* he was used to, but American pie was to die for. Though today, Rafael mused, he would not die for pie but kill for Allah.

"Howdy, stranger," said the man sitting next to Rafael. It was Clarence, the heavyset loafer who maintained the rumor-and-sporting news circuit between the garage, the barber shop, the courthouse, and the Legion. "You from around here?"

"Nope," said Rafael, working on his imitation of an American accent, "I ain't."

"Kinda guessed so," said Clarence. "Where you from?"

"Oh, here and there. I just been traveling around, seeing the country. Nice little town you got here, pardner. Came to visit a buddy of mine. John Mason. You know him?"

"Why, sure," Clarence exclaimed. "Everybody knows ole Johnny. Best quarterback we ever had at Perryville High. Then he went off and entered the ministry, knocked around up in Alaska for a while, then went to Germany to study."

"That's where we met up," Rafael said, studying the man and wondering how much information he could extract from him. "We were students at Heidelberg together."

"So you're from Germany."

"Yep."

"I thought I detected a bit of an accent."

"Yep. But the more of this nasty American coffee I drink, the less accent I have."

Clarence laughed. "That's a good one! Yessiree, Bob. That's a good one. I'll have to remember that." And he would, too. By the end of the day Clarence would have repeated it twenty times at the garage, the barbershop, the courthouse, and the Legion. "So you know ole Johnny Mason. You just missed him. He was just in here a minute ago. He was sitting right over at that table by the window," he said with a jerk of his thumb, "with his grandmother and his aunt and that nigger woman and that pickaninny kid of his."

"A child, did you say?" asked Rafael. His heart quickened. Praise be to Allah. He had helped him find Mason. But the child was here also? It was too good to be true. His left hand strayed into his coat and he fondled the handle of his knife in its sheath.

"Oh, yeah," Clarence blathered on. "This was while he was over in Europe. He was shacked up with some black whore. And when she found out he'd knocked her up she threw herself off a bridge. I mean after the baby was born. So he got stuck with this pickaninny, I mean, what a stink that created around town here when everybody found out. Brother, brother, brother! And so he's working at the garage to make ends meet, and all that good jazz, and who knows what's going to happen next."

Rafael had a very good idea of what would happen next. "Listen, pardner," he said, leaning over and slipping a twenty-dollar bill into Clarence's shirt pocket, "I was talking with Jasper down at the garage, and he said that John was at this place called 'the Clubhouse.' I wanted to come see him as a surprise. Can you give me directions?"

"Oh, sure, no problem," said Clarence, and drew a little map on a paper napkin, detailing the landmarks along the way.

"Thank you so very much," said Rafael as he stood up to leave. "Ah 'preciate it."

"Glad to be of help," Clarence replied and put out his hand. "Come by the American Legion later on. Tonight is fried chicken." Then he saw that Rafael's right hand was maimed and cloaked in a black glove. Awkwardly they shook with their left hands.

"I'll remember that," said Rafael. And he touched the brim of his hat and strode out the door, leaving a ten-dollar bill on the counter and a half-eaten slice of his favorite pie. The hunt was on.

While all this had been going on Rachel had ridden over to the Clubhouse on Milton, followed by a plodding and panting Doxie, who was heavy and about to drop a litter again. TD was already there when she arrived, decked out in his golfing regalia, and with him were two men, similarly attired, and the three of them were lofting chip shots around the lawn with 9-irons. Doxie growled at the men while

Rachel jumped Milton a couple of times over the woodpile like she usually did upon arriving. Milton was feeling his oats and was eager to jump more, but Rachel let him loose to graze instead, still saddled up.

"Hi, Sugar," TD said, and kissed her as she came up to him. "I want you to meet a couple of friends of mine from St. Louis. This is Frank Laclede and his brother Ben."

"How do you do?" Rachel said. "Laclede as in the Laclede Lacledes of ye olde St. Louie?"

"Afraid so," said Ben with a laugh. "Just a bunch of crusty old stuck-in-the-muds, you know."

"Yes," said TD, "the real deal."

"I'm impressed," Rachel said.

"Don't be," Frank said. "Nothing more boring than a debutante cotillion. Bunch of stuck-up rich girls with nary a brain in their head. Now business, that's what gets the juices flowing. Ain't that right, ole buddy?" he said, turning to TD.

"Uh-huh," Rachel responded. "Well, that's great. This is not a real good time to talk business, though. Timmy and I are getting married soon. Are you here to help with the wedding?"

The boys looked at each other. Hadn't TD cleared this whole deal with Rachel yet? Could that be possible?

"Well, not exactly," TD said. "I was just talking with Frank and Ben about this idea I had for development of this property. I mean, you know, somewhere down the line, after the wedding." He was beginning to sweat again. Damn. Why hadn't he nailed this down four months ago when they were newly engaged?

"I'm not sure I follow? What do you mean, 'development'?"

"Well, you know, sweetie, the Clubhouse is such a wonderful place and everything, it just was in my mind that a lot of other people might benefit from spending time in a lovely place like this. Not that we'd do anything to the Clubhouse itself, of course. But half the lakeshore is on our property, and the view is so nice and everything, we could exploit that . . . " TD mentally kicked himself for using the word, "exploit." It was a standard business term, but in a conversation between two lovers it sounded too harsh, too crass. " . . . I mean, you know, we could develop it in some way. That's where Frank and Ben come in. They're interested in investing in a possible resort here. It's a great idea, and its something that would make you financially secure for the rest of your life." He paused, then added, "And your mother, too. Of course. Your mother, too."

Rachel was floored. She ran her fingers through her hair and looked straight down at the ground. She took a deep breath and let it out slowly, then looked TD in the eye. "You mean cut down all the trees and build condominiums?"

"No, no, no, honey, that's not it at all. We leave everything just the way it is. We just put up a little complex over there that people can come to and get a little R and R, and build around the trees. Minimally invasive construction. Won't hurt the environment at all. Like that development I did down in Arkansas."

Rachel shook her head to try and clear it. The prospect was overwhelming, and she was already overwhelmed by the wedding coming up so soon. "Wow, I've got to think about this. I've got to talk it over with Mom."

"But you do have a majority share in the farm, don't you?" asked TD.

"Well, yes, according the provisions of the will. But I wouldn't move ahead on anything without getting Mom's OK first. I mean, that's just common courtesy."

Courtesy. TD chewed on that one word for a moment or two. It was alien to his vocabulary.

Frank and Ben exchanged glances. "Listen, TD old chum," said Frank, "Ben and I have to be running along. Looks like you and Rachel here have some things to talk over. We'll just buzz off here. Give us a ring tomorrow, let us know where things stand. OK?"

"OK, sure. No problem," TD said weakly. This was getting more complicated by the minute. Why the hell weren't things working out the way he'd planned? All of a sudden Rachel was getting obstinate, blocking the road. In football, when somebody tried to block him he'd knock them down. Same in business. Go straight downfield. Use the power offense. Plow them under.

"Listen, Rachel," he said as Frank and Ben pulled away in their Jaguar, "this is something I've been thinking about for a long time. This is something I want to do for you. For us. For you and your mother. To provide well for you. Think of it as a kind of wedding present. More like a million-dollar wedding present."

"You mean you've already committed money to this project?"

"Well... yes, I have. But I mean..."

"Holy cow, TD! And without telling me? I can't believe this."

"No, listen, Frank and Ben have really caught the vision for this..."

"No, you listen to me. I just can't cope with this right now. We've got a wedding in a few weeks and I've been doing everything and you drop this in my lap at the last minute. I can't believe this." She turned on her heel and marched into the Clubhouse, saying over her shoulder, "I need an aspirin."

As she went inside with Doxie following behind, John pulled up in his Jeep with Hilda and Josiah. John went with Josiah into the Clubhouse to get his rod and reel. When he came in he saw her sitting on the porch by herself.

"Hey, Rachel," he said as he sat down across from her. Josiah promptly climbed into her lap, and Doxie began to lick the little boy's hand. "What's the deal with this construction project? Everybody's talking about it."

"You tell me," she said. "I only just heard about it myself from TD about ten minutes ago."

"Are you kidding? From the word that's going around, it sounds like this deal has been in the works for a long time. People are talking like they've got the bulldozers lined up on Rural Route 2 and ready to start knocking down trees."

"I'm absolutely stunned," she said.

"Yeah, me, too," John said. "When I first heard about it I was ready to get my tomahawk and loincloth and go on the warpath..."

Rachel laughed at the comical image. "I can just see you dancing around the fire with war paint on your face." Then she stopped, embarrassed at the thought that John with his lean physique would actually look pretty good in a loincloth. Plus, she wouldn't mind at all having a warrior like him protecting her.

"Yeah, I bet," John continued. "But I cooled down a little bit on the way out here—Grams is the one who's on the warpath; I imagine old TD is getting it right in the neck about now—and I decided that it just didn't add up, that a development project like this would just be totally out of character for you."

Rachel gave John a level stare. He understood her. And she understood that he understood. But did he understand that she understood that he understood?

"I hate to say this, Rache, but . . . well, it would be totally in character for TD to go behind your back like this." He paused. "I'm sorry, I shouldn't have said that about your fiancé."

She continued looking at him. Her eyes seemed bigger somehow, the brown deep and shining, like the eyes of a doe. Her lips were slightly parted again, like they were that day on the dock. He mentally slapped himself back to attention. "I wish you all the best, Rachel. I've said too much already. It's just that I've seen TD pull crap like this before. I'm sure you'll be a good influence on him, though. I'm sure you'll work things out." Then he stood and motioned for Josiah to come with him for fishing.

While John and Rachel were inside talking, the old woman made a beeline for TD, who was sitting on the park bench and looking across the lake where three herons were feeding in the shallows. They looked up and saw TD looking at them. Two, feeling apprehensive, flew up to their nests, while the third went back to his work while keeping a close eye on the intruder. By then Hilda had arrived at the park bench. She stood in front of her grandson, who slumped in his seat and didn't get up.

"Now you listen to me, young man. What's this I hear about some land development scheme out here at the Clubhouse? The whole town is buzzing with it. You've got some explaining to do, and you better make it good."

"Jeez, sit down, Grams, and calm down."

"I prefer to stand, thank you very much. And if you were half a gentleman, you'd stand up when a lady is in your presence."

TD heavily rose to his feet, towering over the little woman, but as so often happens, the big mastiff is intimidated by the smaller, quicker, and angrier terrier. TD shrank within himself and felt somehow smaller than the tiny old lady.

"Well, it's just an idea, really," he lied. "Something Rachel and I have been discussing," he lied again. One lie leads to another and it gets easier and easier until the truth breaks in and disrupts the fiction. "She owns the lakefront property, you know. And, well, this is such a lovely place and all that we were thinking how nice it would be if others could share in that peaceful feeling you get from being here. There are lots of stressed-out people up in St. Louis, and they need a place to go for a few days and get away from the rat race. We'd be doing them a favor if we provided a place for them, you know." Then he got an inspiration, thinking along the track he had been learning from Pastor Dave. "It would be a ministry, really. A place where people could come and find healing for body and soul."

Hilda stood firmly planted with her fists on her hips. "Bu-u-ll. Shit. You're a damn liar, TD. I cannot believe that a grandson of mine would turn out to be a liar. And Millie and Herbie raised you right, too. They took you to church. They took you to Sunday school. They took you to confirmation. Don't you remember the Second Commandment? Let me remind you. 'Thou shalt not take the name of the Lord in vain.' Don't you remember Luther's explanation? Well, don't you? Let me hear you say it."

TD under pressure was tongue-tied.

The old woman shook her head. "Here's what it says: 'We should fear and love God so that we do not curse, swear, use witchcraft, *lie*, or deceive by His Name, but call upon it in every trouble, pray, praise, and give thanks.' I think you need to go back to Pastor Gottlieb and start all over again at the beginning. It's perfectly obvious to me and everybody in Perry County that all you're interested in is making money off this deal, and may God strike me dead if it ever happens while I'm still alive and I'll roll over in my grave." She paused to catch her breath, then added, "Which probably won't be long if you go ahead with this damn project. It would completely destroy this place.

What do you have to say for yourself?"

TD was caught and tried to wriggle out of the trap by more lies. "I was only thinking of Rachel and her mother, trying to find a way to provide for their financial security."

"Bullshit," the old woman said, stamping her foot. "Bullshit, bullshit, bullshit!" But what happened next was not bullshit, but birdshit, for as her rising voice echoed off the cliff, the heron that had been feeding became startled and rose up into the air on its great wings, and it flew across the lake directly over where TD and his grandmother were standing, and as it flew it dropped a big load, yellow and slimy, which fell like a bomb from the sky and hit TD right square in the face and splattered all over his expensive Ralph Lauren golf shirt.

"Oh, God, oh, God," spluttered the hapless TD, wiping his face while the old lady screamed and hooted with laughter, saying over and over again, "Serves you right." And then she went in to the Clubhouse for her morning nap as John came out with Josiah and went to the dock to fish.

Chapter 12 ◦ The Fight

After Hilda went in to lie down in the back room for her nap, TD went into the kitchen where he washed his face, then took off his shirt and began to rinse it out with cistern water. Rachel could see him from the porch where she was sitting, Doxie by her side. Over the past few months he had neglected his workouts and gotten flabby around the middle. She could also hear a car coming up the gravel road. She assumed it was Millie and Miriam coming back from town, as did John, still down on the dock fishing with Josiah.

Rafael had had his car washed after the oil change, but was disappointed that the drive down the country roads had covered it with dust. And in his rush to get on the road, he had not allowed Jasper enough time to work on the accelerator. It was still sticking, though not as badly as before. Normally Rafael was a fastidious man, regular in his habits as befits a true soldier of the Crescent, and mentally he was berating himself for his many indulgences. He had been letting himself go as he traveled through the belly of the Great Satan. He, like so many others, had allowed himself to be corrupted by its luxury and vice. Once this business was finished, he would put away these sins and indulgences and return to military discipline. He would return to Saudi Arabia. He would be decorated for his heroism. He would retire from field work in the Janissaries. He would train other young men in the way of Muhammad (peace be upon him), a man who was both prophet and warrior.

But first he had to get his car to this camel dung Clubhouse over this narrow, godforsaken, rutted, pitted, one-lane, gravel road. It twisted and turned unexpectedly, went over a low bridge with water flowing over it, and missed looming trees by mere inches. To a man used to the Autobahn it was nerve-wracking. Besides, he had forgotten to take his medication that morning, and his wound was throbbing. Berating himself for forgetting, he stopped and took his pills, then took some more, then took a slug from the bottle of Jim Beam he kept under the seat. Then another. Then another. In a matter of minutes he was feeling better. Feeling extremely good, in fact. But when he drove the car again he scraped the passenger side against an oak tree that stood next to the road. "Jesus Christ!" he exclaimed. Then the road got suddenly worse, a straight and narrow way with dense forest on the left and a deep ravine on the right, and just when it seemed it couldn't get any narrower, it narrowed again as the ravine widened, and he had to squeeze around a massive sycamore tree. Sweat was breaking out on his brow as he feared that he would drop a wheel over the cliff and cut off his escape route. But slowly, gingerly, he edged around the big tree, and then he was in the yard.

How peaceful it all seemed, as he took in the scene. Peaceful, but soon to be sundered with blood and death and lovely musical screams. There was the Clubhouse fifty yards in front of him. By it and next to a black Mercedes was parked a red Jeep—John's. Rafael had heard him describe it with affection. Near the house a brown horse, still saddled, looked up at him and then went back to grazing. Hanging from a limb on the sycamore was a tire swing, the kind he'd seen in yards all across America. In the grass was one of those odd-shaped American footballs, the kind you threw and didn't kick. He looked closely for his quarry but did not see it; the dock was hidden from view by the Clubhouse. But as Rafael drove closer he could see on the porch a woman sitting and reading. She looked up at his car. Still trying to shake the drug-and-whiskey fog out of his head, he remembered his training and turned the car around and left the keys in the ignition before he got out. A good soldier always provides a line of retreat.

He took a deep breath and said a quick prayer. It was time. Right now. Why did he hesitate? Allah was merciful and compassionate.

Why couldn't he be the same? Yes, John had wounded him, but he had been a true friend. Like Sinan. And what of the child? He had never killed a child. Why coudln't he just drive back down that road and disappear?

Why? Because he was a soldier. And because deserters were always caught. And shot.

Rafael straightened his tie and his hat and got out of the car.

Rachel was surprised to see the silver Aston Martin. She'd only seen them in the magazines Jasper kept around the garage. She thought it might be one of TD's friends, another business partner perhaps. But a big man in a Stetson hat stepped out of the car, and somehow she knew that nobody in TD's circle ever wore a hat.

"Hey, honey," she called into the kitchen, "do you know anybody who drives a . . . a . . . what's that kind of car that James Bond drives?"

"Aston Martin, at least in the old movies," TD replied. "No. Frank and Ben drive Jags."

"Well, somebody in a big Aston Martin just pulled up."

"No kidding. Our grease monkey John-boy will be interested in this," he said as he toweled off and walked across the porch toward Rachel.

The screen door squeaked as it opened, and there stood Rafael, filling the doorway. He took off his hat without thinking and laid it on the table. TD looked at the man. TD himself was big, but this man was massive. He had on a nice suit, Armani by the look of it, but it pinched at the waist, and his pants had slipped down and were riding on his hips below his paunch. Too many pieces of custard pie. He was clean-shaven but his nose was red and bulbous—a drinker's nose.

"How do you do," he said with a bit of a slur and a combination of American drawl and crisp German consonants. "My name is Rafael. I'm an old friend of John Mason's. Jasper at the garage told me I could find him here. And his son, the little boy. Is the little boy here also?"

"You mean Josiah," Rachel said as Doxie began to growl. "Doxie, hush!" she said.

"Josiah. Yes, that must be his name," Rafael said.

Now Doxie was standing between Rafael and Rachel, her hackles up and bristling. She was about to drop another litter, and was as ready to attack this stranger as she had been John last September.

"Wait a minute," said Rachel, fear tracing an icy finger up her spine, "if you're an old friend of John's, how come you don't know the name of his son?" Then her mouth went dry and she found it difficult to speak for as her mind raced to put things together she suddenly knew she was in danger. "TD," she whispered hoarsely, "when John told us that story last Thanksgiving, what was the name of the man who murdered his girlfriend?"

"His name," said the big man as he reached into his jacket with his left hand and drew out his knife, "was Rafael von Päpinghausen. And still is." The knife was a fearsome thing with a curved blade and a bejeweled hilt. Made of Damascus steel, an art now lost, it had been handed down from generation to generation in the line of Janissaries for four hundred years. It had come to Sinan, and now to him. A skilled hand-to-hand assassin, Rafael disdained the use of firearms. A good knife like this was all he needed. He had killed dozens of men with it, and it was to his everlasting shame that he had been bested in combat by a clumsy American infidel. Rafael was not as good with his left hand as he had been with his right. He knew that, and in his footwork he still instinctively worked to the advantage of the wrong hand. But no matter. What he lost in physical skill he more than gained in psychological advantage. These were peaceable Americans. They were soft. They were not fighters. They had never killed. He could see the fear in their eyes. They did not grow up in a culture of blood and revenge like the men and women of the Arabian wilderness. Even if they engaged him in combat, they would hesitate a second before trying to kill him, and in that second he would turn the tables on them.

But the dog showed no fear. The dog was barking now. This was a problem. A problem that must be solved to get this job done and be on his way quickly. Rafael took a step toward Rachel, brandishing the knife and saying, "I would advise you to collar your dog, and do it quickly if you want to save your life. I am here for John Mason and his child, not you. Call off your dog and I might spare you. If not, well, the choice is yours."

"God, TD," Rachel said, barely croaking out the desperate words, "help me. Do something. Quick. Please." But glancing out of the corner of her eye she saw TD retreating back into the kitchen.

"Now where is the child, please?" said Rafael as he slowly advanced toward her. Damn the dog. He kicked at it. Dogs were too low and too quick to dispatch quickly. But the woman might not know that. "I said collar the dog." He kicked at the dog again. It nipped at him but only caught the toe of his boot. He kicked hard this time and flung the dog backwards, slamming it into the wall.

At that moment Rachel found her voice. "John!" she shouted out as loud as she could.

In the back bedroom Hilda, a light sleeper like all old ladies, awoke from her nap at the noise and shouting and commotion. Down at the dock John had heard Doxie barking and was puzzled, for the dog would never bark like that at Millie or Miriam or Hilda. Then the dog stopped. That puzzled him all the more. Laying down his fishing rod he had picked up Josiah and begun walking toward the kitchen door. When he heard Rachel cry out he broke into a run, tucking the child under his arm like a football and sprinting. His mangled foot was now fully healed, and he ran fast and well, feeling as light as he skimmed over the ground as he once had in high school sports.

On the porch the dog recovered, regained its footing, shook itself, and stopped barking as dogs do when they are ready to attack. Rafael knew the sign and braced himself, for the German shepherd was a big dog, close to a hundred pounds, and was carrying extra weight from the litter inside her. The dog paused a moment to judge the distance, then ran and leaped at Rafael, springing for his neck. But the man was ready. He blocked with his left hand. The dog fastened its jaws around his wrist as the man stepped backwards to absorb the impact, and as the dog sank down he brought a rapid and powerful karate chop on the back of the dog's neck, breaking it with a clean snap. The dog fell to the floor without a whimper while Rafael screamed in pain. For he had struck the dog with his badly infected hand, and no amount of pain medicine and whiskey could cover it up. He wobbled on his feet, his knees buckled, and he almost passed out from the pain. But he was a soldier, and inured to pain. And pain was clean. The pain was pure. The pain cleared his head from the drugs and liquor. The pain snapped him back to full consciousness and keen concentration. He glared at Rachel. "You should have called off your dog. Now you will pay the price, to the last penny."

Gripping his knife again and holding it low, he advanced again slowly, maintaining his balance. Rachel had backed into the kitchen. TD was sidling toward the door. Rachel turned to him. "TD, what the hell are you doing. I'm in danger here!"

Rafael entered and stood by the stove. "Now let's try again. Where are John Mason and the child?" But she didn't need to answer. At that moment the kitchen door opened and John came in with the child, and as he did TD slipped out and ran.

A snap thought of regret like a tracer shot across Rafael's mind, followed immediately by a live round. "There you are, my old friend, and there is the little heir apparent to the throne of Mayangala."

"Rafael!" John exclaimed. "What? Stop it, for God's sake!"

"Which god? Yours, or mine?"

John was dumbfounded to see his onetime friend-turned-mortal enemy intrude upon this sanctuary of refuge, this place of restoration. He had thought that perhaps Rafael had been mortally injured after the sword fight. But then he had gotten the note from him threatening revenge. It had taken such a long time. So much living had gone on between then and now, he had forgotten the hatred of this man, forgotten the imminent danger, forgotten the lust for vengeance in his enemy's heart. Now here he was, bigger and more menacing than he had been in Germany, though at a glance John could see that he was looking at a wreck of his enemy, and not his enemy at full strength as he had been the night he had killed Elizabeth. John was scared, for he was looking at a skilled murderer. He had bested him once, almost by accident. Or by the grace of God. It was unlikely that he would be able to defeat him again. But for now he had no time for thinking. He was just reacting.

With one hand, he picked up a chair and threw it at Rafael. The big man ducked as the chair flew past him and smashed into the wall, narrowly missing Hilda, who was now standing in the doorway. Rafael swung awkwardly with his knife but missed John, who jumped back and grabbed another chair, swung it hard, and hit Rafael in the knee. He grunted and limped backward a couple of steps. By this time he was within reach of the old woman, who had picked up a poker from beside the stove. She jabbed it into his ribs as hard as she could. Rafael yelped at this unexpected pain and spun around. Reacting automatically he swung with the wrong hand—his injured right hand—and struck the old woman across the face, knocking her down and out. But the blow blasted out pain like fire from his hand again, and he cursed and shouted at the fresh agony. Agony and frustration, for this fight was getting more complicated than he had expected. Where was the fear in these people? Where was the whimpering? Where was the pleading for mercy?

Rafael turned again to face John, who was still holding Josiah. Suddenly the child took a rock out of his pocket and threw it at Rafael, hitting him in the eye. Rafael cried out and doubled over in pain. John yelled for Rachel to take the child and run as he came up behind Rafael and smashed the chair across his back. Rafael grunted and spun around quickly on his toes, slashing John across the forehead with his knife as Rachel with Josiah flung herself out the door. "There's a Heidelberg dueling scar for you," he said as he ran after Rachel. "I'll be back in a minute." John fell to the floor, blood gushing from his wound and down into his eyes.

By now Rachel was outside and running for her horse. She whistled for Milton and he came at a trot. John's fight with Rafael had gained her a few seconds, but not many. Rafael was running hard, not far behind her. But the blow to his leg had displaced something, and he was running with a limp even though the overdose of pain killers was masking the pain. He fell. He recovered. Somehow Rachel flung herself into the saddle with the child clinging to her neck and she dug her heels hard into Milton's flanks. The good horse lurched forward and in a moment was at full gallop with Rafael running alongside. But he was on the left side of the horse and could not land a blow with his knife, which was still in his left hand. Rachel kicked out with her left foot still in the wooden stirrup and clipped him on the jaw. He fell sprawling and lost his knife, but in a second was on his feet. Rafael jumped into the driver's seat of his car. Just as he had prepared, the keys were in the ignition. He reached down and turned them and the car roared to life. He dropped it into first gear and popped the clutch, the wheels spinning as he sped toward the horse and rider, gaining ground every moment. Another second or two and he would smash into the horse, breaking its legs and throwing the woman and child. Then he would be able to kill them both easily with his bare hands, and then go back and finish off John. How easy it all was for a Janissary. Allah was with him, giving him power and victory and glory.

Just then John stumbled into the yard. His eyes were blurred with blood, but he saw at a glance Rachel and Josiah on the horse with Rafael close behind. For God's sake, what was she doing running the horse toward the ravine? But in the blink of an eye he understood. Milton was a jumper. If he could jump the ravine, Rachel and the child would be beyond reach of the car and Rafael. But the Aston Martin was closing fast on the horse. It would cut them down yards before the ravine. There was no way he could stop it.

They were almost at the big sycamore tree. From a branch on the tree hung the tire swing. Then John saw the old football lying in the yard. Something clicked. He ran and picked it up and heaved it in desperation at the car. If he could hit it the impact might distract Rafael for a split second, enough to allow Rachel to escape. Then John would have to fight Rafael to the death. The death would probably be his. But at least Rachel and his child would have a chance. Throwing instinctively and without thought, John put a perfect spiral on the ball. It sailed in a clean arc across the yard, flew into the window of the Aston Martin and hit Rafael in the head, then bounced down and wedged itself between the steering wheel and the column. Momentarily stunned, Rafael reacted by pressing down on the accelerator. Then the accelerator stuck wide open—just as Jasper had warned—and just at the moment of impact the horse veered left, took flight, and leaped easily over the ravine. The car screamed forward and dropped down hard like an angel cast out of heaven. It smashed into the bottom of the ravine and burst into flame.

Rachel reined up the horse and looked back. Smoke and fire were ascending from the wreck. She could hear the screams of the man caught inside. He screamed and screamed as the flames enveloped him. The doors were jammed shut from the crash, and his legs were broken. He couldn't get out. He was screaming and dying and crying out to his god, and cursing all his enemies and his enemies' gods. Then he was silent, and there was only the roaring of the flames and the smoke billowing up like Sodom and Gomorrah.

Through the shimmering heat waves Rachel could see John fall to his knees, weak from loss of blood. Her eyes swept over the Clubhouse lawn. TD and his car were gone. John stood up and waved at them. Then he fell again. Holding the reins with her right hand, she waved back with her left, and as she waved at John she saw the engagement ring TD had given her, the big expensive one with the two-carat diamond. She looked at it and without a second thought took it off and threw it into the lake.

Her eyes were on her man, John Mason, as he struggled to his feet and went into the Clubhouse to tend to his grandmother. Then she looked at his child as if he were her own, and the boy was looking at her as if she were his own. She turned the horse toward the Friedensee, and waded him across the shallow place by the spillway and then onto the lawn. Going inside she saw John bent over his grandmother, who having come to was fussing at him for dripping blood all over her new dress.

"Gott dernit," she said, "this cost me thirty-one dollars at Rozier's. This black eye will go away by itself, but how the heck am I going to get out these blood stains. Now go on, git off me and go see a doctor about that cut."

John looked up and smiled at Rachel. Then he passed out. When he came to he was in the back of Millie's old Buick station wagon, his head cradled in Rachel's lap. She was holding a compress on his cut and stroking his hair and it felt good to him. He began to try to sit up, then changed his mind and decided to relax and enjoy the TLC.

Besides, she was smiling and crying over him—always a good sign. "What happened?" he asked.

"Shhh," Rachel whispered and leaned over and kissed him on the forehead. Another good sign. Millie was driving and could see all this in the rear view mirror. She gave the secret woman's eyeball to Hilda and Miriam, who were sharing the front seat with her, and they returned it with a nod of the head. At that moment, a wordless contract was sealed in the family.

They pulled in to the parking lot at the emergency room—Millie had called ahead—and an attendant came out with wheelchairs, one for John and one for Hilda. Both of them fussed about it, but the attendant fussed right back, having dealt with injured but obstreperous Perryville farmers over many years, and made them sit down and be wheeled in. Things were slow in the ER that afternoon, and in a short time Hilda was examined and released, and John likewise was stitched up and let go. The old woman had a bump on her noggin from where she had hit the floor and a nice black eye from where Rafael had struck her, but was none the worse for wear, and in high spirits for having been in a fight. John was worse, having required stitches and a pint of blood.

Meanwhile Rachel had taken the carcass of Doxie to the vet's to be cremated, as was the law. It was a heavy load, for Doxie was a big dog and had been carrying a litter, but Rachel was a farm girl with a strong back, and she could carry a heavy load. Heavier still was the load on her heart, for the dog had been her constant companion for many years, always there for her when she came back from school, always ready to listen to her recent troubles with an understanding ear, always ready to play, always ready to curl up at her feet while she played her guitar and softly sang sad ballads of jilted love. Now her father was dead. And her brother was dead. And her marriage-to-be was dead. And her dog was dead. It was just too much for one little old farm girl from Rural Route 2, Perryville, Missouri. And she sat down in the waiting room and put her face into her hands and wept softly. Then after a few minutes she heard the office door open and saw the vet standing in front of her with a queer expression on his face.

Millie with the old Buick had been doing the running around, dropping off John and Hilda at the hospital, and Rachel and Doxie at the vet's, and Miriam and Josiah at the little playground on the corner of the square. After an hour or so she looped back around and picked everybody up and took them to the coffee shop for lunch, where the whole place was crowded and buzzing with the news. Jasper came in from the garage and sat down with them as they ordered hamburgers.

"J-J-Jeez, what h-happened," he asked excitedly. "Clarence and Merle came in to the shop and said there was a four-alarm forest fire and the Clubhouse had burned down to the ground. I b-b-been worried sick. And God, J-Johnny, you l-l-look like F-Frankenstein."

"Well, I still want to know what happened after I passed out," John said as he sat close to Rachel with his arm around her, and with her nestled comfortably into his shoulder—a detail noted with approval by Old Man and Old Lady Roschke at their corner table. Millie had taken him by his parents' house, where he had borrowed a fresh shirt from his father. His face was cleaned of the blood, and the doctor had stitched up the wound. It had taken twenty-two tiny stitches, and would make a fine scar. "I came to and here was this pretty girl smothering me with kisses."

Rachel said, "Shh," then biffed him in the arm.

"I'd like to know, too," said Hilda, obviously proud of her shiner. "I get woken up from my nap by all this commotion, and I come in to the kitchen and here's this big oofdegoof trying to kill Rachel."

"And where is TD, I'd like to know," said Rachel. "Oh, and I have to tell about Doxie!"

"OK, OK. Let me take a stab at this," said Millie as the burgers and sodas arrived. Josiah in a high chair began to stuff french fries into his mouth as fast as he could.

"Wait, son," John said to Josiah, "wait till we say our prayer."

The child folded his pudgy little hands, his mouth bulging, the end of one fry still sticking out from between his lips. The family said grace together, then Millie continued. "Miriam and I were driving up the road to the Clubhouse and we were just about at the low water bridge when here comes TD in his big fancy car, flying like a bat out of hell, and looking like he'd seen a ghost or something. We pulled off to the side just in the nick of time and he sped right by us. We could see his face as clear as anything. Talk about scared! That got us puzzled and concerned, so we drove ahead as fast as we could on that bad road of ours, thinking there might be some kind of trouble. That's when we saw the smoke. At first we thought there might be a forest fire, which really scared us. And as we later found out the ranger in the fire tower also saw the smoke from the burning wreck and reported a fire. Well, they knew there's no fire truck could ever get up that road, so they dispatched a helicopter with flame retardant to the scene."

"That must have gone out over the police b-b-band," said Jasper, "and somebody told somebody and somebody else and p-pretty soon here's Clarence and Merle telling this wild story to everybody in town."

"Makes sense to me," continued Millie. "So the helicopter arrives just when we do and dumps a load of crud on the burning car and puts it out."

"Is this the c-c-car of that German f-feller that was in the sh-shop?" asked Jasper.

"Yes," John replied. "You remember the story I told you about at Thanksgiving? That man was my sworn enemy, Rafael von Päpinghausen. He had come to kill me and Josiah." He sighed. "We were friends once."

"So that's who that was," said Hilda. "I seen that he was up to no good, so I grabbed the poker from next to the stove and let him have it in the ribs, but he knocked me for a loop. At least I slowed him down."

"And you killed him instead?" said Jasper to John.

"Sort of," John said.

"With what?"

He paused, then said, "A football."

And everyone at the table and everyone in the cafe who was listening laughed and laughed. And John laughed harder than all of them, for he had been in the mortal danger of single combat, and he had prevailed over his enemy, and now the ordeal was over.

"So . . . " Jasper was thinking quickly, "that Aston Martin is still out there in the ravine, ain't it?"

"Why, sure."

"And it would be f-finders, keepers, wouldn't it?"

"I guess so."

"Hmm."

"So then where is TD?" asked John. "He came running out of the house just as I was coming in."

"Who knows?" said Millie.

"Who cares?" said Rachel with disgust as she took a sip of her Diet Coke.

Hilda looked at John. She had seen him in action. There was a bit of the Assiniboine warrior in him after all.

"And Rafael said something about Josiah," John said. "This was after he'd hit you, Grams, and after Rachel had run for it. Something about him being heir to the throne or something. This is all news to me."

Myrtle brought pie and coffee around as Miriam lifted a finger. "Well, it's time you found out, John. You recall the story I related at Thanksgiving, about the song Elizabeth's brother sang, the one with the prophecy in it. I've been corresponding with her brothers, you know, the boys who are still living in England. And they took counsel and agreed that little Josie here and not one of them should be rightful heir to the throne of his grandfather. This little guy here is a true king."

They looked at Josiah. His face was smeared with ketchup and his chipmunk cheeks bulged with french fries.

"Are we supposed to bow down or something?" John asked.

"Maybe later after I change his royal nappy," said Miriam with a smile.

"So anyway the cops finally show up," continued Millie.

"The cops?" said John.

"Yeah. Everybody in the county knows how bad that road is, so the chopper radioed the highway patrol, and they sent a couple of state troopers on motorcycles. They were down in the ravine as we were leaving, investigating the wreck and taking pictures and getting the body out of the car."

"So Rafael is dead," John said.

"Burned to a crisp," said Millie with a shudder.

"I must have been really out of it," John said.

"Out like a light," said Millie. "You lost a lot of blood, poor baby. The hospital said they had to put a half-quart in you."

John and Jasper looked at each other. Both had the same thought, and both said at the same time, "10w-30." And everyone laughed again.

"So," Millie continued, "we threw you and poor Doxie into the wagon and shot off to town."

"Wait," John said, "what happened to Doxie?"

"Killed."

"Rafael killed Doxie?"

"Yes, broke her neck with a karate chop or something," said Rachel. "Poor thing. She tried to defend me while TD was busy saving his own damn skin, and she lunged at him and he broke her neck. But I have to tell you," she went on excitedly, "when I took her to the vet I was in the lobby bawling my eyes out, and the doctor came in and said to come with him. He showed me the most amazing thing. There she was on the table. He said that although Doxie's neck was broken she didn't die right away. She must have been barely breathing or something, he said, and died sometime on the way into town. And when he was getting ready to load her into the incinerator he thought he felt something, a movement or something, very faint, and just on a hunch he opened her up then and there, and to his amazement he found one live puppy among the litter. He could tell she was pregnant just by looking at her, of course, and just assumed that all the pups in the litter had died with her, but there was a live one. Just one, fully developed, and wriggling around and mewling for its mother."

Everyone was saying, "Wow, incredible, holy cow, I don't believe it," all chattering at once. Then Rachel went on. "The vet called me in and showed me this, and you could have knocked me down with a feather. Poor little puppy, all gooey and wet and pathetic, whimpering and squirming and squinting around with its little eyes shut. The doctor knew that a bitch in the pet store across the street had just dropped a litter that morning, so we cut the umbilical, dried the thing off, and I ran it over while he took care of Doxie. As luck would have it the momma dog was also a German shepherd, and when I told the storeowner the story she was just as amazed as I was and said sure, toss him in and let's see what happens. So we put the puppy in the crate, and the mother sniffed it and licked it and nosed it over into the pile with the other puppies, and it found a tit and started sucking away and there you are!"

Again it was, "My God, that's amazing, I don't believe it, that's the wildest thing I ever heard in my life," everyone talking at the same time. At last Hilda said, "Well, I don't know about you kids, but I'm ready for a nap. If you recall, my first nap was rudely interrupted by a murderer!"

"OK," Millie said, "I'll drive you home. Are the rest of you ready?" Miriam said yes and started to put Josiah's diaper bag together.

But John leaned forward and peered into his coffee cup. Then he turned to Rachel. "Can you ... if we didn't ... I, uh, I need to talk to you." She looked at him and nodded assent. Then turning to his uncle he said, "Jasper, could you run us out later on?"

"Sure," said Jasper. "I can close up early. I want to take a l-look at that wreck, anyway."

So Millie took off with Hilda and Miriam and Josiah, and Jasper went back to the garage. That left John and Rachel standing on the sidewalk in front of the cafe. "Let's take a turn around the square," Rachel suggested. "You look like something's on your mind, and the thinking works better when you're walking."

"Yes," John said. "I think you're right. You're right about a whole lot of things, actually."

She walked close beside him. Very close. She took his hand. A surge of hope went through him. He squeezed her hand. She squeezed back. Then he noticed something, and pulled her hand up to where he could see it.

"Where's your engagement ring?"

"I took it off and threw it away."

"You did?"

"Yes."

"When?"

"Today. Back at the Clubhouse. After I saw what a dirty, lousy, rotten, no-good, coward TD was. He did nothing to protect me. Nothing! He just ran off and saved his own skin. So I took off the ring and threw it into the lake. Whoever finds it can have it. And good riddance to it and to him, is all I have to say."

They walked on again, hand in hand, past the memorial to the men from Perry County who had fought in the Civil War. After a while John said, "So the wedding's off?"

"Oh, yes."

Then they walked some more, still hand in hand. Then after a while he said, "But you still have the dress?"

"Yes."

Then they passed the World War One and World War Two and Korean War Memorials. He looked at the names of his relatives, and she at hers.

"Lou Ann said you had picked out a cake."

"Yes."

They passed the courthouse portico. Clarence and Merle were there, sitting in the shade and playing checkers with a couple of other old-timers. John and Rachel waved, and the boys waved back.

"There's something I've been wanting to say to you for a long time, Rachel."

"I want to hear it. I didn't before. I was afraid. But that's over. I want to hear your words, John. I want to hear them now.""

By now they had made a complete circuit around the courthouse and were standing on the lawn across the street from the cafe again. John stopped and turned and looked at her. Her big brown doe eyes were shining. He wanted to dive down into those eyes and swim all the way to the bottom. She looked up at him. His grey eyes were blazing with passion. His hair was long and tousled. She wanted to lie beside him in bed and run her fingers through it all morning long.

"I came close to telling you that day when it was raining and we were on the dock."

"Yes."

"It's just kind of been . . . I wanted to say it, but with you being engaged and all . . ."

"And I knew what you were going to say, and I stopped you."

"But now, I . . . It's hard to . . ." he stammered, then laughed. "I feel all tongue t-t-tied, like Jasper."

"Maybe this will help," she said. And she put her arms around him and kissed him, full on the mouth. And John swept her up into his arms and crushed her against his body and kissed her again and again and again. And he began to cry, and through his tears he said to her in a soft, low voice, "Yes. That's what I've been trying to say. God, Rachel, I love you! I love you with all my heart."

"I love you, too, John."

He looked at her again with the fire of love burning the words off his tongue: "Will you marry me? Please?"

"Yes," she said, "I will."

And they laughed and embraced and kissed again and again and again, and although John and Rachel couldn't see it or hear it, all the people in the cafe were pressed against the window watching them, and when they kissed, the people all began cheering and clapping and whistling and congratulating each other with Old Man Roschke taking bets on the date of the wedding, the winner to use the proceeds on a gift from the coffee shop gang.

Chapter 13 ◉ An Easter Wedding

The great blue herons, which had returned earlier in the spring, had been busy rebuilding their nests and mating and laying their eggs. And now the young in the rookery were hatching and yelping all day for food, and the parents were kept busy soaring down to the lake and the creek for frogs and minnows and fingerlings, hunting and eating and bringing back sustenance for their young. The mourning doves were cooing as they nestled in the strong arm of the old sycamore tree, and robins and mockingbirds kept the forest alive with their song.

Deep in the lake the great fish kept vigil, swimming to the shallows near the shore from time to time to commune with the children, who would come looking for it, and tell it their secrets and hearts' desires. Who could divine what was in the mind of a very old and very large catfish, for in the course of a century of life its intelligence had grown to vast proportions, and it had a way of communicating with little ones. The little dark child was especially attentive to the movements of the great fish, for there was a destiny wrapped about him that drew the fish more frequently up to the shore, even tempting it sometimes to let itself be revealed to the adults who were always close at hand.

So time moved ahead into March as springtime enveloped the hills. Word had gotten around about the heron rookery, and the Audubon Society brought a group out for a day of bird-watching. They paid well for the privilege, and Millie and Miriam enjoyed visiting with them and feeding them. Later on *Missouri Conservationist* magazine sent a photographer out for a shoot, and the picture of a heron in midflight made the cover. This put the Clubhouse on the map for birdwatchers, and caused business to pick up significantly in the warm months when things were normally slow. With Rachel unavailable, Millie hired Myrtle's daughter Ruby, who had grown up cooking in the cafe, to help pick up the slack in the kitchen.

Jasper, meanwhile, had salvaged the wreck of the Aston Martin and was working on it steadily. It was badly damaged from the crash and the fire, but Jasper loved nothing better than a project with some real challenges in it. The frame needed to be straightened and the dents fixed, and he took it over to his buddies at Schultheiss Auto Body. It was in and out within a week. The whole car needed a paint job. Schultheiss took care of that as well. Most of the interior needed new upholstery. That job went to Graumann's We-Do-Re-Do Shop next to the John Deere farm implement showroom. The radiator was destroyed and had to be replaced. But the resourceful Jasper made the rounds of the junkyards and found a radiator from a British-made Rover that fit perfectly. Plus, after studying up on the subject, he learned that English car manufacturers used a lot of stock Ford parts, alternators and hoses and fuses and such. Besides, the drive train—engine, transmission, and differential—were all still good. Bit by bit the big car came together in the back of Mason's Garage, and Clarence and Merle kept the town apprized of its progress, down to the smallest detail. Jasper took particular pains over the stuck accelerator, examining every possible cause of the problem, only to find that it was a pebble from some back road that had gotten itself wedged into the linkage. Not that he minded having made a small contribution, albeit unintentional, to the death of the Janissary, but he didn't want the same problem to reoccur when he presented the restored car as a wedding present to John and Rachel. The case of bourbon he found in the trunk he quietly expropriated.

No such luck with TD's big black Mercedes. He had to sell it at a fraction of its value, since the canceled wedding wiped him out financially. Even with the bridging loan he missed another payment. When Frank and Ben confronted him they learned that the wedding was off. Since the wedding was off, the development was off. Since the development was off, the revenue stream was gone. Since the revenue stream was gone, the $1.5 million loan was gone. They called in their chips, and in order to make good on his debt, TD was forced to liquidate his collateral, which was everything: his business, his development in Arkansas, his house, his Ping golf clubs. Needing to stay in Ste. Genevieve for the welfare of his son Danny, TD had to take the first job he could get, and so ended up as a janitor at the high school where he had once been the star quarterback. His first job was to repaint the dragon, which had once again been redecorated in green and white by teenage vandals from Perryville High. Since school policy required him to wear a work uniform and cap, he got rid of his toupee and began to face life squarely as a balding man.

John's dissertation had been accepted by his committee, and he flew back to Heidelberg to defend and pick up the degree. So now he was the Reverend Doctor John Mason, but there was still no word from any of the church colleges or seminaries. He was beginning to sweat the finances a bit, since work at the garage didn't pay well, when two things happened. One was that the police, who had investigated the accident and found an Interpol dossier on Rafael, showed up at the garage one day and handed John a check for twenty-five thousand dollars. The assassin had been wanted, dead or alive, in a number of countries. On the Perry County economy, that money would go a long way. The other thing was that when Pastor Gottlieb announced his retirement from Peace Lutheran Church, the congregation extended the call to John to be their pastor. After deliberating for ten or fifteen minutes, he accepted. So things were looking up for the young man. He had a doctorate, a call, a fiancée, a car, and money in his pocket.

Rachel had quit going to Pastor Dave's church with TD when she canceled the wedding, and had renewed her commitment to the old Lutheran church where she had been baptized. Pastor Dave's church was now without two band members, which was not a major blow, but the church was now without Pastor Dave. He had not only been ogling the girls like Rachel, but he had been bedding them as well. The lid blew off when his wife caught him *in flagrante delicto* on the couch in his office with one of the beige secretaries. With Dave gone, attendance dropped, the mortgage could no longer be sustained, the new mall-type building had to be sold. They put in a Walgreens and a Starbucks. The church folded. A goodly number of the members, who still retained some memory of the old ways, came over to Peace, filling both pew and plate.

As for Josiah's welfare, the trust fund would provide a stipend for Miriam, who was committed to stay on as housekeeper for the newly-established Mason family, and to teach the child the language, culture, tradition, and, most importantly, the songs of Mayangala. And when the time came, he would be sent off to Eton and Cambridge like his uncles.

As it turned out, Coach Wink won the wedding lottery, having guessed on a lark that since John was a minister he might pick Easter Sunday, which fell on April 11 that year and only the day after Rachel's original date with TD. So they rolled everything into one— the Easter service, the wedding, the baptism, the works. Everybody was to come out to the Clubhouse afterwards for dinner. Normally the extended family would have Easter and baseball at the Gottlieb farm in Augsburg, but this was an exception. They had made special arrangements for the Legion to provide fried chicken, mashed potatoes, and slaw, so for once poor Millie didn't have to spend all day slaving over a hot stove.

So the big day finally arrived, and family filled the church pews right up to the front. John and Rachel with Josiah sat in the very front pew. John's parents, Ralph and Betty Mason, sat beside them with Eileen McFadden, Rachel's mother. Behind them were John's brother Bill, his wife Judy, and their daughter Katie. Behind them in the third pew were John's sister Lou Ann and her son Billy, and Hilda Mason, John's grandmother, who had driven Lou Ann and Billy to church in her old Hudson. Paul and Lori Gottlieb sat with them, along with their son Kurt, now known as Dutch. Next to them sat John's aunt, Millie Pope, and her now-best friend Miriam Seyoum, and both of them were happily crying away and dabbing their eyes with Kleenex. Millie's son TD, minus his toupee, sat glumly with his son Danny in the next row back of them along with Betty Mason's brother-in-law, the Reverend JJ Kolding, and his wife Joan. Josiah's uncles, his mother Elizabeth's brothers Peter and Jacob and Isaac, were absent, though they had been invited. But between Peter's duties as an airline pilot and Jacob's law practice and Isaac's teaching schedule it seemed impossible to get one or two or all of them in the same place at the same time. So, much as they would have liked to have the uncles present, the family decided to go ahead with the ceremonies without them.

The windows of the little country church were thrown open, and a soft, fragrant breeze wafted through and over the congregation. At ten o'clock the sexton rang the bell—an old German church bell that had been brought over by immigrants in 1839—and the service began. The old pipe organ wheezed to life and the people rose to their feet and began to sing, "Jesus Christ is Risen Today, Alleluia!" First came the acolytes, attired in red cassocks with white surplices, followed by the thurifer, casting incense like the smoke of the morning sacrifice of praise that drifted up and around and over the people, enveloping them in a sweet savor. Last of all came Pastor Earl Gottlieb with his old shepherd's crook, given him long ago in Mayangala. He stood on the floor of the nave, stooped and reverent in his old age, as the children lit the candles, including the lamps of the presence, for it was a high feast day with the celebration of the Eucharist, and the thurifer censed the altar.

With no announcements, no phony shake-hands-and-say-howdy-to-your-neighbor, and no show business, the old parson simply turned to the congregation and intoned the ancient words, "In the name of the Father, and of the Son, and of the Holy Ghost," as he made the Sign of the Cross, and the people likewise crossed themselves in remembrance of their baptism.

Then he turned and faced the altar and knelt down upon the floor, and the congregation also knelt, and as penitent sinners they said together,

> Oh, almighty God, I, a poor miserable sinner, confess
> unto thee all my sins and iniquities with which I have ever

offended thee and justly deserve thy temporal and eternal punishment. But I am heartily sorry for them and sincerely repent of them, and I pray thee of thy boundless mercy and for the sake of the holy, innocent, bitter, sufferings and death of Thy beloved son, Jesus Christ, to be gracious and merciful to me, a poor, sinful being. Amen.

Steadying himself with his crozier the old pastor rose to his feet and faced the congregation, his face beaming, his eyes twinkling through the thick glasses, and he said in a loud voice, "Upon this thy confession, I, by virtue of my office as a called and ordained servant of the Word, announce unto thee the grace of God, and in the stead and by the command of my Lord Jesus Christ I forgive thee all thy sins in the name of God the Father, God the Son, and God the Holy Ghost. Amen." Again he made the Sign of the Cross, and again the people crossed themselves, and sat down.

He motioned for John and Rachel to come forward, and as they got up and moved toward the chancel Pastor Gottlieb said, "We have a rather full service today—a wedding and a baptism, along with the regular order of service and Holy Communion. I may have to cut out the sermon." A murmur of gentle laughter went through the congregation. Raising his finger he said, "But not the collection!" Again they laughed.

John and Rachel stood before the pastor, with his brother Bill as best man on his right and his sister Lou Ann as maid of honor on Rachel's left. Rachel's dress, the one she bought off the rack at Rozier's, was made of white satin with lace ruffles on the sleeve, and a long veil that trailed down behind. John had on his plain old preacher's black suit, with a white shirt and blue silk tie. Bill, who with a size 19 neck never wore a tie, had for the occasion squeezed himself into his one and only suit, a light blue polyester thing he'd bought at the old Kmart and wore only at Christmas and Easter, and kept fingering his shirt collar to loosen the tie a little, when he wasn't fumbling in his coat pocket for the thirteenth time to make sure the rings were still there. Lou Ann had gone all out and run up to St. Louis to a fancy women's boutique at the Galleria mall, and her mother Betty had picked out a good-looking robin's egg-blue dress for her with matching shoes and purse. She had lost a bit of weight and with her hair newly done and her gum spit out she looked like a million bucks, a detail not lost to the observation of the three or four bachelor farm boys who were in attendance that day.

"Dearly beloved," Pastor Gottlieb began, "forasmuch as you purpose to enter upon the holy estate of matrimony, which is to be held in honor by all, it becometh you to hear what the Word of God teacheth concerning this estate." And from his little black book, the little agenda that contained all the rites and ceremonies in common use among Lutheran churches, orders for baptizing and marrying and burying ("hatch, match, and dispatch" as the preachers say amongst themselves), he read the Scripture lessons from Genesis that described the wedding of Adam and Eve, and from Ephesians where St. Paul admonishes husbands to love their wives and wives to submit to their husbands, and then went on, saying, "Into this holy estate you now come to be united, and that all men may know your mutual consent in holy wedlock to have been sincerely and freely given, it behooveth you to declare, in the presence of God and these witnesses, the sincere intent you both have."

To the congregation he said, "If there be any here present who can show just cause why they may not lawfully be joined in marriage, let him now speak, or ever after hold his peace." Then came that awful moment of tension that happens in every wedding, when all are in dread that someone will speak up and abort the wedding. "I do," John thought to himself. I was born in sin and in iniquity did my mother conceive me. I have committed adultery. I have a child out of wedlock. I am a sinner. I have no right to be standing here today. "I do," thought Rachel. I have made a wreck out of my life. I got pregnant, then had an abortion. God should cast me away from his presence, and make an old maid of me. Just then Pastor Gottlieb caught them both with his eyes. He looked at them, and through the thick glasses and grey hair and wrinkled skin both the man and the woman, penitent sinners that they were, could see the face of Jesus looking at them as he had looked at the woman caught in the act of adultery, and it was the face of divine love and mercy and forgiveness. And they looked at each other, and the woman could see in the man she was about to marry the face of Jesus, who on the cross was all sinners rolled into one, and the man could see in the woman he was about to marry the face of Jesus, who in his body received the sins of the world. He was about to take her to wife, and she him to husband, and Jesus in his eyes said to her and Jesus in her eyes said to him, inasmuch as ye have done it unto one of the least of these my brothers, ye have done it unto me. And thus they resolved before God and men to do good to one another, so doing good to Christ himself who was present in the other, to love, to honor, to cherish, to obey, to keep the bond of wedlock holy and unbroken till death did them part.

Pastor Gottlieb, still beaming at John and Rachel, pronounced them husband and wife, and as John drew back the veil and kissed his wife, Pastor Gottlieb looked out over the congregation he had served so long, and that he would soon be leaving. There were the farmers, there were the wives, there were the children and grandchildren, most of whom he had baptized, there was the Mason clan, and there, sitting in his great-grandmother's lap, was little Josiah Mason, in the pew next to the aisle next to the window. The grandmother with rapt attention was looking at the bride and groom. A small yellow spring butterfly fluttered in the window beneath the picture of Jesus blessing the children. The child saw it, and craned his neck when it flew out again. A moment later the butterfly flew back in to the church, circled down, and settled on the palm of the child's outstretched hand. The little boy gazed at it in wonder, then popped the butterfly into his mouth and ate it with a rather peculiar expression on his little face.

It was all Gottlieb could do to keep from falling over with laughter, while everyone in church assumed that the joy of the Lord had come upon him, for he alone had seen the child eat the butterfly. With an effort he regained his composure and said, "We proceed with the order of Holy Baptism. Let the candidate be brought forward."

Deep in the Friedensee the waters began to stir.

Rachel picked up Josiah and carried him to the baptismal font, which stood in the center aisle just behind the wedding party. Bill and Lou Ann, who were doubling as both witnesses to the marriage and sponsors for the child, moved to the font.

"Dearly beloved, forasmuch as our Lord hath commanded Baptism, saying to His disciples in the last chapter of Matthew: 'Go ye, therefore, and teach all nations, baptizing them in the name of the Father and of the Son and of the Holy Ghost,' it is meet and right that, in obedience to his command and trusting in his promise, you should bring this child to be baptized in his name." As he was speaking these words Pastor Gottlieb began to be dimly aware of a commotion up in the balcony and toward the back. Some of the young people, who always sat up there fidgeting around and daydreaming during church, were looking out the open window and whispering to each other. Refocusing his attention, he plowed ahead. "Let us pray. Almighty and everlasting God, who according to Thy righteous judgment didst destroy the unbelieving world by the Flood and according to thy great mercy didst save faithful Noah and his family . . ." But he paused, distracted again. There was some loud noise coming from outside. It sounded like a tractor.

". . . who didst drown obdurate Pharaoh with all his host in the Red Sea and didst safely lead thy people Israel through the midst thereof, prefiguring thereby this washing of thy Holy Baptism: and who, by the Baptism of thy beloved Son, our Lord Jesus Christ, didst sanctify and ordain Jordan and all waters for a saving flood and an abundant washing away of sin . . ."

What the dickens was going on out there? The kids were leaning out the window now and pointing at something, and the adults in the balcony were starting to look at the kids who were looking out the window, and the people in the nave were starting to look up at the adults in the balcony who were looking at the kids who were looking out the window.

". . . we beseech thee, of thine infinite mercy, to look with favor upon this child and to bless him in the Spirit with true faith that, by this salutary flood, there may be drowned and destroyed in him all that he hath inherited from Adam and himself added thereto; and that, being separated from the number of the unbelieving, he may be securely kept in the holy ark of the Christian Church..."

Now even the ushers, who always dozed in the back of the nave until the sermon when they went out on the front steps for a smoke, had become aware that something was going on and were up out of their seats and disappearing into the narthex.

"... and ever serve thy name with fervent spirit and joyful hope, to the end that, together with all believers, he may be accounted worthy to attain to everlasting life; through Jesus Christ our Lord. Amen."

At last, thought Gottlieb, that interminable Flood Prayer of Luther's was over. Hopefully the ushers would get whoever it was on the tractor to move along and give them some peace and quiet. Why on earth would somebody be out on a tractor on Easter Sunday, anyway? All the farmers in the area were sitting right here in front of him. Except for Jamieson, that hippie agnostic organic farmer, but he was seven miles down the road and across the creek and plowed with a mule. There. The motor had shut off. Good. On with church. A nice, sedate, well-ordered church service, right out of the book.

He turned with a smile to Bill and Lou Ann, who by now were holding Josiah and ready to say their vows as baptismal sponsors. "Who brings this child to be baptized?" said Gottlieb.

"We do!" cried a ringing, resonant voice from the back of the church just as Bill and Lou Ann were about to answer. All heads turned in the direction of the sound, their eyes popping and their mouths hanging open as they saw three tall black men with spears and shields enter the church and stride down the aisle, dressed in bright array, wearing the traditional wedding festival garments of Mayangala. In the lead was Peter, the eldest, and he was dressed in a robe of gold cloth that went from his shoulders down to his feet. After him came Jacob, swathed in iridescent purple, and walking with the perfect posture of a king's son. Last came Isaac, the tallest of the three, and he wore a garment of many colors—red and blue and gold and green and more red and purple and more and more red. Each man wore upon his head a plain gold circlet that indicated the rank of prince. Miriam seeing them clapped her hand to her mouth and cried out with joy. They had come at last! The whole congregation was abuzz with amazement as the men walked with utmost dignity to the baptismal font, then knelt before the old pastor and bowed their heads. Gottlieb went to each man individually and spoke a word in the Mayangalan tongue, and touched him on the head, whereupon he rose and stood by. Peter spoke: "We apologize most sincerely for creating a scene. I'll explain later. But we wanted so badly to come and also stand as witnesses at the baptism of our king."

Gottlieb with tears in his eyes looked upon these princes, each of whom he had baptized long ago in the kingdom of Mayangala, and said with catch in his voice, "You are most welcome, my sons."

The congregation beheld all this in amazement. Then Ralph Mason stood up and walked with high dignity to the baptismal font and joined the group. Looking at the old pastor he said simply, "We need one more sponsor to balance things out. Three from the mother's side, and two from the father's. I want to stand up for my grandson."

"William and Lou Ann, Peter, Isaac, and Jacob . . . and Ralph, it also behooves you as sponsors . . ." and then he choked up and couldn't go on. Tears filled his eyes and he began to weep, his shoulders shaking with sobs, and he cried with a loud voice in the midst of the congregation of God's holy people, and they wept with him as he leaned upon his shepherd's staff, that out of all the death in the world God could bring life, that out of all the pain God could bring joy, that out of all the hatred and evil God could bring love. It was a little cloud, and soon it passed. The tears of joy ceased to flow, and in a voice now stronger than ever the old man continued, "it behooves you as sponsors, while confessing in this sacred act the faith of the Christian Church in the Triune God, in whose name this child is to be baptized, to bear witness publicly in the child's stead that by Holy Baptism as a means of grace he obtains and possesses the saving faith in the one true God and renounces the devil and his wicked works. Moreover, after this child has been baptized, you should at all times remember him in your prayers, put him in mind of his baptism, and, as much as in you lies, lend your counsel and aid, especially if he should lose his parents, that he may be brought up in the true knowledge and fear of God, according to the teachings of the Lutheran church and faithfully keep the baptismal covenant unto the end." And here the old man got a lump in his throat again, for these young princes had indeed lost their parents, and it had fallen to Miriam Seyoum and her husband, Shadrach Teseney, their sponsors, to bring them up in the nurture and admonition of the Lord. The old man looked at the sponsors and parents and said with utmost gravity, "This then, you intend gladly and willingly to do."

They answered, "Yes."

"How is this child to be named?"

John and Rachel looked at each other, then John spoke. "Josiah Earl Mason."

Then Peter added, "Lion Slayer, Shepherd of His People, and King of Mayangala."

"I now ask you to answer, in the name and in the stead of this child, the questions which I shall now address to him, to signify thereby what God in and through baptism works in him. Josiah Earl Mason, dost thou renounce the devil and all his works and all his ways?"

The parents and sponsors and congregation said, "I do."

"Dost thou believe in God the Father Almighty, in Jesus Christ, His only Son, our Lord, and God the Holy Ghost as we confess in the Apostles Creed?"

"I do."

"Wilt thou be baptized into this Christian faith?"

"I will."

And taking water from the font in his hand, the old pastor poured it over the head of the child, making the Sign of the Cross and saying, "Josiah Earl Mason, rightful King of Mayangala though in exile, I baptize thee in the name of the Father and of the Son and of the Holy Ghost. Amen." And this rite being done, there followed another as the child received a crown from his mother's brother, Peter of Mayangala.

At that moment, deep in the Friedensee the great fish awoke from its slumber and rose to the surface.

The young African men put down their spears and shields and joined the congregation, squeezing into a front pew with an astonished farm family. The service went on, the old pastor delivered his sermon, dairymen who had been up at four milking dozed off, only to be awoken by the babies, who like all babies waited until the sermon to begin screaming their heads off.

"Dear brothers and sisters," the old pastor began, "there is a word in the Greek that I want you to hold up to the light and take a look at. That word is *chortazo,* and it means, 'to be filled.' It comes from the root, *chortos,* which means 'grass.' The image here is of cattle grazing. And as we all know in this farming community, cattle with their four-compartment stomachs—the rumen, the reticulum, the omasum, and the abomasum—can eat quite a lot. So when applied to people it means to eat and eat and eat until you couldn't possibly hold another bite.

"Now some of us are going over to the Friedensee Hunting and Fishing Club for a wedding feast after the service. I expect we'll have a lot to eat. I was there for Thanksgiving, and I can tell you they fed me pretty good, especially with Millie's sausage dressing!

"In Bible times, though, there were frequent famines, and often people didn't get enough to eat. So when they had a chance, they really packed it in. One such incidence is the feeding of the five thousand, as recorded in John chapter six. It says that a large crowd followed Jesus to hear him preach, and the Lord tested his disciples and said to Philip, 'Where will we buy food so that these people can have something to eat?' And Philip, who was thinking in human and not divine terms, couldn't answer. They didn't have enough money to buy enough bread for the crowd. Then Andrew found a boy with five loaves and two fish, but observed that that wouldn't feed but a few. So Jesus, having painted his disciples into a corner, now worked a miracle. He told them to have the crowd be seated. And everyone sat down, five thousand of them, counting only the men, and the text says that there was a lot of *chortos* in that place—a lot of grass. But Jesus wasn't going to feed them grass. He would give them good, nourishing bread.

"Jesus took the loaves and the fishes and gave thanks, and distributed them to the disciples, and the disciples in turn distributed them to the people. And everyone ate and ate and ate, as much as they wanted, and when they were done, there was enough left over to fill twelve baskets. So the people were filled. *Chortazo.*

"That's the basic miracle. Jesus fed the five thousand. It shows his divine power. It shows that he is truly who he said he was, the Son of God, who would confirm his message with miracles, with works of divine power. A lot of those hungry people, when they saw what Jesus did, wanted to take him by force and make him king. A bread-king, that's what they wanted—someone who would feed them. But Jesus eluded them. He did not come to be a bread-king or any other kind of king. He came to be a suffering servant, to give his life on the cross for your sins, so that if you believe in him you will not perish but have eternal life.

"Later on Jesus said to the people, 'You seek me because you ate of the loaves and were filled.' There's that word again, *chortazo.* They were filled in their stomachs but not their souls. So Jesus goes on to say, 'Labor not for the meat which perishes, but for that meat which endures unto everlasting life, which the son of man shall give unto you.'

"What about you? Are you spiritually empty today? Do you have a hunger deep in your soul that only God can satisfy? Do you find that material bread—the things of this world, money, wealth, property, cars, status, prestige—doesn't leave you satisfied? That's because it is temporal. It is transient. It doesn't stick to your ribs. When this world comes to an end all those things will perish." He was looking straight at TD as he said this. "And if you have tried to fill yourself with them, you will perish. Do you understand what I'm saying? You will go to hell forever. The Blessed Virgin Mary understood this when she sang, 'He has filled the hungry with good things, and the rich he has sent empty away.' Some will be excluded from the Kingdom of God: those who are rich in their own eyes with their good works and their own wisdom and poor toward God who demands sinless perfection.

"But that's not what God wants for you. God loves you and sent a Savior in Jesus Christ to redeem you from all these vain material things. God's son Jesus Christ was not a bread-king. He himself was the Bread of Life. As bread is broken and consumed, so Jesus let his body be destroyed on the cross. There he suffered and died for all of your sins, including the sin of materialism that we're talking about today. In his death he paid for all of your sins.

"But it doesn't end there. Jesus rose again from the dead on the third day. That is why he said in this chapter, 'I am the living bread which came down from heaven. If any man eat of this bread, he shall live forever. And the bread that I will give is my flesh, which I will give for the life of the world.'

"The five thousand ate bread and went away, and a few hours later they were hungry again. In the Old Testament the prophet Elijah was given bread by angels, and it so sustained him that he went on the strength of that food forty days and forty nights to Horeb, the mountain of God. Tolkien translated this biblical image into his epic tale, *The Lord of the Rings*, where Frodo and Sam are given *lembas*, the waybread of the elves, for their journey. And just a bite of this bread of heaven as it were enables them to travel a long way through the Land of Mordor.

"We do not live in a fantasy realm. We live in a real world, full of evil and temptation. We are tempted at every hand to seek Jesus only for bread, only for healing, only for success, only for deliverance from trouble. And once we're full, we forget about him.

"But dear friends, look at the altar. There is the bread of heaven, the true body of Christ prepared for you. As Jesus says, whoever eats of my flesh will never hunger, and whoever drinks my blood will never thirst. Put away the things of this world, which do not satisfy. Fill yourself on this true bread, the bread of Life, Jesus Christ himself, who alone can sustain you in your pilgrimage to his eternal city. Amen."

After the Credo and the Sanctus and the Pater Noster it was time for the celebration of the Holy Eucharist. The old pastor stood up at the altar on that Easter Day, like thousands and millions of pastors were doing just at that moment in churches great and small all across the wide world, and like thousands of pastors had done in the past on the "little Easter" of every Sunday in churches great and small all across the wide world in an unbroken line of tradition going all the way back to Christ himself, who gave his body on the cross for the sins of the world.

"Our Lord Jesus Christ," he began, taking the wafer from the paten and repeating the Verba with utmost reverence, "the same night in which he was betrayed, took bread, and when he had given thanks he brake it and gave it to his disciples, saying, 'Take, eat, this is my body'"—and here he made the Sign of the Cross over the host—"'which is given for you. This do in remembrance of me.'" Then he poured the wine from the flagon into the chalice and lifted it up, holding his right hand over it and saying, "After the same manner also He took the cup when he had supped, and when he had given thanks, he gave it to them saying, 'Drink ye all of it; this cup is the new testament in my blood'"—and here he made the Sign of the Cross over the wine—"'which is shed for you for the remission of sins. This do, as oft as ye drink it, in remembrance of me.'"

In the Friedensee the great fish began to swim. Beginning in the center of the lake, he began to swim slowly in widening concentric circles, with each circuit becoming closer and closer to the shore.

In the church, the heart of Timothy David Pope was smitten by the words, "on the night in which he was betrayed." He looked down at his hands, now rough from honest manual labor. He thought of the sins he had committed with them, from cheating on his golf score to delaying payment for the contractors at his Arkansas resort to clipping and holding penalties he'd gotten away with in football to opening the door and running away when his fiancée was threatened by a killer. TD looked down at his hands, and he was ashamed. He was not overcome with powerful emotion. He did not weep. He did not wail. He simply repented. Then he looked up and saw that the usher was at his pew, signaling with his hand that it was time for his table to go forward. TD hesitated, then got up and walked down the aisle. Turning aside at the front pew, he went and stood before Rachel, who was at that moment looking into her hymnal and singing stanza six of number 458, Luther's hymn based on the Lord's Prayer:

Forgive our sins, Lord, we implore,
Remove from us their burden sore,
As we their trespasses forgive
Who by offenses us do grieve.
Thus let us dwell in charity
And serve our brother willingly.

"Rachel," he said.

She looked up at him in surprise, then stood up with a rustling of her voluminous wedding dress.

"Yes?"

"I'm sorry," he said simply. He had sinned against a hundred people that he knew of, not counting those he had forgotten and those he had offended without knowing.

She looked at him with pity. So he was a sinner, too. Well, big deal. So was she. They were all sinners, everybody in the whole church, Ralph and Betty and Millie and Miriam and John and Josiah and Pastor Gottlieb and Ann and Bill and Judy and Katie and Lou Ann and Billy. And TD. And even Jesus himself. Even Jesus was a sinner when he hung on the cross. In that hour he was every sinner that ever lived, for in his Baptism he became sin for us, that in our baptism we might become the righteousness of God in him. She took his hand and squeezed it. "That's OK," she said. "Don't worry about it. Now go on up and take Communion."

He nodded a thank you and went forward to the altar rail, and there knelt down and received the true body and blood of Jesus Christ. He didn't feel any different, but on some objective level he knew that the slate had been wiped clean.

At the Friedensee under the surface of the water the great fish was circling the lake and moving toward shore.

Chapter 14 ◉ A Sacred Meal

After church the congregation spilled out the door and stood in little groups on the lawn, talking about the extraordinary events that had taken place. Jasper, trailed by all the young men, made a beeline for the parking lot, for there in the shade of the hickory tree was a 1988 Morgan Plus 8, long and low, British racing green with a tan leather interior, and looking like it was going a hundred even though it was standing still.

"... and when I heard the noise coming from outside, I thought it was a tractor," Pastor Gottlieb was saying to Peter.

"My sincere apologies," the young man replied. "We flew over by special permission of British Airways—my company, you know—and they were good enough to let us take the car along in the cargo hold. But something jarred the muffler during transport, and I'm afraid that's why it sounds so bloomin' loud. And to make matters worse, you Americans drive on the wrong side of the road, and we forgot to do that and got pulled over a couple of times as we were going through St. Louis. So that's why we were late. Plus, you know, three black men in costume—with spears!—well, the local bobbies couldn't resist getting a closer look. Sorry about interrupting the service and all that."

"Don't worry about it, Peter," Gottlieb said. "Not much happens around here, so this will keep the folks buzzing for a long time."

"Speaking about buzzing, we should be buzzing off to the reception, shouldn't we?"

"Yes, everyone's invited to the Clubhouse for dinner."

"Is it over a country road? These Morgans are pretty low-slung."

"I don't think it will be a problem. They've recently graded the road. Just go slow. They've put down fresh gravel. Don't want to put a ding in your nice car."

"I'll keep that in mind," he said over his shoulder as he walked to the car. Of course by now there was a knot of admirers clustered around the sports car, and the boys were obliged to let some of the young men take the car for a short spin down the county road and back. Jasper claimed seniority and went first, and his face was pure joy as he came barreling down the road with a cloud of dust kicking up behind. "*Mach Schnell! Mach Schnell!*" he cried. "*Viel spass!*"*

This all took a half-hour or so, during which time the rest of the family and guests were assembling at the Clubhouse for the Easter dinner/wedding reception/baptism celebration. Millie and Betty and Miriam were setting the long table, which they had moved outside under the shade of the sycamore tree. There was also a buffet table where family members had brought covered side dishes and salads and pies. The American Legion would be delivering the fried chicken soon. The men were standing about sipping beer and talking. Among these were the Reverend John Kolding and his nephew and namesake, the Reverend Doctor John Mason.

Kolding looked morose. "Well, Johnny, I suppose I must congratulate you on getting your doctorate."

"Thanks, JJ. Somehow you don't look overjoyed."

"I just would have thought that a European education might have given you a more progressive outlook on theology and life. I just don't understand how, given the achievements of modern thought since the Enlightenment, people could still be so pigheaded and superstitious and cling to these outmoded traditions. I mean, here we were in church today—traditional wedding, traditional Baptism, traditional Communion, tradition, tradition, tradition!"

The young man grinned slyly, "You're beginning to sound like Tevye in *Fiddler on the Roof*."

---

* Go fast! Go fast! ... What fun!

"Don't poke fun at me, young man!" Kolding said irritably. "I'm being quite serious. Things are going to hell in a handbasket. The labor movement of the early twentieth century has dwindled to a shell of its former strength. The socialism of the Thirties that FDR brought into American government was overturned by Reagan and his troglodytes. The promise of the Soviet Union came to nothing. The counterculture movement of the Sixties fell apart. The hippies all went into business. The women's liberation of the Seventies and the gay liberation of the Eighties have gone nowhere. And our own Missouri Synod—we had such hopes that the stodgy old conservatives would be turned out and replaced with some progressives."

"You mean like Dave Henderson in Ste. Genevieve?"

That brought Kolding up short. He had to think of a response. There was the roar of an engine and the Morgan came speeding into the yard, with Jasper driving—a beatific smile covered his entire face—and the three young Africans hanging on for dear life. Jasper gunned the powerful engine one last time to hear the music, and the boys all piled out. In the silence that followed, the old crank telephone in the Clubhouse could be heard ringing, two longs and a short.

"It's for us," Millie yelled from the table, "somebody go catch the phone."

"OK," Lou Ann called back from inside. "I'll get it."

"JJ," said the young man, "do you really want me to end up like Henderson? He committed adultery. That's a sin. His wife is divorcing him. He had to resign from the ministry. He's been removed from the clergy roster. This is bad, Uncle John. I know it's bad."

"But..."

"Let me finish," John continued. For once he was finding the words to answer, for once he wasn't tongue-tied. "I know where this stuff leads. I followed you. I looked up to you. I took your words to heart. I let myself be open to all these new experiences you were talking about. 'God is love,' you kept telling me. 'God is love, God is love. Love, love, love. We need to follow our bliss.' You know what that bliss is, Uncle John? Nine times out of ten it's sin. Just plain, old-fashioned sin. And look at the result: I got a woman pregnant. I had an illegitimate child by her. And as a result of my stupidity I got her killed. It's in the Bible. Romans six: 'Are we to continue in sin that grace may abound? By no means!' This is the basis of the theology of the Third Use of the Law, Uncle John. This is Catechism 101. Just because we are forgiven by Christ, that doesn't mean we can live any old way we want to. Then you end up like the Gnostics in the second century, or the Ranters in England in the seventeenth century. Or the liberals today. No! Christ saves us and fills us with the Holy Spirit and motivates us and enables us to obey the Law."

"But..."

"No, Uncle John, you listen to me for once. I just wrote a whole dissertation on this. Plus I've had to find out the truth the hard way by bitter experience. I know what I'm talking about. 'We were buried therefore with him by baptism into death, in order that, just as Christ was raised from the dead by the glory of the Father, we too might walk in newness of life.'"

Kolding sat down on the park bench and looked out at the lake. He glanced down toward the beach by the dock. The children were there, wading in the shallows and pointing to something in the water. The Africans were strolling nonchalantly toward them, still in full wedding regalia, spears in hand.

Jasper approached the park bench. "Hi, b-b-b...b-b-boys, how ya d-d-doin'? Whatcha talkin' ab-b-b-bout?"

Kolding looked at the mechanic condescendingly. "Just a point of theology. I'm sure you wouldn't understand."

"I d-d-dunno, t-try me."

Millie called out from the house: "John, can you come here a second? We've got a problem."

"Will you excuse me," John said, and walked across the lawn toward Millie.

"Simply this, Jasper," Kolding replied. "At issue here is the theology of the Third Use of the Law. Modern theologians such as Käsemann and Bonhöffer have argued that this was a fiction imported into Lutheran theology from the Calvinists, and that Melanchthon rejected this concept in favor of a Gospel-centered ethic in which the redeemed person is a free moral agent not bound by the strictures of Old Testament legalism. *Lex semper accusat. Verstehen Sie alles, Herr Mason?*"*

"*Ja,*" Jasper replied, pursing his lips. "*Ich verstehe ganz gut. Aber Sie haben dieses Wort vergessen, Herr Kolding, wie auch Chemnitz in dem Formula Concordiae hat geschrieben: '... obwohl die recht gläubigen und wahrhaftig zu Gott bekehrten Menschen vom Fluch und Zwang des Gesetzes durch Christum gefreiet und ledig gemacht, dass sie doch der Ursache nicht ohne Gezetz seien, sondern darum von dem Sohn Gottes erlöst worden, dass sie sich in demselben Tag und Nacht üben sollen.' Sie sollen sich daran erinnern. Oder veilleicht es ist besser, dass Ich Lateinisch sprechen?*"

This Jasper spoke fluently and without the trace of a stutter, leaving Kolding staring with his mouth hanging open. The old mechanic got up. Before the bench and directly in front of The Reverend John J. Kolding, M.A., D.D., was the tub of beer. Jasper bent over to get one. As he did so, he cut a big fart right in Kolding's face.

"Arrgh! Feh!" exclaimed the distinguished clergyman, to the hilarity of the men standing by. He fled to his car, got in, sat down, and sulked.

"John," Millie said as Betty, Miriam, and Lou Ann stood by. "That phone call was from the Legion."

"Yes?"

"They can't bring the fried chicken!"

"What? What happened?"

"I took the call," Lou Ann said. "They were expecting a big

---

* "The law always accuses. Do you understand everything, Mr. Mason?"
"Yes," Jasper replied, pursing his lips. "I understand very well. But you have forgotten this word, Mr. Kolding, that Chemnitz in the *Formula of Concord* has written: '... although men truly believing and truly converted to God have been freed and exempted from the curse and coercion of the Law, they nevertheless are not on this account without Law, but have been redeemed by the Son of God in order that they should exercise themselves in it day and night.' You should remember this. Or would it be better if I spoke Latin?"
[Jasper is quoting *The Formula of Concord,* Epitome VI, "The Third Use of the Law: Affirmativa 1" in F. Bente, ed., *Concordia Triglotta* (St. Louis: Concordia Publishing House, 1921), p. 805.]

shipment of chicken from the supplier in Arkansas. But there was a wreck or something. The shipment didn't arrive last night or this morning."

"What about Johnnie's Poultry right there in Perryville?"

"It's Easter. They're closed. Besides, the chickens would need to be killed and plucked."

"Walmart?"

"No."

"Rozier's Grocery?"

"No."

"So we've got thirty-five people to feed and no meat."

"Yes."

"And no chance of getting any."

"Right."

Just then a window opened and Rachel called out, "John, can you come here? I want to show you something." Then she closed the window and drew down the shade.

"OK, coming." Then turning to Millie he said, "Boy, I don't know what we can do. Maybe give everybody a fishing pole and see if we can catch anything. Have a fish fry."

"To feed thirty-five people? We've got the oil and the kettle. But we'd need one of those miraculous draughts of fishes, like in the Bible."

"Well, let me go see what Rachel wants. I'll be back in a minute. We'll think of something."

"Maybe just fill up on dessert," offered Lou Ann.

"Wouldn't the kids love that," replied Betty. John walked slowly into the Clubhouse, through the screened porch, then turned left down the long central hall, until he came to the last room on the left, his old bedroom and study. He turned the doorknob, but it was locked.

"Is that you?" came Rachel's voice from within.

"Yes." There was a click as she turned the key from inside.

He stepped into the room. With the shades drawn it was dark, just a bit of light seeping in from the edges of the shade. As his eyes adjusted to the darkness he could see the white of the wedding dress draped across a chair. Then he smelled Rachel's perfume, and he took a deep breath of it. He heard another click as the door was relocked, and she was right beside him in the darkness, with nothing on. "You are my husband now, John Mason," she said softly.

"And you are my wife," he said.

"I demand my conjugal rights," she said.

"And you shall have them," he said as they lay down on the bed together. "Rise up, my beloved, and come away," he began.

"For the winter is past," she continued, "and the time of the singing of birds is come."

And the man knew his wife, and she knew him, and they became one flesh, and found joy in one another.

On the front porch however there was sorrow, for the women had prepared a feast but there was no meat, and no possibility of getting any. There were a few side dishes and a few desserts, but not enough to satisfy the hunger of so many.

"I just don't know what we're going to do," said Millie.

"Have we thought of everything?" asked Lou Ann.

"Where's John?" asked Miriam.

Millie looked at Miriam over the rim of her glasses and raised her eyebrows.

"Oh," said Miriam, and put her hand over her mouth.

"Maybe one of the farmers nearby has venison in the freezer," ventured Betty.

"But even if they did, how long would it take to thaw?" asked Miriam.

"And then cook?" said Millie. "Let's face it, we're sunk."

"The McDonald's out by the highway is open," said Lou Ann.

The other women shot her a dirty look. Lou Ann shrugged her shoulders, then said, "I'm going to go check on the kids."

Lou Ann went out the screen door, and it closed behind her with a squeak and a bang. As she walked toward the lake, she saw the children gathered together in a bunch, talking excitedly all at once and pointing at the water. "Pishy book, pishy book," she could hear Josiah shouting. "Book! Book!" He was jumping up and down. The three

African men were standing by the children, and one of them, Peter, the eldest, was taking off his clothes. Lou Ann quickened her steps and in a moment was at the shore of the lake. "What is it," she asked. "What's going on?"

"Look, Aunt Lou," said Bill's daughter Katie.

"Yeah, Mom, look at that fish," said her son Billy.

She looked into the water and uttered a sharp cry. There, lying on the sandy bottom, was the most enormous catfish she had ever seen in her life. It raised its head and looked at her with its deep black eyes. By now Peter of Mayangala was stripped to his loincloth and had his spear in hand.

"What...what?" she asked.

"It's Old Methuselah," said Billy.

"He comes to visit us sometimes," said Katie, "and here he is. He talks to us somehow."

"What does he say, Katie?"

"He says, 'I am given for you.'"

"Oh, yeah, sure. Right. He sure is a big one, though."

By now Peter had waded cautiously into the water. "Quiet, everyone, please," he whispered. But the great fish was still, as if waiting for the end. Peter's two brothers, Isaac and Jacob, stripped for battle and came in behind him, carrying their war spears. They were real spears that had been used in battles long ago. Now they were merely of ceremonial use, though a king was still expected to use one to kill a lion. So the points were kept sharp and at the ready.

"All together now," said Peter softly. "Ready...steady...GO!" And at the signal all three men drove their spears into the flanks of the mighty fish. It thrashed powerfully, churning the water. Its huge tail came out of the water and struck Isaac on the chest, knocking him down.

"Hold on to the spears, lads!" shouted Jacob, trying to drive the point deeper into the fish. "Don't let him get away!" Isaac splashed over to the melee and caught hold of the staff of his spear, but the fish lunged again and knocked him sprawling.

Peter with a grunt extracted his spear from the fish and stabbed it again, burying the point deep into its flesh. Blood was pouring from its wounds and staining the water all about. The fish was fighting with all its might, and with its size and weight it was more than a match for three grown men. It rolled completely over, throwing all the men into the water again and loosening two of the spears. The men were breathing heavily from the battle as they scrambled to regain their footing in the shallow water. Jacob recovered his spear and struck again as hard as he could. Now the great fish leaped up, almost completely out of the water, twisting and writhing with the spears in its side, then came down again with an enormous splash that sent a wave across the lake.

"Try to grab him by the gills," shouted Isaac, "we'll drag him to shore!"

"Right-o," said Peter and Jacob. "Now!"

The two men plunged under water and each put an arm into the fish's gill slits. They heaved, and moved it forward a few feet. They heaved again. Another foot. The thing was tremendously heavy. Then they looked up. Jasper and Ralph were in the water beside them, still wearing their Sunday best. The fish was still for a moment, weakened from the wounds and the struggle. "Heave-ho, boys," shouted Ralph. "Let's go!"

Peter and Ralph were on one side, Jasper and Jacob on the other, and as men do when they work together, reading each other's minds and sensing the signals of their bodies, they lifted and surged forward and dragged the fish up onto the bank. Peter, exhausted, fell to his knees, and as he fell his crown fell from his head and landed on the head of the fish. Josiah came forward with a stick, his face stern, and he lifted up his hand and struck the fish. It gave a shudder, and then was still.

By now everyone had heard the commotion—everyone but John and Rachel—and had come to the shore to witness the battle. They looked upon the great fish with wonder and awe. It was not a story. It was not a legend. It was real. And the reality was greater than the old stories that had been told and retold and handed down and embellished with oral tradition. The legend was true. The fish was over eight feet long. Its weight they could not determine. In its body were five wounds.

"I don't believe it," said Kolding as he stood on the edge of the crowd.

"*Aber hier ist die Tatsächlichkeit,*"* said Jasper, looking at him sternly. "*Mein Herr, Ich glaube dass, Sie sind demythologeziert.*"

"It's miraculous," said Millie.

"Boys," said Miriam, "you killed him like a lion."

"Well," said Ralph with a laugh, "he is a big cat."

"But who gave it the death blow?" said Miriam. "Did you notice?"

"Yes," said Peter softly, "I did. It was our king. He is a fish-slayer."

"Let me ask a question," said Millie as she stood with her hands on her hips. "Can we eat it?"

Ralph looked at the great fish for a moment. "Well, I don't see why not. The big ones often taste muddy from laying on the bottom, but with one this size, I couldn't say. We have to slaughter him first. Bill," he said to his son, "you and TD get a fire going. And put the big iron kettle over it. Millie, you said you had oil, right?"

"Yes."

"How much?"

"Five gallons."

"Well, run fetch it. That should be plenty. Jasper, we need to nail this critter to a tree to strip it. How are we going to do that?"

"We j-j-just use one of them spears, and drive it in real g-good with a hammer."

"OK. We'll need a couple guys on each side to hold him up. Peter, you and me on the left, your brothers on the right. Here we go." And the men dragged the fish over to the oak tree and lifted up its head, and Jasper drove the spear clean through the head and hammered it down.

"Wait, does anybody have a camera?"

"I do," said Rachel's mother Eileen as she rummaged through her purse. "Everybody line up next to the fish and say 'cheese.'"

As she snapped the picture, Jasper said, "Can this thing be stuffed and mounted?"

---

* But here is the reality... I do believe, my good man, that you have been De-mythologized!

Ralph thought for a moment, then said, "Good question. Let me call Maier's Taxidermy and find out. He might know a better way to skin it. Go ahead and gut the fish while I call Elmer."

As the children watched with fascination, Jasper, having fetched the tackle box, drew out a fishing knife and ran it down the belly of Old Methuselah, spilling his entrails out on the ground.

"Eeeuuww!" said all the children as they looked at the steaming mess.

"Are those his guts?" asked Billy. "What's that?" he said, poking with his stick.

"That's his gizzard, B-Billy," answered Jasper.

"What's that?" he asked, poking again.

"That's his intestine."

"What's that?"

"That's his stomach."

"What do catfish eat?" asked Danny, TD's son.

"Oh, most anything they can find on the b-bottom. Crawdads, frogs, you know. Any garbage that's thrown into the l-l-lake. We can open up his stomach and take a look if you really want to f-find out."

"Eeeeuuuwww!" the children exclaimed.

But Danny said, "Yeah, wow, sure! Hey, Daddy, come look at this."

"Be right there, Danny," replied TD as he lit the fire. "Bill, watch this for me, will you?"

"No problem."

TD walked over to the tree and looked at the pile of fish guts. "What is it, Danny?"

"Daddy, Uncle Jasper's gonna cut open the fish's stomach and see what's inside."

"OK. Probably just fish heads, maybe a tin can or two. Catfish eat anything, you know."

Jasper gripped the big, slimy, purple stomach with his left hand and made a careful incision down the length of it, and the contents spilled out. The children crowded in for a closer look. Someone whistled. Someone else said, will you look at that! There on the ground lay a silver dollar, and next to it a ring.

Just then Ralph came up. "Elmer's coming over. He wants to see this thing, and take measurements for a mold. He'll show us how to skin him the right way... hey, what's this? A ring? How the heck..."

"I d-dunno," Jasper said, pushing back his cap and scratching his head.

"Didn't you say these fish were bottom feeders?" asked Peter.

"Yes," answered Ralph. "They gobble up whatever they find, but... say, what's the date on that silver dollar?"

Peter turned it over in his hand. "1911," he said.

"How about that," said Ralph. "The year the Clubhouse was founded. Boy, what a strange day this has been."

TD felt a shiver go up his spine. "Can I take a look at that ring?"

"Yeah, here," said Ralph, tossing it to him.

TD looked at it with dumb amazement. "This is really weird, guys. This is the engagement ring I gave to Rachel. She said she threw it away. But here it is."

"Well," said Peter, "finders, keepers, I'd say."

"Yes," said the astonished TD as he put the ring into his pocket, then drew it out and looked at it again, "yes, I suppose so." And it began to dawn on him that the value of the ring could stake him to a new start in business. But an honest start this time, with no deceit, no double-dealing. "Excuse me," he said. "I need to sit down for a minute." And he walked down to the dock and sat down in the little chapel and bowed his head.

Meanwhile Elmer Maier came bouncing up in his pickup and whistled as he saw the body of the great fish. "Hoo-eee, fellers," he exclaimed. "That must be Old Methuselah, the one the old-timers used to talk about. Lordy, that there's the biggest dang fish I ever did see." He took out his tape measure and stretched it from tip to tail. "Eight feet, four inches!" He measured it across the width behind its massive head, and then brought out a collection of skinning knives. "Let me go to work on this here thing," he said, and made careful incisions behind the gills and working swiftly and expertly in a matter of minutes had removed the skin of the great fish in one piece, exposing the pink flesh. "OK," Elmer said, "now git me a big bucket over here and we'll fillet this thing right quick. Millie came up with two five-gallon buckets and Elmer cut strips of the flesh and tossed them in until they were full, then with the men hauled the carcass of the fish to his truck and drove off.

"Ralph," Millie said, "go check on the fire."

"OK, Sis," he said, and when he had gone he called back, "it's good and hot and the oil is bubbling."

"We're about ready, then," she called back. "Eileen and Betty, have you got the cornmeal?"

"Yes, we do," they answered. And Eileen added, "I whipped up some hush puppy batter, too."

"Great! Then boys and girls, we are ready for a fish fry!"

They had done this many times, and each person knew his job. TD and Bill kept the fire under the kettle going. Betty powdered the fish fillets in flour, then handed them to Eileen, who dipped them in egg, then handed them to Millie, who dipped them in cornmeal, then handed them to Ralph, who put them into the kettle of boiling oil and watched them sizzle along with the hush puppies, then when they were done took them out with a big wooden ladle and put them in a tray for the grease to run off, and when they were dry and still piping hot Ann Gottlieb took them to the buffet table and put them on a platter, golden and crisp and steaming as the hungry children crowded in to be first in line. By now John and Rachel had sleepily emerged from their den and were greeting people with bashful expressions. At last several platters of fish were ready, and Millie called out, "Pastor Gottlieb, will you say the prayer?"

The old man stepped forward looked at his people, the people of his heart, and said with a soft voice, "Thank you very much, but I wish to defer to the new pastor of Peace Lutheran Church," and extended his hand to John. Rachel had Josiah on her hip and whispered in his ear, "Fold your hands, honey." And the small boy put his little hands together.

John took a step forward and spoke in a clear voice, "*Sollen wir beten.* The eyes of all wait upon thee, O Lord, and thou givest them their meat in due season. Thou openest thy hand and satisfiest the desire of every living thing. Lord God, Heavenly Father, bless us and these Thy gifts, which we are about to receive from thy bountiful goodness, through Jesus Christ, thy Son, our Lord. Amen." Then after a pause he began the old common table prayer in German, "*Komm, Herr Jesu,*" and everyone joined in, saying, "*sei unser Gast, und segne, was du uns aus Gnaden bescheret hast. Amen.*"

And the people filled their plates and filled their stomachs with fish, and hush puppies, and cole slaw, and dinner rolls, and lime jello salad with little marshmallows, and beer, and soda, and brownies, and seven different kinds of pie, and coffee. But the Reverend John Kolding was standing off to the side by himself. His wife Joan came up to him and said, "John, why aren't you eating?"

"I don't know," he replied. "Just lost my appetite, I guess. I'll be all right. Just feel kind of empty."

John and his wife Rachel sat with Pastor Gottlieb and his wife Ann. And after seconds and thirds on everything, John looked at the old man and the old man looked at him, and they both had the same thought at the same time, and nodded their heads in agreement.

Epilogue • Healing

It was September, and seeds were falling all around from the weeds and the brush and the trees, and the doves, which are ground feeders, were feasting and fattening themselves for the coming winter. Their cooing filled the quiet air. The heron rookery was empty, for all the great birds had flown south, except for the one lone bachelor who stuck around and looked after things in the off season. John had taken up his new duties as pastor of Peace Lutheran Church and was settling in well. He and Rachel had taken his bounty money and were building a little house on her side of the lakeshore. During construction they were living in John's old room at the Clubhouse, and Rachel found she had her hands full looking after a two-year-old boy who was into everything. Millie and Miriam carried on like sisters, happy to cook and clean and care for others, and talk about books as they shared a reading lamp on the front porch, Millie with her coffee and Miriam with her Earl Grey tea. Over the mantle there was a new trophy, the true body of Old Methuselah, startling in its size, and visitors to the Clubhouse never failed to stop and gaze at it, along with the history and legends of the fish that Jasper had collected and written up.

Things were stirring in Mayangala. News that a king had been born and survived an assassination attempt had electrified the people, and even though the Muslims were still firmly in control, late at night around tribal campfires the elders were taking counsel, and young men were discovering a fire in their belly to fight for a return to the old way of life, and at the end of the meetings they always sang in Mayangalan the words of the old Lutheran hymn, "Lord, Keep

Us Steadfast in Thy Word." One day the child Josiah would have to reckon with his African destiny, but for now he was kept safe in the old American way of life as it manifested itself and was lived at the old Clubhouse, and day by day the guardian angels kept watch over the mantle clock as its hands moved ever so slowly and inexorably toward the world's last hour. Within the tradition there was change, and the tradition absorbed the change and included it, change such as the interruption of the stasis brought about by John's unexpected return, and all the things that that event had engendered—the advent of the Africans, the life of the child, the death of the Janissary, the broken engagement, the marriage, and, most of all, the changes in the heavenly places that had taken place by the rituals of the church: the confessions, the absolutions, the Baptism, the Eucharist. So on a morning in September John lay in bed with Rachel, and she lay nestled in his arms while out in a great limb of the big old ever-living sycamore a dove called to its mate, and there came a scratching at the door.

"Wake up, John."

"You wake up. I'm still asleep."

She kissed him.

He kissed her.

"Eeeuw," she said, "your breath is so bad it could burn the barnacles off the bottom of a battleship."

He thought for a moment. "Yeah? Well, your efflorescence is so foul it could flame the fleas off of a flapping flamingo."

Rachel laughed. The scratching continued.

"Come on, you have to get up."

"I don't want to get up. Why should I get up?"

"It's Sunday. Today is church."

"I don't want to go to church."

"You have to. You're the pastor."

"Oh. Right. Who's at the door?"

"Three guesses," she said as she reached over and turned the doorknob.

In bounded the puppy, the one that had survived the death of its mother Doxie. One leap and it was in bed and licking John's face.

"Agghh, it's slobbering all over me! Go away, Mooch, you little pest."

"Well, if you wouldn't spoil him, he wouldn't get on the bed."

"Well I wasn't raised on the farm like you, so give me a break."

"Look who else wants in."

"Let me guess."

Josiah was by the side of the bed. "Mommy, I'm cold."

Rachel reached down and patted his bottom. "That's 'cause you're wet, your little wet majesty, you." With a swift hand she took off his pajamas and his diaper, wrapped him in a baby blanket, and placed him in the warm spot between her and John.

Mooch, who had slept at the foot of Josiah's crib, wriggled in next to him. After a moment the child said, "Warm now."

"Rachel, I can smell coffee in the kitchen. Be a good wife and bring me some."

"No. I don't feel good."

John turned to her and leaned up on his elbow. "Really? I'm sorry. How do you feel exactly?"

"I'm sick to my stomach."

"Jeez, I'm sorry, Baby. Can I get you anything?"

"Yes."

"What?"

"I want a dill pickle and some chocolate ice cream."

"God, that's disgusting. You're kidding, right?"

"No."

"Well, I think we have some pickles in the pantry, but I'd have to run into town for the..."

Rachel started laughing. She laughed and laughed and the little boy started laughing because she was laughing, and the puppy was wriggling all over because he was laughing, and the more she looked at John with that stupid blank expression on his face, the more she laughed.

"What..." he said, "what?"

"I'm pregnant, you moron." And she laughed so loud and long that

Millie and Miriam in the kitchen began laughing, too, even though they had no idea what was going on. Then John began laughing, too, and jumping up in bed said, "Really? Really? No! Really? That's amazing. I don't believe it. Really? Oh, God, oh, man, I'm so happy, this is the most amazing thing... this is wonderful."

Then Rachel looked at him quietly and said in a soft voice, "It is wonderful, isn't it. It happens all the time. That's where people come from." And giving it a moment's thought, she continued, "It's happened before to both of us, hasn't it?"

"Yes," he said simply.

"Yes," she replied. "But this time it's all right, isn't it? I am filled with life."

And they embraced each other and kissed and embraced their child and kissed him as the puppy licked everyone indiscriminately, then piddled.

"OK, now scram, go get me that pickle."

And as John shuffled across the hall toward the kitchen in his robe and slippers he said to himself, "*Chortazo!*"

◉ ◉ ◉

Clubhouse Recipes

Clubhouse Recipes

At important junctures in the five novels of *The Diamond Quintet*, family meals are described. Many of these meals feature dishes that are unique to German-American culture. For those who wish to get a taste of this culture, the following recipes are provided. These are taken, lightly edited, from Gerhardt Kramer, ed. *Heritage of Cooking: A Collection of Recipes from East Perry County, Missouri.* Fifth printing, revised, 1981. Published by Concordia Historical Institute, 801 Seminary Place, St. Louis, Missouri, 63105. Used by permission.

Sauerkraut

Cut cabbage with kraut cutter. Pack in quart jars 2 inches from top. Add 1 teaspoon salt (sack salt is better) to top of quart of cut cabbage. Fill with boiling water, then seal tight. Let stand about 5 weeks or longer before ready. (Use jars that have glass clamp lids. Due to the fermentation, zinc lids will deteriorate.) *Veralda Bach*

Spätzle

  3 cups sifted flour
  1¼ cups milk
  ¼ teaspoon nutmeg
  3 eggs
  1 teaspoon salt

Combine all ingredients in a large bowl, beat well. Force batter through a large holed colander into boiling salt water. Scrape batter from bottom of colander with knife which has been dipped into boiling water. When cooked through, remove from water with slotted spoon. Serve with sauerbraten or rouladen. Spätzle may be drained and sautéed with butter in skillet, if desired. *Mrs. Selma Hiller*

Rouladen

- 1½ pounds sirloin
- ⅛ teaspoon pepper
- 2 slices bacon, cut into squares
- ¼ cup lard
- 2 cups water
- ½ teaspoon salt
- 3 tablespoons onion, chopped
- 6 dill pickle strips
- 3 tablespoons flour

Cut beef into a 10×4 inch piece about ¼ inch thick. Sprinkle with salt and pepper. Cover with onion. Distribute pickle strips and bacon squares over meat surface. Roll up as for jelly roll. Secure with toothpicks or string. Brown in lard or shortening on all sides. Remove meat. Add flour to pan, blend well, stir in water and cook, stirring until slightly thickened. Add browned meat, cover and cook for 1 ½ hours or until meat is tender. Season gravy to taste.

Gritze Wurst

For 1 gallon, put 1 ½ pounds oatmeal (or steel-cut oats) in large pan, pour broth over (from kettle of cooked meat) until oats are cooked. Add ground cooked meat (pork shoulder, hogs head, or any kind that is left over from butchering) to make one gallon mixed together with oats. Add small handful salt and 2 ½ tablespoons pepper. Mix all together. Maybe put in freezer in milk cartons or other cartons. Before eating fry until brown, breaking it apart as it fries. Eat with apple butter or jelly bread. *Mr. Martin H. Dreyer, Mrs. Fred W. Baue*

Hasenpfeffer

2 ½ pounds rabbit, cut into pieces
¼ cup vinegar
3 bay leaves
2 teaspoons salt
⅓ cup flour
2 tablespoons brown sugar
1 ¼ cups water
1 onion, sliced
10 whole cloves
½ teaspoon pepper
⅓ cup lard or shortening
1 cup sour cream

Place rabbit in bowl and cover with mixture of water and vinegar. Add onions, bay leaves, cloves, salt (1 teaspoon) and pepper. Cover tightly and set in cold (or refrigerator) for 2 to 3 days. Remove rabbit and coat with flour and remaining salt. Melt lard in in a heavy skillet. Fry rabbit golden brown, turning frequently. Gradually add 1 cup strained vinegar mixture and brown sugar. Cover and simmer until tender (about 1 hour). Add sour cream before serving. Heat, but do not boil.

Kochkaese

Place 1 gallon sour milk in a warm but not hot place; standing it on the pilot light of the gas stove is just about right. After it begins to clabber, pour into a cloth bag or sack and let drip until all the milk water is out. Crumble the remaining cheese very fine, adding a teaspoon salt. Cover with a plate and set in a warm place again. Stir every day until it changes to a yellow color. Then melt a spoonful of butter in a saucepan, add the cheese mixture and cook over a low flame. If mixture is too stiff, add a little sweet cream. Add ¼ cup caraway seed and cool before serving.   *Mrs. Leonard Ochs*

Kaffe Kuchen

  ¾ cup sugar
  1 cup mashed potatoes
  1 teaspoon salt
6 to 7 cups flour
  ¾ cup shortening
  1 cup milk
1 ½ cake yeast dissolved in ¼ cup lukewarm water

Make into soft dough. Set overnight. It will rise and push the lid up. Next day, pinch off a little ball of dough and pat into a greased pan about ½ inch thick. Let rise until double in bulk and bake in 350°oven about 30 min. Top with crumbs or any desired topping. *Mrs. Hildegarde Weinhold*

Walnuss Kuchen

1 ½ cup sugar
  1 cup milk
  3 cups flour
1 ½ teaspoon baking powder
  ½ cup butter
  4 eggs
  ¼ teaspoon salt
  ½ pound walnuts, finely chopped

Blend sugar and butter, add eggs and milk. Sift flour with baking powder and salt Add walnuts. Bake in greased and dusted round cake form for 1 hour at about 350°.

Mohn Kuchen

- 1/2 pound butter
- 5 eggs, separated
- 3 level teaspoons baking powder
- 1/2 teaspoon salt
- grated rind of 1 lemon
- 2 cups sugar
- 2 1/2 cups sifted flour
- 2/3 cup poppy seeds
- 1 teaspoon vanilla

Cream butter until light and fluffy. Add the sugar and beat again until fluffy as whipped cream. Add egg yolks and beat again. Sift flour, measure, add baking powder and salt and sift again. Add this to the first mixture. Alternate with the milk in 3 parts. Then add poppy seeds, lemon rind, and vanilla and mix thoroughly. Last of all, fold in the stiffly beaten egg white. Bake in greased and dusted loaf or round form pan, at 350° about 45 minutes or until the cake shrinks from the side of pan and springs back when touched lightly on top with fingers. *Mrs. William Popp*

Crumb Topping

- 1 cup sugar
- 1/4 cup shortening or butter
- salt
- 1 cup flour
- 2 teaspoons vanilla

Mix well with fingers. Prick top of cake with fork. Sprinkle on dough and let bake on coffee cake.

Christmas Stollen

    1 quart milk
    3 cups sugar
    5 eggs
    ¾ cup citron
    2 teaspoons almond extract
    1 teaspoon salt
    4 cakes yeast
    1 pound butter
1 ½ cups raisins
    grated rind of 2 lemons
1 ¼ pounds mixed candied fruit

Scald the milk and cool to lukewarm. Add 1 cup sugar. Dissolve the yeast in this mix. Add about 5 or 6 cups flour to make a sponge. Beat this 5 minutes. Set in a warm place. Let rise 1 hour. Then add fruit and other ingredients, beaten eggs, melted butter, and flour to stiffen. Let rise about 3 hours. Make into loaves and let rise 1 hour. Bake in moderate oven. Makes about 8 loaves.

Snickerdoodles

    1 cup lard
    2 eggs
    2 teaspoons cream of tartar
    ½ teaspoon salt
1 ½ cups sugar
2 ¾ cups flour
    1 teaspoon soda
      flavoring

Mix with hands. Chill dough 4 or 5 hours. Mix 2 teaspoons cinnamon in a small dish. Roll 1 teaspoon of dough into ball. Roll in cinnamon and sugar mixture. Place on cookie sheet. Bake at 400°. *Mrs. Mollie Winter*

Springerle

4 eggs

Beat for 15 min, then add:

¼ teaspoon baking soda
1 pound powdered sugar
vanilla or anise

Stir in flour—just enough so dough isn't too stiff. Spread on board and roll out ⅜ inches thick. Press picture form on the dough, cut in squares and lay on floured board overnight in a cool room. Bake the next morning (not too hot an oven). *Mrs. Wm. Oberndorfer*

Rhubarb Pie

3 cups rhubarb, cut small
2 tablespoons flour
½ cup orange juice
1 cup sugar
3 egg yolks
¼ teaspoon salt

Mix sugar, flour, egg yolks, juice, and salt, and pour over rhubarb in unbaked pie shell. Bake about ¾ hour at 400°. Spread with meringue made of stiffly beaten egg whites and 5 tablespoons powdered sugar and bake in 350° oven until nice and brown. *Mrs. Arthur Fassel*

Apple Butter

Peel and core apples (a fall variety preferred). Wash apple pieces and put in copper kettle and cover with water (enough water so that apples will swim). To each bushel of apples add about 6 pounds of sugar. This is added when the apples are of apple-sauce consistency. Cinnamon and anise are used as flavoring (whichever is preferred), according to the taste of the individual. 4 pounds granulated and 2 pounds brown sugar makes a good combination. Cook until no liquid forms around the edges when a spoonful is put on a saucer to cool. Fill jars and seal immediately. *Mrs. Edgar Heinbokel*

Dill Pickles

- 1 cup salt
- 1 cup vinegar
- 3 quarts water

Let come to a boil and pour over pickles that have been washed and packed in jars. Add leaves and dill and seal. They will ferment in jars and some juice will run out, but this will not spoil them. *Mrs. Emilie Katt*

Home Remedies

Spring Tonic: To thin out your blood in the spring of the year, drink a tea made from sassafrass roots boiled in water.

Backache: To prevent backache always carry three chestnuts in your hip pocket.

Bee or wasp sting: To draw out the poison from a bee or wasp sting, chew some tobacco and put the moist leaves on the sting. Cover with a bandage.

Ringworm: Cut a slice from the hull of a green walnut and rub the moist section over the infection.

Laxative: Chewing the bark of the root of a slippery elm tree is good for a laxative.

Constipation: A tablespoon of flaxseed is better than all else for relieving constipation.

Warts: To rid yourself of a wart, rub raw potato on the wart and plant the potato. If the potato doesn't grow, the wart will disappear.

Farm Remedies

Lice: To combat lice on chickens, put some cedar twigs in the hen house and nests.

Fleas: To rid a dog of fleas, wash it in a solution of tobacco leaves cooked in water.

Hollow Tail: If your cow has a hollow tail, cut it open 6 or 8 inches and put in pepper and salt and forget about the cow.

Sweenied Horse: If you sweenied a horse, thread a thin poke root under the skin as long as the sweeny so that it will drain.

Groundhogs: To discourage groundhogs from undermining a house vegetable garden, plant a castor bean in the corners of the garden.

Insects: To keep insects from invading the garden, put cigar butts around the perimeter.

Eggs: Tie a nail to a human hair and hold it in your right hand over an egg in your left hand. If the nail spins clockwise it is a pullet—if counterclockwise, it is a rooster.

Skunks: To catch a skunk with your bare hands, look it square in the eye and keep looking while slowly advancing. As long as you keep his attention, he will not turn around and squirt. *Mr. Alvin Meyer, Frohna*

Birthday Cake

3 measures of Faith
2 measures of Courage
2 measures of Modesty
3 measures of Unselfishness
2 measures of Endurance
1 measure of Neighborly Kindness
1 measure of a Good Neighbor
1 measure of Fraternal Love

Combine the Great Principles of Faith, which binds and holds us fast to God, with Courage, the source which enables us to overcome danger, physical or moral. Add to these the Power of Modesty. Stir lightly, fold in lastly Unselfishness. Mix well and use and icing of Kindness of a Good Neighbor and let the crowning decoration be that of Fraternal Love. *Mrs. Roland Winter*